PRAISE FOR JODY S[...]

"[*Passing for Human* is] one of [...] [...]science fiction novels you've never read."

—Charlie Jane Anders, *iO9*

"Anyone who appreciates the offbeat (and the off the wall) will enjoy Scott's [Benaroya]. Benaroya is a visiting alien, whose mission (to save the human race from an evil alien invasion, and to have a good time while she's at it) is complicated by her inability to understand why human beings make a fuss over such inessentials as death, pain and the physical universe. Wearing an attractive assortment of bodies, including those of Emma Peel and Virginia Woolf, Benaroya shows herself and the reader a riproaringly magnificent time. …Quite unlike anything anyone else has ever done."

—Neil Gaiman

"Protagonist comes to alien world whose natives and absurdities are of course not at all 'alien' but refractive of the human condition. The tilt of alien perspective however enables the insanity of that condition, perceived by a faux-naif, to be the more clearly perceived… This is the greatest employment of science fiction in the service of satire; we've had notable satirists—but Scott alone refuses to sentimentalize."

—*The Magazine of Fantasy & Science Fiction*

"This satire was first published in 1977, but its biting commentary still registers strongly today. Scott carries on the tradition of Mark Twain, using outside observers to remark on society. A light touch keeps the moralizing from getting too ham-fisted, and this cautionary tale calling for a better world is a message needed now more than ever."

—*Publishers Weekly*

"A joyously and at times scatologically tangled Satire of the post-industrial Western world from a Feminist point of view that wittily verges on misandry."

—*The Encyclopedia of Science Fiction*

"The rapid non-sequiturs Scott puts into Benaroya's mouth and her aside justifications combine sharp jabbing observations and great humour. Those who seek to deride feminist SF often suggest that it is too serious, po-faced, but Jody Scott's wild imagination, seemingly scattershot but tightly controlled, makes [*I, Vampire*] an absurdly

comic romp of unexpected juxtapositions and witty asides."
— SF Mistressworks

"Jody Scott does it again [in *Devil-May-Care*]. Her latest book, presents us with a startling vision of life on planet earth as seen through the eyes of alien beings, disguised as famous humans. Fasten your seatbelts and brace yourself for a tumble through the universe with Virginia Woolf, Abraham Lincoln, Nancy Reagan, Douglas MacArthur, General Patton, Heidi's grandfather and, of course, our favorite vampire. [*Devil-May-Care*] is the third book in The Benaroya Chronicles and I promise it will keep you on the edge of your seat."
— Amazon 5-star review

"Jody Scott is like a mad cabby who knows most of the streets in town and knows where the laughs are—get into her rig and she'll take you on a fast and furious spin through America's ideological terrain."
—Michael Shea, World Fantasy Award-winning author

"I liked *I, Vampire* enough to check it off on the Nebula ballot. I'm still of the humble opinion that it is the equal (in a couple of cases, the superior) of the books that are apparently on the final ballot."
—Pamela Sargent, Nebula Award-winning author

"Scott is a superb social satirist."
—Samuel R. Delany, Nebula, Hugo, Lambda Award-winning author

"The best unknown SF writer."
—Barry N. Malzberg, John Campbell Memorial Award-winning author

"Jody Scott [has the] amazing ability to look askance and detached at humanity and human affairs, all the while passionately involved. Huge enjoyment of Scott's vitriol, her hilarity, her delineations of action and excitement (and indeed, one can read for these facets alone and gain many times the price of admission). A further, truly remarkable achievement of hers is her ability to describe a steamy, passionate love sequence without being explicit. My. How unfashionable. How very refreshing!"
—Theodore Sturgeon, SFF Hall of Fame inductee, Hugo and Nebula Award-winning author

THE BENAROYA CHRONICLES

I. Passing for Human
II. I, Vampire
III. Devil-May-Care

DEVIL-MAY-CARE

THE BENAROYA CHRONICLES III

JODY SCOTT

Strange Particle Press

ISBN 9781539349426

Copyright © 2016 Mary Whealen for the estate of Jody Scott
Published by arrangement with Mary Whealen, Jody Scott's life partner and heir.

All Rights Reserved.
This book may not be reproduced in whole or in part, without permission.

For further information contact:
Digital Parchment Services
digitalparchmentservices.com

*For Mary Whealen
and for The Sage LRH on Rysemus*

PART ONE

THE DEATH OF VIRGINIA WOOLF

ONE

Whack.
General MacArthur got hit in his sleep by what they called a Nightmare. And it was a corker.

Whack! A Mafia word meaning to shoot, stab, strangle, hang on a meathook, or otherwise molest until dead, the squirming bod of your enemy. The victim is required to: (a) Squeal loud apologies. (b) Cry, wriggle, and implore. (c) Volunteer his or her immortal soul in exchange for freedom. (e) Writhe and yell unabashedly, while soiling Jockey Shorts if wearing them. (f) Whimper softly. (g) Die.

WHACK! Doug thought it was Scaulzo, which meant...worse torture was on the way! Because now...he was engulfed in a warm, sensuous dream...and that could only mean...the Big S. was...toying with him...

The General was on vacation in Heaven. Or maybe it was just the Capital of Peace and Understanding. He, Douglas MacArthur, walked down a fabulous street, gaping at marvels on all sides.

There was a FOR RENT sign on a building. Doug grabbed the sign and began climbing a flight of stairs. The place stank like urine trickling down a tombstone but he wanted to live here *more than he'd ever wanted anything in his life.* He rapped on the Manager's door. No answer. He gave another loud rap. The door opened...just a crack.

Doug saw something moving in there. Something that smelled like an open grave. His heart just about stopped. The hinges began creaking. A hideous, drawn-out sound. He knew that behind the door lurked a THING so awful that *to see it would drive him mad!*

There was a hand. Part of one. Ugh! Clutching the door. The hand was rotten. Decayed flesh fell off ivory bones. Doug didn't want to see the body it was attached.to. He would scream! He'd turn into a gibbering madman—he'd foam at the mouth, wet his nicely pressed uniform pants and look ridiculous. The men would laugh! It would be *a thousand times better to die*—except he couldn't die! He was Supreme Command with a whole Galaxy riding on his shoulders. He'd just have to confront the HIDEOUS CORPSE lurking behind this door...and WHACK the sucker.

A terrible, ringing noise sliced the air. Doug turned to run but his feet were rooted! The door opened wider—bits of rotten flesh peeled off the fingertips. His heart was banging in his chest. In another second it would reach out for him—a ZOMBIE returned from limbo.

"Don't open that door!" he tried to yell but his lips wouldn't move.

The door fell open—

Doug woke with a scream clenched in his throat. He grabbed the phone with a hand so wet, the stupid instrument fell (sweat was running off him in rivers) and he had to lean down and scoop it off the carpet with a half-sobbed:

"Yo."

"I have correct core Virginia Woorf," said Tokyo switchboard with grim self-satisfaction.

"Patch her through to Lincoln," barked the General.

"Rady say love you all to pieces."

"Tell her to get stuffed."

"She cry and cry—"

"Tell her, we haddum locked in a cage! And this is just the beginning."

"Warns that General in serious danger."

"Tell her: 'If only you had examined *the long-term consequences* of your actions, you two-timing twat.'"

MacArthur hung up with a bang. Virginia Woolf, ohhh, yeah. When last they'd kissed goodbye she had simpered

"Ooh, lover...I have SUCH A CRUSH on her," referring to that honey-haired blood-lapper Sterling O'Blivion. It was a sabotage thing. Practicing being human (as every anthropologist had to do down here examining the pathology of Earth social customs) the bitch only wanted to humiliate Doug in front of his men as women always did; but she'd be punished for it! *The whore would wish she had never been born!*

The General had signed into this hotel after an exhausting journey, rushed upstairs, collapsed on the bed and fell asleep only to have that *(could it have been prophetic?)* terrible dream. Now he was wide awake gnawing the handsomely-buffed nails of his long, sinewy fingers and wondering how in fuckinghell the trouble-shooter Virginia Woolf had verified his location in Tokyo (a city seething with happy Japanese who worshipped MacArthur, their newly crowned Emperor—*go check your history book if you wanna dig how nuts humans are* as Patton would say)—him seeking a place to crawl away from the world and think a mind-wrenchingly complex situation through...

Virginia Woolf. Who'd have guessed what a slut she'd turn out to be—like all Earth babes? Supposed to be down here cracking the puzzle "Why do humans generate a chronic state of war and hysteria?" and what does she do but go play hide-the-salami *(oh no no no!* Christ. The very thought made his head throb) with Scaulzo himself; the demon incarnate...*devil in the flesh*...the Big S.! who had terrorized this primitive species since pre-cave days, forcing them to love it. And now the whole incredible, hypocritical mess was gonna blow sky-high if he couldn't—couldn't—

Doug chewed his nails.

A merciless psychopath, Scaulzo destroyed his victims after "having his way with them" as the saying went; and as luck had it—four billion citizens were hot to dance the boogaloo with him, while swearing on a stack of bibles that they weren't! Which meant: Omark was now an army commander. Nothing easy—oh no! He hadda be the dude licensed to WHACK until the folks would kiss his feet—for being a weird combination of gushy Hallmark card and serial killer; a guy able to decimate an entire population and then appear on TV with tears in his eyes giving toys and Granola to a bunch of raped, starved orphans— oh yes. Mr. Macho needed gallons of self-pity, mixed with that beefwitted lack of understanding of how every single act of every man's, affects everything in the universe like a stone tossed into a pond—for then and only then could the salient points of a sour culture where there was no relief from crimes of violence and ripoffs of the environment under the holy name "Defending Our God-Given PROPERTY (including animals and women)" be grasped by a scholarly, alien whale like Omark in a dude suit. Wearing a sidearm. *Ouch.*

Yep: saving humanity was a matter of infinite hope. And this ol' teacher found out real quick that if you were your natural, loving self...they'd WHACK you.

He could see it coming. Folks' morbid fascination with horror and paranoia could only mean that—Christ! Omark'd wanted a shot like this for years; and now that he had it...

But field reconnaissance aside, on top of learning paranoia (a skill so complicated it was driving him absolutely nuts) he had to work full-steam on his thesis. Back home on Rysemus the theory had seemed fundamental. A clean, flawless leap into the Unknown. He had pared it until it could be expressed as a simple question in basic English. This was that question. *Should human leaders be allowed out without their mothers?*

Then suddenly the ax fell. Yesterday, in one of those compulsively dreadful moments that were happening all too often all of a sudden, *"something"* made him open his big fat mouth and tell the men the true story of how MacArthur had lived with his Mom while attending the U.S. Military Academy. The very memory of it made Doug's face twitch, it was so humiliating...

It happened at a briefing in the War Room of the Pentagon. He'd been slashing at a map with a rubber-tipped pointer (one of his better skills) and whacking toy tanks off a layout, pointer in fist and sidearm on one hip (a sidearm, Omark had gathered, was symbolic of the fact that you possessed a dick almost embarrassingly big. Your hand was supposed to pat your sidearm lovingly—also symbolic. Most of what humans did was symbolic but you couldn't take a chance on wringing any of their necks because you could never be certain what the savages were up to, even if you were the senior Squad Officer down here, right?) Anyway he was giving it his all, slapping toys off a board as he boomed in that deep-throated, masculine voice of authority that made men hang on his every word; when suddenly—everything he had built up so carefully came crashing down around his ears.

He thought they'd be mildly surprised but appreciative of his homely honesty. *Hah!* First: that mortifying ripple of laughter. Apparently the men were laughing *at* their General, not *with* him! Soon they were guffawing like rubes at a sideshow—who'd have dreamed that Moms were not valued here as bunkies, messmates, negotiating partners, offensive strategy consultants—when females were obviously the sex with the brains? If any human could be said to have any brains. Why, there wasn't another tenth-rate

DEVIL-MAY-CARE

pesthole in the Galaxy with a policy so suicidal.

And Doug hadn't known how to fix it. He tried the old reliable butch swagger, picking his teeth with his knife and scowling like an Easter Island idol but no soap. Then fumblingly he tried explaining that the Orca whale lived with its mother all its life and was the most successful big animal since the dinosaur (or would have been if you erased humans from the picture which might not be too bad an idea—Doug had twice voted to have them put out of their misery but Virginia Woolf, Harry and H.G. outvoted him and Patton)—anyway, the men *just about split their guts* laughing and it was a demoralizing blow to Omark. He'd been helpless to keep from blurting that stuff out. Was he going nuts? Or could it be...*something* had hold of him? *Something* from the vast, dim halls of Eternal Evil—the Agony Organ in other words?

The tough part was sorting out the ordinary craziness people considered "normal" from attacks of the A-0 or demon possession sent by Satan as these rubes called Scaulzo. That bastard...he could WHACK an agent...that *nozzle!* He'd soak you with "subconscious" crap: distinct memories of things that never happened or he'd make you say things that needed to be said but you could get your wally blown off for saying them—and if the General was under attack whose fault was it but *that literary slut, Virginia Woolf?* Doug feared there'd be plenty more nasty surprises waiting for him. Already his penis wouldn't behave. It got erect at the slightest provocation like a junior high school kid's, always at the wrong time...which boded no good.

Scaulzo. A hideous, dark, unclean thing (the worst of it being— *they had the bastard in a cage* until the crazy floozie turned him loose!) driving a man right over the edge; nor was this the first time for Doug. Once, he'd been able to resist any A-0 attack but now? Too much TV and sleazy horror literature maybe. And when you immersed yourself deeply into a savage culture like this one, it could be fatal. You were always walking a fine line; but that was the challenge. That was the fun of it. If you could survive.

The big S. always looked so great when he wore a human bod dressed in a thousand-dollar suit. Clean-cut, with a fine and appealing voice, hair neatly combed, he had beautiful manners— everything Kosher. The idol of every generation, the bad dude never said "Mofo" or any of those words that upset Earthies so bad they couldn't think rationally (butter wouldn't melt in the archfiend's mouth; yet in his native body he was a basilisk so hideous they'd scream and turn to stone at the sight of him) and yet: being superstitious savages, unable to take control of their own lives, they went on their knees to him. Billions applauded the idea that *the Boogieman was Lord* and they were only helpless pawns; and now Doug would be required to immerse himself in that mind-set while not letting it destroy him if possible — or be discredited, sent back to the minors. And it could happen. Even to one with Omark's spectacular academic standing. Ouch.

The old hotel creaked. Otherwise all was quiet except for overhead fans clacking. Now a radio down the hall played a boohoo song about tears on a guy's pilla each morning — "*I cry when I dream about you,*" quavered the voice. It was sad, very sad and Doug tried to get into it. He got sad too. There was no rock and roll way back here in the fifties, there was drugs and sex but no rock and roll...so he got sad.

He really loved Virginia Woolf. And the dumb cunt was probably suffering *horribly*, trapped in some snafu of her own making (*flake that she was*) — and yet Doug had a hunch she was mixed up in this more than he knew. "It is time for me to deal with you," he'd say in passionate tones and smash her across the chops. For Woolf had made her choice. "So that's where she belongs — with him, not with me."

Woolf was her own worst enemy. She *flirted* with that sadistic hypnotist. *She lured him!* "I love you so much but goodbye," he'd tell her. For she had done the unpardonable — driven by what she called her "Inner Spiritual Light." Yeah, right! "*The courage to face evil, the faith to subdue it*" — give me a fucking break. Doug knew she was *really* drawn by that unruly lock of *black hair* that fell so *sweetly* across his rival's brow. Yeah — the devil was smart enough to show up with lots of hair. Humans *loved* hair, as long as it was attached to the appearance of wealth and a smooth line; which explained why they voted for the Big S. every time. The Rysemians were always unpopular compared to Scaulzo. Doug didn't quite know why except *they were the real thing* and not just a well-advertised tub of expensively coutured lawyer pudding with Mafia funding, and yet...the reactions of his staff pained him terribly; but no matter how bad it got, or how much they taunted him, the General loved those cathartic memory trips to the good old days at West Point with his Mom — the best of Doug's life.

DEVIL-MAY-CARE   17

She used to say, "Doug darling, the secret of success is having a dream and having the courage to run after it. Reach for the stars!" and bring him chicken soup. And the day he took the Point's tough entrance exam she said, "Heroism is an equal opportunity employer, my child. Put honor first and you'll be President one day." *Was that a coach or what?* Omark felt that every General should stick with her Mom from cradle to grave like the Orca whale, and why? Because a mother knows. A mother can tell. A mother is unbeatable at helping a fellow face the storms of life. Hadn't it been proven that with a trainer like Mrs. MacArthur in his corner, this General not only graduated first in his class, but almost got himself elected President? Not bad for a rich white kid from Arkansas.

"Virginia's trigger-happy, boyfriend" (as that hoarse-voiced, *big-screen pussy, Sterling O'Blivion*—who would as soon drain a decent man's blood as look at him; yet considered herself a "hermetic scholar" in love with her own glitzy past but was only a dotty old broad who should be booted off the Squad—but of course wouldn't be as long as Woolf protected her and the Chief backed it up—*always called Omark*) thumped his pillow but sleep would not return. *He* was the one in grave trouble here, not Virginia Woolf! He had put in to be MacArthur because the assignment looked like a plum. Frimble put in for Doug as well (Frimble was the engineer who devised the "Mousehole" system linking galactic poles that brought the Rysemians to this dustmote in the first place. They were never attracted to the dump; it just happened to be near Grid 8 which might cause a problem) and they tossed for it, Omark "won" and now Frimble rode the cat seat. All he hadda do was grunt "Bombs Away" and blow the balls off two cities while Omark sweated blood here in Tokyo because Harry Truman was out to get him. It was unfair!

The phone rang steadily. Doug figured it was Virginia Woolf the woman he had loved and lost "to another woman," how humiliating! but screw her. Or again: it might be Commander in-Chief Abe Lincoln and that was equally distasteful.

Rysemians had no use for "authority"—a barbaric device leading to dysfunction and early extinction. What was needed was either a thoroughgoing use of the N-bomb by his people (Patton wanted that—not that it'd make a hell of a lot of difference in light of the total oxygen rip-off that was coming in 2123 A.D.) or:

a draining of old poisons from each and every human individual (Heidi's Grandfather, the head of the Mission, wanted *that*, with all his sweet little ole goat herder heart) followed by your basic training in Ethics. If a species had Ethics they didn't need authority. If they didn't, authority didn't work.

But Ethics was a bad word around here because psycho bigwigs could make "serious money" off of mass confusion—unaware that they already had all the "serious money" there was to be had.

Punishment? A joke. How could you punish beings who were acting terrible because they'd already been punished too terribly? Oh, it was a paradox for sure. Nothing could solve the mess. Still, they were giving it a try. The phone rang steadily...

He'd be walking into a coffin if he answered.

TWO

This was ten years after the Japanese bombed Pearl Harbor. The 'real' General was in cold storage on the star cruiser Vonderra and would never know the difference if all went well; but safety was a thing of the past and it was MacArthur's fault! For not getting tough with Benaroya and that quiff she was romancing (or "seeing" as yups called it) but mostly for not being in mint shape so he could fight the psychological pressure of the Agony Organ.

Doug sprawled under a revolving fan, glad to get away from the demands of a wife, child and far worse (he closed his mouth and shuddered): from Harry Truman. He was AWOL because he had to work on his thesis and Truman kept sticking his big, fat nose in. The thesis was frustrating enough without convoluted attentions from a dapper, fedora-topped little crook — Harry was A-1 at the political talent of deflecting argument from any real issue but otherwise like all CEO's he was an ignorant spearchucker. As top Squad anthropologist Omark knew his Barb Behavior cold — he could knock off any type degradation or trivialization but these tribal chiefs, yi! And now his dear comrade Frimble (the erstwhile Dirty Harry) opted to be Pres. Harry S. Truman in person...just to give his ole pal MacArthur HELL.

Doug put the section of pipe that goes between the lips between the lips, puffing and thinking...it rankled deep in his gut. The whole U.S. Army was slowly turning against him — why??? Simply because he was not dull, dense, and an emotionally retarded adolescent as they were. But how was that possible? He'd done fine here on Earth in Civil War days in the body of Charles Jennison, a crafty, crotch-tugging Old West gunfighter; but now things had changed. How could you account for it? How could you account for a regression as sudden as THAT (snapping two fingers expertly) with no cause that anyone could see?

"Have I gone nuts?" he asked himself.

He wasn't crazy enough to try making sense out of the insane, because the insane was by definition "crazy" meaning that you'd go insane trying to make sense of it, although countless millions did that for a living, and yet: it was a General's duty to get fully paranoid and stay that way. A General had not only to "fit in" which was nutty enough, but actually to lead the craziness of his men and do it with a certain flair and elegance. MacArthur did not—nor could he ever—do it as well as the bandit Jennison (a guy "in touch with his emotions" as they said around here) stealing two hundred horses with a week's growth of beard on his handsome mug. But still, Doug did it with a fair amount of class. So why should the riddle be beyond solving?

These were the facts.

For two hundred years, American officers had been hell-for-leather cavalrymen. Shy, kindly, Gary Cooper-type fellows. Lean, clear-eyed, fine-looking lads who said "Aw shucks" in a winning way while nudging pebbles with their toe. (The Rysemians knew this from having seen every movie ever made on the subject), then by degrees they turned into pod persons. Cold, hateful bureaucrats who spoke a glib, hard-sell gibberish instead of the quaint, honest Yankee speech.

But how? Why? What had spoiled the good life? Who could explain why a nation of cowboys with the sweet smell of horse manure on their heels, turned overnight into corporate entities in Gucci loafers and Rolex watches, driving a Japanese car, and nine times out of ten having been forced into sex acts with larger or more powerful males while saying they didn't so as not to be laughed at and/or get in trouble with the Authorities? Omark, seeking a root for these unwholesome and frightening trends, had come up with two theories.

One theory was far scarier than the other.

The mild theory was: the downtrend began when that sidewinder Truman organized the diabolical CIA. Once all the sneaky, sadistic, underhanded tricks began, all the fun and innocence just plain evaporated and before you knew it—bang! An undeclared war in Korea. Followed by the paralyzing shock of Vietnam that caused a weakening of American moral fiber.

The harsher theory pointed to an alien invasion.

Scaulzo the Sajorian, widely worshipped in 18 galaxies (this one was Gal. #13) as The Devil, had been pulling off outrages of this magnitude for eons and getting away with it. The smart money said he either didn't exist, was a group hallucination, or: must be worshipped. In other words it was a never-ending battle — nor would it come as a shock (Doug sighed) if Woolf's sly loverboy was embroiled in a massive take-over of this ditzy little globe.

And why not? He had all the obsessive drive and PR skills it might take to worm his way into any power structure on Earth. He had fine manners, a nice exterior. "The devil never says fuck," Doug grumped to himself — even Benaroya had been heard to gush that Scaulzo was "So *soigne!* So *distingue.* So nasty and sexy like a soap actor."

And that was only the beginning.

General MacArthur switched on the lamp, grabbing his handmirror. Was the competition unbeatable? There was no time to waste. To come forty thousand light years and then make a clown of himself — ouch! What he needed was drill. H. G. was up there keeping tabs on the whole squad; time to toughen up. Be a mensch! Go over and over it.

"It is my sacred duty to become the collusive, mob-funded puppet that people vote for," he growled to the cool gleam of eyes between thick lids.

Not bad. Not Hall of Fame maybe but it showed promise.

"Look Ma, I'm a General. How's your wife? Compared to what? My wife is so fat that — Take my wife. Please." No; those were old Borscht Circuit numbers. He needed something out of an old war movie. How about (MacArthur positioned his aviator's shades and corncob), "All right, ladies. This is a dark hour. I wanna see more skulls tacked to trees. How else will we know we're men? Let us not get our *cojones* caught in the wringer for not kicking enough ass, you pussy-loving buncha goat blowers," clearing his throat.

Excellent! The voice resonated with GI appeal as Doug continued, "The Treaty of Versailles was a sadist plot. It brought you Hitler," he bellowed. "You liars really know how to hand-craft a vicious dictator and say you didn't," with a friendly smile — but no; that was too direct. Why was he blurting this classified material? It could only be...

Impossible. The Big S. had been whipped once and for all! Even if Woolf removed his slimy carcass from that cell on Vonderra to parts unknown she certainly wouldn't—she absolutely WOULD NOT—

Unless driven mad by female hormones, or...

Doug bit his pipe stem. Okay, kid. Smoke and mirrors. Just take a deep breath. That underlying sense of horror—you could play with it—and not fall into the trap—if you were good. And he was THE BEST.

"Long Dong Silver saddles the Supreme Court with his law school diploma in one hand and his dick in the other," he exploded, lighting the pipe with hands that were not too steady... But he had to get very sincere here. "You better shape up, Cell Block B, or I'll put the wolves on ya. Fifty guys will get atcha in one night—" No, no! That was *warden* tough, not *General* tough. There was a subtle difference. The only way to seem honest to these confused locals was to lie and have clean, shiny fingernails, not forgetting that you had to use theatrical devices. Otherwise you wouldn't sound sincere and they'd think you were using theatrical devices.

"We're gonna step on some toes here. We're gonna kick ass and take names. Get your butt smoked." No, no, that sounded too much like Patton. Try again.

"You want a sweeping look at your universe you dirt-clod humanoids?" he snarled, watching his teeth in the mirror. "You've heard of the Empire? Well let me tell ya, this Confederacy consists of 75 planets and we're fighting a battle that'll singe your shorthairs. And where's the black hole at? Sajor! The eons-old root of your trouble if you but knew it—where your favorite serial killer is God. Ladies, this is a holy war. The guy in the red pajamas has got you hooked on wicked games. Don't fall for it no more. Just say no! Say no to horror, folks. Cowabunga." Doug grinned at his own foolishness.

The weather-tanned chin looked hard as a rock, the large nose stuck out impressively; the sinewy hand clutching the mirror was perfect and with a little effort he could make his nostrils flare like Katherine Hepburn's but still—

"Now people. We must prepare to fight the international Communist menace which in forty years will prove not to have existed; which is a nice joke on your species which has less sense of history than a monkey"—good. His nostril hairs quivered sincerely. "Harry-boy, you tellin me not to bomb China after you unloaded those mushroom-shaped clouds over Japan? Is that what you call FAIR? I'm gonna DEEfuckingSTROY the Chinese unless they negotiate with me personally—what is this, some kind of immoral compromise with evil? We must go in there with a full blown invasion..."

Oh great, that was wonderful! And his mind was perfectly clear; no A-O problem whatsoever. Just for practice, the anthropologist did a pretty fair imitation of the loathsome Sterling O'Blivion—his whole body writhing.

"I've worked the streets but seldom as a hooker. I used to shack up with Henry James after a thrilling fling with his big brother Bill—but it was Victor Hugo that I taught how to parse a sentence." *Ugh!* What a disgusting bimbo she was. Vampirism was a serious affliction, yet she made light of it—but Doug needed to concentrate here.

"It is my destiny to defeat Communism because old soldiers never die, they just fade away—" (Excellent. The mouth-twist alone bordered on sheer genius.) "Only God or those in Washington will keep me from this great goal! The long gray line has never failed us in stumbling from crisis to crisis pouring our country's blood into sophisticated missiles, pseudo-sophisticated, counter-counter missiles as we create the Supreme, Grand Master Missile of the Drug Empire of the future beyond anything your dirt clod brains have as yet envisioned—"

Woolf's in trouble.

Fine. She asked for it.

Yeah, she did maybe but...Scaulzo's A-O beam was total evil, he used people as puppets by playing on deeply buried fears when their guard was down. That hypnotic grip made a victim blurt, yeah you got it, *blurt*: spill your guts as it planted seeds in your mind making you do BAD THINGS when everyone around you thought YOU were doing them—and—and—to confront and blow the deeply buried fears was your only defense but—if you got mired in social convention as Doug had to do for his role, oh God—

This time the pain was so bad he nearly screamed. His eyes rolled up in their sockets...and when they came down they were staring at MacArthur's own eyes in the glass, him lip-synching along with a billion voices in weird places and dates of this globe (while the only sounds were the radio down the hall, and his own heart thumping) *Oh no, the Vietnamese weren't comfortable in the jungle, they were all city boys, they had no idea what was going on. We played tap dances all over'm all the time. They never successfully ambushed once. I captured one guy one day, it was kinda cute. I was in Recon battalion by a lake, these guys were throwin guns in the lake (to look like civs), I followed these wet footprints to his house, his wife was cryin, I checked the house out and the room out and spotted him beneath the bed. I flew a trip flare in there, the Chinese grenades sparkle just like a sparkler, he thought it was a brigade, I hit him in the chest when he came runnin. Straitjacket time, you literally go nuts. To survive the insane situation you go nuts.*

The flare landed against the wall of his house and burned his house down, the first prisoner we ever captured didn't squeal like a rat. The Germans helping the French had a horrible reputation. This one put the gear on and the prisoner talked right away. "Hey Dave your prisoner ain't talkin," I started sharpening my bayonet. He squealed like a rat. We looked nasty crazy clothes fallin off, been in the jungle for months. You shoulda seen these Iraqui kids burnin like flares and no food, these kid-legs like skin over a coupla bones where babyfood cost $40 an ounce and water $20 a quart after the Bushmen hit and it's cold, so cold here in Valley Forge—

Doug screamed, throwing the mirror at the wall (where it broke. Seven years' bad luck)—holy *shit*. That had been a brainlink! across centuries with the caveman voices, drumbeats and everything coming through hard and clear...Doug wet his lips. He had to dive back into the acceptable trivia of the day, but fast. Especially when his public esteem was crashing and he missed his dear old Jennison body with the powder burns on the trigger finger—

"Harry's gonna lynch me," he snarled. "Yet everything hinges on inflicting huge casualties, people! Please note that all I'm doing here is drilling that grim, goose-steppy style of delivery you psychotic mobs go gaga over, so-let's tie a yella ribbon around our neck and give it a good hard yank in honor of the fact that we all get off on the time-hallowed sound of a rifle being cocked. Right? Now listen to me, you foolish savages." (He was panting heavily. This was *the worst A-O attack yet*...He hoped he'd come through it alive.)

"It's a garbage detail to go around pinning medals on combat casualties, especially on little boys who are either corpses or soon will be, which is how I got in big trouble last week. I was doing the required medal-pinning and when a kid died as I pinned his pretty medal to his corpse, I told key members of my staff:

"In addition to having unbounded admiration for my Mom, you ice-holes, I, your General, am from Rysemus! Yes, my home-world is a planet far off in the Milky Way — so far you can't imagine the distance with your puny little custom-deadened brains. Otherwise you'd see at a glance that ALL war is a demonic attack. LRH, our own Rysemian scholar, defined it thus, 'War is chaos. War only brings anarchy. War is having to exert bad control because good control was not exerted in the first place. ' In short we're looking at a mass tantrum of frustrated babies — whether or not glorified by trillions of savages over trillions of years of psycholic dramatization that solved nothing whatsoever. But why does it always happen to poor little YOU, you ask? I think Holden Caulfield summed it up when he yelled, at the top of his goddam voice, his historic remark: 'Sleep tight, ya morons!'"

And then what did Doug blurt to Harry Truman himself, oh God..."Have fun, dude. Relax and keep smiling as you fall on your knees to the sadness, the blasted dreams of forever being EFFECT and never CAUSE so that the good guy gets wiped out by the killer manufactured by a complex bureaucracy and it's so SAAAD we can't do anything about that or anything else, just throw our apron over our head and have a good cry, because us poor little humans are Married to the Mob and, boohoo! Gulp, sob, sniff! Boohoo, men; we're so helpless we must go WHACK someone — which is how you humans solve all your problems," he sneered in the President's astonished face.

On God! What an idiot! Oh Jesus Christ...And then the capper. "Being in an army doesn't mean you're a hero. It means you're a wimpy puppet with no mind of your own," MacArthur told Truman.

Oh sweet Jesus Christ...he bit his nails. He couldn't enforce authority, couldn't gain respect — it was terribly sad but at least he'd learned the bitter lesson of how you feel when you're *not even part of the crowd*, let alone a leader.

Now Omark with his fine, polished style knew that Scaulzo was laughing his head off at him and his ears burned. The men thought he was the worst type of ice-hole (his anxiety level was shooting way up: good) but at least it was educational. A daily, hands-on exploration of how to play hardball in $300 sneakers on a court greased with human blood while you probed the bitter irony of this bugshit job of MacArthur's, the Last of the Good Guys.

Doug grabbed his long legs in his arms and squeezed hard, head resting on knees. He cried. He cried hot, salty tears that splashed on the blanket. It made him feel a bit better...Abe Lincoln was correct. To be convincing again he'd have to get that Sajorian snake off his back.

But now—he heard an elevator stop at his floor.

The phone was ringing hysterically. Doug picked it up and smashed it down (it was either Woolf or Truman and they could both go piss up a rope) and—someone was banging on the door.

"Who's there?" he yelled.

"Trampy, hosebag," came a high-pitched, surreal giggle.

"Who?"

"Miss Roundheels," with another awful giggle.

Doug grabbed his skull with both hands...he had an overwhelming fantasy that it was *himself*, the self that was suffering horribly in this pre-dawn Tokyo bed, who would totter over and open that door with a hand that had flesh rotting off the dead fingers

"WHO?" he shrieked.

"Pwetty pwease," the awful thing standing outside the door begged him.

Doug was horrified! Last week in Washington, some wit of a Major General had sent up a prostitute for him. He'd had to climb bodily out the window to the street; then yesterday in Korea a floozie with teased hair and a flouncing walk almost cornered him in a lobby saying she was from the NEW REPUBLIC—and as always, the basic dread was: this could be a killer sent by Scaulzo's people to freeze him into his body. To a Rysemian, that was a fate worse than death. Any death. Any time, anywhere.

"Go away!" Doug yelled. But the door was opening—very slowly.

THREE

"Ohhh baby, baby, *bayBEHHHH!*" Sterling O'Blivion sang in her shower.

"*Multosque per annos errabant, maria omnia circum,* tum tetum" — warbling lyrics from the poet Virgil whose heart-tugging, old, very dead language the vampire had learned at her Mother's knee in an age when not to know Latin was a disgrace —

"Arms I sing and the woman who, exiled by FATE, first came to ITALY from the coasts of TROYYY!..."

Sterling's Latin had a rough Transylvanian twang, but she knew secrets about those wars that had been fought beneath the lofty walls of Rome long ago; oh yes. But! she had to hurry now. In a minute Nancy Reagan would stick her blow-dried head through the curtain with a, "Hush. We must act ladylike, Sterling, and do it all *by the book* so no harm comes to Virginia Woolf" — her lips twitching. Old Miss Roach Clip Just Say No. Nancy drove the vampire right up the frigging wall.

But if any harm *did* come to Woolf it would be Douglas MacArthur's fault, not hers. The General did everything in his power to break the two of them up ("But darling: I've made you the Star of my Heart and that ole soldier can't part us! We'll be hugging and kissing again soon, I swear," the vampire vowed silently to her lover as she soaped her lovely legs) and he was going to suffer for it, she promised herself grimly. O'Blivion hated Omark. That big snob of a Rysemian scholar treated her *like dirt under his feet* and nobody, but *nobody*, could get away with that!

The warm water felt so good, so soothing...Gratefully she tilted her head and closed her eyes, letting its gentle fingers caress her face. Ahhh! That was better. It washed away the cruel tortures Woolf's people were inflicting upon her, up on their ship where she was still in the preliminary stages of DETOX — commonly known as *cold* turkey.

The Cure had its compensations though. She could see Earth through the spaceport, looking pretty in its cloud-wrap 200 miles straight down (no, straight up!) — they were parked over *(no, under)* Chicago where Virginia waited patiently for Sterling. Woolf wanted her dear friend to be cured of blood addiction, then popped out of the profound hell that all of humanity struggled in — the never-ending valley of agony that went on day after day, year after year, century after century, for everyone alive on Earth. And afterward: "The doors to Immortality shall spring wide!" Woolf had vowed. It was almost too much to hope for but —

When Ster was...well, *clean,* the two would have a life brimming with fast-paced action, adventure, romance, suspense, and high monogamy "Just like in a 1940's Cary Grant/Katharine Hepburn movie every day of our lives!" Woolf said. They'd dance into the sunset together, she promised. But now...

Ster whimpered with disappointment. She felt totally worthless — she shouldn't have put out on the first date! She had so looked forward to working in tandem every day with her idol Virginia Woolf but now that her easy routine was all shattered — Woolf just kind of, well, *dumped* her and took off saying "You've got to trust me, kiddo," leaving the vampire so forlorn...

But. She was thrilled to be part of an adventure this big; and after her habit was kicked —

"Eons ago," Woolf said, "people enjoyed a state where promises were kept and hearts were never broken. We shall put your feet back on that Path to Wisdom, until you can command your own destiny. How about it, babe?"

"Are you sure?" Sterling had asked, leaning forward anxiously.

"Of course I'm sure, for cryin out loud! But in this game your soul could get ripped off. Are you prepared to take that chance, you luscious big tough dame?" Woolf wanted to know; going on to speak of *"the greater pattern,"* and *"the re-discovery of innocence"* and other matters that Ster didn't get the import of — but — Woolf's lips had tickled so delightfully...

And so it all began. After eight centuries of wandering, O'Blivion had come home. Or at least she hoped so. Love! Such a thing hadn't happened to her in years — she'd about given up hope; but now —

It was hard for the vampire to grasp that this was no joke, no send-up of the cartoony bullshit that people chuckled about—aliens monitoring our thoughts from a far planet and suchlike, ha ha ha ha ha! But as it turned out, just because a million paranoid schizophrenics swore by an idea didn't meant it was untrue. In fact, everything tended to be the exact opposite of what was taught on Earth. How had Woolf put it..."Your sun is a pinprick, your days numbered like the mayfly's, but now? Off to exciting futures with the woman of your dreams!" she had laughed gaily.

Sterling had been wanting to do something a little bit different. Stretch a little. And this seemed like an unparalleled opportunity. But here on Vonderra she was forced to look at a lot of weird, alien artifacts (*some nice,* some *nasty*) though; and there were many veiled, mysterious things going on...What *have I got myself into?*

It mainly started the day she was seated at her desk watching a storm on Lake Michigan as she sipped Lafite Rothschild out of a Diet Pepsi can so the staff needn't be jealous. Ster was Manager of the best dance studio (Max Arkoff's) on Chicago's Miracle Mile where she loved to sit looking down on Michigan Boulevard when a storm blew up on the lake, watching rain slash at the window, and towering waves crash on the shore, as lightning flickered and thunder boomed. Chicago's wind-wracked coast was wilder than the Pacific Ocean and the champagne had gone straight to her head, when in walked—guess who!

How would *you* feel if Virginia Woolf, undiminished, strode into your workplace dripping wet and grabbed you, kissing you on the lips and palms and inner elbow? Well, that's just about how Sterling felt. Blown away. Woolf was in Chicago recruiting for the Vonderra Mission but Ster didn't know it yet, but she found out soon enough, but by then she was so crazy in love—the poor sap. She fell hook line and sinker, why not admit it; that's how she felt, in her inmost heart.

Never would she have admitted to being a weak-kneed fan, swooning in a hopeless crush on a major celebrity (for wasn't Virginia Woolf, whose body Benaroya wore with such style and flair, the most innovative woman writer of all time?) to her Yuppie friends back in Chicago or her Physics Department pals at Wellesley who'd only roll their eyes and dismiss her with their usual sophisticated contempt—so screw 'm. Virginia Woolf had always been the vampire's idol. She wished she could be half as good as Woolf!

It was too bad that on Vonderra you had to learn more than you wanted to know about the interstellar battles that constantly raged. Sterling was part of the whole thing now, a very tiny part, true, but still: Heidi's Grandfather tried to teach her some odd things. *"A commercial that warns about disease is actually laying a curse on you. An anti-drug campaign sells drugs quickly.* Peace is the *only* effective war" — pointing out how cockeyed local customs were. As far as Sterling was concerned it all went in one ear and out the other — but the clincher was — a million people had been interviewed for this job, and she alone had made the cut. Why? Was the whole thing a set-up, some kind of trap; a sting being pulled on her? But whether it was or not, on an impulse she had said yes. Yes, yes, YES! Take me away, you perfect woman, I'm yours!!!

Well — it seemed like a good idea at the time. For one thing she was so far in debt there was no way to climb out. She remembered the day Woolf entered the picture; the staff straggling back from lunch at Leon's where they cracked "This nun went into a bar — " jokes nor could you scream "SHUT UP!" at your own staff; and was she bored with the hollow mockery of her big-salary, managerial position and the whole rat race in general? Does a bear shit in the woods, do medicos snort cocaine, does the Pope wear one single pretty little gold nipple-ring under his official robes? "Bite me," as Sterling would say.

Her personal life in the pits, the law had a tap on her phone... no doubt of it. Her glittering notoriety drew those lawmen like flies. Last year in Tennessee she'd managed to slip through a state-wide manhunt, complete with bloodhounds, and didn't know if she could pull it off again; she wasn't as young as she used to be — and the thought of a shaky future preyed on her. She should be dead by now, but wasn't, and hoped to keep it that way — a woman who'd had been whipped in the streets, Sterling knew what pain was. She'd spent years in jails all over the world and knew that locking people up was worse than stupid, *it was a dangerous disgrace* — but mainly, O'Blivion always needed to be doing something scary and terrifyingly difficult or she wasn't happy.

"Play over your head" had always been her motto. And because she wasn't servile or tame as most women are trained to be, she often got in the glue with small-minded men who accused her of heinous crimes — cannibalism (*now wouldn't that be a tacky turn-off* in spades?), grand theft (true but it was only the Mob she stole from), being a Russian, Cuban, or Israeli spy; arson, assault with a deadly pussy, being caught wearing black leather boots and nothing else while wielding a bullwhip (only did that once, didn't much get off on it); being a pimp, Dominatrix, serial killer and many times jailed as "potentially offensive" — oh yeah, she'd been down that street so often she thought the law was a sick joke. The whole Govt was, in fact, a complex and deadly scam run by a master criminal, H.G. told her in her daily lessons.

"You are an anti-social personality," one robed magistrate had shaken his finger while passing sentence. "You've committed the most disgusting act of humiliation and degradation any decent citizen can suffer. A long record of felony indictments proves to me that you — YOU!" (his mouth pulled a moue) "are VIOLENCE PERSONIFIED!"

What a mealy-mouthed hypocrite, twisting his flabby lips around the lies she was forced to stand there and take! And both of them knowing all the time that you *had* to hurt and scare people or they wouldn't tolerate you — or as she told the arresting officers, "In a masochistic world, even your *prose* has got to hurt. Otherwise you won't be taken seriously," but cops always hated O'Blivion. She was too cocky. Fast, mean, and street-wise, she took no shit from anybody but lipped off and didn't appear the least bit sorry for what she'd done; in fact, seemed proud of it.

"You are a dangerous beast," gasped that judge. "You are diabolical! The ELECTRIC CHAIR is too good for you. I'm only sorry we have no DEATH PENALTY in this state" and on and on. Ster yawned, thereby earning herself an extra thirty days...

Shit. Can you teach an old dog new tricks? Ster had been "interrogated" so often and so cruelly it had messed up her brains like when you pick up an egg, "This is your brain, darling." Crack into a sizzling pan: "This is your brain under our male warlord system, any questions?" and that about summed it up.

"Excuse me but life's an adventure, you tired old dick," she'd bawled in that courtroom standing in her favorite pose of chin upthrust, hands on hips, tossing the honey-colored shoulder-length hair out of her eyes as she shouted "Five billion bods slouching to Bethlehem chomping pork steaks as they practice Position 87 from the Kama Sutra and you yell at ME for lapping six measly ounces, where's your sense of proportion you pompous asshole?" she had squalled as they took her away. "Even tots know that our society is founded upon violence which is the key to power and what I do sure beats dying of old 'age in one of your degrading retirement homes," she howled as they stuffed her into a cage —

That was two generations ago. But Ster remembered it as if it happened yesterday. That judge was so mean she wanted to kill herself! She needed to get rid of all that anger, piled up for so long with no release and you can bet if she'd had a gun, razor blade, bottle of Lysol, anything, she'd have committed suicide right there in her cell. But when she got out: back to business at the same old stand.

"That very night, wearing only a coat and high boots, I had the Governor. And we're not talking copulation here," Ster smirked into the cameras in her only interview with Oprah, face fuzzed so no lawman could get a make on her.

"I'm always well groomed," she told the D.A. — a sleazeball so intrigued with the raw voltage of the gorgeous O'Blivion (admittedly a batlike beast of prey but cute, shapely and incredibly sexy) that he had a tent-pole erection right there at his desk, the jerk! "I approach my victim in a non-threatening way," she explained politely. "He or she feels very safe, very flattered, which is what those who choose to live a consumer life without dignity adore. But me: I carve out my own destiny. What *I* adore is the excitement of the chase! Everyone needs excitement to survive other than as an intimidated, despicable couch potato," she pointed out.

A major change after nearly 800 years, excuuuuuse me? It wasn't in the cards. Leading a double life had always been O'Blivion's way. She was a clean, sober female who made her own rules and would not conform to any tradition whatsoever — which was precisely why the Rysemians picked her as Special Liaison in the first place. Oh sure, the promise of a new lease on life was attractive as hell; even though something inside of her kept whispering "You'll never be seen alive again!" and yet — hey. Most human beings simply could not handle the fact that the Rysemians were serious game-players who were more than a million years advanced from them; and, think of the fun of having your mind expanded! And yet...her captors were obviously totally mad, according to her own long-held standards — or else *she* was. But be that as it may...*where in the holy hell was Virginia Woolf* about now when her beloved was suffering so badly?!!?

DETOX. Hateful! Why couldn't they let a person BE? True, like

Scaulzo, Sterling was a very good actor but there the resemblance ended. The Sajorian was the original Prince of Darkness. But she herself was GOOD! A warm, sentimental lady who in her slap-dash way, loved the thrill of conquest, what was wrong with that? She only lapped six ounces, remembering when she was a tiny girl her Daddy would plunk down bags of gold to get bled by the town leech, a hunchback with a white pole that had bloody rags wrapped around it—that's how barber poles got started. In bygone times doctors LOVED to bleed people which only proved how two-faced they were and also that, far from being an abominable crime, vampirism was not only a wonderful release but a tonic better than kelp or Vitamin C. And O'Blivion was extremely proud of her Body of Work. She'd sucked some highly important people. And would suck plenty more before she was through. With luck.

Gratefully she picked up the bottle of shampoo, letting the hot water stream down her back and thighs and basking in the pleasure of it as she poured shampoo into her palm, it smelled so good! Everything on Vonderra was first rate—very plush, what she'd seen of it—except for her cell, it was crummy. Sterling soaped her head, massaging her scalp gently, cleaning her ears with her fingers. Ahhh, that felt better.

"Oh baby baby baby, baby baby ooooh!" she jived; doing an Elvis better than the King himself if she did say so. But then—
"Wait a minute—"

Her face went pale. *Only my imagination.*

No.

Oh yes. Yes it is. (*Something working inside her—uncanny*)

"Cool it! No reason to panic."

But this light-headed feeling all of a sudden. *No. Don't give in to it.* Everything was hunky-dory as it should be. What she'd felt (*and almost-seen*) was a twinge of imagination; no big deal.

Sterling picked up the soap and laughed.

(Oh no)

Her own laugh prickled the skin of her neck. Years ago, a malign spell had been cast on her, and even now—*Oh God!*

What came out was a froggy, weird croak that formed in the back of her throat from *way down deep where you can't control it*—

She crammed her knuckles into her teeth, hard.

FOUR

(C ouldn't hold it back)
Sterling doubled over, trying not to yell. The water was turning red! It had a thick, coppery reek to it—oh shit. She saw with dawning horror that it was *blood!* Welling up, trickling out and cascading over her neck, breasts, belly and—

She gaped in stunned disbelief, knees trembling...then the cramps began.

Stomach cramps. Painful, oh God! But it wasn't time for her period. She'd just had one. No, this was more like a knife in the womb *(that she could feel going to work on her).*

NO! This couldn't happen because if it did *(if the thing got a foothold)*...Groaning and shaking her head, Ster bit her lips hard but *(no stopping it)* out came a jet of slimy, green bile. Projectile vomiting! She'd once worked in an E.R. and knew that vomiting like this came only with massive cranial damage, a crushed skull, bone pressure or a ruptured brain stem or impacted frontal lobe or—*holy shit!* that wasn't the worst of it.

A ghostly green, wavy LIGHT came bursting through her lips! Oh God, the source of the horror was HERSELF *(her own body)* transfixed by a shimmering, polished-looking, yellow-green BRILLIANCE *(trying to swallow it back was a joke)*—as if some killer had buried a body down there long ago and it turned into a gassy, decomposing BEAM writhing out of her, enveloping her neck, bare shoulders and breasts in that cancerous, lighthouse BEACON! like meltdown in a nuclear power plant—or—the burning death ray the vampire had seen *(and laughed at)* in the worst of horror comics! And now exploding out of her was—was—oh lord God!

Cockroaches.

She gaped, lips puckered with disgust. Then she was thrashing in horror as a sticky wad of bugs literally gushed from her open mouth—earwigs! Army ants. Sawflies—

The vampire yelped in shock and pain as hardback bugs the size of a quarter, waving feelers, snapped their pincers on her nipples and soft parts...and after them came a bushel of tapeworms, maggots and snakes that poured, twisting and slithering, coiling and uncoiling, from her nose and mouth—

She shrieked, trying to beat the vile things off—moths fluttering down—*a big hawk moth clung to her leg beating its wings*—

Her eyes bulged with terror. She tried not to scream again (*as yet part of her said wryly: "See, asshole? This is just what you deserve"*) when quarts of slimy, hairy mold gushed out, thick with lumps that seemed to be embalmed, decaying fingers (*oh God it's* — !) pink-mottled, gray lumps (*fingers*) clutching bloody eye-sockets blinking, twitching in seas of horrid filth pouring from her own lips—

Spiders by the hundreds! crawling frantically over her cheeks and forehead and wriggling down her body, as a huge gout of blobby stuff came out—stuff that was dark, oily, smeary, gristly and it was the *stinking, furry bodies of alien beasts!* choked to death by yards and yards of greasy pink intestines exploding from her mouth along with...rotten bones. Teeth. Bones with meat decaying on them; pulsing, glistening brain tissue, sweetbreads and other thick, gruesome shapes upchucking from her guts, and the more she struggled to fight off the shock and not scream, the thicker it got.

O'Blivion had always been terrified of choking. A huge fat freaky lizard, a *basilisk!* got stuck in her windpipe; she choked, frantic to spit the squirming thing out and...and...*here it came*...it plopped on the smooth, hard tiles...Ugh!

Pools of blood rattled into the drain and clotted at her feet.

"FUUUUUUCK!" she shrieked.

Blood trickled down her body, sheeting all over until the whole stall was smeared and dripping—and still more rivers of blood ran down her legs, drenching everything as clots of bloody worms gouted from her mouth, sluicing out of her rectum, vagina, urethra, nose and ears. She staggered, reeling back to the wall—groped wildly for a towel, anything! but slipping on a wad of wiggling sowbugs (*they popped, splitting open under her bare feet—ugh! That was the worst*), the vampire twisted her ankle painfully.

A groan rolled out of her. Her eyes went blank.

"Oh Woolf," she whimpered in delirium. "My woman from

the stars. Your face sticks in my heart, I've got to think only of your body now, your lovely body...*oh, how could you turn into a traitor and sadist and dump me here among tormentors!* How could you—oh baby baby I'm in PAIN!" the vampire moaned—hardly knowing what she said.

She was blinded by blood, covered with the stuff, her mouth full of it. It began to clot on her skin, worms and flies getting stuck in it, squirming as fresh rivers of blood oozed down her caked, befouled body.

"Oh Virginia Woolf! where are you when I need you," the vampire howled.

(*Ohhh God I can't stand it—I did not sin bad enough to bring such punishment on my head*) driven half crazy—sicking up vile clots of unspeakable nasties—they sluiced from every body opening, even her very pores. But little by little it tapered off, slowing to a trickle; then only glints and flashes came, and finally, nothing. It was over.

Pure water began drumming on the tiles again—draining away the last of her panic, as the attack quieted down. Sterling sagged with relief. Her heart gradually slowed to a normal beat.

At last she was clean! She dried her body on a warm, fluffy Cannon towel that smelt faintly of a nice fabric softener; wondering exactly what in the hell was going on...yet knowing that the nasty outflow hadn't been part of her "Detox."

No way, Jose. She had a long way to go before she'd be fully recovered, yes, but: that kind of a tasteless Junior High gross-out? It wasn't the Rysemian style. Detox was supposed to be a time of growth and new beginnings—

But *something* triggered it. Anyway, the worst was over *(maybe)* but somebody sure meant business. Oh yeah, she understood who was behind it: *Scaulzo!* And he had been warning her. Oh, he'd come too close. Something hideous was going to happen, because Woolf was the focus of his passion; oh yes, he'd unleash all the devils of hell on you and make you squirm but what he really wanted was *Woolf's heart spitted on his bayonet*—

The vampire swore under her breath, staring down at Earth where she needed to be...a pretty little globe that lay wide-open to any invader from the cold wastes of space—a rape always in progress! The AO that had slacked off would only start again worse than ever. The Big S. enjoyed knocking the props out from under people, squeezing the maximum pleasure out of them—

She'd been told that Earth was invaded constantly, always had been and the Authorities had no way of knowing it; nor could they have done anything if they did, except punish the innocent in their own terror...Scaulzo! That unspeakable demon had fed advanced technological data into a caveman society with disastrous results—all for his own twisted pleasure.

And now, Ster had been fingered by Sajorian shock banks. Like a deadly mental germ, the AO left you confused and scared—but at least it had been mercifully brief. And Sterling had broad shoulders. She'd survived many traumas over the years; she was a tough cookie, except...there was one thing she could not confront. Not ever!

She hoped and prayed they wouldn't force her to re-live the death of her daughter.

The AO teased and taunted, sometimes putting voices in your head that came back to haunt you. Ster would be glad to think it was Patton or maybe Doug torturing her—but—she didn't understand the corrosive effects of what Scaulzo did, but knew it was *the road to madness, not sanity!* True, the Rysemians were putting her through hell—forcing her to brush up on her riding, archery, swordsmanship and other semi-lost skills, locking her in a narrow cell with only a shower and toilet, hard cot, wind-up gramophone and a stack of F. Scott Fitzgerald-era records (*My Blue Heaven, Ain't We Got Fun, The Sheik of Araby, Ramona*) along with Nancy Reagan; but a relentless tide of insects spouting from your mouth and every orifice you had? No: that could only be the spook-beam that caused the world's crime, war, disease and poverty, as it intimidated billions. In any case...she didn't dare tell the Chief (ole Abe Lincoln) or H.G. or she'd land both herself and Woolf in hot, hot glue; because—

The thought of her once-beloved Benaroya messing around with that demon, exposing all of them to unthinkable outrages like what had just happened to her...

"Oh Woolf, I believed in you!" Sterling whimpered. "I loved you! You sold me down the river, you filthy slut, and now I've got to escape or die. I've GOT to get out of this awful place! And I only hope you understand. But if you don't...fuck you, you two-faced bitch of a woman! You're just like all the others."

Wincing on the sprained ankle, Sterling gritted her teeth and told herself to think. "THINK! Get a plan, asshole."

Her clothes were laid out on the bed. "Put 'm on quick while you think. Use your brains if you have any, you jerk." (Sterling was often quite mean to herself. "Adequate justifiable self-contempt," Patton called it. She spent too much time scolding herself; even though H.G. said it was a *First Dynamic Crime* according to their big Sage, LRH, back on their home planet.)

Time meant nothing up here on Vonderra but it meant everything to the flip, hip vampire, who wished only to stay forever young-looking but was in a terrible fix! She'd had a bad scare. Without fresh human blood she'd soon look her age *(nearly 800 but who's counting)* and that wouldn't be too great for business. Oh yes, she could laugh at herself and her foibles but it was no joke—without the Ruby she'd swiftly age, die, and become a horrible dried-up mummy. *("For Chrissake rack your brain, you stupid turkey!")*

The shuttles and smaller craft were kept on a mind-bogglingly enormous flight deck. O'Blivion had seen that great big deck when she first got here. Now she tried to imagine where it lay in relation to her cell.

Sterling had grown up in her family's Transylvanian castle high on a hillside, with its colorful banners snapping in the breeze, and hidden passageways concealed by figured tapestries (depicting scenes from the Crusade her father had fought in) hanging on tall, stony walls—but, Vonderra? Mere words couldn't describe this ship—a living diamond bigger than Rhode Island, she contained life-sized duplicates of every city in the world past and present (including Alexandria complete with fabled library). But if Ster could somehow manage to reach the flight deck and steal a tiny escort or even a patrol ship for that matter—if she could commandeer one, then figure out how to fly it—then head for home all by herself—and why not? *If she didn't shake her booty but fast she'd be written off anyway.*

"I see no reason why you folks don't have a paradise on Earth," Heidi's Grandfather always harped at her. "We're here to bring a timeless message of hope, but nobody seems to want it and yet: intelligence will come—in time—when you stop thinking you already have it."

(Excuuuuse me?)

H.G. socked her with that "Your future is bounded only by the imagination!" guff in every session. "And don't let any materialist scoundrel tell you different," he'd say.

"You call yourself a scientist," he'd shake his head sadly. "You say you've been taught to put your faith only in things that can be seen, felt, measured. But when it comes down to the short strokes, it turns out you maniacs think that life grew out of matter somehow. Lightning struck, and little buggies started dancing the two-step in a peat bog. Creepy! and, dehumanizing.

"This weird theory of yours is a neat trick—mind showing us how to do it in a lab? No, O'Blivion, I'm afraid all of us spirit beings made matter, energy, space and time. Then we did so many crimes with the stuff we got amnesia about it. These are some of the course headings you'll deal with in Ethics 101."

To cap it he said: "We plan to put an end to people's horror-addiction and start you being creative again. For openers we'll bring your 'Science' and 'God' together in a way that is natural and sensible." *Eeooo.* H.G. was little, and sweet, with very pretty, white, thick, unshorn, raggedy hair and shaggy brows (plus a wallet stuffed with snaps of baby Heidi that he often bored Sterling with) but if the old geezer only knew how many bejeweled gold, silver, wood, or plastic crucifixes the vampire had pried from the fingers of her squealing, pleading victims before enjoying the hell out of them—*(She smacked her lips, remembering)*

"Your sage Emerson once called Man 'A god in ruins' and boy howdy, dear, that was no lie—"

Poor little H.G. used every cliche that sophisticated people roll their eyes and shrug at—he made you wince with embarrassment! "You have limitless power. To believe you are powerless is to get that way in a hurry," he said. "But the time is ripe to take you back to your heritage, lead you to make the discovery yourself—ah my child. Soon, like a Thing in a cocoon, *every human shall awaken to a new life!*" nodding his pious old, fraudulent head...But H.G. was at least sympathetic and intelligent, unpretentious, and far nicer than Woolf's crude, sneaky boyfriend Doug MacArthur or that male chauvinist swine George Patton, her worst teacher.

("I could have the pair of them WHACKED for a measly ten grand apiece!" fumed Sterling, who had contacts in the criminal underworld and knew how to hire thugs when she needed them...)

Was that a vent in the ceiling? A vent with a screen over it?

The ceiling was forty feet up but if there was a vent in it no matter how high—

The whole thing started the day Woolf came to the Studio to invite Sterling out for dinner in a five-star restaurant and Heidi's Grandfather (who kept goats and smelled like it but she'd never hold that against the old sweetie) crashed their party. Pretty soon Woolf and H.G. began dangling a shimmering dream before her—a dream that all too quickly turned into this drug rehab center where she was being treated to tortures right out of old Roman law!

"But only till you kick your wicked habit," Nancy Reagan smiled, pushing forward her breasts—oh yeah, dear Nancy always tried to undercut Woolf. "Give her up. She'll break your heart. Choose me instead," batting her eyes.

Sterling would draw herself erect.

"And your point is?" she would say frostily.

Oh yes: "Old Miss Nose Candy Hotpants" as Ster called her, was one of a kind—the wrong kind. She got a thrill out of toying with and punishing the vampire. She was a bottom feeder, and Ster vowed that one day she'd kill and drain her!

No...Forget Nancy, and forget the vent. The price was too high. What she should do was settle down for a good night's rest. First thing tomorrow, a session with General Patton was scheduled for her...No!! Anything beat staying here and being cut to ribbons by that macho redneck sexist oinker.

Setting her bunk on end, Sterling crawled on it and began feeling for cracks or bulges in the wall. She'd seen the rock-climbers on PBS; if she could find a crack or two and be very, very patient and not lose her head, and if there really was a vent up there, or any kind of hole big enough for her to crawl through—

"Let me go. I'm no addict, I can stop whenever I want to!" she yelled (in case Nancy or someone was listening).

Then she thought of Woolf and chuckled to herself. Thoughts of The Bloomsbury Superstar always comforted the vampire and put her in a cozy mood. She loved Woolf with every fiber of her being. That was the truth. Even though the two-faced cooze had maneuvered her into this cell to rot...damn her gorgeous eyes!

Ster emptied her pockets. Nothing useful. Except a tube of white lipstick from the sixties—she threw it away, and dug an itty-bitty nailfile out of her bag.

Was that vent-frame attached with screws? The only tool Ster had was the file; it might do. Barefoot, she stuck her fingers in a crack and began climbing.

Stabs of pain lanced her ankle, but NOW(!) had to be escape-time. If she kept her wits she'd be out on the street again, a free woman, creeping along Walton Place near the Studio and hitting on necks where she could find them. The L station was ideal on a cold night. You'd slip your mouth under some shivering guy's wool scarf, people thought you were an engaged couple, they'd smile—a charismatic woman, Ster knew how to hold her victims up skillfully when they sagged and groaned and she always felt she brought a little sunshine into the windchill factor of the average Chicago life. *Yes: everything would again be as it should be...*

The wall was a hard climb. It leaned first inward then out, never straight up and down; kind of like her daily fights with Gramp.

"As a good liberal I feel we should forgive our own weaknesses and those of others," she'd argue.

"It you really love your fellow man, never modify your expectations," he'd answer—give me a break! "Step this way into our magical rocket to Bliss. Have an immortality sandwich, see the lion lie down with the lamb; hold your hat, young ones, we're off." *Eeooo*

And to think that Sterling, in all her sequined sophistication, fell for it! She bit on it like a box of Buddy Squirrel dark chocolate creams (her favorite). Woolf and H.G. threw stardust in her eyes, luring her out of her easy, comfortable life and she didn't even say to herself, "Now girl, keep your head! Remember: they are outer space monsters." No. But at least they were fair enough to warn her that weird things would happen—but it seemed like a wonderful adventure at the time.

"I trained against the Nazis in Czechoslovakia," she had bragged over the soup course (trying like mad to impress the stunning British novelist). "I've gone places and done things that would curl your hair. I can handle any job you've got."

"But if you are hooked on blood," H.G. began—

"Hooked?!!? Are you daft? This is no addiction, it's just a colorful little eccentricity of mine—my way of helping people by furnishing a fabulous Myth to take their mind off their bondage, fear, and trouble."

"Woman born of woman is of few days and full of trouble,"

clucked H.G. as he forked spinach into his beard—That was another thing about Woolf's people. "Learn table manners!" she wanted to scream, but they took their identities from novels, comics, TV and films and had to practice like mad to escape detection, yet were infinitely wise—advanced (it was said) to a point where it couldn't begin to be grasped by the human mind. In their native bodies they didn't even have sex. They had "Union" which was supposed to be a mighty, shuddering, thrilling fusion of Pure Spirit that would atomize the likes of her. Or so it was said.

"I know you can lick this thing, my darling," Woolf had murmured into her ear.

Whew. Sterling had never felt so turned on! But now disaster was sitting on her forehead, as her old granny in Rumania used to say.

"I'm your woman," she had whispered, turning her head so that their lips met. "Just so I can work with you."

"Deal," murmured the world-famous novelist as they kissed. This wasn't the *original* V.W. of course—*that* Woolf was *dead,* a suicide, by drowning in a river in England in 1941. She had been Sterling's Role Model since one night in 1923 when they met at a poetry reading given by Woolf's husband Leonard for his bud, T.S. Eliot. *This* Woolf was a gigantic *sea pig* or *whale* in her native body (all Rysemians were clone sisters)—a lovely, innocent soul, who possessed wit, wisdom, beauty and authority, and with whom Ster had a deeply touching, non-Platonic friendship that was exquisitely steamy. They clicked right off, tuned to each other, having madcap fun—

(*"Will you love me forever?" Virginia Woolf had whispered behind her hand* as T.S. Eliot *sipped his cocktail*)—but even just touching and being close, Sterling felt it was unrealistic to expect it to last. It was too good, she sighed...And yet! Confronted with the agonizing prospect of actually losing Woolf...

Sweating freely, her toe in a shallow crack, Ster reached for a jagged hole and drew up (she'd like to get on the outside of a good dinner first but that drip Nancy wouldn't serve for hours yet), climbing as fast as she could. But—she had to confront the thing that really scared the bejeezus out of her. The Rysemians had taken Scaulzo prisoner but Benaroya released him saying "I caught the 'sucker, I can open the cage if I want to!" with a toss of her dark, Woolfian locks. And Mersoid, honest Abe, told Sterling:

"I fear she's doing shameful acts with the Evil One. Perhaps even *sleeping* with him. So get your habit kicked, then go tail her and report anything unusual to me."

"*Sleeping with the devil?* Bullshit!" Ster fumed. "You're telling me to cop on my best friend — do I look like I'm inclined to squealing? In the first place she wouldn't do anything dirty. In the second place, you want the juicy details *go get 'm yourself.*"

Ten minutes of nimble climbing and Ster was twelve feet up. Pausing to congratulate herself, she made the mistake of glancing down.

She slid, flopped, hit the floor, lay stunned. She was unconscious for a minute or two but: "Stay cool," she growled.

Big toe in a crack (she was leaving a fresh trail of blood but screw it), sliced-up fingers grabbing a knot in the wall, O'Blivion slithered up, soon attaining a nerve-jangling altitude — egged on by thoughts of Patton and what he did to her; the torrent of abuse he dished out every day, insulting the shit out of her as if his "training" wasn't horrendous enough.

"You, the ex-physicist pioneer who tapped the field of time travel," he sneered. "The woman who opened up the portal to the past — and look at you! Impossibly irresponsible, blood all over your teeth — creepy druggie. You are pathetic."

Interesting what happened to men's mouths when they called you 'pathetic.' The lips pulled down. A shy, red tongue poked out when they said THEH, middle syllable of that stupid word 'pathetic'...*eeooo!* Especially the way Patton did it. He was ship's captain Boolabung, an ugly misogynist who should be killed and his kidneys fried with onions (like a certain hideous proto-human Nazi Sterling had just barely managed to evade, used to do to his victims). Men like that should never get born! These and other vengeful thoughts kept her climbing until —

"Don't look down!" Dizzy, she grabbed some bricks; the floor was a postage-stamp. But the hard part was still to come.

The vent was four feet out. Ster found a chunk of masonry to stand on and leaned, slipping the file into a screw.

Pinggg! The screw hit the floor. She prayed Nancy wouldn't hear. Caught in the act of escaping! What would they do to her? It was roasting up here at the ceiling, dust clogging her nose, making her eyes throb — she wedged fingers between grating and plaster, unscrewing every screw. The grating fell with a clang (almost taking her with it but she grabbed the opening at the last second).

Sneezing, dangling, Sterling looked up...The opening was just big enough! Thank God, oh, thank God. If she could manage to kick and squirm, pulling herself through—

Heart pounding, the vampire did a pull-up. Every muscle in her neck was standing out. Her eyes rolled up to see...

"No!" she screamed. But it was too late.

Tongues of fire leaped at her. (*Oh God, did it have something to do with Pentecost?*) The upper room was a blazing inferno, flames shooting out and licking the vampire's hands. The agony was unbearable—her fingers turned into bubbling, ruined blisters but she couldn't let go. Panting, dangling, her eyebrows were seared off; an orange tongue blackened her face, but she hung mesmerized—

One spot was not afire. One tiny spot, way back in the dim distance. Racked by coughs, Sterling couldn't keep her eyes off that spot. The spot was black. Black as the pit of hell. It hovered in the shadows.

She peered at it, her flesh sizzling, scorching, burning off. It was a funeral wreath, bouncing and sliding on waves of fire—

Did she remember that wreath? From a long-ago funeral perhaps? Knives of fear jabbed her when it bounced closer.

There was a clean white, satin sash across the front.

Trembling with effort, her features melting and running together like wax—the vampire had to strain every muscle to read the words on that bit of white cloth. She was so afraid she'd see her daughter's name on it but no: what it said was—

YOU LOSE.

She had opened the door on flames.

She read the message with numb horror—and lost her grip. The cell resounded with her screams.

Arms wide, legs flailing, O'Blivion dropped forty feet. She hit the cement with a noise like a watermelon cracking open.

FIVE

The door was opening. Slowly.
Trickles of sweat ran down Doug's ribs. He cursed himself for not being armed except for the duty piece snatched from a drawer.

The hotel was unpleasantly still...This .45 would blow the head off any human assassin. But if the Presence behind that door happened to hail from Sajor--

He needed the bulk of an H-2 unit in his mitt! The Chief had made it abundantly clear he shouldn't be tempted along those lines, and there'd been no point in arguing but he'd be a liar if he didn't admit Woolf was behind this--

No time for recriminations though. Doug leaned forward, elbows on knees, sights trained on where a pair of eyes would show up. This intruder might think MacArthur was a cornered rat but when the bastard revealed himself--he'd "lose face."

Bad luck if he happened to be from Sajor. Change of plan! Throw this peashooter in his teeth, try to grab the unit and with it, usher him into that world of torture Doug himself knew so well. He had been struck by H-2 fire once...just once. It had stamped a deep impression on Omark. "A fate worse than death. That's how you've got to think about it," he told his students. Stranded on this planet, frozen into this bod, a bag of kneejerk meat, oh God! It was unthinkable--and Scaulzo's men were a gang with a grudge. Doug scowled, fingers tightening around the .45's cold grip as he strained to hear...the sights unwavering, his breath coming deep and quiet--

But why was the door opening so SLOWLY?

The H-2 had been invented on Sajor (of course. Who else would do it?) and it was the only thing in the known universe this squadleader would run from. A festering, unspeakable horror, awaiting any Rysemian unlucky enough to be hit by it.

Doug licked his lips, keeping his sights on the door moving open with agonizing slowness. Whoever this was, would get his head blown off in about two seconds but—odd sounds came from the hall. A grating, unpleasant kind of a squeal—then nothing. Radio off. Only the ominous silence. What did it mean? Doug heard glass tinkling. (A bomb of some kind maybe?)

He wanted to yell, "Show yourself!" but could only wait.

He had to remember that the Korean War, called a mere 'police action,' was the bloodiest war in recent history. A million women and kids had been killed in it so far. It wasn't too farfetched that some relative might feel irked enough to try and murder the General—

The door flung open with a tiny crash! against the wall and in popped, thank Gods, only the hotel maid, name of Miki. Miki had introduced herself to the General last night when he got in. Now she pushed a wheeled tray loaded with breakfast goodies under silver domes along with a tall water glass and a silver vase with a rose in it. She crossed to the window and pulled back the drapes. Sunlight stabbed through the panes. Doug winced. Miki, for her part, stole sly peeks at the long, silent figure hiding a .45 under tangled sheets.

Ever since that weird day when Doug accepted the Japanese surrender aboard the battleship Missouri he'd been ruler of Japan and...be honest. It was part of the reason he'd accepted this job—come on! Who wouldn't want to be Emperor of a whole danged country? It had sounded like fun even for an overworked anthropologist, except that ever since he met Miki she hadn't tried to hide the fact that she'd love to crawl into the sack with Emperor MacArthur. And so did everyone else, but women did it even in public. As second class citizens they had to chase men, the richer the better—forced to seek "Johns" to support their young instead of being permitted to earn an honorable living at a fair wage. He knew Miki didn't care for him, only for what he represented—which was rather a pity; he'd like to see how women would react without the institutionalized slavery.

In any case, it was rough enough putting up with a wife of his own! Doug hoped he wouldn't be forced to allow Miki to crawl into the hay with him too. Life on Earth was one long anticlimax but—he should complain? Next time he'd carry a good ol' H-2 unit and screw Abe Lincoln and his faggy orders. And yet—

When Doug shoved his .45 under the pillow and sat up to eat, it was clear that he'd gone to bed with his General suit on.

The shirt was open at the neck the way it should be, but he had his sunglasses and pipe on. Miki's eyes widened in surprise and disapproval...followed by a knowing wink.

Omark cussed himself for forgetting the petty but ironclad rules about putting your General suit on, taking it off, putting it on, taking it off, over and over; inane details you were expected to do not only with flair but a genuine liking. Shave the cheeks. Comb the fur. Tie the tie. Floss the teeth. Floss them again. Floss them again. A lifetime spent dressing, undressing and playing with a G.I. Joe doll—it could drive a sane being nuts—you had to chew apples with your incisors, carrots with your molars and be ostracized or laughed at if you mixed them up—God Almighty.

He grabbed the phone when it rang, chewing a mouthful of egg.

"To the service of humanity," said Abe Lincoln.

"Serve humanddy" growled Omark around egg.

"Why are you avoiding Virginia Woolf? Lady says you refuse her calls," Chief Mersoid's voice rang out in Abe Lincoln's sonorous baritone.

"I think you know the answer to that one."

"Switch to commlink. I want to see your ugly face."

They switched. Miki wasn't surprised to see the iron-willed leader in frock coat, swallowtails, stovepipe hat and brand new high-button shoes made in 1860, scowl heavily as he walked up to MacArthur's bed—she knew that Americans could do anything.

She poured the hologram a cup of coffee but it refused it. "What are you digging up in the way of information? Not you, young lady. I'm talking to the General here," Lincoln snapped.

"Along what lines, Mr. President?"

"Along the H.L. Mencken lines, General."

"I don't know what you're talking about."

"H.L. Mencken," Lincoln said patiently. "Not that it matters but he was an American writer born 1880, grew up to be a mordant satirist, twitted the popular writers of the day and for a while made'm love it. Called'm 'the booboisie'; but poor Mencken was a sauerkraut-eater of German stock so when the big bad bang came, the booboisie cold-shouldered him into a pauper's grave. Americans born in Germany were under investigation at the time—not tossed in concentration camps like the Japanese in World War II but still—"

"Do I look like I give a whizz?"

"Gray-faced male, sunken-eyed, pecked-looking, often seen lurking in shadows smoking a wet cigar?"

"Beel!"

"Or one of the other lieutenants, so tell me. Why in holy hell did you let Virginia Woolf give that Sajorian demon a freeze release? Why didn't you stop her?"

"Me? ME?!!?"

"You. YOU. Let's recap, and don't interrupt." Lincoln lifted an index finger, ticking off points. "Frimble invents the Mousehole. Its terminal exit happens to be near Earth, an infinitesimal and heretofore unimportant planet at the rim of Galaxy #13. Tailing us for booty and evil games comes Scaulzo, who begins playing with humans, turning them into psycho puppets in his war dramas. Benaroya showing great heroism traps him for capture by yourself and Frimble, the great scientist, having fun as Dirty Harry.

"Meanwhile you develop a freeze release negating the effects of the H-2; you use it on Benaroya when she gets hit and later she uses it on you, saving your life—but never, God forbid, on Scaulzo, frozen into the body of the dashing Count de Falke—a highly attractive but dangerous human male. Woolf herself has frozen him, captured alive, held for study aboard Vonderra to 'test the basic components of evil,' says she. Then for no reason we can fathom she frees him—"

"No reason we can fathom," said Doug sarcastically.

"Yes, well, hear me out. Here's what we know. Woolf took the prisoner Scaulzo from his cell on Vonderra. His whereabouts are unknown and there's no way we can force her to divulge information. Her only logged statement is 'I'm gonna drop the net on him once and for all'—whatever that means. But the crunch now becomes: his A-0 is pushing you to the brink of tolerance and don't deny it."

Doug rolled his eyes, but held his peace.

Lincoln puffed out some breath. "It's your skin!"

"And yours, Harry's, George's and don't forget Woolf's! My guess if you want it, is: she's got the devil stashed away somewhere, frozen in his carcass and nice and ready for, uh...clandestine purposes of her own, to put it delicately. Could be she's slow-torturing him. While jumping his bones. I wouldn't put anything past her."

"Sounds more like her loverboy has you by the throat—"

Doug stared back at him. "And you? Remember the last time we saw each other? The day before the assignment began, we were in that bar. Remember?"

They'd been walking past houses with lights in the windows, just surveying the situation for practice and to get a handle on smoothly breathing air—

"Now tonight," Abe had said, rubbing his hands together, "we officially kick off what I think is going to be the best in-depth ethnology probe to date. Ethnology: the study of what man does. All those deep, dark secrets the cute little sucker will not confront. Is this going to be exciting or what?"

It was twilight. Purple shadows crawled on walls. They passed a bar with music coming out of it.

"Like a brewski?" Abe asked, moving his neck and head in the exaggerated mannerisms that proclaim your wish to be viewed as a macho, heterosexual male and no mistake about that buddy and if you call me a faggot I'll beat the shit out of you. It was the accepted routine in this kind of a joint where sexuality was always iffy; men avoiding the fact that men were always far more interested in men and their activities than in anything that had to do with women (except as women enhanced the appearance of the man's own sexual prowess in the eyes of the other men who fascinated him).

"I've heard of this place. They make the best darn chili in the world," Abe said, turning into the bar on East Pike Street just as smooth as if he'd done it all his life.

Inside, a gang of loggers bellied up to the bar chugging brewski while having their inner ears punctured by blaring non-music. Doug, very new in his body, needed some practice in suppressing telepathy, intelligence and other social skills while seeing how drunk he could get without throwing up; learning to hold his liquor like a real Earthguy.

"Two brewskis," Abe ordered; chin tucked in, mouth pulled down, doing the whole routine to look tough, with his legs stretched out under the table—and those legs. Lincoln's legs were nine feet long and then some.

"Get your foot off mine," MacArthur had objected mildly.

Immediately, Abe's lips pulled back and his face got stiff. God! But Abraham Lincoln was a fierce-looking mofo when he was angry. Doug recoiled a bit—he couldn't help it. Their faces were inches apart; and when your face is inches apart from Abe Lincoln's face, your breath gets noisy—not out of lust, that was different, but because the man was awesome.

"I'll need a full report of everything you see and hear beginning tomorrow!" Lincoln barked.

And Doug was a little upset. Abe didn't need to bluster and pull rank the night before the action started—but now it struck him. That pallid creep with the cigar. Hadn't he seen him lurking in the background in that stinky beerjoint? Omark could never forget how, disembodied, he'd had the "pleasure" of watching his own autopsy performed by a couple of joking medics in an Italian morgue. It's how he lost his well-loved Jennison body, and ever since then he had a tendency to see a Sajorian lurking behind every bush—

Abe started bragging, Doug's first clue that something was wrong. The cool Chief never stooped to boasting—but tonight, with his long whiskered chin sunk on his bosom, and his lids raised over somber eyes to peer at General MacArthur, he looked precisely like the robot ringer of himself that totters onto a podium and intones the Gettysburg Address at Disneyland—odd that nobody recognized him, or his drinking comrade either.

"You have no idea how cool I'm able to be," Abe bragged, sucking brewski out of the bottle. "In a scene abounding 'n corruption I keep 'm guessing to a point where they never realize the whole Civil War was a shuck! Hell—the slaves were about to be freed, it cost too much to feed them and new machines were being invented every day, and if I wanted to keep every state under my Presidential control whether they liked it or not, which in fact I did, I could have thought of a far saner way to do it than the massacre I helped bring on-—but—fact is, Douglas: we were all of us cannibalizing a new, pure land so that by the time we got it stripped bare, the whole locust-routine would go down the tube. What I'm saying is that none of us had anything to offer except bigger and better exploitation methods, so nobody showed an ounce of sense including me."

"That's too technical for me." Doug puffed his pipe.

"Yeah well the point was that nobody ever provided for the future at all. Yet all us pols of the governing elite, we're worshipped as gods. Can you explain that? But what concerns me is, it's not considered at all queer that men love running off to war with other men more than they love anything on God's formerly green Earth. Is that peculiar? Or what? Why can't they just come right out and admit—"

Doug's pipe had gone out. He flicked a match afire with his thumbnail, enjoying the flare as he touched it to his pipe and inhaled briskly—smooth as silk.

"I'm considering a Civil War rematch," Abe was saying. "That'll excite the lads! Spend plenty money, order brand new uniforms and swords and all, maybe let the South win this time and see if things turn out any better."

"Yeah—you can reel off the Gettysburg Address and it's heartwarming but it don't butter any bread on a black lady's table," Doug agreed. "But enough about you. You're boring. Let's talk about me. My problems are more winsome."

He was just drunk enough not to give a damn if Lincoln got mad.

Abe, though, chose to switch the conversation to how the Yanks left the Iraquis in 1991. "No electrical power; no drinking-water except some fairly pure stuff in gutters, only a little oil and pee in it. Bush said they were going after the head honcho, but they let him continue living richly while they bombed women and children as always." He stowed away the chili (it had been set on their table by an apple cheeked boy waiter) into his six and a half feet of gaunt height. Doug watched the muscles in Abe's jaw work as he crushed crackers into the chili and ate'it off a big spoon—Doug himself wasn't hungry. A gnat had flown into his mouth was the trouble.

"Luckily," Abe was saying, "our boys know that little children die quite easily. They don't make long-winded deathbed speeches or anything like that to disturb the distributor-consumer relationship that keeps our economy healthy. Please pass the hot sauce, thank you, General."

Abe kept craning his neck toward the bar.

"Bring your eyes into focus on that booth over there," he murmured. "There's gonna be some thumpin'."

Six or eight men seemed very interested in what the ex-President and the wannabe President were up to. That seemed to tickle Lincoln. He used his napkin.

"Check it out," he said. He blew into his fists.

"Shall we stroll about the city?" he grinned.

Doug didn't need to be asked twice. This would be fun: half a dozen punks in fatigue pants or jeans, stompin' boots and green-and-black or red-checked lumberjack shirts, deliberately not-watching Abe slap down bills to pay for the beer and chili.

Into the rare pale twilight they sauntered. Fresh air tasted fine after the smoke curtain, and Doug risked a glance back over his shoulder—yep; here they came.

"Ah, the city," Abe was saying. "The ancient, mysterious human pile bearing the scars of state-licensed ick and dehumanizing neglect, umm..."

Two perfume-scented bodies brushed past them.

"Hookers, poor dears," Abe breathed. "They are called 'ho' or 'chippie.' They Do It For Money! If we had an extra ten minutes—"

MacArthur shook his head.

But Abe was in his element. "Tell me, Dougie, is there something about me that says I'm too old and venerable to whip the crap out of ten punks of an alien race? Tell me the truth, now. Do I look middle-aged?"

"Well..."

Both men were a little drunk. They walked unhurriedly down the street, rounding a corner into light spilled from backdoors. It was the alley (reeking of wet garbage)...scuffing feet sneaking up behind them.

They both said, "Ahhh!" while taking a blissful pee against an old brick wall. Looking up, Doug saw the star carpet known as the Milky Way. Rysemus and its sun were too far off in the center of the Galaxy to be spotted from out here in the boonies—this tiny rim system was in the Back of Beyond—but it looked so pretty it would tear your heart: that barely-visible ribbon of white diamonds, flung across the black velvet of the sky. Then as they zipped up, the other men closed the distance.

One pair kept to the rear; the rest grinned and swaggered in front.

"Gimme da wallets," their leader smirked.

Abe shook his head sadly. "Tsk! Violence confronts us everywhere, I'm afraid."

"Shall we give him our wallets?" Doug asked Abe, very seriously.

Abe looked gravely at Doug. "Gosh, I don't think so. I'm too scared to move."

"Me too, so I vote we pay them off."

"Aw, let's tease 'm a little first," Abe answered, joy creeping into his tone. His eyes were clear, bright, and sardonic as only Abe's eyes could get.

"Don't you think these men are dangerous?"

"Oh terribly! Maybe we should scream and plead."

The thugs looked like they couldn't believe their ears—then, they bristled and moved in. Abe was grinning happily.

"Whenever you're ready, maestro," he said.

"Oh, let's not rush the pleasure." They bowed solemnly to each other and shook hands.

"Gimme yuh fukn money yole fukfaze!" their attacker yelled at Abraham Lincoln.

"Only if you say please—"

A fist shot out at Abe's face. He ducked, and Doug smacked the fist's owner in the forehead—not a completely smart move as it made his knuckles sting something awful--

Then there was a burst of activity. Everyone involved began smashing heads and cracking chins, wet smacks sounding as Abe and Doug, jumped by a bunch of muggers out for mere loot (as if a primitive couldn't get all he needed by using his brains if he had any! and if he hadn't, what the devil was he doing running around loose?!!?) heard the gratifying sound of the pop, crunch and snap of breaking bones as they sent men flying, but they stopped short of taking them out. Mersoid never permitted his people to kill without roundly chewing them out for it so he could hardly do it himself—but they did kick the living shit out of them, leaving six mangled bode draped on boxes, ashcans, and a fence—limbs twitching, but not in death.

They didn't kill them, just disabled them but good.

Doug grinned as he remembered Abe Lincoln on his toes with that cool footwork of his weaving, hammering with his roundhouse left fist; the first attacker instantly on his knees going "Bleh. Bleh. Blooah" as gallons of used brewski tumbled from his unhappy mouth-parts. And the others were squealing as they bled and made gagging noises—their fight ebbing quickly.

Abe and Doug didn't wait till the dust settled. They strolled off licking their knuckles and male-bonding, making remarks like: "Wow, gulp, what an adrenaline rush. Except after it's over you get this big letdown so what's the point? And remarkably enough, humans have been doing this and then asking the same questions afterward for umpteen trillion years, are they hung up on the time-track or what?..."

But that was then, and this was now. Abe Lincoln was giving Miki the eye—as, all at once an oompah band began playing in the distance, probably in celebration of MacArthur's victory.

Doug felt irritated though. He couldn't stand Miki, true; but— he had seen her first!

SIX

"I'm here on your planet to WHUP THE DEVIL!" shouted the naked woman.

She hopped onto a bandstand in Lincoln Park in Chicago, where a grinning youth in a Speedo swimsuit pushed a mike into her face (which was darn nice of him).

"My name is Virginia Woolf and a great big SMACK from me to you," blowing kisses as iron boxes on poles went Ooolf-oolfsssssmooo. "But something has gone horribly wrong! You are being invaded under the master plan of Scaulzo, Grand Intergalactic Crime Boss heading up the CIA and MAFIA and all those who've sucked your being RIGHT OUTTA YA."

There was laughter and a sprinkling of applause.

"Is this a fairy tale?" Woolf yelled, getting red in the face. "Oh my brothers and sisters, the simple holy truth is—there are bitter days ahead but don't go 'way! Lots more entertainment coming," pushing the hair back from her forehead. "Now, I'm hip enough to know that YOU the CONSUMER are POWERFUL and will switch me off if I'm not spellbinding. But where in all this hoopla and whoop-de-do can you find the truth? Huh? You live in a fantasy world right out of the Twilight Zone, but hey. I see you dudes ignorin my words as usual and lookin at this body. Ain't it a beaut? Fresh outta the Shop. Feel that muscle."

Woolf bent to let her breasts plop into outstretched hands. As her bicep and naughty bits were grabbed at, her long hair swung in their faces.

"Squeeze me," she shouted. "Is that a hard one or what? And check out the paps, so bouncy yet soft with firm, yielding contours. Are those luscious or what? Take a good feel, grab a BIG handful of ENTERTAINMENT. The mass of human tits will soon outweigh the planet—but—go on and play your scarcity game, you poor shortage-lovers," she teased.

"Burn baby burn," encouraged a voice out front.

"You got it right," Woolf brayed. "We got a LIVE show for you today and speaking of LIVE, friends, none of this would be possible without the help of our good pals upstairs," raising an index finger as she closed her eyes and swayed.

"Now today as we kick off the official Anti-Antichrist Rally all across this great, rich, rolling land of yours—Shut up and listen!"

Woolf knitted her brows darkly. The crowd, after some tittering and shuffling, settled down.

"Oh my poor bushies," her voice rolled and thundered.

"I've seen scads of savages but none as tragic as you. The hollow in your heart must be filled" (ILLD-illd-illd-illd went the iron boxes) "cuz you need a brandnew way of seeing things, not knowing the rules of life cuz you've been BROKEN, not a person at all but a Composite Sketch drawn by an underpaid cop artist. They gave you a mental lily-foot, deprived of genuine humanity, wired into slavery and told you are free rich and peaceful—now that's something for your imaginations to get hold of!"

Woolf laughed uproariously. The crowd clapped and cheered. They sensed her political rightness as they ogled her nudity.

"You can-blame Scaulzo getting off on your jails and drugs and sorrow in the colleges that make mental cripples outta ya— he's running a con here! Wake up, dudes! The thing is blowing up in your face, which is why I feel a heartrending compassion for you," closing her eyes against sudden vertigo.

(Hey...what was going on???)

Tears began running down her cheeks.

"You know what that spells, little brothers? It spells TROUBLE. It spells TERRIBLE THINGS COMIN DOWN on your poor squashed melons," the speaker screamed, every cord in her neck standing out. "I'm here to straighten out the old Good and Evil hassle once and for all. I'm working with PURE EVIL today and oh boy he's more than I reckoned on! So I'm asking you to help me WORK FAST. The Big S. is doing something to my head right now—at least I think he is—unless it was my lunch—ULP!"

Woolf threw up, she spewed, she hurled, but only a bit and quite tactfully so's not to upset the front row.

"Oh my brothers and sisters," she then continued, raising her arms like the crackerjack Evangelist she was determined to become (no matter who said what! *and that went double for that dumb old, sexpot Douglas MacArthur* who wouldn't answer his phone — yes; Woolf longed to get off the train in all these drowsy little, pretty American towns and preach THE GOSPEL as soon as she found out what the hell it was—)

"Your cowardly complicity gives you an illusion of safety, which leads to yet another stalemate as time runs out on al-laya. I'm warning you of the vanity of combat, and asking you to KNOCK OFF WAR. Us Rysemians could vanish this whole planet by lifting one finger, therefore SEE HOW SILLY YOU'RE BEING?" she roared. "But oh my poor lost lambs: on this tiny foreign globe, in this brief flicker of eternity, under the blazing blue dome of heaven I have come to bring SPIRITUAL ENLIGHTENMENT followed by unheard-of power, freedom and joy for every human alive—"

"Can we meet after the show?" a tenor voice requested.

"Now you're talkin! This little world coulda been successful if you'd resisted Scaulzo from the gitgo—I admit it's a tough proposition; he puts out sexual sensation (which you believe you lack) and bucks in your wallet which is the kind of offer most people can't refuse unless you're a REAL warrior, a HERO! Which is what I'm here to talk to you about."

There was a smell of popcorn on the warm summer breeze... and other tantalizing smells that she opened her nostrils to breathe in—and this was a fine speech if she could keep her mind on it—but—hey—

"I used to be incredibly snobbish! Virginia Woolf the Bloomsbury Snob they called me! Then I found GOD! And for your sake I added the JUDEO-CHRISTIAN ZEN ETHIC and came to bring light where there are shadows to all you poor wretched little cannibals whose ignorance, you know what it spells? It spells TRUBBULL. It spells TERRIBLE THINGS COMIN DOWN on your poor little melons! unless you can get down to the root of yourself. Can you hear me back there?" she squawked.

"As I told my lesbian girlfriend Sterling...'As a mere human, all you got is mortality and failure. BUT all you gotta do is ASK and I will take you away on my starship' I told her. And she had the guts and the heroism to ask! And now my buddy and I, two tough bulldykes who are unbeatable as a team, we plan to enjoy a lifetime of TRUE LOVE together with the approval of MOSES

AND JESUS!"

EASES ozez eazez ozez cried the iron boxes—

There was whistling and a few angry glares, but hey. She shouldn't be saying ANY of this stuff, should she...?

"Of course I could be shining you on. Who knows? As a squadder I'm under strict orders to behave like the species I'm studying and if that species happens to occupy a sinkhole of lying barbarism, well, boy howdy damn-me all to hell!!!"

(Woolf cleared her throat. The crowd clapped and laughed while the sun shone merrily out here in the fresh air where a breeze ruffled the flag and all was cool but...*was she losing the thread, perhaps? The attack had caught her by surprise. She wasn't geared for this, uh,* blur *in her head all of a sudden —*)

"As any fool can see, I am an alien spy on a secret mission out here in this backwater among you natives whose cruelty is muttered about and deplored among species you never heard of," her voice boomed out. "You, riding your billion-year war machine and say you can't stop—ZAP! The devil's at your throat, SCAULZO! decreeing a ruined life for each and every one of you—(*Whew: she was outta practice* trying to beat the eerie sensation...*numbing. Her guts all knotted up in a ball,* hoooo this was something bad) And are you even vaguely pissed about it? Do you get mad when you think of it? NO! Just the opposite. You eat Scaulzo like jujubes, whereas I, a marine animal, far more sane than you, am here to provide you with the inspiration many of you have been praying for."

She did a little dance step, flashing the thumbs-up and victory signs before plunging on.

"Doug MacArthur's gonna break my chops for blowing my cover so totally (and I have no idea why the hell I'm saying these forbidden things to you!) but hey. The kids back home where I hail from? My schoolmates deep in the heart of this wonderful Milky Way of ours? OH, they gonna turn green with envy. Say. When do THEY get to see a real live alien up close enough to sniff its butt, pull its eyebrows, run your tongue in its ear and yank its li'l wingwang while jumping into bed on your stork legs as you gab with your tireless tongue about the never-ending human gossip that means not a plugged nickel in eternity? HAH?"

The speaker paused as if momentarily bewildered, tugging a bit of pubic hair and twirling it around one finger. Her mouth went slack. *Whatever it was, this bad feeling, it washed over her again and again — a disturbing flicker of A-O maybe* but oh that couldn't be; anyway it was just a cat's tongue but...awful.

"Get her down from there," ordered a cold voice from the rear.

"You can yank my wingwang any time," smiled the youth in the speedo.

"Put your spears down and listen to my favorite story," Woolf bawled, recovering herself. "What a goodlookin crowd you are! My my, and what a great show I got planned for you. I tell ya what, I'm really excited—" shading her eyes from the sun's dazzle, "and you know what? I think this gonna be the best wake-up call any of you ever got," with an involuntary belch as she flexed her knees.

"Lesson One! You live down here in a war zone where you get zapped repeatedly, given implants till you remember nothing, not your past existences or which way your butt is screwed on even. Now! Who's at the bottom of this outrage. Who's the deadly tentacle setting you up for the big take over? I'm tellinya it's SATAN! AKA my prisoner Scaulzo the Sajorian who, I'm beginning to find out the hard way, has slippery tentacles that get in everywhere BUT! I don't have to tell ya — you could create something magical out of this mess if you wanted to — you could have the greatest bliss any soul is capable of. Like it was this guy, what'zizname Moses, or was it this guy Jesus who said 'Resist the devil and he'll flee from you?' THAT'S ALL YOU GOTTA DO! Isn't that easy? Whereas I, in the white hat? Whatever it takes, I shall try to bring order out of your confusion."

This bandstand was only a block from the beach — she could see the beach from where she stood — sunbathers wedged in so tight they all had to turn over at the same time — OUCH! a stone knicked her belly. Another grazed her hip, dammit and double damn ouch! She was losing 'm. Better do something they approved of.

Woolf walked on her hands shouting "You've massacred whales! You wouldn't want my people to come out here in a war canoe and massacre you? You are not better than animals. I'm an animal. Hurt an animal and you get diseases and new diseases pouring in now and doctors can't help you. AND!" flipping to her feet and bouncing up, "I know I'm not universally loved, who the heck ever is? I'm a little alarmed right now folks; it feels like I'm losing not only my mind but the mob's attention...Oboy."

The anthropologist took an invisible handkerchief from a non-pocket and fanned her face, neck and other parts with it, then wiped her underarms, balled it up and threw it to the crowd. "Heyyyy! I've studied your artifacts and know what delights you utterly. I know what you will ACCEPT: nothing but TITS and ASS and BLOOD and HORROR!" she laughed. "Now I'm gonna press those bushie buttons that please you. Just you watch."

There was something very wrong — her skin goosefleshing even though it was hot out...aside from the fact that poor ratings mean you're dead in the water. You have to have the edge. You simply CANNOT GO NUMBER ONE ON THE CHARTS (as Woolf had every intention of doing) without two hundred million people responding wholeheartedly. She needed a slick new formula and had better get one fast.

Throwing both clench-fisted arms in the air she began running up and down high-leggedly wiggling the hips, then grinding the pelvis at the grandstand, legs spread, knees bent, as she had seen Football Heroes do it, actions idiotic enough to make Bushies cheer their heads off, applaud, and whistle — as many now did.

That was cool. Yeahhh! She bumped up and down toward the ground — they liked that. They liked it a lot. And now for the horror part...or at least a taste of it.

"MacArthur says it would be kinder to give you euthanasia like a sick old cat!" she panted with a frank smile. "General Patton agrees on an anthropectomy. Ectomy: a combining form denoting surgical removal. But ME? I stick up for you in our meetings, but holy smoke, how come you dudes show no sign of evolving? You've been here since the dawn of time and haven't changed a hair and now they're asking me — hey. What if you hop off the planet and kill innocent people? Like ummm the wolf and the Indian and so many species? See then I'D be guilty of murder, see my position? So meanwhile what we're offering is not for everyone; but I want to help as many of you little brutes as will accept it while there's time. The rest is up to you."

The crowd fell into uneasy silence — some actively disliked her, in fact were quite pissed so Woolf pulled herself together; she HAD to please them. "Work them like a trout" as H.G. taught her.

Smiling seductively, she mimicked unhooking a bra, and dropping it with a sexy wink; then stepping out of a pair of nonexistent panties (the folks didn't even clap now. They hardly breathed!) and pulling off, slowly — slowly — with her teeth — while giving sly little glances at the audience—an invisible glove, slowly-slowly VERY SLOWLY before kicking the panties and the glove to a suddenly dead-quiet mob—

Their roar burst on the air.

She was a surprise hit! How wonderful. A little polish and she'd be a media conglomerate all by herself, except...uh oh. There were those ladies who always looked nasty at her. Their cold, pruny faces and glittering eyes meant she offended them. Deeply disgusted, lips pinched in a white line, they wouldn't rest until she was crucified. Now they snuffed cigarettes and gathered wraps preparing to leave—and call the cops, Woolf telepathized (*which she should not do! Absolutely NO psionic talents were to be employed in any capacity whatsoever while on this planet and the agent knew it— now what in the forever heck was going on with her?!!?*)

"My home body's in storage on our cruiser," she boomed, jerking a thumb at the clouds. "Yes folks, I come from way out in the vast, glittering show of stars and I am here to bring you a new life. You don't know what HORROR is yet. You should see this place in 200 years as I've done. But there is still hope! Our magnificent Rysemian sage, LRH, has taped the way out for you. His ideas must flood the world! So step right up, come to me and I'll give you personal instruction; step up and sign up. I can help you unleash your tremendous, dormant powers but every moment is precious—the clock is ticking. You're in a coma, poor little ones; hypnotized in an abusive relationship with the Sajorian demon and all of your dysfunctional relationships especially WAR IS A SMALL-POTATO dramatization of this basic horror! He finds new ways to terrorize you, oh yes my brothers and sisters, even on a sun-filled day like this one. And me, oh my darlings? I am overwhelmed with grief at your coming extinction," she wept openly, the tears streaming down her face. "Your little voices stilled forever, I mean is that sad or what? To think that something so splendid could slip away in one little day," she cried bitter tears—

(*Holy mackerel. Jumping the gun with classified data what was she saying* AND DOING!??! It suddenly hit Woolf full force that she was starkers, yes, bare without a stitch on. EEOOOO. Where was her wide-brimmed white straw hat? Her elbow-length gloves? Her silk stockings, her girdle, her flowered silk dress, her matching pumps??? She'd been interviewing passers-by in a wealthy shopping mall just an hour ago, learning everything there was to know about the human race and the work was fascinating until something prompted her to — to —)

GAG ME WITH A SPOON.

As a trained field agent Woolf was fully aware that to reveal your nipples, buttocks, and particularly the springy dark V-hair with the little pink lips inside (that hair was STRICTLY VERBOTEN — not to mention the puckered brown rectal orifice behind it which was a TOTAL NO-NO) was considered the worst mistake on this whole planet! Second only to shooting off your mouth, and she'd done both.

(oh jeez, she had nothing on but a Chicago Cubs baseball cap)

Woolf swaggered up and down sticking her chest out, imitating birds...and couldn't stop. Oh God! This had to be the A-O striking without warning and she'd been targeted but lucky for her she knew how to handle it. Otherwise, you made foolish mistakes. It you had a speech to make you'd get it tangled. Make an ass of yourself, maybe wet your pants like when you were new on the job, always flubbing sphincter control or how not to gasp for air while you teetered on spindly legs. These bods — she'd destroyed dozens of 'm before catching on, sure, but now her career was hanging by a thread. Doug MacArthur! She tried calling that big mean snob three times this morning and he wouldn't even pick up the phone. Oh sure, both Omark and Frimble had heavy academic schedules on top of their Earthie roles, but that was no excuse at all.

He was jealous! Jealous because she and Frimble landed the cool jobs. And that was bad news...because her longtime mentor Omark was not only a cool dude, but their larger-than life, All-Star master of disguise who could "do" any bushie behavior no matter how depraved and enjoy it, even while bitching bitterly, non-stop, if bitching was part of the guy's makeup — which it was in MacArthur's case — and then go home and write a book about it. But now she had an uneasy feeling about Doug, fighting all alone back there in the watershed Fifties. He was a driven man, always needing to do something a little bit extra; but if he didn't start drawing the line, before you knew it he'd be a burnout and a sitting duck perhaps even "Going Native" as they called the disease — getting into punk rock and trying to re-grow his hair while buying shiny new cars, condos, film studios or whatnot, obsessed with appearances while the world around him fell apart. Omark (the big lug!) (Benaroya really loved her dear Teach; he had saved her bacon at least twenty times and she saved his once) was a real artist, a genuine master — their #1 anthroponomist, Rysemian Ironman and Biggest Enchilada, who worked miracles with the tools of his trade and he was one great, beautiful guy all right, but!! If he kept taking these subtle risks. She might never lay eyes on him again, whose fault was that? She didn't want to examine that question too closely, nossir. But if Doug continued to fool with sordid details and forgot the big picture, like oh gosh — would it be HER FAULT if he wound up all Macho City? Like maybe a morbid-boohoo, self-pitying, blind Kerouac-Hemingway environment thrasher, sad unknowing male in grief due to his gotta-go-kill-animals-or-dump-babes-to-feel-anything BLUES that other men paid a fortune for in bookstores — oh, sweet Mary in Heaven! Then he'd probably fall in love with a handsome bullfighter or young jail-kid and say it was some woman, right, then shoot himself in the face or drink himself to death, whichever was easier, while the crowd cheered.

BAD NEWS.

She only hoped Doug had worked his shield out tough, and hadn't dived into his part too deeply cuz —

The advance unit, uncoordinated, at Scaulzo's mercy. A small wave of terror washed over her.

("What kinda mess have I got myself into?" Woolf now had the good sense to ask. Every eye was upon her, flashbulbs popping as Earthies snapped pix of her breast, wings, forbidden hair and drumsticks from every angle — all cuz she'd felt that mental shift that shoots you right into Lala Land, a cloying deathgrip if it gets under your skin...And she knew this was only the beginning of the demon Scaulzo's sadistic pleasures.)

"Everything gonna work out, folks, we're gonna float a rainbow here, but keep your eyes on the prize!" she hollered. What she needed was vim, vigor and focus — cuz she was in over her head(!) by the mere act of taking the cruel demon from his cell on Vonderra.

"HEY!! You're a great crowd. We have lotsa talent here today — but — the shark is circling, folks. He is the curse that feeds by night on your goodness while you sit enjoying a scary story, getting all larded up with soapy advertising flattery my poor brothers and sisters," running her hands down her upper thighs—

Hundreds had turned out. What a success she was! More were even now rushing up here from the beach to look, listen, and hopefully to be saved. And yet...

(*an unspeakable, subliminal horror making you do things you weren't aware of doing.* Woolf ticked off in her mind the times it happened before, what she'd done to squeak out of an attack. She'd developed good tricks but with the odds stacked against her as they were today...she had a sudden, cold apprehension that...)

Yeah, she took him from his cell but—not because he was CUTE and the idol of teenagers, children, and adults in every country. Scaulzo was CUTE all right with his sly grin, clean-cut features and air of authority—a sociopath can be phenomenally attractive; it's his business. No! She did it because she knew it was the right thing to do), after mindlocking the creep so he couldn't play with her brain and yet: somehow...somehow...she couldn't put her finger on it but—the Mission was being plunged into terrible danger)

Something could happen that was far worse than death.

"She should be run out of town," a gray-whiskered gent with a long, bony skull shouted.

"Oh my darling," Woolf moaned. "Would I come all the way to nowhere just to step on your corns? Nah, your world's strategically unimportant and didn't even exist until Frimble's Mousehole went through Grid 8"—but explanations were useless. She was in the soup here. All had gone routinely up to her "fatal decision" and even then there was only one flaw. Scaulzo got fixated on Benaroya. *Obsessed* with her. "In love" as he told her every time they met—(eeooo!)—meaning he was on a sexual quest beyond anything ever known or dreaded by the Rysemians—something like a nostalgic trip back to pre-Eden, pre-*space* even, with *her* in chains this time. And it had far-reaching implications because...

"Call the police!" Billy Whiskers hollered, thumping his cane—Lake Michigan was smooth as steel today. She caught a glimpse, on the far horizon, of a barge and a steamer going by and it sure was nice here—

Oh boy. It was a real jam. She had to amuse these savages! She loved how Billy's oral slit puckered and fluttered as the hair went in, then out, then in then out as he yodeled "Call the po-LEESE!" with slipping teeth and the cane whomping and whacking yet

Jeez! Fun was fun, but she was in a fix.

Entertainment! Never forget it; the thing that fixated their attention. Nothing else mattered as long as bushies were being entertained.

Woolf was tall, long-legged and fully fleshed. She flexed her knees, churned out a cartwheel or two — then did one slow, dramatic split while singing "Buffalo gals wontcha come out tonight???" in the down position, followed by half a dozen backsprings.

They watched with staring eyes! Heads jerked back and forth, following the arc of her glistening thighs and split beaver. The day was mild, with puffy clouds piled up over the glassy lake, as more kids came shouting to each other — great armies of boys and girls pedaling bikes or balanced on skateboards, shading their eyes as they gaped.

"And so the great General won't answer my calls," the agent yelled ruefully, panting from her exertions as she flapped her elbows to dry the sweat. "He says I'm comin on like a religious fanatic — bull. We don't have your kinda religion but I can *duplicate* it as a way to get through to you, okay? so that's what I'm up to. ANYTHING to get through to you before you self-destruct is my motto. If I can ignite religious passions, maybe we can slice through the baloney! But Doug sneers. Is that jealousy or what? But I must talk fast. The enemy is on the way."

She waved at the harness bulls who, having piled out of their squad car, were stuck in the fringes of a crowd that refused to budge as it stood rooted for Woolf's next number. And that was a lucky break for her.

"Listen listen listen, I have much to tell you in just a few seconds. We got a lot more entertainment comin' right up...!"

Her voice rose, hypnotic, commanding.

"The Unknown is the biggest chunk of real estate there is, folks, and you've got to quit stumblin' around in it. Get a road map! Listen. Fifteen minutes after you die you are programmed to be born in a baby bod, in other words fetuses have nobody in 'm till just before birth, so you make a lotta fuss about nothin! Bodies? We can make all you need. "You're spirit using flesh and you deserve to be happy! So don't befoul the sea you'll swim in later, what are ya — brain dead? What you need is full information on these taboo subjects and you came to the right place," she bawled —

Oh sweet Lord in Heaven, Woolf was doing and saying all the things she'd been briefed not to do and say and was making an awful ass of herself—true, she'd acted like a worse maniac when she first got here, but a raft of problems wised her up and by now she should be smart enough not to play the bigmouth; having gradually learned the intricacies of how to walk, talk, and keep the mask up like humans did except—

waves of faintness. head spinning something terrible

A bunch more cruisers pulled up behind the others. Reinforcements with dome lights circling, scattering their ruby rays as men stepped quickly in her direction and hey—

One unmarked, slowly moving Plymouth. The FBI! She'd been in trouble with those guys before and—if she wanted to save this crowd, she better hurry because the bulls were gabbing excitedly into their handsets, looking as if somehow she wasn't just your ordinary neighborhood bust (no pun intended). The FBI car drove slowly as if watching her—

"In your world of lives, each one precious, you bring EVIL down by hiring cops who only know how to beat people up and fuck 'm one way or another. Your existence has been flagged and that's too bad BUT: you do not have to be trapped in the flux of time, or believe you're stuck to bodies as you've been forced to do under the devil's reign! 'EEEE. OOOO. Meat on a fork. Ick on me, I'm only long pork!' But ah how fortunate it is my sisters and brothers that you are far more wonderful than that. You are immortal emptiness, less substantial than the light that dances on the edge of a sword—then little by little you were drawn into a REAL horror not just some TV hype—"

Sirens wailed nearby. Woolf edged back and talked fast as six cops with drawn guns came running.

"Gotta end off—thanks for listenin'—love ya—have a good day!"

the PA system racketing, cops breaking through and closing in fast but luckily nobody paid any attention to her WORDS, *only her body-parts*.

"I shall return!" Woolf yelled.

She made a stiff bow from the waist, cartwheeled to the bandstand's edge, hopped off and began bucking toward the beach. A marine creature, she'd be safe in the cool green depths of Lake Michigan if she could avoid the paws grabbing at her.

SEVEN

"There's been an accident," Nancy Reagan's yell resounded through the corridors of Federation Starship Vonderra.

The semi-conscious vampire was in horrible pain: multiple ruptures, massive internal hemorrhaging, fractures of both femurs, spinal nerves severed (*never would she walk or talk again*); neck broken, skull crushed, jaw and face bones smashed, third degree burns over ninety percent of body—

Nancy heard the SPLAT! as the woman literally exploded on the floor ("Exactly like," Nancy shuddered, "those *cantaloupes* David Letterman drops from high places on his excellent show") and rushed in to give mouth-to-mouth.

But Sterling's mouth *(like her bra and panties)* brimmed with blood. The death rattle was in her throat; an arm nearly torn away, her face a barbecued mess, the pain so bad she began to hallucinate.

She was a clay flowerpot that somebody knocked off a ladder in her hometown of Sibiu. But it was lovely being in the quaint, droll village in medieval Romania with its pointy roofs and weathercocks and as she hurtled through space she heard a soothing clop-clop of hooves, rattle of harness, creak of wheels, bells pealing from a steeple...voices calling in the street...

(you're dreaming)

"No I'm not! I hear the beloved speech of my childhood—and around this corner'll be the kids I grew up with—no longer mouldering in their graves—but singing the homely old songs, how I miss'm—people don't realize—nobody ever stops to care—"

PHLUNK!

Her flowers and dirt spilled out. Her tears froze to the cobblestones. It was freezing out. A little dog, strolling by, peed on her. That made her warm for a minute but afterward she was even colder. So cold!...being placed on a stretcher and hauled away; two Nancy Reagans trotting alongside.

"You have a bad attitude. You tried to escape," said one of the Nancies.

"Shut your yap," Sterling tried to mutter but nothing came out.

"It's for the best," Nancy said complacently. "Now you can discard that vile body; and you know what I hope? I hope you slide right into HELL and endure tortures day and night, and never forgive yourself—which is why everyone should always JUST SAY NO and not make problems for others."

Was it a threat? The delirium closed on her brain. She *thought she was home again, after so long...*

Rushing up the stairs to the bronze door with the battle scenes on it, she screamed "Mama, Papa! Tell me you love me! Oh please PLEASE say you forgive me!" and as they pulled the huge door open, she felt her parents' arms around her—as happy to see their child as she was to see them.

(In reality, the dying woman's face glistened with sweat which Nancy, sighing sadly, mopped off). But all at once...

A foul smell came. (*Was it delirium?* No, no. A true bad stink) as they rushed her down Vonderra's bowels—right down to the crazy, echoing half-light of the Body Shop—

(*oh God*) Sterling wanted to cross herself (puzzled by the *burnt* smell of herself: blackened skin and muscle peeling away). *Her lips were burnt off,* teeth grinning in a Hallowe'en mask, but pain absent. Had they given her something? She couldn't move a finger. She was forced to stare at literally thousands of...of unclothed... men and women...

Naked bodies! Hung like

(obscene)

cattle in a slaughterhouse: on rising spirals like an enormous DNA staircase or (*oh God—no!*)

an Aztec amphitheater where they sacrifice people and—and— up there was *the High Shrine!* where priests *snatch out your beating heart* and hold it up—or maybe (she thought incoherently) I'm in a museum; a place eerily big and—out of scale, the corners *(were there corners?)* disappearing high up where blue light spills over a million *dead bodies* in glass coffins—

(*I can't look!*) at this horrid meatmarket because it is SICK (*my familiar belief system...undermined...*)

There were great-looking girls who'd be all laughing-eyed and tangle-haired if they could wake up...flanking lugubrious males with neck polyps — teratisms, medical anomalies, women with mustaches and saggy breasts, every shape and color of the human animal — Madame Tussaud's wax figures but LIVING! in wisps of evilly-dripping steam — famous men of past and present (*it was beyond blasphemy!*), noted beauties (Liz, Marilyn — *was that Cleopatra in the kohl?*)...and kings, poets, scientists, tattooed hunks with long hair and muscles; here a stately blonde matron, there a bald dwarf or brawny Schwarzenneger that put shudders in the vampire's blood...a bleached Michael Jackson keeping company with the Elephant Man unmasked in a line of diseased freaks that had black stumps for teeth — noses eaten away; and now — backed up to Luke Perry and that cast of teenage misogynists with doting parents from Beverly Hills 90210 — *their eyes sealed* under waxy lids — *their limbs moving* like fetus limbs (yes! In a kind of amniotic fluid)

Whose bodies were these?

(*ohhhh*. O'Blivion felt horribly sick to her stomach)

"We are the drowned," clamored a chorus of voices. And suddenly (*appallingly*) in the middle of them the vampire saw...*Natalie Wood*.

"Mother of God!" she muttered.

"I'm not the one who's dead. *You are*," Natalie smiled that charming smile of hers. The actress was immediately recognizable — shockingly so — and was beckoning from her glass tank! A horrible panic took hold of Sterling.

"Not dead, vampire," Natalie's lips seemed to form words. "*Not dead at all. I am drunk with eagerness for life...and I'm going to climb out of this coffin...and kiss you and tell you all about the night I drowned: the untold story nobody knows...for your ears alone...*"

Sterling's hands would be clenching and unclenching but she couldn't move — not even to close her eyes (*the lids burnt off!*) or grind her teeth together (they were black, *her mouth full of an ashy taste*)

and she was feeling so lonely.

Then suddenly behind Natalie and the drowned people was — yes! HIM! The Bonus Prize — she wanted to look but there just wasn't time (*did this mean...was she dead*; was this her last chance?) and the smell. Sickly sweet...*she remembered that stench* from Black

Plague days. Dozens of stiff bods stacked like firewood, hauled away on carts (*do you remember that smell?* Like used Keds. Rotten meat. "High," they used to call it. Sickly-sweet, *oh yes*: amid bawling noises of blubbering friends, relatives, wives and children who sometimes followed the wagon all the way to the burning pit, when was it? and where? *London.* Around, oh — 1665) — ideas began whirling in the vampire's mind — the churchy silence broken only by Nancy's alarming whispering.

"Pray for us now and at the moment of our death, birth, death, birth, death, birth," Mrs. Reagan mumbled over and over to her beads — to a dim, faraway buzzing of what had to be those unthinkably horrid *placenta-feeders* that nourished the bodies (Woolf had told her about them and at last she believed it) —

Yes: the smell definitely was...decaying meat.

Byproducts. Chunks of rotten human *flesh*. Sour bits of the protoplasmic *goo* they manufactured here — in clumped cells forming tissue forming organs, forming forms: nerve chains, eyestalks, ovarian tubes, brain folds — a horror, yes! but: *where there was rot, there was seed.* More valuable than all the treasures of the earth (*O'Blivion was very tired, wavering in and out of consciousness*) —

But even in her death throes the vampire knew enough to keep "*Un' occhio alla padella, uno alla gatta*" — one eye on the frying pan and one on the cat; having been forced for years to score blood or money or both, while escaping danger or warding it off — and if she could only solve the mystery of this place (*can you understand, can you understand?*)

(*but I'll go mad*)

The possibilities! If you had the guts, the energy — what they were showing her now — some would call it *the face of God* all right — but — what it really was was — *was* —)

Near death, she drifted in and out of consciousness. Then her bearers took an abrupt left turn and were in Heidi's Grandfather's office (*or at least it looked like it*) and he was asking questions and people were fussing with her.

"Lighten up," B.G. said in matter-of-fact tones. "All this is *perfectly commonplace*. Where'd all the goofy considerations come from, anyway?" he asked gently. "It's no conjuring act: I promise you. There is birth, growth, decay and death. If you get tricked into thinking these things are 'horror' it's like having your limbs hacked off by the Devil," he smiled, picking pizza topping out of his beard.

"Are you telling me I'm going to die?" Ster squawked—her voice ringing loud and clear.

She was alone in a little room. A technician came in to say: "And fix your lipstick," pushing her into the corridor.

"Wait! *I've been hurt*! I need a priest, a lawyer, a doctor," she yelled.

"Never send for rich men who prevent you from learning the skills needed to survive in the jungle of Earth," the guy said. "Get back to your cell! You have punishment coming."

"No," the vampire screamed—longing for get-well cards, flowers, needles, pain; the confused attention of General Hospital where the obsessive days drag on and on as interns clown in corridors, pious nurses react and then (snorting coke) they copulate in an examining room. But she had to face the fact that she was healed! And it meant...back to what she'd been trying to escape from in the first place—DETOX. A real bummer.

"Wait, dammit. This can't be all there is," the vampire sobbed—she who loved the fuss made when you were sick, or fainted. As a reward for not appearing threatening to other Twinkles (*a Twinkle being any coddled person born after 1930—in Ster's hook*), illness made you feel so good (only temporarily though; and never good enough to give up bloodsucking for: it being a mere side benefit), the vampire found it offensive to be healed just like that—snap! She didn't like it one bit. It was even more *declasse* than Detox, being treated as a *thing* instead of a person, an *important body* who not only wanted but *needed* to be disabled in an attractive way; but this business of no drugs, no bandages, no casts, no doctors snubbing your frightened little queries as they rush off wealthily to shoot a birdie? Why, it was like being cheated out of your modern-day birthright! Because "life" (as Sterling and most folks knew it) without the occasional meaningful convalescence was certainly not worth living.

Yes; like many consumers in our unwholesome milieu, Sterling had gradually learned to get off on sympathy. She loved holidays from work, being brought chicken soup and told what a good girl she was for offering no competition—illness being universally accepted as a no-threat condition. And Sterling badly needed consolation. She longed for a hastily scrawled note from her fellow con artist Henry James: "I was distressed to hear that you were ill," suggesting they do lunch when she got on her feet, written in about ninety pages of convoluted prose that would make your average sophomore in English Lit positively gasp! But...more than that...

Being crippled would have got her off the hook, true; but it'd also have made her important enough to bring Woolf running. Wasn't that how it was taught on TV, plenty of passive suffering and gooey doctoring mashed into the fine, sadomasochistic tradition (which she belonged to in spades)?

"Oh darling. If I could but CALL you! We'd drive to some little bed and breakfast in Port Townsend and—ohh—crawl between the sheets and make passionate, outrageous, wild, all-night-long FORBIDDEN LOVE and have multitudes of climaxes," was the thought-wave she sent Benaroya and then...

Sterling winced, shut her eyes, opened them, touched her head, looked around—Nancy had escorted her back to her cell. Nor did Mrs. Reagan give a damn that the vampire was shuddering violently, in such desperate need of blood that she was ready to kill for it.

"I don't know why I saved you," Nancy complained. "You're never grateful! Here's an inkwell, a quill pen and lots of parchment. H.G. wants to know who you think you are, what you want, why you're here and so forth. He requests a full biography by dinnertime."

"And if I refuse?"

Mrs. Reagan smiled as she locked the door. "Finish quickly. It's almost time for your daily torture and degradation. The General is looking forward to it. But not as much as I am."

Sterling heard her heels click-clicking down the hall.

"Fuck you!" she wrote savagely, breaking the pen so Nancy was forced to bring another.

She bit this new pen and frowned, looking out at the blue planet with gauzy swaddling (it was possible to watch dawn creep from London to New York, to Philly, to Chicago, to Denver while the West Coast snoozed in their beds except that Vonderra was always parked invisibly over Chicago)—*oh, shit!* She didn't have energy for this. The fall and its aftermath had really scared the crap out of her. Her heart was still beating too fast. She was used up, depressed and tired; dabbing at her wrists and forehead with a hanky dipped in cognac...that old fossil H.G., he asked too much! But: now a plan was gradually taking shape in O'Blivion's crafty, devious mind.

My dear Grandfather *(she wrote in her spidery, old-fashioned hand).*

You ask for my biography before supper. *Swell!* Just what I've been wanting to jot down.

Born in the family castle in 1282 I can boast of a rich and brilliant past. What'll it be: an exhaustive recounting of every detail of The Life? Or just the highlights?

I first sucked blood at age thirteen. He was a priest who sexually molested me during confession. Angry, I bit; I lapped. The pig ran to his Bishop, who ran to the Sheriff. Thus began the hell on earth that became my life.

I am a vampire! No other aspect of my personality has been so misunderstood; because...I am Pop and Classical mixed together in a tall shaker. Add a dash of bitters, pour into two crystal, long-stemmed goblets. Our toast? *"Ant-seething city, city full of dreams, where ghosts by daylight tug the passer's sleeve"* –

Baudelaire. CLASSY! Miles above those ghetto-esque, heavy metal Brit/Yank organ grinders in my humble opinion — so kill me. As the condemned man told his executioner: "I am beyond that." I write this not to annoy you Grandfather, but because I am The Eternal Refugee. A literary snob, an exile having suffered bloody persecution at the hands of a vast number of subliterate oafs who thought they had A PERFECT RIGHT to misuse me, because I AM WHAT I AM!

You poke into my affairs with your morbid curiosity — try this on for size! Forever looking over my shoulder. Fleeing to a New Life in a New City, getting terrific at dropping out of sight; ordering another new passport, sidestepping Immigration and Customs, dodging tiresome questions — and be advised that I stood up to them every time! I'm no yellow-guts even though I've suffered sad losses — do you have any idea how much it hurts to lose EVERYONE? Home and parents, friends, lovers; the old tongue, that the mis-educated Twinkie of today would laugh at — I have suffered! My generation long dead and dust — *oh how I miss you, every one.* We were all so ignorant, uncouth, and don't think they didn't ostracize me.

Then came poverty like you don't know. Twice, I felt the hangman's hands at my neck.

Mama and Papa drove me out of the house. Nanny Blescu the old woman who wet-nursed and adored me, sided with my parents. All alone! Only thirteen, I was ordered never to darken their door again (*just for sucking that stupid man's warm, freckled neck* — the illegitimate son of a tenth-rate minor Lord, he wanted to see me brought down. I think it was because I wouldn't fuck him but was an "arrogant," flashing-eyed, magnificent brat if ever there was one), for 400 years I lived in isolation — twice coming close to winning the Nobel Prize for my work in physics and literature but *passed over* because I am not only a woman, but a woman who will not flatter, cozy-up or, unlike far more successful female authors (Twinkies one and all!), suck anything but necks. They passed me over for this reason, that I can prove through qualified witnesses, to wit: *winning prizes depends on what a woman will suck.* This fact must be made crystal clear, or what follows will make little sense.

A little over a year ago, I informed the U.S. Govt. I had built three original types of nuclear weapons and was storing them in Gary, Indiana. Chuckling, the government man began groping me. When I protested he laughed me out of the office; calling me a *"silly, headstrong Anita Hill"* as he pointed at the door. This Authority Figure seemed to regard me as worthy of no further consideration. I was angry! But later over a Big Mac, fries and a chocolate shake, I talked myself out of being angry. I mean WHY should I give a shit? I now possess what practically every Third World nation also has: nuclear weapons. And: being rejected as I have been all my life, I feel entitled to do whatever I like with the fruits of my labor; particularly if it includes arms deals with the Middle East. I definitely intend to place an ad in the Personal column of major publications, *"Need nukes?"* along with my phone number. Perhaps I'll also fry a few cities on my own. Washington D.C. is my top choice of the moment.

Yet remembering the baby daughter lost so tragically — she was only three. Two dozen of my sons and daughters have been born, grown old, died. But it's always Stefanya I want to buy Christmas toys for.

But I can't sit here scratching out this tripe when I am dying. You MUST let me go to where I can drink a little Ruby and if you won't: my death will be on your head! *You filthy whoremon* — (paragraph blocked out).

And yet dear Grandfather; I recall what you said about TIME. "You aboriginal gook-fellas don't have a whole lot of it left." That's when I agreed on a cure—because I love Virginia Woolf and must be made worthy of her. "You will do your part to save the world," you said. *And I'm trying.* I am desperately trying.

Then there is the matter of my Bonus Prize. I saw that great secret, locked in your Shop, among those glass-cased museum exhibits with the nasty THINGS moving inside them like embryos (*even though most of them are adults!*) and I recalled your inspiring talk on the subject, Grandfather:

"As a reward for good behavior you'll be allowed to do something that will terrify you—and at first seem, to an untutored savage like yourself, disgusting, creepy and weird; till you learn to lay back and enjoy it."

You were hinting about the possibility of doing something speculated upon by our great philosophers over the millenia, since time immemorial. Many have been obsessed with that craziest, most far-out act imaginable (*far creepier than simple vampirism* which is actually rather ho-hum) and yet: the most natural thing of all! It's only our Puritan training that makes us believe doing it is wrong and bad; but as you say—we must abolish Puritan considerations if we are to enjoy life as it is meant to be enjoyed.

I felt funny as hell but I did it. Now, it seems like a dream. *Did it really happen?* I can't believe it. And you—the things you told me! "None of us are finite, my dear; and in order to insure your joyfully aware immortality, you'll be asked to switch bodies from time to time; a warm, powerful sensation that brings a wonderful sense of completeness."

Right away it got under my skin. (*Just a little joke* Gramp.) You showed me how and said: "Relax, babe. Go with the flow. Don't fight it. It's merely an empiric function of a spirit without which every one of you warped wasps is doomed to a ball and chain for the rest of eternity," and very quickly (no doubt because it was addictive; although perhaps 'psychotropic' would be a better word?) I became SO enchanted with DOING IT that now I want to DO IT ALL THE TIME! As you knew I would.

So do we cut a deal? You let me use the Spock equipment and for my part: I agree to snoop on Woolf. I'll give as complete an account of her thoughts, plans, and actions as I possibly can. *Those are my conditions take it or leave it.* I think you get the message.

Now! What else? I crossed the Atlantic to find religious freedom and ran into a mob of Fundamentalists who tried to burn me. The great American tragedy, right? I think you're beginning to realize that after many hassles, Grandfather, I KNOW what humans are. You've seen the 947 crucifixes in my personal collection, each one taken from a terrified victim on his or her knees in front of me. I've seen them pleading; how they cringe back, crossing their index fingers in the form of a cross while pleading for mercy (*I love it*). But if the hypocrites really believed in those sacred images they'd get off their knees, wouldn't they? I mean you had to be there—really. Heads bobbing up and down, making weewee and poopoo right in their pants, you should see people the way I've seen them. It arouses a feeling of pity and absurdity—and not just because I've left the stamp of my art upon so many throats; or been stoned and spat at by bad boys on the street. Right?

The first time Virginia Woolf and I had sex, she said:

"Ohhh God. It feels so good. Ohhh!...don't ever stop." You hardly realize that this is a tremendous metaphor beyond your grasp, my sweet; because with a human you have to break up the ideas and spoon-feed them with suppertime stories cooing '*Open the hangar door; here comes Mr. Data's Pretty Space Ship*' which is why we came here, Sterling" and right then—oh God what an orgasm I had! It went on and on...ohhh...because for centuries, you see, I'd wished for a romantic love affair like in the movies; complete with convertibles, the moon, and Glen Miller. I wished it on a falling star! And then one day—Virginia with all her gaiety and wit, fell into my arms. Which may explain why I flatly refuse to believe that my adored one is mixed up in anything gross.

You see, Grandfather...*we madwomen love beyond the five senses.*

Virginia is the kind of bewitcher who makes your heart burst with excitement when she walks into a room. Would such a paragon go to bed with the devil? *Use your head.* She's funny, sophisticated, chic, sympathetic, warm, lovely, friendly, stunning; brilliant, talented, cool and clean; she gladdens the heart—she's the end of the rainbow, my shining star!

But there are two sides to every coin, and the flip side of this coin makes me terribly sad, because...*how can I ever know that I'm worthy of the honor?* I am master of great secrets. True. *But!* They are nothing compared to Benaroya's wisdom. I'm very much out of my league with a Rysemian. How many of us have wished with all our hearts, that a loving E.T. would come to us—as I wished for Benaroya? And now? *I feel inadequate*—she's beyond me—I can merely hint at her excellencies. Touching her is a glorious sensation. She would not waste her exquisite sexuality on the likes of a Scaulzo; she hasn't a mean bone in her body. It may seem to one who doesn't know her, that something physical is happening between her and the Prince of Darkness but take my word for it—but enough about Woolf. It's me you wanted to hear about, correct?

No wrinkles, no lines, no facelift. How do I do it? How do I keep this Peter Pan act going? I can tell you in one word. *Blood.*

B-L-O-O-D!

Fresh, bubbling hot human blood; my tongue hangs out for the Ruby. *I need my ration NOW for the love of God.* Am I not even allowed to come decently to a tragic end, like in the books and movies? Does this mean, then, that everything we are taught is as false as Rimbaud said it was? That all our highly respected rituals come down to a bunch of hooey—just a lot of going ON, and ON, and ON? God! No wonder I refuse to believe it. I mean like: if my body is not a temple, and my spirit is just one more tenth-rate fuckup of a ghost going "Wha—?" as it forgets to get the license number...then you've GOT to let me go home for an hour. *Please! I'm begging you.* Let me put on my black velvet dress for one single hour, and walk through the Drake Hotel lobby into the bar, and pick up some Prudential exec or maybe a nice young Microsoft hacker...mmm!...*I can taste it* now...remembering that I am the only woman who ever said: "Tonight I will suck Napoleon"—and did. I'm the only woman who ever said: "I will master the Night," and did!!

Excuse me Grandfather. Is my face red! Didn't mean to hot-focus my singular aberration; only to say...Long an inhabitant of the underworld, I no longer consider it charming, exotic or any big deal and yet jaded as I am, you *must* realize that my value depends on world demand. I enrich lives, taking minds off responsibilities which might require genuine hard work and confrontation to handle—hey, *we humans are not exactly heroes!* We have a chain-of-pain going on our planet. It would behoove you not to break that vital, important link, ME! You're tampering with forces you know not of, *you stupid fish* (blotted out).

My masterworks in science and literature scorned, my great

novels unpublished, they being the work of a true artist rather than the accepted, market-oriented hack—a woman who may possibly, occasionally, kill *(by accident!! I never kill on purpose and don't you forget it)* but always in an Upbeat way; what did I get out of all that labor? Only the indescribable joy of creation, like the late Vincent Van Gogh—him cutting off his ear; me, being forced to find epic realization in vampirism.

And so the foolish world bumbles on, crying for "something NEW" *even as it rejects it.*

Offended orthodoxy may abhor the idea; yet what other field is open to a non-conformist female with surpassing genius? Hauled through the streets in a cage, I wound up with emperors kneeling at my feet *(well, one emperor)* and more recently was on Oprah, appearing in silhouette confessing in sepulchral tones (which the idiots lapped up as always); yet it was *a dangerous thing* for one who has suffered so terribly at the hands of cruel men. Often manhandled by Officialdom's surly brutes, O'Biivion is the only human alive who can speak the truth—the basic truth that every nation is founded on blood. The police, you ask? Well they sure don't work for us ordinary people! Their existence is to enforce the fact that we don't respect anything but violence on our once-green planet.

And don't jive me with lip service about. 'sharing and caring'—people only *respect* a nine milly automatic held firmly to our head. Nothing motivates us better. Earth may be a troubled place but it's a *community.* We're all professionals here. Witness my superbly controlled skill! I am a seducer, not a rapist. Would you rather have your daughter sucked by some amateur? I think not! I am *superfinissimo,* at the peak of my native talent. The unexpected twist is what makes me great. Wake up and smell the hemoglobin. What do you think keeps me from eye bags, from neck wrinkles—from death itself? No, my friend; I'm a vampire and will never give it up. I'm a legend! You can't kill a legend, you cock

(Ink covered the next page. Then Sterling appeared to gain control of herself again.)

It was I, ME and none other! who served as model for three out of five of the heroines created by the American novelist Henry James, *so don't taunt me,* you fat fish. I try not to capitalize on poor Henry's crush on me at the turn of the century (we met in Geneva where I taught him everything he knew about writing. I stressed the nuances that his big brother Billy, a philosopher rather than a novelist, did not understand, nor was William able to pass them on to Hank—*and don't get me wrong*, I was crazy about that cute hunk of a big bro William James, I still get off on Billy's *Varieties of Religious Experience* but you must understand that art was foreign to his nature, particularly French fiction of the realist school which I originated and passed on to Guy de Maupassant in a few steamy nights. But it was in Geneva that Hankie James, Bill's shy kid brother, appropriated my feeling for English style without a qualm although the truth is: Hank and I never made out aside from a little petting from the neck up. I'm afraid Hankie was in love with Robert Louis Stevenson the whole time. He was jealous of me; they all were, because *The Portrait of a Lady*—for the first time I'm revealing here that I wrote it and let Henry publish it under his name because he needed the credit so badly, whereas I—a true hero, snapping my fingers at Fate from a position miles above the crassness of Fame or the mob's base adulation! And this, the TRIUMPH OF THE HUMAN SPIRIT—is, I am sure, why you chose me as part of your team.

Now please take this information to your fellow blubberfish so they can at last understand where all those pale-fingered, aristocratic, satin-bustled bimbos came from in the first place!

(*Inkblots covered the page.*)

I'm sorry Grandfather. I hope you'll excuse the Attitude but I'm under great pressure here. You've got to remember that I CARE. I care deeply! I'm trying to change, *I really am* and all I want to be sure of is, will you keep our bargain? *Is it a deal?*

("Oh Woolf. If only you were in my arms" the vampire muttered—and a minute later: "She's forgotten me," she mourned, completing her task.)

Grandfather, good night. I kiss my fingers to you! I'm counting on you to let me lunch with Woolf soon at which time she can make a Judeo-Christian out of me. I long for a sight of the face of her whom I love—but *yes*. I'll spy on her as you ask. Yes, *yes*, I'll do whatever it takes! This is *my life* I'm talking about; my comic, tragic life that—

Hearing Nancy's key in the lock, the vampire put the pen down with a grimace.

She didn't look forward to seeing General Patton. She knew

he'd beat her bloody! But Nancy had brought lunch, her favorite—an excellent year of claret, plus a delectably-seasoned pea soup and French bread that broke into great, toothsome chunks she dipped in the piping hot soup—

For the moment, all was peaceful.

Maybe nothing horrible was going to happen after all.

EIGHT

"Come on, let's go," Abe said.

"I'm *sick*! My head's throbbing and my throat's rawer than an uncooked Religious Rightist—why wear ourselves out?" Doug growled from bed.

"Because I have a terrible feeling there's something right in front of our noses we're not seeing."

Lincoln stood motionless, his arms folded and his dark eyes brooding solemnly down on the traffic that hummed in front of Doug's hotel. He was a surprisingly tall man with stooped shoulders, an austere dignity and a long, sad face that people adored. "*My hero*" they'd cry with that sappy look on their face; they never tired of him *(he mused)*—but only because he was no longer alive.

If he was *alive* they'd tire of him in *six months*—roughly the frame for a warmish fad to run its course. The record was something like: 4 days for Tiny Tim, 40 years for Frank Sinatra, 400 years for Elvis, 2000 years for Jesus and *that's all folks*—ol' hook reaches out and snatches you off the stage! The only major figure who could manage to survive for over 2000 years would be Shirley Temple, Lincoln thought morosely.

"So, Chief; were you always a manic-depressive (although painted with a bland brush and having a halo stuck on your head)—*or did I say something*?" MacArthur asked sourly. Doug felt cheated. He'd wanted another Guy Day replete with bashing, swaggering, get tanked on whisky, shoot a little pool but Abe had decided they'd plan his next campaign.

"Pure depressive, General," Lincoln said cheerfully. "Behold a very complex man with great depth of feeling—a man not made happier by the existence of a sallow, sunken-eyed satirist lurking in shadows, a cigar tilted in his mouth..."

Beel. Why couldn't Scaulzo's button man find some other planet to rape? As if Abe didn't know.

"I want to be *used*," he cried softly, tugging at the drape cord. "I want to DO something for mankind! to make up for that ridiculous Civil War I authorized."

"Ahhh, they loved it."

"It was wrong of them."

"Think you got trouble now? *Shit!*" Doug said glumly. "You wanna inflict a *wanton insult* on humans by turning'm into what they hate the most — enlightened beings. That's cruelty! Ramming it down their throat...why hell, you're an object of veneration; but me —"

Abe shrugged. "An object of veneration about which they want to know nothing except that it's 'far above' them which means they can never even *begin* to catch up because every role is set *in advance*, therefore nobody has responsibility for anything which is not only false and infantile but is what's wrecking the planet!"

"Exactly! Which is why we've got to bomb China right NOW before brunch! Because we sure as hell can't go around saying 'Oh, you *stubborn homunculi* — walled off from reality for which you've substituted the chilling narcissism of *ditzy sitcoms*' for Godsake!" Doug exploded.

Lincoln slanted his eyes toward the long figure on the bed.

"Do you need a hug?" he asked tentatively.

"Social moralizing is crap! Humanism is demonic! Conventional knowledge is self-mutilation! And keep your dirty paws to yourself!" MacArthur howled, arching his back as he tapped his crown on the bedpost for emphasis.

Abe shook his head slowly. "It is with piercing regret that I look back to the mistake of the pompous, costume-ball Civil War," he mourned. "I've said this twenty times — slavery was obsolete, we all knew it but I had to go and order Sherman's march and suspend freedom of the press because the public ate it up, they kissed my feet, beating drums and swooning at how *cute* they looked in their suits — it makes my *flesh crawl*. And did they ever view themselves as preening, *adolescent gangmembers*? Even Walt Whitman, bravely registered field nurse that she was, never saw herself as a dramatizing twit playing a bad scene."

"Hell!" Doug exploded. "If you hadn't done what you did the U.S. wouldn't be a big world power — and *you* wouldn't be a great big, soulful-eyed, sit-down statue either."

"Oh yeah? Well maybe life would be better for the common people after all," Lincoln argued. "Look at their products, man! Don't you see what Scaulzo is up to? An ever increasing dose of artifacts, chemicals and Tom Brokaw, acts like a drug—in fact it *is* a drug. We gotta save this teeny globe, for Godsake! Gotta make it fly."

"Get a grip. You sound insane."

Lincoln shook his head. "Now I know why Presidents in encyclopedias are always so grim and self-important. There's no joy in life for them! It used to impress hell out of the voters but no more, I'm afraid."

"And your point is?" Doug asked snottily.

The Squadders were drilling their roles. The more terrified of Beel they got, the harder these maniacally alien, fathomlessly imbecilic walk-ons had to be crammed, crammed and crammed some more.

"I have talent; now what I need is big hair," Abe said.

"Big hair?"

"Big hair and to be *short*. Gangly is out! Voters now demand, not a gaunt giant with warts like me (the post-Pepsi generation is positively *not* gonna buy *that* image) but a diminutive, taut, timely, smooth-faced Wonderwoman sweeping into the White House in a certain splendid disorder."

"Oh yeah. Squeaky-voiced, *pouf*-haired and self-sillying," MacArthur said sourly. "Runs knock-kneed with tiny steps waving its hands, oh yeahhh: who'd trust *that* as Commander-in-Chief?"

"I'll tell you who, General. Voters! *Tout le monde,* buddy. The pendulum is swinging and I plan to swing at its very tip. Look at them down there," he pointed. "There they are: the clean and shining young, the beat and shocking old—each undergoing a giant, bloated, demonic invasion, unawares! And how do we clue'm in—so all the crap stops? By getting me elected President again! And by golly that's where O'Blivion comes in. *She knows what sells!* She can manage my campaign."

"She's a she-devil. A sick, dangerous woman," Doug snarled.

"Come come! The vampire's merely getting a fresh grip on her *chutzpah*. It's a long road, kicking a drug habit on your own away from everything familiar to you! Her quest for self-respect will overcome—"

"You'd like the job botched?" MacArthur sneered.

" — feelings of worthlessness and self-doubt, a problem shared by females everywhere. Let us not forget: Sterling is capable of many special powers that she, like all mortals, have denied with bug-eyed terror so they can 'fit in' to an unthinkably hideous, dehumanizing system."

"I'd rather not discuss it."

"True, she's a firebrand, a woman of strong emotions—"

"Yeah. The main one being to make the earth shake with *my* star cadet Virginia Woolf!"

"How insanely jealous you are. Ster's a fugitive from justice— the CIA has plans for her gangland-style *WHACK!* Just like John Kennedy and the others they creamed. The quiff has no choice but to do as we tell her."

"I'll bet you a year's pay—"

"She's smooth, she's elegant, she needs to lose herself in something."

"Something like *saving humanity*? Don't make me laugh."

"With us she'll attain a multidimensional command over time, space, forms, and thought! She'll take off like a—well, like a spiritual jackrabbit. What a proud day it'll be for O'Blivion. She'd be nuts to turn down a deal like that."

"She's nuts already."

"No. Not her. Her habit is nearly kicked. I think our *cidevant* vampire will quite soon find her place in the scheme of things," Abe wagged his head.

"You live in a fantasy world right outta the Twilight Zone," Doug groaned, turning over.

"I'm a great American patriot. Do you know what that means? It means, who else would spend twelve trillion dollars to beat down the Soviet Union that was never a real threat? No, what I'm saying is—it may be a real tragedy that we sold our inheritance to finance our wars; but we've got one thing in our favor. We're too dumb to feel shame."

"Listen, Chief, if the man on the street knew we were here, do you know what he'd say? 'Why don't you just bring your leader to our leader? Then you can sit down and decide what to do.'"

"Oh yeah, right!" Abe hooted. "Me in my basic body. It even makes *you* wanna throw up. You know what they'd do if they saw one of us in our basic bod? After they got done vomiting—" He sliced a finger across his throat.

"Yeah, how we look, they'd want to kill us for it..."

Abe's rough-hewn chin sunk to his chest. Tears ran down his cheeks. "I'm upset with being forced to replicate the contents of the paranoid mind over and over because Scaulzo has rigged it so the marketplace has *no reality* on any higher state, sure," wiping his face with his 1860's hankerchief. "But the sad part is: if they saw me in my native form they'd WHACK me and be proud of it."

"Yes, but to repeat it twice is being a masochist!"

"No, it isn't! We'll not have this argument again. The barbs wouldn't just brush us aside as lightweights who in their view are not to be taken seriously, oh no; they'd *whack* us. Torture and snuff us — what's wrong with your head? They don't let anything as physically repulsive as us *live!* You must be *cute* to be given a license to survive on Earth."

"You sayin' they'd *snuff* us it they saw us in down-home Rysemus bodies?"

Abe nodded. "*Squashed*. Like bugs."

"You're wrong. We're made up of the same biological material, aren't we? Whacking us would be bigotry, and they *hate* bigotry."

They both chuckled, and Abe said, "Picture the average man finding out we reproduce by cloning and consider sex a dubious, *ho-hum*, obsessively overregulated rite that is *featherweight at best*. Don't be naive, boy; they'd kill us as *sexual deviants* — they *persecute* what they think of as sexual deviants with an ingrained, self-righteous hysteria! What's more: if I'm correctly informed they would despise *all* our traits. No hostility? No *shrewdness?* No *self-hatred?* No *pecking* order? Nothing but a magnificent, soul-lifting *love and understanding* 24 hours a day — why we'd be a living reproach! And you know what *that* means: *whack*. No, let's concentrate on boosting my popularity."

"You want *popular*, have Woolf stick her head out the window and yell '*Heyyyy everybody. Free sex!* Here 'tis!"

"How about a catchword: *ABE*-solutely! Can't you just see that on campaign buttons? Think it'll get the votes? Is it sleazy enough, does it reach out and grab the balls of the lowest common denominator?"

"At this time—"

"Yes yes, how right you are. We must *outcruel* 'm — but with *compassion for all*! Which boils down to lofty, well considered ideals replaced by calendar art loaded with whatever is darling and/or scary. Nothing counts but mass markets! *Numbers!* That's where it's at. It's a numbers game—"

"Don't you have any pride, Chief?"

"—until I get my break. My big break! What every actor-politician dreams of. I just need to be *noticed*. I'll be the IT guy. I'll finally—"

But the man on the bed was quiet.

That stung Abe, as MacArthur had hoped it would.

"Think I can't cut'r? I'll show you, boy—where's that little yumyum Japanese piece of yours? It's time to dip the old wick so I can get happy again." Abe made squeezing motions, hands lifted at his breast pockets with the palms out. He smacked his lips.

"Honk! Honk!" he said, rolling his eyes.

Doug sighed. "You'd never make it in today's market. What're you up to anyway—behind that machismo pose?"

Abe stared at him, then said: "You have no guts."

"Just what the hell do you mean by that?" Doug screamed.

"Only that we must gamble on making our dream come true! We *can* pull this world out of the soup! But the people need *briefing*—in the form of a bolt from the blue. From *me?* From *you?* Who knows? But we've got to *act*."

MacArthur flexed his muscles with a grunt. "If you really wanted to run again and get elected—think you could pull it off? Seriously."

Abe shrugged. "Yeah, if I specialized in the ever-acceptable SOMETHING EEEVILLL IS OUT THERE AND IS COMING FOR US! *(AND WE ARE HELPLESS)* crap—that brings on heart attacks, cancer, stroke, diabetes, war, crime, death and *everything but the truth*, the whole truth and nothing but the truth! Which we Rysemians shall continue to serve, from this day forward, with devotion and single-mindedness"—fingering his beard with a glance at the tense body under blankets.

"*Something juicy is about to happen,*" Doug muttered.

NINE

Woolf ran fast. The way out was over the beach and boardwalk to the lake.

At the bridle path she veered, hurdling a hedge and bent-over cleanup man spearing trash *(he* screamed! but not as loud as her "GoodAY-AYYY" that reverberated on air) when

(out of the blue)

An angry jab from the vampire. *Mad and sad:* bemoaning cruel things happening to her.

"Hang in there, my vixen—" Woolf tried to jolly her.

"Fuck you!" Sterling lashed back. "Bitch! I hate you! You BETRAYED me! I BELIEVED in you. Without blood I'll turn into a MUMMY, an ugly CORPSE and it HURTS and I HATE YOU because they say you've been DOING THINGS with SCAULZO!"

"That scaly razor-tooth? Pah," Woolf soothed. "Come what may, we'll stand by each other till the stars burn out."

But Ster flipped a Sicilian arm-chop—*Oboy was she mad!*

"Have you forgotten our unspeakable happiness? Now listen. You do exactly as I say—"

"Go to hell, lying motherf—"

"Or Mankind'll be extinct forever; so we must play it close to the vest till he swallows the bait and I swear it—afterward: *showtime!* Two swashbuckling heroes, *you and me*—spending Eternity in the most romantic, dangerous duty just like you wanted—" Woolf nimbly sidestepped a man in a turned-around collar who pantomimed that she locate and don her garments and cease offending him ineffably with headlong nakedness.

Ster gave the finger.

"Aw come on baby," Woolf messaged. "Your golden skin tantalizes me, true, but more important: you're a joy to work with and if I'm not mistaken *we have more fun than a barrel of monkeys* or are my memories playing me false?" but Ster wouldn't listen. They were having their first fight—*telepathically!* Woolf had to patch this up. And fast.

"What a *fine-looking woman* you are, Sterling O'Blivion. My lips are parched for sly, mean, sexual YOU—the best thing I ever saw, so don't crap out on me, *hear?* You gotta give a little, take a little and let your poor heart break a little. That's the story of, that's the glory of love and you'll be a *powerhouse Squadder* if you c'n just hang in there—"

Not that Ster (*even in the act of dying*) would get these messages, not really. Ster sent a powerful signal but like most humans didn't pick up thoughts—hadn't even learned *how* to do it, let alone keep herself from knowing she *was* doing it as every Rysemian agent did as part of the job description.

"What're they sayin about me an' him?" Woolf asked (*but Ster was gone*).

Past a frozen yogurt joint, bare feet thumping—soft breeze ruffling her hair—a sweet kiss from this lovely July 10, 1999 with its cloudless blue sky—

OWWWK!

One small flash of the mad, howling abyss that was *the mind of the Big S.!* But—no big deal. Really it was kind of interesting—it was what the Sage LRH called *"The Glee* of Insanity": a dank, bottomless pit of...silence. Broken by *giggles and gibbers*, snow, *commercials*, soaps...voices pretending to be some *hideous version* of your *dead lover..* . knife-twisters like that...all CRAP...but it made your flesh CRAWL...it was subliminal as the net of the Media itself...a *direct tap* into Scaulzo's loony-tunes thinktank...UGHHH.

Woolf whipped her head around. The uniforms were moving in and—*OOOF!*—she'd badly underestimated the hammerlock on her brain, coming at spaced intervals impinging (*YIKE!*) her puny, rusty deflectors—a weak bulwark against the bland, sneaky *WAVE* that comes humping, slithering like a Congo eel—pretending to be part of your own inmost thoughts—which was why she'd lost her cool up there...*WHUMP!* trapped in a formidable mind-crunch so intense it whacks your brains out-—not that THAT was an acceptable excuse for bungling an important job! and hey—her appearance sure caused a flurry. Cars were crashing up on Michigan Boulevard (lights and sirens impacting the very street where Sterling worked and where they had met) and sunbathers pointing with wide eyes, gawking at the intolerable, *other-worldly view* of a fleeing nude member of their species —

"Don't be shook. It's only me," she called. "Just one Earth-friendly little alien called Benaroya—" (oh yes! whose *big mouth outran her numbed brain*).

There was a new religion exploding in America known as Devil Worship — the foundation of Scaulzo's invasion plan. Teenagers were killing themselves, adults wallowing in horrorific sadomaxies that were not only plagued with killer diseases (among folk who should be DISEASE-PROOF!) like the Iatrogenic Medicine of AIDS, herpes, hepatitis-B, the brand-new Titan Crabs and the oldtime "White Man's Burden" of cross-burning, gaybashing and woman-smashing plus ever newer ones for which tons of preparations including hairspray, deodorants, fancy cars and liposuction had to be bought in advance, until all the fun was gone; the psychic torture escalating with one painful claw-nip after another as Sajorians played mindcontrol with hapless Earthies like mice under a paw until all of a sudden — *Woolf herself, all alone,* had kicked off that good ole Fatal Attraction by attempting to bargain with Scaulzo. No crap: the big ole donkey Girl Scout really thought she could TALK the DEVIL into being GOOD! But now realized with stunning finality, what a dumb ignoramus she had been

(*You got it, scout. Make no mistake. Your Executioner is on the way*)

when a stream of bikes and speedskaters blocked her path — whining sirens to the right; blue suits, left.

And yonder lay the wide, flat beach.

She had botched this badly. She shoulder bailed! Laid low instead of

(*getting nostalgic*)

for her sanctuary called HOME with its crystal clear rocks... waving fronds...that sheltered a nice little grotto...in a dim, heavywater sea 300 fathoms deep —

Tears wet Virginia Woolf's cheeks. Her home was SO FAR AWAY that she started to weep n'wail but — HEY! *(letting a psychic attack crowd out rational thought? she called that suicide.)*

One thing for dam-sure: *the devil is not unbeatable!*, even if his emotional spasms are so darn REAL when they yank your chain so...gotta spit in his eye, remember?

Here goes nothin.

Screaming traffic belched its poison, clearing space for her to jacknife, roll herself up in a ball and pop under a truck—the truck was not speeding but to coil yourself and whip behind the front wheels in one swift, rolling motion, as you crossed your fingers that you'd make it out before the humming rear tires flattened your crunchy skull—eeeHAH! That was real sport. No pansy fare like ol' hockey and football, hooEEE! and onto her feet picking up speed as she ran to a chainlink fence with a gate that was solidly padlocked.

Woolf flexed, skinned up the jingling links and threw one leg over the top *(ouch, barbwire!! No fair)* and then the other leg. Then she dropped, *thu!)* into the fragrant depths of lovely, sweet-blooming vegetation.

Nostrils quivering, she raised her noble chin to snuff like a deer. Flies lighting on bloodied calves stung the hide, as unknown creatures investigated the gorier parts—then quick she's snaking her sweat-slicked bod under drooping foliage amid good, mushroomy smells and suddenly...

Sterling came back.

"You cheater! I'm a nervous wreck because of you. Why aren't you *here with me*? I thought you were *trustworthy*! Now the truth begins to register."

"Some day you'll be able to understand—" But what could be said, after all? A feisty, glitzy turn-on, the vampire was A KIND PERSON under her smirky arrogance; but—she'd had so many jail sentences—kicked, teased, raped, starved, spat on, ridiculed, ostracized and all the usual stuff that poor ignorant humans pretended would make their society BETTER if they sanctimoniously did it to each other (ohhh were they ever NUTS!) that she was now a classic NEED-CASE or walking example of the self-doubt humans drummed into each other from birth on; and H.G.'s priority was to *heal the vampire's wounds*—which would be a grand, transcendent achievement, sure; but the glitch was—only The Sage knew anything about the bent human psyche and how to cure it—but they were doing the best they could; and with luck, soon the vampire would be Empowerment trained, her timing spit-polished and drilled till she KNEW she was a Co-Developer!—the very knowledge that humanity had lost under Scaulzo's lash, and finally: a seasoned specialist, she'd be rehearsed to work with Benaroya as Trouble Shooter on the "assault team" attempting to free the human spirit WHOLLY of its time worn, clanking chains! Yet at the moment...

The dashing O'Blivion was a caged beast! Her anger and humiliation knew no bounds. She was hurting! It was raw fear. Woolf knew fear when she saw it. And she knew what to do about it. *(WHACK!)*

"It's your GUILT that makes the fear stick," she telepathed — and poof, *Ster was gone. Just like that.* Cuz *remorse* was the heart of her problem. But Woolf had bigger problems right now such as

(if you wanna live, concentrate)

the unseen terrorist pumping his lethal poison into your soul without mercy — same way his grip on the masses through the media was near-total: shoveling out terrible images behind "the social facade" *(owwww!)* as he set the public mind running in circles as the needling voices began — in between being treated to their *spoonful of pablum* taking their minds off the *catastrophe to come* — (HELP!) and under normal circumstances, she'd be cool as Superwoman compared to these folks but now — when the Sajorian A-0 poured on its payload — shooting her reaction time to hell — she knew exactly WHO was doing it to her and WHY —

A man loomed in her path *(uh-oh)*, a medium-size geek but a big presence: piercing eyes, gaunt face, a kind of sallow, *oily dude* licking a big, black cigar. He raised questioning eyebrows at her —

Who was this bird anyway? Leaning his bulk against a dumpster, watching Woolf with cold amusement —

Right away, things began popping. Woolf's popularity was again spiraling — Holy Zeus! Her fanship must have grown from a potential 2 billion to 6 billion just this afternoon! And she knew it when a line of laughing ladies in bikinis bore down on her with autograph books and ballpoint pens — as simultaneously a gent in tights who'd been juggling plates and bottles, dropped his plates and bottles and cried in fluting, soprano tones,

"This is in the worst possible taste and I love it."

The man with the cigar — smiled — or more correctly, yanked his lips off the tusks gripping the stogie — his eyes not smiling at all. There was *something evil* in those icy, depthless eyes *that gave her pause*...but here came many a hunkazoid, autograph hound! Woolf began signing books, casts, tushes in speedos; whatever they, in their celebrity mania, breathlessly presented for her signature —

It seemed she was wildly popular! A much bigger hit than the real Woolf—forced to self-publish because no established publisher would buy her books—had been when she was alive. *(They liked her dead a ho-lot more, though.)*

She hesitated briefly, then plunged on—but not before letting the crowd jostle her against that man with the ice-water stare and the cigar.

"You forgot your wallet," she smiled politely, handing it to him.

O.K.: who WAS that seedy-lookin jabeep? He wore Tony Lama boots with pointy toes—*his I.D. said he was H.L. Mencken,* she'd swiftly noted...

Moving full tilt, Woolf gazed over her shoulder but saw only the beach crowd—the dude had vanished; yet she'd SWEAR she knew that name from somewhere—but now heard running feet and her pursuers yelling "STOP THIEF!" and "HEY! GRAB THE BROAD" as she reached the tarmac.

Uh-oh. A line of troopers had fanned out on the ridge above... *("H.L. Mencken," huh? She smelled a major rat here.)*

"I'm not lookin for trouble," she called to the law. "I'm offerin to shake hands!" and stuck up a hand; waggling the fingers in friendship. But the cop-cold faces hardened.

Oboy...she *could hardly wait* till those sparkling Lake Michigan waters closed over her melon CUZ...Scaulzo's thirst for vengeance was apparently far from satisfied. Mix that with a warped sex drive *(and SHE was the one marked for his gloating, lip-licking pleasure)* and you had something right out of the psychotic, never-closing Auschwitz/Buchenwald files—the TRUE EARTH HORROR! Legs pumping, Woolf reached the dunes picking up speed. Sun glinted off the lake—

Ohhhboy. Here it came. Her thoughts drifting back to the jailed, vengeful vampire (just as a man with his arms outstretched in a dark jacket, tie, and wingtip oxfords, grabbed the runner; took a heel in the groin, doubled over—his howl failing to halt or even dent her insanely racing thoughts—).

"My nipples are getting hard just thinking about you," Woolf couldn't help but telepath to her absent lover. Oh yes! she did *so* love the smile wrinkles around her dear O'Blivion's eyes—little lines indicating that Ster had the brains, guts and pride to do a job well—cuz she was a brassy, sassy, fiery, RIPE WOMAN who loved a challenge, who longed for romance and had a MAJOR

CRUSH on Virginia Woolf.

"I want to get to know you better," she had whispered that first night, both so excited and...so deliriously happy: *Woolf's fingers running lightly over Sterling's bare shoulders* — they'd dined by candlelight staring into each other's eyes and turning each other on (H.G., also present, was easily ignored) — Sterling thrilled to be dating her long time idol Virginia Woolf in the warm-lipped flesh. And so the greatest love story of all time began — on a night that was all champagne and stars —

But now — the bitter irony was (and of course had to be), that both Abe and the hard-bitten George Patton were talking of putting the screws on Sterling right away.

"Scare the bitch. Rough her up, teach her a lesson she won't forget" was their plan of attack. "Burn 'r if indicated; no big loss. She's half mad," they said. Nonsense! She wasn't. They were just practicing their male stereotypes as they griped, "We can't get anything out of her." Of course that was the Earthie roles talking and not the real Mersoid and Boolabung (well, maybe the Captain a *little* — for this mission his shtick was to be the worst bully in the whole bunch of clone sisters). But luckily H.G. was running the show up there. H.G.'s genius was to peel off the lies, the intricate design of plots and counter-plots that Earthies clung to with tooth and nail, even as it meant their world would become a smoldering cinder.

"The vampire is being exposed to sanity — an agonizingly unprecedented thing for a human; but we expect a breakthrough soon," H.G. promised.

Sure — Ster was having a tough time but she'd come around. And when she did, Woolf and O'Blivion would then co-star in a full-action buddy movie FOREVER! Swashbuckling around the galaxy saving civilizations, doing heroic deeds, having rip-roaring adventures as they made wild, passionate love. In light of that, the cure was actually going quite well. Naturally Ster hit a few bad days. When her Need flared up she got Patton's roughest handling, which, combined with Nancy's smarmy Good Cop Routine, was no doubt kind of hard on her. But none of them ever forgot that this absurd, pop bloodlapper was the key to a plan that could free up a power greater than Earthies ever imagined they had. (...Hey. *Pay attention here.* Concentrate! *if you like life.*)

Over the rise was the sunny beach. From there all at once she sniffed good things a-cookin. The redolence of hotdogs and sauerkraut, wafting under her nose in wavy lines...like in her fave *Classic Comics*, ahhhh...coming from a hotdog stand under what looked like a funny green parasol — NOT. It was a great big PICKLE!

Her belly craved food. Ravenously hungry! She hadn't eaten any lunch yet. And Woolf was crazy about pickles. She must now stop to order a heap of hot, smoked kielbasas on buns with lots of Grey Poupon, onions and ketchup and juicy, tangy sauerkraut plus (on the side) half a dozen BIG pickles to munch as she raced to the water —

Holy Gods on their thrones! *What was she thinking of?* But oh... the entrancingly green, slick pickle was over *ten feet long* over a sign that said: !!RED HOTS!! and if there was one thing Virginia Woolf had never been able to resist, it was to gorge on any kind of food that was a small replica of a glossy, maddening, promotional model of itself; especially a nice big *shiny, tangy, semi-translucent* cucumber PICKLE, glittering and twinkling in mouthwatering, juice-drippingly glaucous EMERALD, jade, citrine and glimmering laden with a provocative, fir-black shadow under each and every wart...an exquisitely winking, shimmering PROMISE of burst after burst of rich, exotic, tangy, other-world pungency to be squirted onto your quiveringly youthsome, unjaded tongue — OH, HOTSY TOTSY!

One time she'd seen a promo sized, Cheese Whiz spread come gooshing right out of a billboard — it made her so hungry she went and bought a gallon of the delicious orange goo and consumed it in one sitting. And when the Oscar Mayer truck, shaped like a wienie on a bun with lip-smacking relish, chopped onions and mustard drooling out, rolled by, the anthropologist ate five dozen franks and was sick all night.

She stuck her hand in the pickle jar on the counter.

The attendant frowned.

"Boy, am I revellin' in the sheer joy of bein'," she explained with a grin as she fished out a luscious-looking green pickle —

Oh Jesus Christ on a slide trombone. *There was something wrong. Terribly wrong.* She had neither pockets nor money and all at once...the popeyed gent whose driver's license said he was H.L. Mencken was standing right next to her ordering a hotdog with sauerkraut *(OWWW!)* and THE LAW was moving closer —

Steps thumped behind her as Woolf sped down the boardwalk, weaving through people in cut-offs and swimsuits but unfortunately hitting a wet patch—she took a tumble. OWWW! Her lower cheeks got skinned and stinging—then BANG a bluesuit jumped her, his service revolver drawn—

Bad news. *Meaning no harm at all* she twisted the poor little animal's head around! Right round on his too-bony neck: crack, CRIK, craaack! *Oh shit. Oh dear:* she'd been ordered many times by Abe Lincoln NEVER to do that and was in deep trouble; would lose her credibility, her Squad career in the toilet—

On the beach, radios sobbed and complained on empty blankets, the humans having rushed to where Woolf had been forty seconds earlier. And boy howdy—they were giving her a standing ovation! A loud roar of applause hung on the air over the platform where she'd kicked those imaginary panties to a panty-starved crowd; the crowd now growing denser and denser—whistling, clapping for Woolf to cartwheel back onstage. A few toddlers remained on teeter totters, watching as men with assault rifles ran along a seawall.

She took one lope to dry white sand, one to brown sand, one into shallows and one to breaking waves, yeahhh! Home free.

Uh—not quite.

A lifeguard shinnied down from his station, spoke briefly to the guy with the cigar and came after her. Woolf swam a couple strokes. She'd intended to go deep and lay low but—change of plan!

Four cruisers bearing Coast Guard insignia were vrooming in from the deep; skidding, slapping full-throttle in the troughs. Woolf's eyes began to widen...

(O.K., *wait wait wait*...Your mind keeps trying to push it away, weakly, till it becomes a SM game you play with yourself; you *internalize* they call it. You push your own buttons—but it's not YOU doing this kind of thinking at all. It's HIM. Scaulzo. Your 'lover' in chains. OOF! And that's what powered Earth's madness *and now*—her own!) *Oh no!*

Woolf took no chances with the A-O; *it scared her silly* and this time—as *the icy finger* touched her heart, it was a real gut-twister, making her falter and uh—

"'Scuse me sir?"

—The lifeguard had her by the throat! A look of triumph on his face, as with painful tightness his hands fell on Woolf's neck. Her feet flew out from under her—she almost couldn't believe this! When she tried to jerk loose, the guy's stiff fingers could not be pried off.

Quickly he got the Rysemian in a lock. Nothing had prepared her for losing control—the juice drained from her willpower. All of a sudden she was being forced underwater

and couldn't break loose! floundering three feet deep under a dude's heels. Her cheek pressed into a sharp stone.

The guard was standing on Woolf.

She couldn't breathe! And it brought...*panic*. She did not learn this in Omark's class. It was what you AVOIDED but...whew... *what now?*

The guard leaned down and pinched Woolf's flesh between a thumb and forefinger. OWW! She didn't gasp—a sure way to drown. *Just hang on. Hold your breath.* It's okay to let out a bubble or two but whatever you do, don't inhale.

Don't...in...hale...

Hoooo! Thank God at least he hadn't used an H-2 on her. How horrible that would be. Separated from your mother ship, *frozen in a body,* you'd rot here, *marooned,* as inside your chest a heart beat frantically day and night...a freaky, four-chambered worm that squeezed off a Lub-dup *(beat.)* Lub-dup *(beat.)* once every second squirming as it pumped gallons of gore all night and day, day and night, night and day you are the one, only YOOOO beneath the moon and under the sun—

URP! *What was happening to her?* Uh....

As silver bubbles streamed from Woolf's mouth and nose, she began thinking about air. Great, gulping breaths of AIR as she fought not to draw water into her lungs—and yet...oddly enough... she'd never given a thought to how the original or "real" Virginia Woolf had lost her life.

Virginia Woolf drowned.

She drowned in a river in England.

Of course, *this* was a *homicide* and the *real* Woolf's death had been *suicide*; but the weird part was—*this* Woolf thought she was able to catch a kind of blurred version of some of *that* Woolf's dying thoughts. And they went like this:

"I gave what I could. And now that I'm properly dead, you make your fortune off my life and books. And I have learned the two things you hate! The first is GREATNESS because *it isn't done by formula.* And the second is: LIVE WOMEN. Live women are *dangerous!* They too are anti-formula. And when these hated things are put together — please: I invite you to ask the poet Emily Dickinson who was never published in her mortal life, to explain how REAL women writers are *unacceptable* to your paltry, *formula-driven,* shortsighted, *genocidal,* mass-market conventionality —"

Whew! That wasn't really real — of course — except in essence maybe — but right now...

Soon Woolf'd cease to be conscious. She'd be fresh outta skin; dead!!

(—dying—)

with little X's for eyes...*Drowning: the quiet death.* You'd drift off to death the way you drifted off to sleep — so the important thing was: to shoot off a last little, goodbye message to her dear O'Blivion.

"Oh my darling. Will we never meet again in this life — our love so new, a song unsung? Will I never hear your sweet, whisky-voice again; *is everything ended before it has begun?"* she asked.

But hey: no use succumbing to despair, not yet. Just hang on one more minute. *Thirty seconds!* That might be enough.

A sonorous phrase rolled in her head; the clanging of a big bell that said "For she has found a watery grave" — the A-O, crowding out what was called "intelligence" and it was what these damaged people suffered night and day — day and night — oh, *how sorry she felt* for poor humans! but

Woolf was dying. Going numb all over, the breath locked in her throat. Her oppressor held her down under his clever feet. If she had a pocketknife she'd stick it right into his hairy calf! That would be so cool — but she couldn't even wiggle — tried to crawl up the ladder of his legs but no go. Then suddenly, *too late*...she got a make on that beady-eyed savage with the cigar.

She had to warn Doug — *had to!* but: she was entering the stiff, heavy feeling you get when you're on the verge of drowning and your bod's turning into a piece of wood. She was feeling all langorous which means: *"Time is up,"* as the final seconds drag along.

Woolf's hands clenched convulsively. Dying was a simple, routine piece of business *(time stands still when you are drowning)* but — she wanted her life! She wanted AIR!

"Oh Sterling: the wonderful things are yet to come," she telepathed.

Ears roaring, Woolf now moved into the death zone, hearing

at the last—a voice murmuring up there. Over the thud of her heart the guard was waving men off yelling "SHE WENT THAT WAY." Then the darkened shapes of boats turned around.

Woolf expelled most of her breath.

Her eyes dimmed. Her store of energy faded. But then. Something happened. In a last spasm—she got it together!

Rolling out from under the guard's foot, she took a good-sized bite outta his ankle. And surfacing, her breath exploded out as his angry scream just about deafened her!

The guy was so mad—Woolf had no choice but to turn the wannabe killer's head around CRAAACK and let him slump (*would this mean a demotion* by Abe personally? Hey. *It was worth it!*)

Then taking a wonderful lungful of air, without further delay she went deep with the fishes.

TEN

"Bomb China, *bomb China!* Is that your sole goal in life?" Abe asked peevishly. "To ape the Hemingway ideal of WHACK'm while you schmooze bullfighters in terminal self pity? Pooh. *Going native is the dumbest thing you can do.*"

"Shut up!" Doug swallowed that yell—his face muscles rigid. *A man was what he was!* It was all he could do to keep from blowing up at Lincoln. The guy refused to put a sock in his big mouth and stop picking on MacArthur.

"A man can't change his inmost thoughts," he growled.

"*Sez who?* We have no way of knowing what IS and IS NOT *possible* for these barbs—which is why we've got to annex Sean Fontana before it's too late."

"You mean the kid who used to be King Arthur? *Why?* He's a juvie delinquent for Chrissake."

"If the boy king can provide a keystone...something brand new but very old; great principles once known but now lost—based on what the mind really IS from an engineering standpoint, don't you see? If he can demonstrate how to tell a psycho from an ordinary person, and *how to deal with one,* they'll get a handle on their problems."

"Uh-huh, and if Santa Claus brings me an H-2 unit I won't have to keep begging for one!" Doug was much angrier than he wanted to let on—or the Chief would just turn around and take it out of his hide; you couldn't win a set off ole Abe no matter how you sliced it and the truth was: neither man wanted to confront the real problem. They couldn't get a fix on Woolf, hadn't heard Word One all day and were growing increasingly worried. Especially in light of...the disgusting part that Doug didn't want to think about.

Abe was unruffled. "Listen to me, General: war is a form of

punishment. Punishment is committed by psychotic people who first punish *themselves*. In secret, of course. They deny themselves a favorite food, whip or burn their arms with cigarettes, shotgun themselves to death and everything in between. The public believes this is *normal*. So, the root of war is a *secret*. But you can't keep secrets from a telepath which is what WE are which is what THEY suppress viciously in themselves using *punishment*."

"Scaulzo keeps it secret too!" Doug yelled.

"That's why he always *wins*. He messes with their minds and *kisses up to'm*. And makes'm believe they are helpless, get it? The human then guilt-trips himself so bad that his inner being is smashed to pieces while he chases money and the approval of his fellows and the point is, *we're here to help 'm!* Not get sucked down into it."

Doug bit his lips. He had to rein in this feeling—or risk an open fight with Mersoid—who didn't have to PLAY THE GAME directly but could stand there and shoot off his mouth theorizing about the stress of enduring human traditions all the time—the way it weakens a free being—dumping him into a living hell of isolation. Take last week: his aides, so puzzled—he could tell when that funny look crept into their wind-browned young GI faces—*was there something wrong* with the hardheaded MacArthur *or what?* He'd been inspecting injured bodies by the mile ("troops" they were called. Troop meant teenager from the Bronx or Georgia) as army docs told him how troops get wrecked. The troop he was looking at had stepped on a land mine. Both arms and a leg were blown off but the other leg was perfect, beautiful, untouched. The MASH doc wrote a symbolic poem about it that got published in *The Paris Review* and won a thousand dollars and a plaque—and the next troop was even worse: croaking at the exact moment that the square-jawed, steely-eyed General was pinning a *shiny medal* on him—tucked in between scores of other burn victims and thousands more examples of torn flesh displayed by young men with ruined lives who hadn't yet died but were barbecued, smashed, blinded or had both ears burned off; and although it was true that war inflicted untold suffering on them and every victory was a staggering loss, the bulk of Earthies continued to adore war and even while dying, instead of just lying there calmly observing the futility of violence, these wounded loved to read (or if blinded: be read to) about the glories of slaughter; while watching movie after movie about these subjects.

Yep, he'd learned a couple things about the military that'd flip off the masses if they knew. *Triage* for instance, meant that when there were two wounded troops the less wounded would get the fastest, best medical attention; which was sensible. How could you patch up a seriously wounded kid enough to send him back into battle? Besides, the only person who'd give a shuck was the dying kid's Mom—and *she never knew!* The Authorities *spared* her that knowledge; shipping her boy back in an attractive box with a free flag. If he was rich, he'd also get a heartwarming 21-gun salute. A gun salute was far more prestigious than just being alive. A gun salute was used to demonstrate the chief difference between a dead *rich* male and a dead *poor* male.

Aside from the gun salute, both rich and poor died in exactly the same way—like rats in a trap—and once dead, rich and poor were both dead as doorknobs. They'd never show up at the family reunion; no, *never again*. The General felt the tears trickle down his face just thinking about it. These macho asininities were the saddest thing on the whole sad planet.

Abe leaned forward. "Listen Dougie—it might not be a bad idea for you to grab a little R&R on Vonderra about now. Polish up the old shield; then go trace Woolf, find out what's happened to her."

"I can't. I have important things to do right here."

(MacArthur knew *something was terribly wrong*...but...couldn't quite put his finger on what it was.)

Abe watched him narrowly, rubbing his beard. "Let me try and put this in perspective for both of us," he boomed. "What have we got here, point by point? Fundamental point: the H-2 *freezes a being into a body.* Trapped! Cruelest and cleverest torture ever devised. Never forget it's how humans were wiped out and conquered over a trillion years ago. Once almighty free beings but now—still hypnotized with shock, they are *unthinkably* degraded, trying to kill or maim each other, their only other game being to '*get ahead*'—ahead of *what*, to *where*, for *which*? There's no place for them to go. "And yet the power, intensity and reality of their lost life are *even today* experienced as dim, fleeting memories and dreams by millions of Earth people. I call it a living hell. Am I right? It's like they remember their Home Universe as Paradise Lost—and oh God *what a sad condition it* is.

"But now for the true horror. Along comes Scaulzo. He gets

off on the situation—ourselves being put in jeopardy when your cadet Woolf makes a crucial error! And now the question is: *can we restore humans to full power*—even as the Big S. *toys* with the puppet-like carcasses the poor little beings consider 'themselves'?—it being obvious that they're possessed by demons. The devil has them on a chain," he said gloomily. "O.K. As researchers you Squadders have got to immerse yourselves in this crap up to the ears—"

"You knew what it was like here when you made the decision—!"

"And get so paranoid you're practically useless—not that I'm *blaming* you; it's the pickle we're in. Because what is inevitably coming is an all-out war with OUR butts on the firing line! So the time to act is *now,* old friend. Not tomorrow or the next day."

Doug puffed his pipe. Furious as he was, the vague premonition suddenly began haunting him...What was Abe *really* saying? Why was he acting so strange; *was the Chief hiding something?* It signalled that Abe wasn't quite what he should be...that he'd been *tampered with* somehow. A thought so terrifying that MacArthur had to suppress it *fast*...or lose his mind.

"I need my gun," he barked. "And I don't mean this li'l cop-whacker!" He'd taken the .45 from the drawer and was dangling it contemptuously.

"Your H-2 unit? Are you nuts? Whadaya think I've spent a solid hour telling you? Bear in mind that it takes infinite care and unhurried patience to make an eons-old dream come true," Lincoln growled, his eyes fixed on the traffic outside the hotel window. (So he didn't have to face MacArthur? Obviously—as the General had feared all along.)

"What the hell has that got to do with me?" Doug exploded. "You want me to walk into a tiger's mouth for Chrissake—when what I'm worried about is an H-2 death! The most horrible, drawn-out death trapped in a writhing human carc while bad men TORTURE you!" he squawked.

"You got out of it once before, didn't you?"

"That's easy for you to say," Doug shouted.

Abe shrugged. "My hands are tied."

MacArthur screamed.

It was hardly his fault that his trigger finger suddenly tightened, blowing a hole through the wall over Abe's head. He was sure Miki'd come running—but she didn't.

"See what I mean?" Lincoln turned with a smile (as if he was GLAD that Doug had demonstrated his A-0 woes to him!)

"*You don't even care!*" Doug yelled.

"On the contrary. Your welfare means everything to me."

"Bullsh—" All Doug knew was that *something out there was REACHING for* him…its fingers bent into CLAWS!

"I need that weapon," he almost sobbed. "You've got to issue me one for a few days at least."

"Oh no, can't do'r," Abe said laconically. "In the shape you're in you'd be nothing but a beacon."

"That would beat a stinking death!"

"There's no possible chance, General; the question's been discussed and decided. If you weren't strung out on the A-O you'd see that for yourself. I'm telling you, humans are nearing the fatal crossroads. Your task is to find Woolf and put your heads together—develop a plan so O'Blivion can snatch young Fontana out of the danger he's in."

Doug swallowed hard. He had to shut his teeth. First scope it out; then, *act*. "Why is that important?"

"I've *told* you. O'Blivion will be sent to weird Chicago, the megatropolis of the future where the boy lives. Timing is critical! He'll be brought to Vonderra to be nurtured and developed. It's a slim hope but it's the only one we've got—and Sterling must pick him up with the care of a jeweler tweezing up a priceless gemstone—or his mind gets smeared all over the track, you got that? Lost forever (and the road pussy'll die too which is of little consequence)—meanwhile, your job is to help give her some idea of what's going on. Some perspective."

"No way. That's Patton's job. You're not paying me enough!" Doug groaned.

Abe checked his watch. "I'm setting up a meeting between you and Woolf at oh-eight-hundred. Her welfare is up to you! Got it? Now pick up that phone and confirm it with her."

"She won't answer. She's in dutch and we both know it."

"I know nothing of the sort."

"In any case she's forgotten everything I ever taught her," Doug shook his head wearily.

"So, take her in tow. Make her see the light."

"Do you mean *her*, or both of them?" Doug asked with bitter sarcasm. "Am I supposed to include Miss Graveyard Dust into the bargain?"

"'Smatter, the vampire too much for you? What is it, 'fraid she might reject you as a man? What do you hate most about our road pussy—the *chip* on her shoulder? Or is it those over-the-edge mammary glands—"

"Shut your mouth!"

"Or is it her sharp wit? Or maybe the way she moved in on you with that cute face off a wanted poster and the full, curved mouth, perfect figure, *um yum*—rounded hips and bosom, muscular but nicely-cushioned buns—" Abe was smacking his lips and doing Squeezo with his hands. "Plenty style and pizzaz, *hot*! Ever think about a roll in the hay with'r? I wouldn't mind. What say we try, you and me? I bet she's a burner. *Hoo-ee*, she'll rattle the bed a little."

The thought of O'Blivion in that context—ugh! It made Doug break out in a cold sweat. The bitch was a blood junkie! And, worse: she had *"found her true love"*—and it was his own Benaroya.

MacArthur knew Woolf and Sterling shared a secret joy he wasn't part of... and it hurt.

"Why those things never entered my mind, Mr. President," he said sweetly. "But now I'm wondering. Does getting WHACKED by an assassin's bullet change your *political* viewpoint too? I mean—if it could make Abraham a drooling womanizer did it make JFK a *monk?*"

"Sterling's our interface, you moron! I order you to treat her decently. She's taken more punishment than any man alive and lived to tell about it. Now how about it... shall we ring your little Miki for lunch?"

"Fine! Fine; but keep your sexual-harassment mitts to yourself. Is that understood?"

ELEVEN

"These are your textbooks. They contain vital, *vital* information: all *top secret* up to now," said H.G.

Wearing her reading specs, O'Blivion settled at the desk by the window where she could look down on Earth. Clouds hid the entire Midwest today; weather reports said it was raining in Chicago, and in Sterling's heart it was dark and rainy in sympathy... she felt so cut off from the world!

The trouble was: she hadn't seen or heard from Virginia Woolf for over a week now. Was that strange or what? H.G. brought what he called THE TECH OF SAGE LRH and the vampire fully expected to have to wade through pages and pages of boring, same old "same-old" like the hundreds of textbooks she had read and even written a few of...feeling more and more positive that this Cold Turkey Cure of H.G.'s was nothing but some kind of weird, intolerable con job! And if it wasn't—*where the hell was Woolf?*

Nancy had been treating her badly too.

"There's never been a human who recovered from vampirism," Nancy pointed out with that patronizing LOOK of hers all stuffed with hidden meanings. "Are you planning on trying any more games? Think you can escape from here? You're supposed to be an intelligent woman, or is that an oxymoron? It's not worth dying for is it?" and on and on and ON: *ad nauseum.*

One thing was certain. They were making the vampire spill her guts and confess things she'd never revealed to anyone before—not even *herself!* Secrets that were so deep a part of her she'd thought they WERE her! And her whole personality structure would collapse if they were removed. But oddly enough...it hadn't. All that happened was, she felt better. But was still only partway through the Cure. And she knew the worst was yet to come! She'd have to play it by ear for the next little while—H.G.

looked feeble and puny but had tons of bullying power. And Ster knew he wouldn't let her off—no matter what she said or did.

She began turning the pages. Soon her mouth became a round O of surprise, terror and pleasure all mixed together—*this stuff was incredible!*

Parts of it really gripped her imagination—it seemed the data didn't hold true for Earth alone. It had been researched on many planets and applied, apparently, to every form of life; a universal law of existence. And Sterling recognized it at once! This Sage of theirs had laid down axioms and principles she'd always felt were *true*—but only somewhere down so *deep* that she'd never been able to look at them in broad daylight. Or broad ship light, Ster thought; grinning down at her misty ol' Earth-globe...

This was *The Answer*. To all the basic questions that people always asked, and then some!

It said here that she was already a god, creating the stuff of reality. She had forgotten how she did it...but would be re-taught the steps one by one! Until she regained Total Freedom.

The Sage spelled it out. That precarious planet down there was not her home and native land, for openers. It would be a mistake to say that the inhabitants had GONE crazy; they had BEEN crazy since an incredible disaster overtook them trillion of years ago; but today, there were too many of them for their planet to absorb all the craziness they inflicted on it—

The paranoia was finally paying off. They were out to get each other. They were weaving a noose for themselves, as a species. WOW!

Sterling felt dizzy! Reading this stuff was supposed to speed her healing process but how did she know it wasn't... maybe...a *chilling scheme* to FORCE humanity into evolving mentally? The quotes around LRH's words looked a mile high, " " like the tracks of some gigantic Alien slithering out of its awful lair; knowing everything—and insisting upon sharing *every crumb of* that apocalyptic knowledge with the human race—*whether it liked it or not!*

And it seemed the Rysemians lived by this knowledge. Once upon a time they'd been barbarians like her own people, raining fire upon each other. Then the Sage was born, did his research and passed on to be deified in the form of a forty-foot, stuffed pig-whale mounted in a heavy water museum on Rysemus. Flipping ahead, Ster didn't understand the lore revealed in the advanced volumes but was intrigued, partly because—unless the whole myth was a dirty lie—IT WORKED. The Tech appeared to have saved the early Rysemians from ruin; and who knew? *It might do the same for her.*

"You are learning to use The Force," H.G. smilingly encouraged when he poked his head in. "Onward, toward the Sublime! For what other goal is truly worthwhile?"

Queer stuff indeed! The vampire knew she was in touch with an awesomely lucid intelligence...except...she felt overwhelmed... her own role in The Future (till now so clear in her mind) taking on the aspect of a frightening dream *(if I can't cut it —)*

She read what she herself had written only this morning:

And through it all, my yearning for my Star Woman remained. I was sure she'd come to me some day, a fairy godmother with a magic wand; and she'd release me from this malign SPELL I'm under—and she'd give a splendid pattern to the interwoven threads of my weird, sorrow-crammed life—

"God help me, I've been *kidnapped and brainwashed!*" Sterling yelled (but not aloud. She didn't want Nancy waltzing in)—feeling she could at last understand the subtle torments endured by those poor wretches who report they've been "Taken aboard a space ship and probed and examined and *it was awful and*—oh God—I don't know what happened next" is what they say on TV, looking utterly zapped and violated. And everyone sneers at what a publicity-hound this kook must be to make up a nutball tale like that—but!

There was a revolution going on—temporarily ignored by the scientific and publishing worlds. A tale as old as time. Once widely known, now suppressed. The "fact" of death was nonexistent. Bodies die. People don't. Your memory, blanked between-lives with pain, drugs and hypnosis can and must be restored...but it can't happen if you've been so EVIL that you cannot confront *the past*; now...or ever...forever...

and she had so much GUILT!

(dizzy) in which case the cycle'd start again...

Sterling let out a moan! She grabbed her pen and began spilling her guts in a frenzy onto the crackly parchment—

Jimmy Hoffa. Does the name ring a bell?

Fame is fleeting. All the inane stories you hear about Jimmy bring a wry smile to my lips...The public thinks the Mob whacked this Teamster boss, burying him in cement under third base in a New Jersey stadium. Sorry, chumps; nothing could be further from the truth.

'75 was a bad year for me. My career in the toilet—how can a tenured professor be fired from her Wellesley job you ask? Grow up, my friend! I was onto something (in my field which is particle physics)—a torrent of ideas threatening to wash me out of the pond. And when I'm IN IT that deep—I'm wide open to attacks from jealous colleagues. Top scientists, unaware that life does not happen in three dimensions only—men so retarded they defy belief! One of them informed the Dean that my scandalous secret would be printed if I wasn't cut from the Department. The ax fell. I fled—like a coward.

O.K.: in '75 I was into drug and alcohol abuse. I'm way past it now; but at the time I was your typical, broken woman numbing herself out—living on the edge in a haze of prescription chemicals. This is a highly recommended role for the American female especially if she's past forty. Flattened by the Dickmobile that crushes everything like a steamroller, she drifts up and down the turnpikes of life dabbing at her eyes with Kleenex as she wanders wraithlike past motels, billboards, fruit stands, ski lodges...sobbing her eyes out, wildly trying to extinguish her thoughts—and herself if she can—which is a story for another time; but that description about sums me up (little knowing that in fifteen years I'd be one of the richest, most successful dance studio franchise operators in the business—and *fuck science!* Science hates women; in a sneaky underhanded way, of course, not wanting to lose their funding).

Going bugs one weekend, I climbed into the old Ford truck that I slept in and zoomed up the Interstate. I'll be the first to admit I'd had a snootful. Warm pints of Jack Daniels nipped from the car flask while smoking pack after pack of Camels—my self-esteem at an alltime low; my truck needing work, air conditioning shot, fuel pump coughing like an old, sad, once-lovely call girl that nobody gives a damn about any more—

I lurched into the side lot of a tavern and proclaimed to the dark night:

"SHIT!"

Now I'm in a cool, quiet bar nursing a Scotch rocks and listening to the gossip. You think I'm a snotty type? Wrong impression! I am *extremely nice* to people, as an aristocrat should be; so forthwith feeding dimes to hear Janis Joplin and Jimi Hendrix — I love rock and roll — so much a part of this nonstop century with its wacky, hypnotic mourning over our fumbly, Wannabe-Sexpartner ineptness pridefully concealed by the technology of steel guitars and drums, not to mention condoms with hopeful messages of clean health and sexual prowess printed on them — "*O lost and by the wind grieved ghost*" as old Thomas Wolfe used to complain (and poor Tom didn't know the half of it back in America's palmy days, right?) — my thoughts wandering all over the place.

Suddenly the man on the next stool leans to me. Uh-oh. A pick-up attempt? In any case, it beats depression.

"Buy you a drink?"

"Thank you," I smile, batting the lashes a bit.

What the hell. Everyone wants to be noticed.

We talk. Pretty soon I recognize who he is; the Union Czar himself, unshaved in an open-necked Hawaiian shirt and cream slacks — perhaps I haven't made it clear that we're not alone. Even in that crummy little bar Hoffa was surrounded by adoring ladies hanging on his every word, or pretending to as custom demands — males insist on such behavior from women, indeed take it for granted which is what makes them so boring. These males are forced to 'act superior to women' in public under pain of being insulted and ridiculed by their fellow males — which to my mind is a cry for help. I mean what is the pontificator really saying but: "*Boohoo*. My whole sex is *obsolete*. We are Old Hat — we are Past It! Please, *please!* Euthanize me...don't let me suffer like this...but meantime, *blah blah blah*; me me me, *I, I, I...*" which reaction is of course, *abnormal*; a malignant social cancer undiagnosed and untreated. There can be no two-way flow with a male; only his own compulsive outflow — and women are forced to play up to his *me-me-I-I* not only because they hunger for social approval but they FEAR being PUNCHED, ostracized, or called a DIRTY DYKE by him. I usually try to avoid such symptomatic cliches but tonight I "*needed somebody*" and here was a Big Name — the vampirization of which is, after all, my specialty. (Sorry for the digression Gramps; I was just tryin' to set the mental stage for you.)

"You're a wicked female," Jimmy grins.

I'm sitting there in my blue jeans and sweaty T-shirt with WELLESLEY across the tits, right? A far cry from the slinky black with sequins that I usually wear under a cloak (occasionally switching to basic lipstick and leather).

"You don't even know me," shrugs the cool, quick-witted O'Blivion. We spar verbally a bit—

Jimmy was absolutely unafraid of me. I like that in a victim. He was your wholly typical male; had to be the center of attention, women crowding around and cooing like under-secretaries with wine coolers in their manicured fists.

Without warning Hoffa leans forward. "What do you charge to suck a neck?" he whispers in my ear.

I about fell off my stool! Where had he heard such a thing— was it entrapment—it wouldn't have been the first time. Who told him? Was he toying with me? Or was the guy a tiny bit smarter and kookier than average?

We chatted. Jimmy said he'd seen me on Oprah. I said no way. My face had been fuzzed. He wanted to drop it. He was losing interest. I couldn't let that happen. I began cooingly agreeing with him like the bar chicks with the tiny umbrellas in their wine coolers. Soon Jim began eating out of my hand—please don't forget: I belong to the Middle Ages. It's not for nothing that I call modern people "twinkies." I'm a thirteenth century woman! Whereas Hoffa was a New Age male—swamped with luxury, pampered on all sides—and like an immature Roman emperor they get bored very quickly. I was scared of entrapment but he came off quite sincere about paying for services rendered—

A weirdo. Nothing to do but lead him on.

"This is a rare bit of insolence," I flirt; belting the Scotches he buys me (on top of all-day car-flask nipping) and soon we head for a motel. But we never got there. Instead, we wound up in the Men's Room. Alone together.

It was no big trick to put the willing Jimmy into the trance—he on the floor, me straddling him, hoping no one could peek through a crack or something. What a picture we must have made! I punctured his neck *(a beautifully thick, strong, bronzed Slavic neck)* with the usual two tiny holes; then the moment of excruciating pleasure—the sweat! The heat...the *impenetration*...his coppery blood bubbling in my mouth...I lap ever so delicately...*deliciously*...striking through to the living core and essence as I sip from that rich, red fountain...and lovingly run my fingers over the swooning victim's face, neck, and arms, in an ages-old intimacy partaking of the sorcery of heathen practices—tinged (I am forced to admit) with my own religious awe of this pre-Christian obsession of mine *(Oh Christ!* the hot *ancient* taboo-smashing Rubysucking thrill...it's why I chalked up so many years in flophouses, lowlife cafes and dimly-lit passageways loitering wherever bare necks abound, and every passerby is a potential victim)—and: like all great athletes...I make it look easy.

A complicated, driven woman, the caring parts of my personality dictate that I LAP GENTLY! not SUCK; and take a mere six ounces. Six is all I need. I absolutely *hate* killing people. Compassion! That's my watchword—sneer as you will. Killing is far too outre and Norman-Schwarzkopfy for my taste—but...I don't know how it happened—Hoffa was a juicy one. Possibly I lapped too much; maybe eight or ten ounces—I was swacked out of my melon, barely standing. And he'd asked for it hadn't he?

So then without a word of warning, the stupid wuss goes and has a coronary on me! I recognized all the symptoms. Oh shit! What a total drag—Jimmy just slumped. He went stone-cold dead under me. Believe me when I say it was the LAST thing in the world I wanted! I'm not sugarcoating my past when I confess that my Compulsion, or Bad Habit or whatever you choose to call it, comes over me in a kind of frenzy; then I MUST DO IT. But I only LAP! Never SUCK to leave a drained, dry HUSK or steal a wallet, peek at genitals, or take other cynical liberties with unconscious bodies (such as rape, or painting amusing slogans on their butt and so on). And anyway this job was consensual, don't forget.

I had invented an attachment for my Swiss army knife, a laser-like little jigger that could cut through flesh and bone like butter. Quickly I used it on Hoffa starting with the toes, sawing him up, and when he was sliced clean, flushing every part of him down the toilet, slowly, so the mechanism wouldn't back up and vomit a bunch of toes and balls and so on; you know how it is; I'm sure we've all had the unpleasant experience of a toilet vomiting back at you, and there was no plunger in there.

Men kept rapping on the door—I worked as fast as I could. Pieces of kidney and offal came back up a couple of times—goosh! I had to pick everything up and toss it back in. His eye—that was the worst. It just wouldn't go down no matter *how* hard I flushed, sweating and cursing under my breath; it just rolled up to look at me out of the toilet.

I sometimes think of that eyeball twisting up LOOKING AT ME, I swear, Grandfather! As if there was *sight* in it. And it was JUDGING me! while men who wanted to go to the can rapped and knocked on the door.

"Fuck off. I'm taking a dump," I said in lordly, masculine tones; making my voice brusquely commanding. And they did. I worked as fast as I could — then found a can of Comet and scrubbed down the whole john, cleaning up all the blood spatters and finally the toilet and myself.

When everything was sparkling clean, I walked up to where the good ladies give free coffee to tourists and downed four or five cups, smiling wearily. I had got what I needed. The two C-notes in Jimmy's wallet would fix up my truck. I had flushed his I.D. down the toilet knowing he'd be magnanimous enough not to give a shit (after all, *what goes around comes around* — I myself often tucking a few bills in a pocket if a *suckee* is down on his or her luck as I was) and decided to forget the whole incident as I always do.

But !!...

Earth. A total house of horrors. It lets you rest just long enough to get set up for the next horror.

TWELVE

"*Her people*," as H.G. called them, were in great danger.
These fat books of the Sage's were a DOOR. The kind of door you'd slam shut under normal circumstances — because you were programmed to steer clear of *The Force* as it was called in the film STAR WARS. You were supposed to think a power like that could exist only in some *fantasy* or other. Surely YOU could never learn to use it. Using it might prove UNCOOL for *The Evil Empire* — whose minions had done the big brainwash job on your whole race, *eons ago!* Then along comes cute little Heidi's Grandfather saying "We can help you remake your world but only if you CONFESS EVERYTHING." *Outre!*

It was either *pure hooey* — or just plain *wonderful*.

Sterling's hands shook, clutching her pen.

I never knew when or how my parents died *(she wrote)*.

When they kicked me out bodily, I was but a poor little orphan of the storm — the event took place at four P.M. on a dark, wintry Sunday. A lowering sky spat hail; a gusty wind blew branches off trees...*I can see me now*. The child weeps. She huddles by the stone wall edging our property. "Our" property? Ah, my dear, never call it that again! The ancestral home has slammed its door to you. You are HOMELESS. Like legions of far worthier young people.

My parents. God-in-heaven, will I ever forget their expression? A look of dread mixed with utter loathing — the bulging eyes and tightened mouths as they shrank away — from ME! the girl they had all but worshipped (as I did them; we'd been a happy, close-knit family) suddenly revealed as a *MONSTER! A Dracula daughter.* The worst thing that could happen to a 13-year-old who wouldn't have her first period for 6 months yet *(or recognize what it was when she did!)*

What was to become of me? Had God passed judgment on me for getting raped by a priest? I tried to kill myself many times — I'd have welcomed death — sweet death that would put an end to my torment —

There was humiliation everywhere. Curses and spiteful words rained down; manure, rocks, fiery arrows — myself dazed in shock, wanting Mother to fold me in her arms again; old friends screaming that I'm a freak of nature — WHY?!!?, I kept asking. WHY ME?!!? Bawling like one of the witches I'd seen burned at the stake, I shook my fist at the sky and cursed God. "Why? WHY?" I yelled. Why was I drowning in devil piss while the rest of the world rolled happily on?

The bitter part was that I had lost my best friend Greta just a week earlier (the angels took her away, I'd been told — *it was enough to make me hate the fucking angels' guts!*) and so I ran, tearing my hair out by the roots — many a cold night had to be struggled through — the moon illuminating every stone and hillock of the moor I was forced to roam, weeping for what I had lost: my little bed, food, indulgent parents, good reputation — even the kindly Sisters (my last hope) paid bowmen to send me packing (I have a scar on my shin to this day from one of their arrows). And when you ask, "Did you know?" — *I am without an answer.* Possibly I WAS aware that Scaulzo had singled me out to lay his clammy spell on my head; *but hardly consciously.* There were many hints and suspicions but the shock was too great. I was only a terrified kid — although since he returned from the War (the BIG war, the IMPORTANT war! not one of your shabbily absurd C 20 baby-tantrums) my father had regaled our guests with stories about *Jujus* and *Hexes,* baleful Spirits sealed in bottles — the Holy Land bristled with every wicked tale and portent. But they were *stories*: not personal to me.

Years later, I began trying to fit the pieces together. This thing that happened to me; people call it weird. But I believe stuff like this happens *all the time.* And also: could it, by any stretch of the imagination (and at least in my case) be *a blessing in disguise?*

You spoke of The Evolution of Consciousness. So I must ask myself...*what's so good about being "normal" anyway???* Normality (if truth be told) is cruel and stupid. To be "normal" one must put oneself in subjection to the laws and whims of a killer Civ. — and I escaped that! I was LUCKY! Now I realize what made those

Judges so furious. I mean what *really* pissed'm off until they practically *foamed at the mouth,* over and beyond my Rubylust — was the horrible fact that I had tapped, somehow, into the *Fountain of Youth* And that is a CRIME! The biggest NO-NO of all. Because it hints at a Power that could *break Scaulzo's hold over us.* YES! It begins to come clear to me. Normal people are subject to delusions. And our laws render us *passive,* malleable. But the Sage's books are an *escape route* from this. Am I right?

In point of fact — vampirism (I much prefer the word RUBYLUST) helped dull the ache of loneliness — YES!!! I sucked blood; YES YES YES I always felt *guilty as sin for Chrissake* why can't fools stop asking that question? The answer is obvious. *Who wouldn't,* under the circumstances? Thrust into a world I was totally unprepared for, I struggled through one tribulation after another — wore rags, ate rotten vegetables, stayed alive by the skin of my teeth. I've been tortured, scourged, raped, sodomized (*and I'm going to describe every filthy detail* of how it feels to be sexually violated and molested — repeatedly — in a minute. It's a hideous story; I hold the record for being *the most-raped woman ever born* — 532 times! Several were army-sized gangbangs). I've been roped tight, arms pinioned behind back with bright lights flashing in my eyes for hours by a circle of frustrated, rude, stupid, sweaty morons who don't have the brains God gave little green apples but are, in every generation, society's appointed Guardians of Authority; which serves to reveal how non-survival "society" (the *sworn enemy of happiness and creativity*) is.

And now as the Cure pierces my consciousness, I see the truth of history...and realize we have a tiger by the tail. With Scaulzo in power the future *(just like the past)* will be controlled by the men who control the CIA, KGB, AMA and other gangs of state-sanctioned psychotics; all of them hung up on Authority and chain-of-command. Women don't go for the chain-of command stuff; but many men are addicted to it. I only met one man in my life who wasn't — my husband the good Duke whom I loved so much that I pronounced him an Honorary Woman — the highest rank a male can attain; but who died of old age while I stayed young. (More about the Duke later). That's why I feel giddy realizing that at last, *the current of history must turn!* The eons-old law of brute male force must be brought to a flying WHOA! *if humanity is to survive.* Our petty wars have got to be dumped. The limp-wristed violence now thought of as 'masculinity' must be abolished. I'm beginning to understand that these 'Guy Things' as they are called, are a small scale dramatization of the ongoing space war we've been trapped in for a trillion years or more—*unaware!* Unable to see what's in front of our very eyes.

O.K. Grandfather: I now see that horror has no social value at all. It's not "catharsis" as I always used to say. All it does is help Scaulzo keep his grip on us.

The truth is: *I was wrong!* No more wrong than plenty of others, true—but we failed to take care of our world's future. We never clarified what we were trying to BECOME. We never made up our minds! We were too busy *cannibalizing* each other—getting *richer* to buy better *toys*—

Hell!!! Trying to sustain your *concentration* in this dump...Nancy Reagan sashays in. "Sterling: you are writing a bunch of lies," she whines. "I've given you a second chance to attain the Unattainable and this is the thanks I get."

"I demand to see Woolf NOW!" I yelp; *slamming* this Confessional (thwarting the jerk's attempt to read over my shoulder).

"Only one thing can bring you and your red-hot mama together again. Know what it is? Your success in snatching King Arthur from Armageddon—the *jaws of death*."

"Take a hike," I command as nicely as I can. "Don't come in here and insult my intelligence, *dizzy bitch*."

Whereupon she nuzzles my shoulder murmuring: "You are tough-talking but with heart-stopping beauty" and, butt-twitching out, locks the door. (What is the cooze *up to?* I don't even want to *know*.)

Nancy has said it not only "left deep emotional scars" but triggered a life of bloodsucking, when, while being pinned and sodomized by that pederast priest—I turned and bit his sweaty, freckled *neck!* "You went bad because of preadolescent *sexual tension*," is her mournful psychobabble that only underscores how misunderstood not only I, *but all natural women*, really are...Alone; so alone and *desperate for love*—so desperate that soon I was glorying in my shameless passion three or four times a week.

But THAT DAY *(that hideous day!)* I was an innocent virgin. Yet: knowing what a huge market there is for details of sexual misconduct and how quickly the reader (possibly even *yourself*, Grandfather?) gets bored with anything that is not violence, gossip, betrayal and the grand favorite, *sex-as punishment* —

I made my confession. Priest told me to say five Hail Marys and enter his booth behind the grille. I rattled off the Hail Marys glad to get off so easy (my *mortal sins* were disobeying Papa, nut-pelting a fat monk, peeing in the lute of a bowlegged minstrel who sang like a frog). Little did I know it would be my last confession *ever* —

I entered the booth. Whereupon, swiftly bending me over my confessor *pulled down my panties*. I of course didn't protest; I thought it was a legitimate punishment — a bit odd perhaps, when he *spat on his dick* (I'd never seen one in a stiff condition before; and only from a distance in any condition) and breathing like a walrus he spread the cheeks of my bum, thrusting "himself" in the direction of my tight, virginal *rear orifice.* (I find the fact that men call their dick "himself" quite significant — as in: why bother with the rest of the body, *particularly the brain,* when we could just have a whole lot of little *"himselves"* crawling around the planetary surface and Senate floor?)

The priest was stronger than I. The hand that moved between my legs felt like iron. I thought this was God's chosen punishment. His dick pressed with lustful force against my rosy rectum; which all at once yielded for a deep, spit-slicked penetration — then he was moving in and out going "SSSSS!" with teeth clenched and eyes shut, I noted upon turning my head.

Did it hurt like *hell?* Like *fire?* A redhot *poker* up the back door? Of course; but I didn't yell — him gulping air, moaning raggedly and going "Uh! *SSSSS!* Oh YAY-sooo!" over and over as he slap-slapped against my ass. I'd like to drag the scene out for you but there wasn't a whole lot more to it than that; the guy came; fluid dripped out of me; with a deep, satisfied sigh he began the in-out for a second time — a third time — it really turned him on. I know that many male novelists are obsessed with this scene, describing it over and over. I'll tell you why. *They have a prostate.* When a prostate is rubbed, an *orgasm* can result. Women *have no prostate.* Contrary to male opinion, women are not panting to be screwed in the butt for a very simple reason: it's *boring*. They can't come that way so why bother? No; for such an activity, I'm afraid males are stuck with each other. Although let me add that AIDS was originally spread by men thus using their wives in Africa (as a birth control measure), the rectum being much more easily torn for germs to enter than the tougher vagina (and here I must say that some of *my dearest friends* have died of AIDS and I mourn them every day — although I myself am immune to just about every disease you can name, I don't know why. Part of the curse, is my guess).

Now comes the really *bad* part.

I don't know how it happened. Afterward, I prayed that the clock hands would move backward, and the sodomization would not have occurred! Or that I simply grinned and bore it; letting myself be repeatedly buggered and then forgetting it as thousands of women and male prisoners are forced to do — *no hard feelings, buddy, what the heck.* But: I turned, as I say. And suddenly found myself biting his neck, which put him into the trance. His dick became about an inch long! The way the thing shriveled absolutely amazed me! Then I lapped — not very much, but enough to ruin my whole future when he ran to the Authorities that afternoon —

The first weeks passed in a kind of dream. Then one night I crept close to my old home for the last time. The snow was knee deep, more of it drifting down. The castle blazed with light but my little high room was dark. I saw the sputtering torches of guards that had been posted to drive me away. I heard their hearty laughter. It sounded *hollow* in the biting cold. Then all I did was skulk in shadows and weep. Around three in the morning the truth sank home. I wasn't too bright, perhaps — freezing to death, face swollen with crying — a dumb young girl.

The sun's first glow found me climbing up beside a peddler in his cart. *I would try my fortune in Spain!*

Poor little whelp — her future was bleak indeed. I know you have more important things to do so I'll rush over my first view of the pink light slanting down on Barcelona —

When I finally got arrested, the rape that took place was what actually deflowered me; I mean in the *vaginal*, not the *rectal*, way — which I've already described. I'll tell each painful detail of this violation in a minute; but first —

Soon I began building my reputation — one victim at a time, gradually coming into my own in the Spanish countryside as I ripened into THE vampire of southern Europe. My black cloak and pale face became a fixture around many towns — which was absurd but what could I do? My whole life became a joke — masking a *bottomless depression* I wouldn't confront. Often I went to church and prayed that *death would end my agony* and the worse it got, the more I wanted The *Ruby,* my only solace; but all God sent was more of the same and it really hurts when brats stone you and their gorgeous Spanish mothers cut you dead on the street!

And all I had was victims — this scenario reenacted many times, my actions having made a considerable stir around town once again, as again I had to move — please don't think I'm offering arguments in support of vampirism or that I don't fear Lucifer's fire, the writhing flames of the *Bad Place!* The Suits in their smug outrage always question me about guilt — *I don't tell'm shit!* But oh boy. You say "God help me!" as on and on the torture goes; your heart languishing, the memories rotting in your mind — you can't quite be sure it ever happened and ask yourself, "Hey stupid, did you really suck the man's blood? *You're fukt.* Is this your only means of communicating with the outside world?" and on and on until you develop a poor self image.

So after the first arrest I lived in dread of it happening again. For months I only came out at night. I scolded myself: "Your soul is a muddy pond, you fukn-blud junky. You better start fearing the diabolic consequences!" with furious self-disgust. There was rage piling up — what had happened to me was beyond mortal endurance — but now looking back, I see *a tremendous value* there. Perhaps it *weakens* a person to have clots of admirers patting you on the back and handing you perks and awards. That could be just another of Scaulzo's control mechanisms! "Live like a warrior," Don Juan advises — welcoming being alone and at bay. How else can a woman accomplish anything? I mean look at the bland, boring books on the shelves — all the work of pampered Yale graduates born after 1930! But me — I was granted the chance to *develop my character.* I lived an outrageously daring lifestyle; my passions being all that kept me going during hard times. My first duty was to stay alive; and as the love of my parents faded into history, I soon realized that I had a talent verging on genius and what I really needed was a place to work.

I needed money to develop the theories that were tumbling through my head; bizarre ideas about *time,* and how the universe is really put together — so came out of hiding and created an identity for myself. I faced overwhelming odds and suffered years of misery; but when my Duke died of old age I inherited a great deal of money.

Young chickie-broads always think that being in love with some hotshot male is *so cool*. Little do you know he'll only dump you — one way or another — so what should you do with your life? You're a problem-solving animal, kid; solve the problem! (As I told myself when my dear Duke died.)

What is mass? What is energy? How does what we think of as "time" relate to the spatial and other dimensions? I got a grasp on a path heretofore unknown to science; and finally made my breakthrough, three centuries ahead of Einstein.

Albert Einstein. An adorable little guy with fuzzy white hair, and a cute sense of humor; but Al made a simple error in confusing the definitions of words — because he had the *victim* mentality *we are all taught* and not even an Einstein could see beyond it; although he was admired by the whole world — which would have laughed him to scorn if he'd been a woman. (*And don't you ever forget it!*) Anyway, I laughed and shivered — astonished at the simplicity of a discovery which turned out to be my supreme triumph, eventually bringing me to Virginia Woolf's attention.

Yes, it was my blazing, brilliant oeuvre in physics and the novel that attracted her...or perhaps it was *my brilliant pudendum*. Did you ever look that word up, Grandfather dear? In Webster's dictionary it says: "That of which one ought to be ashamed. The vulva." Suggesting that you should crouch down and chew your toenails wailing "Oh God, look at that! *How shameful of me.* A vulva, for land's sake! Now why did I want a distasteful organ like *that*? I can never hold my head up in the village again. Why didn't I get me a meat weapon like decent folks? What good am I except as a slave? Oh, boohoo. *Boohoohoo!*" — crying and crying; the approved condition for women to be in. A real no-threat plight.

The male language is so seeded with boobytraps for women of good will, it will have to be disinfected before using. A society full of such bullshit must be dismantled like an old stove you're cleaning before it blows up in your face — all right. End of bitching, Grandfather: I'M LUCKY! and I know it. And in light of that historic confession —

I must have a glass of wine before launching into a blow-by-blow of the *brutal rape* that happened to me next.

THIRTEEN

"Circumcision," Abe snarled.

"What?" Lunch over, Doug lay gloomily on the bed, hands entwined on chest. "What's eating you now?"

"Don't be so quick to judge," Abe said excitedly. "What have people been crazy about for millennia? Genital-trimming! In light of that, here's my new speech — *Africa!* The veldt. *Tribesmen.* The war is over! *They put down their spears.* It's time to cut off the labia of all the women of the tribe with a *rusty ax.* All clitorises will have to go too — *blood's flowing everywhere* — then: *Huh. Hoon. Huh. Hoon!* In marches a platoon of fine-looking soldiers. They carry signs that say: NUTHIN TO BELIEVE IN. 'We will fight hard for our beliefs!' they roar in unison and the war with the tribesmen begins. JOLT! TWIST! *OH NOOOO!* and then I put in a little uplift. *Bait-and-switch!* Voters always go for it if you grease well with vaseline — then the Headman delivers a speech about how all genitals everywhere must be cut, mutilated or removed by Authorities as soon as possible or God will be *displeased* and *hurt us.* At that — KCHFF! The blood begins flowing. SHNNKK. Kreee-AASHHH! JOLT! TWIST! AaiiEEEEE...THUDDD! And they sue each other for outrages, infringements and malpractice. Do you like it? It's my updated Gettysburg Address," his eyes sparkling.

"Let me tell you something—"

"Next paragraph! Ninety couples copulate frenziedly as a clown tortures a boy scout duct-taped to a flagpole, a mummy dressed as a Nazi rapes a beautiful spread-eagled Jewish actress with Faulkner's corncob and scientists destroy helpless dogs and cats, telling the public that this saves lives; you get the idea — my Address, updated for sophisticated tastes! How else can I get re-elected after all these years? CONK. *Ouch.* POW! *Take that,* you burning-eyed seducer," he yelled.

Doug burped wearily. Abe shook his head.

"Don't you get it? We must be audacious! Inspired! Because the more troubled and stressed-out humans are, the more their little minds rush to feed on the very paranoia that mashes their endocrine system into a disease-receptive state! How else can we build a consumer demand for sanity in an asylum than by first offering stiff doses of the poison that drove them nuts in the first place? A housewife amputates a man's feet with a hatchet—give that author fifteen million bucks a year!—as plates of hamburger with blood drooling off 'm are served at McDonald's, while Earth becomes one big, stinking tomb—you get the idea; if it doesn't *hurt and bleed,* if you don't *put 'er in reverse* again and again and run over the poor little fluttering bird until every bone in its body is *mashed flat,* whatever piece of fiction you're trying to create will never, NEVER be sold on the mass market, General—and time is running out on us. I've GOT to be reelected! It's a death race. People are beginning to get terrified! Dumb as they are, they sense something's wrong that just possibly might be fixed with half an ounce of sense," Abe declaimed, waving his hands.

Doug puffed his battered corncob and rolled his eyes. "Misery is their portion, chief. They aren't happy with anything else."

"I don't buy that! All I want is for the American people to see me, and love me. But it's certainly true that every human tested so far has failed the Turing test."

"The which?"

"Turing test! How you can tell a genuine human being from a look-alike machine, AI, artificial intelligence. I'm saying that we MUST appeal to whatever hearts they have left and do it NOW."

The Battle Hymn of the Republic began playing softly in the background.

"That song..." Abe said, remembering. "It calls to all that is noble in us—" The orchestra came up. "It tells us: have the guts to GO FOR IT! Just DO IT as the good people at Nike say. Because no tawdry, advertising bullshit can match the simple grandeur of the truth—the truth that every person knows in her deepest heart; which is why I ask one simple question. Can Man have greater freedom?"

Abe had to laugh at himself. "Imagine saying these things not as satire but as simple honesty! What a brave thing I do...and so I must lead them (this time without crossing my fingers cuz I'm so scared of the other men) not only to Freedom, but to the Promised

Land! And when the music swells—when tears appear in all of our eyes—then we'll know that the scumbags have not won—but the strong American heart still beats brave and true; and that brave heart—a hero's heart!—which is too wise and sincere to opt for anything as corny as some pissant Award—thirty pieces of silver for selling out—" Tears welled in his eyes. "Because like God himself, it just IS. And truth WILL conquer in the end."

Doug was moved. Who wouldn't be? But Abe had to play a balanced role here. "Now please tell the Asian bimbo to get lost. We have important white male business to discuss," he said with a confident gleam in his eye.

"The coffee's cold," Doug snapped at Miki. She grabbed the pot and left...but MacArthur was trembling all over. He was ashamed; he hardly knew why, as Abe talked on.

"Just think of it. Every subject flunked the Turing test; a series of questions given to a computer or a person to find out whether or not there is real understanding. The test wants to know, is this computer really alive? Or is it just a machine? Now the word 'understand' is defined by our sage LRH on page 454 of his masterpiece (the title of which H.G. has translated into English as THE TECHDICT) as follows: 'Understanding is knowingness of life. It is composed of affinity, agreement and communication.' *Voila!* None of the humans we tested could be shown to have any knowingness of life. Also: quite often the subjects proved to be mere bodies with no being in them at all (although two were chewing Bubble Yum and ten were political candidates).

"Now! We know that a society that has war cannot have understanding. You yourself defined 'war' in one of your books, Omark; I'll read what you said.

"'War: that enforced homosexuality seized upon by male humans as an escape from the frenzy of the boredom imposed by an endemic suppression masquerading as 'rationality,' which leads to an inhibited imagination that ends, unfailingly, in the degraded pop culture and robotic stupidity that precede a painful, horrible, self-mutilating death for an entire ecosystem.' So! To get the ball rolling here—"

"You want my cooperation? Dump her," Doug said angrily.

"General, be reasonable. None of us like the vampire but we need recruits—a very few but *important* ones. Who else can attract them for us? She's being prepared for a career in deep time.

It isn't easy with a paranoiac like her. Patton has to work'r down pretty fine—"

"I hope he kills the tarted-up twat."

"Look at it like this. She has everything it takes. Is one of the top competitors in a grueling sport admired by all; has always lived on the edge, has plenty of glamour and best of all, *a rotten self-image.* One of the many forms of slavery endured by female Earthies for no good reason, but it ties her to us."

"Then make her into a Turkish mute! Cut out her tongue so she won't blab our secrets."

Abe sighed. "Sterling'll keep her lip zipped. She'll never go home again, that's the beauty of it—but the hour's getting late; every moment is precious. The plan is to bring back an ancient band of warriors from a place called Wales in the A.D. 500's. They were widely known as the Knights of the Round Table. Their leader is presently impounded in the 22nd century. Arthur (he is now named Sean) is deep in that brainwashy, deadly amnesia humans call 'normal'—a teenager without the slightest knowledge he's the Once and Future King! Isn't it sick how none of them have any ghost of a memory of their past lives? I simply can't get over it. How could any being think he's stuck in some crab-shaped bag of offal on sticks, with toes? At any rate O'Blivion must go there and if she survives (which isn't bloody likely) she'll bring our man back for rehab and training. If anyone can clean up this planet's mess the original King Arthur can."

"Send me instead! Please, Chief! I'm wasting my big chance buried alive in a dead-end G.I. role—"

"No way, General. You made your bed. Now lie in it. Hold on. I've got call waiting."

Lincoln vanished. In sixty seconds she was back, far more comfortable as Mersoid in her tank in her native form.

MacArthur gagged; his hand went involuntarily to his throat... To human eyes, it was a sickening shock to see a Rysemian blubberfish—the most ugly (although the sweetest, smartest and most loving) creature in the known worlds.

"You disgust me too," Mersoid growled—telepathic to the gills of course—and what hideous gills! Nauseatingly horrible, they rippled pinkly as the unsettling fins curled around the thirty-foot, mottled, asexual, uglier-than-sin hulk lolling at ease in the scummy tank. Doug looked away, fighting to keep his breakfast down.

"Ster's a hand-picked, classy dame who's led a harsh, wretched life that toughened her up for a real achievement. She's survived against all odds, is perfect for espionage purposes—you'll treat her with ordinary male contempt hidden under a respectful social veneer till our difficulties are resolved," the fish burbled. "Is that clear?"

"I can't and *won't* fake respect for a 'sucker. I don't care what a hotdog she is," Doug said, looking calm but wiping his palms on the bedsheet.

The way Abe looked at him brought on the cold sweats. "I'm noting physical signs of stress," Lincoln said coldly. "Listen to me. This vampire *takes the punishment*. Nothing fazes her for long. Fights her way back like a salmon going upstream, doesn't know when to quit, shows rudiments of understanding, passed the Turing test with flying colors—hell, she can crawl up the side of a building! She's the *one person we need* to attract the ones we *really* need."

Doug bit his lip until it bled. No use bucking the Chief when her mind was made up.

"Now!" Mersoid barked. "I need to know two things, two small things about Virginia Woolf and Scaulzo. Are they involved romantically? Is he going to have his evil way with her? Have they fucked?"

"That's the most revolting thing I've ever heard," MacArthur screamed.

"You call yourself an anthropologist?" sneered the Chief. "Hiding in a sleazy hotel; you're the Emperor of Japan for Chrissake. I want you settling the score with Woolf and her vampire tail—and I mean before the sun sets."

"You think just because I'm in bed I'm lazy, I'm not thinking and suffering?" Trying not to puke, Doug forced his eyes back to the monster's (clone of his very own self! It just didn't seem possible). "Do me a favor, Chief. Your looks make me sick, O.K.?"

Mersoid winked and waggled her whiskers (an obscene come-on; an affront to human sensibility—the fat blob was sexless as a damned paramecium!), then vanished with a snarled, "Being in a human body may be dangerous to your health. Never forget that you're just as nauseating to me as I am to you," returning a few seconds later as Lincoln—just in the nick of time, it turned out.

There was that same knock on the door—that giggly, whispery tap-tapping that had scared Doug so badly half an hour earlier.

It was Miki. With hot coffee which he gulped gratefully, burning his tongue a bit...but...he was ashamed. He'd been rudely jolted, thinking it was a Sajorian at the door instead of Miki, the sexy hotel maid who now stood batting her eyes suggestively at both himself and Abe Lincoln (what a slut she was, like all women, especially Woolf, that traitorous bull dyke lesbian!) and he was understandably embarrassed by it. But not Lincoln.

"Hey baby, smack-smack, you wanna gamahootch with me, hah?" Abe was leering at Miki, making silly hand gestures.

Doug drew his knees up wearily. "Don't encourage her, you ice-hole."

"Why not? You scared of women? She doesn't even speak English."

"Are you implying I'm less of a man than you are?"

"You call it *implying,* you tiny-dicked wuss?"

"Prove it," MacArthur exploded.

"You damn right I'll prove it," Lincoln roared. "The time has come! I'm ordering you to screw this cute little Miki *right now* on this bed. Look at her, how she wants you, with her powder-blue eyelids, a ton of lipstick and little pointy feet. Come on, cut yourself a slice of nooky and then I'll hop on too if she enjoys pulling a train — an old fraternity term for a gangbang."

"Cut one yourself!" Doug screamed. "You're implying I'm not a true man!"

"You could fix her up. Buy'r a nice dress. She'd be a *fancy piece* on your arm like a gold watch, hashmark, or trained falcon; isn't that the approved way?"

"Nobody's immune," Doug cried bitterly as a new thought struck him...A thought so horrible he didn't even want to consider it.

What if—? *But no.* It couldn't be.

It was just a vague idea, free-floating without roots and yet: it was a whip that stung across his face. It was just possible that Mersoid had been corrupted. That he'd fallen into the net and the Miki woman was...was...a part of it somehow—oh *Christ!* He could be being set up; framed in an elaborate sting, when all he wanted was to see his home again and be safe and happy, experiencing wild joyousness in the twinkling deeps where things were really real, unlike this haunted place...this floating graveyard of life-hating pirates who'd whacked each other's testicles off for more millennia than the newer suns had existed!

"Nobody's immune." Maybe he shouldn't have said that. He'd have to be more cautious. Abe was fooling around with the sexy maid (or could it be a mask? Part of the sting—how could you tell? *You couldn't.* That was the problem).

"I'll do it myself," the tall man was roaring. "I'm not only far better at human sexuality, but, mine is bigger than yours any old day."

"It is not!"

"It is too! And I can prove it."

"So prove it!"

Miki left quickly, slamming the door behind her as the two leaders sat on the bed proving that Doug's was indeed slightly longer and thicker than Abe's, but not by much.

"It's merely because when you're a hologram, the optics appear to *foreshorten* whatever is too enormous to appear as it really is," Abe said good-humoredly.

"Yours is ropier, like your forehead."

"Yours is squatter, like your neck."

"Yours is adorable though."

"Yours is adorable too."

"Good! Now we don't have to go to war."

"That's not the only reason they fight," Doug said gloomily.

He was fed up with sex talk—he really wanted to tell the Chief about his Truman woes—the mental torment he was in, swept up in a world of political corruption, his true self smashed to pieces behind the silly surface of it all—yes! He had to lay the pain out before Mersoid (for what it was worth) because his Chief had no clue to the pressure MacArthur was under. Those young aides of his, so quick to pounce on any tiny slip...He could feel them waiting with bated breath for him to do something so goofy it would confirm their total lack of faith in their General.

"When I eat a napkin by mistake, their eyes bug out like frogs and if I forget to zip the stupid fly or when from this mouth comes that drawn-out, involuntary BRAAHHP! that makes people's heads snap on their necks—these less-than-shining moments are mounting up; just when America is heading into its ten thousandth international crisis and I'll be expected to play my role to perfection," Doug complained.

The clear vision—that's what he needed. But how to get it? His *"little woman"* was a *"wonderful lady"* everyone said, meaning she played the 1950's upperclass feminine role of the woman who "needed" a man with gravel in his voice who was accustomed to conquer and would soon, she hoped and prayed, become President so that together they could sneer at Harry Truman without getting bent. Yes; his little woman adored being wedded to an iron-willed, shambling, towering, pipe-smoking, steel-jawed adolescent in khaki shorts who'd say "You're my finest soldier" gruffly twice a week while assuming top half of the missionary position. It was the fifties boutique-y ideal—you were supposed to hate Commies to the point of rabid murderousness; and although they posed no threat whatsoever, you were supposed to hate their guts as you jumped under your school desk during the daily bomb drill, because rulers got rich by tricking the gullible.

As to Harry Truman, Doug's nemesis—that guy: he made anti-war speeches thumping tables, "We must end war before it ends us!" he'd storm, not admitting that war was the multi trillion-buck business that supported him and his ilk. The public had bought this nonsense for upwards of a million years which was quite remarkable. A thirst for massacre like that, it was almost Sajorian in the purity of its insanity—not to mention the fact that Earthies were now hot to rush off into space, but their barbarian phase was far too severe to let it be unleashed on harmless strangers—

"Calm down," Abe yawned. "You sound crazy."

"Crazy? You're the one who's crazy! Look at the facts, I'm butch as hell—I *love* being a General! I'm *nuts about being Emperor of Japan!*" he screamed. "I *love* deploying tanks and artillery and shuttling troops around protecting weak spots and all that garbage. What makes me ralph, is the *lying lying* lying! And the *dead-baby count* turns me off a little too but not much! so don't jump to erroneous conclusions about my virility."

"What kind of soldier are you if you can't stand a few dead babies?"

"The best! Virginia Woolf should be half as good," Doug shouted.

"They don't get better than Woolf. She's the core of our asset."

"Bullshit! She's lost her credibility. An agent's most precious asset. Oh, she's resourceful all right and awfully persuasive—*criminally so!* Who else could sell Patton those lunatic theories of hers about appealing to Scaulzo's 'underlying morality'? And that cowshit about 'training evil to be ethical' based on the fact that 'everyone is basically good' according to her—*she's* the insane one, not *me*."

"But don't they make a hot couple? Just picture all that charm and elegance buck naked in a steamy bedroom scene," Abe teased. Abe's face was slightly misshapen, sharp lines drawn from nose to mouth. Videogenic—no. But could he get down-and-dirty enough to make it in the next election? Doug found himself watching those ropy forehead tendons twitch as Abe spoke.

"Now I know you're in love," the President sighed.

"Shit! My aides are wondering where I am. They still love me for the Inchon landing but how long can I trade on the real General's achievements for godsake?"

"Let the Americans take care of it, they'll soon stabilize the economy by selling the Japanese every small town, giant redwood and seaport in America so you needn't worry about it." Abe drummed his fingers thoughtfully on the wooden bedstead. Then his eyes stabbed up, gleaming.

"PR, that's your job from now on," he said.

"What?"

"Inject some sane input! We can judge sanity by what a species considers its 'history.' If it's—*these* buttheads conquered these *other* buttheads and in turn were conquered by some assholes—they are *raving*. Why not make'm confront it? Scaulzo's forcing our hand, man! The cartoonish fruitflies have all of a sudden become absurdly important to the future of our Confederacy. We can't afford to let their lunatic life go bumbling along—"

"We can't?" Doug yelled. "What're we hitting but their inability to think for themselves—the basic definition of a barbaric culture, *a slave can't change his mind!* Jesus Christ! *I need my H-2*. I'm walking into a trap here—what they'd do to me—" His voice was as snotty as he could make it without arousing Lincoln's ire. "Where's the engine that drives their confusion if you're so damned smart?"

"That's for *you* to figure out!" Abe yelled. "Ignorance; not knowing that war is ALWAYS and ONLY a WHACK—the sharkstrike of the Unseen Terrorist—*no matter what tear-jerking justification,* wars are made by the Dark Powers—their own Bible says so but they've twisted the meaning until it bites its own tail. And this is what I want you to *straighten out*. YOU! With Woolf and Harry, NOW! Clear enough?"

Doug let out a shuddering sigh. "I'm on it, Chief, I'm slicing it—you know what the real source of our problem is? O'Blivion. She draws the enemy. She's the weak link."

"Don't be paranoid. Ster's incredibly hip for a human. She has to travel through time for Godsake! She'll be wearing a wire, but you know how hard it is to maintain contact. If she falls into the wrong hands and is tortured, what then? She must learn the trick of silence—and I promise you one thing, General. It can only be based on an agent's skill in exiting a body at will without being dragged back by pain."

"Good luck," Doug sneered. "How do you plan to sell that idea to a humanoid?"

"Simple! To think you *are* your body is a *psychosis*. Hell, three-quarters of Earth population knows you're not; *even Shakespeare knew* it. 'Whip the offending Adam out of you, leaving your body as a *paradise* to envelop and contain *celestial spirits*,' that's Henry V. and who's Hank talking about? Exactly who is a celestial spirit, General? You; me; your *maid*; the *vampire*—"

"Yeah, well, they don't go for that Truth stuff since shrinks took over. Today, a human's considered a stimulus-response machine. A body and no soul. A computer with pheromones. So much for Shakespeare, Mr. President."

Abe sighed. "Apparently the art and practice of being a piece of raw meat on the hoof is very dear to them. We'll work it out but first: O'Blivion must get her hands on that boy king *without delay*. He's the key person in our whole structure—what are you so nervous about?"

"Who, me? I'm not nervous."

"Yeah? Remember what you taught Woolf about resisting these attacks? *'Always bounce back,'* you said. 'Anyone can be a mental hero with a little practice.' Which means that all we must do, is go out and tell the woman in the street!"

Abe's bearded face was expressionless—a face on a copper penny—Doug had a handful of them in his pocket. It made him laugh. "You wanna get poleaxed? Secrets like these have to be kept from ordinary mortals."

"I couldn't disagree more! We need a resurrection of the human spirit, General—they need brand new, *great principles* never before discovered—and potent symbols of a new religion based on our Sage's teaching—which is so mind-blowing it'll make them forget all that simpleton goosh they eat with spoons today.

Right? *Back to innocence and the golden days!* I'm sure that if we just honestly tell people, they'll see that man is asleep and must wake up; because the hounds of chaos are baying on the ramparts."

"Boy. Are you naive," sighed MacArthur.

He climbed out of bed, stripped off his uniform and jumped into a hot shower. "I say cut 'er loose! I'll take her place," he yelled over the pounding water.

"The risk is enormous and we can't throw you away," Abe yelled back.

"If anyone can do it I can."

"I have better plans for you, and a few for the human species! They have no future unless they make *changes* — changes that'll restore the power taken away from them. Otherwise we'll have to clean up after a species slain *without a struggle*. Embarrassing? An utter disgrace! No; the old ways of life must be altered completely. We've got to turn their stodgy thinking upside down."

"That should be easy."

"People worry, and cry, and go on suffering. They are their own worst enemies. But we must believe in them when they don't believe in themselves!"

"Just so we make the sale." Doug soaped himself.

"Don't be a cynic. After a great deal of heart-searching I at last understand that the perfect form of Govt is anarchy," Abe said in his Fourscore-and-ten, ringing tones (*oh, that wonderful voice of his* — it put goose-shivers down MacArthur's spine). "The people must be able to act ethically and make their own decisions! Then they have *no need* of a central governing authority. No doubt remains in my mind that any time you have a CGA it will be corrupt and chaotic, for the simple reason that if you *need* one, you'll *never have* a good or advanced society because you're *below* being able to have one! What's the solution? First we must show them they already have life eternal! The problem being to get 'm to believe it on an individual basis. They need a complete change of heart! The *bright new vision* — the evolution of a New Spirit — they'll be overjoyed that Man does NOT have a bad, corrupt nature, but is gloriously PURE and NOBLE when you remove the Scaulzonic brainwash! What a *thrill* it'll be for them. Think how they'll love it."

Doug turned off the taps and grabbed a towel, chuckling.

"They love fascists in steel boots more," he grunted.

FOURTEEN

Punishment is EVIL. Why? Because all it does is cause the unwanted thing to persist *(O'Blivion wrote)* – as anyone but a moron can see.

I grew into adulthood as a *wild beast*. Born 1282, I am 13th century for the luvva Mike! – the only dame you'll ever meet who spent her teens, not at West Beverly High but in a feudal dungeon *(where she freaked right out)*.

Time passes slowly in that vaulted donjon connected to a torture chamber. At best, you don't get enough sleep. Of course in these plush times you can go out and BUY a cute little Dungeons game made for spoiled Twinkles who'll never have a genuine experience in their lives – yet grow up to run the governments of the world. Is the New Age a *comedy?* Or a *tragic farce?* All I know is that it makes me laugh wildly...as chills run up and down my spine.

Today, I sit in mournful thought – counting on you, Grandfather, to respect my disinclination to dwell on these humiliating subjects and yet...*what is a dungeon?* A cesspool made, by men, of hewn stone. The floor seeps water. Even in June the walls are limned with frost. If you're lucky there'll be a handful of straw for frantic rodents to scuttle across in the dark (and it's dark 24 hours a day). If you don't starve, go mad or have your throat cut by some guard or other prisoner, you'll last the full 100 years that a well-fed Judge laid on you (his indignation at the boiling point) in his blindness, stupidity, and childish ignorance of the fact that your punishment *will escalate genocide*.

"Let me out! I want to go to church and pray," I screamed pounding the wall. Can you imagine – my first night in a dungeon. Those words had worked for me in the past but now: young Sterling was being forced to grow up and smell the ratshit. And after about twenty minutes in that dump, she'd gladly have sold her *eternal, immortal soul* (or anything else she might own) for a momentary peek at a ray of light on a single blade of grass! But such was not to be. The prisoner had too much to learn. And a cruel jailer, whip in hand, to teach her. I am a living example of the fact that PUNISHMENT DOES NOT WORK. The devil's tool, punishment feels SO GOOD to the punishers—*ooh how satisfying it feels* to get that FIX of disciplining a culprit!—while booby trapping your own future. Any State that has PUNISHMENT should be destroyed before it causes REAL problems—such as universal death. It never occurs to pompous AUTHORITIES that they are using a drug that will kill them, slowly and horribly—along with all the good, kindly folk in the world—but hey—*excuse me Grandfather; I'm lashing out! And nobody wants that. Nobody wants an old vampire's philosophy no matter how insightful and true. So hey. No more preaching.* ACTION ONLY! I'll cut right to the rape. I'll go directly to the lip-smacking sexual outrage that I suffered at the hands of a brutal, leering, dandruffy booby one fine day. (Hold on please; one moment. Is that Nancy I hear rattling keys? *Yes!* The gossipy snoop *has an ear to my* door. Politician's wives. Are they *all alike* or is it just Republicans?...)

Pale, heavy-lidded, cloaked in black, and graceful as a gazelle, I had an irritating effect on the whole town. But my 'sin' sat lightly on my own conscience—yet my soul was filling up with shadows. I'd changed *in a horribly grotesque way!* Rejected for it, I lived with hunger and thirst, the rain on my head—guilty of a sin He was punishing me for. That's how we thought in those days. Alone at night, whimpering with cold and solitude *I heard the echo of ghost voices* on the wind's keen edge—but don't forget who you're dealing with! *I am my Father's daughter.* Stern Crusader blood flows in my veins—and my reputation was ripening.

A familiar figure in those parts, beholden to none, yet forced to steal and hustle, I'd walk into town with a swagger. I had begun perfecting that market-pleasing shtick that would shoot me to superstardom *(but at the cost of everything worthwhile in life; as it always is whether we care to admit it or not)*—every day, dodging a mob on my heels—assholes crazy to chase me down—it became a game—I got expert at eluding the smelly savages—in two shakes I'd be far away thumbing my nose at the superstitious jerks—luck was usually with me—zipping through cobbled alleys under swinging signs and laughing over my shoulder. They considered me a *Spirit of the Air,* a demon and fiendish witch giggling merrily, bringing them grief and unhappiness. I was something far beyond their ability to understand (*and still am,* today more so than ever) — they couldn't tolerate my freedom. When had they ever seen a girl who wasn't BROKEN? A sassy one; not on her knees from the *brainwashing* and *slapping-around* that *girls get* in this society? Why, such a thing didn't (and still does not — *don't kid yourself*) exist!

You, B.G., pointed it out. We humans live in a male chauvinist, insane asylum. There's a basic, pervasive mental affliction (you said) — the chief symptom of which is to deny that anything is wrong — explaining why humanity is a scorpion stinging its own tail. Under Scaulzo's prodding, the deadly disease infects many *women* as well; those who stab at you *spitefully* under a cloak of Niceness — I mean baby, *they are the broads to watch!* They'll hurt you worse than men do. *Ask me.* I know my misogynists. But at the time of which I am speaking, I thought I'd scoped out the whole scene and had it well under control. *Yes indeedy.* Until one terrible day...

Raggedy-ass Vampire goes down to the river on the outskirts of town to wash her silks (all she had to wear aside from a *stiff leather cloak* and *pair of shoes*). A cool green day; Spring is mumbling to the sleek mud — I'm on a mossy bank humming a little tune and dabbling bare feet in cool water, at about ten in the morning. Peaceful warmth, lulled by flickering sunbeams...when...*dazzling vision!* Face to face with a wild boar. Shaggy. Young. A sylvan god, he stands in tangled fern with his curly white tusks —

My soul had longed for a simple, honest beauty (unlike people! *Sharp tongues* poking out of *flat,* ugly faces — thinking they're so *superior* that every other life form must be sacrificed, poisoned, burnt, oil-slicked, shot, or tortured in labs by them —).

My boar snuffled and drank. He looked at me and lapped. It was reassuring for both of us. *I loved him so much.* And he loved me too! I was having a direct contact with the Fabulous. (This of course, long before it was shat upon by six billion, plastic flat-faces.) And so: utterly forgetting how my world had blown apart, I became immersed in one of those beautiful childhood dreams we all get — dreams that come only when eyes are fresh, life is good, colors thrillingly bright and we take a marvelous delight in the world around us. I drifted into that rich, *calm cogency* that the soul-killers hate like poison; those creeps who, militantly coplike, worship bureaucracy and get off on calling themselves "rationalists." At any rate, my mind dozed off. What happened next was my own fault. I know that most rape victims say "It was my fault" for mistaken reasons, but in this case it WAS my fault, as you will see.

If this were a European movie, the boar would now be speared by arrogant human males priding themselves on making his warm blood spurt out. In this exact (Heming)way, European men have murdered every fox, badger and boar; as African men murdered the elephant, Japanese men murdered the whale, American men murdered the buffalo, until the whole planet is dripping blood and the stones cry out—at which point the buttheads may ask God to forgive them. *Or shoot themselves.*

Recently I rented and watched the movie "*Beauty and the Beast*" in memory of my fine young boar. And here's a capsule review. So *jealous* are males, they must kill anything that is *beautiful,* wild, or even a bit saner and happier than they are. I sadly hang my head to think that humans are *monsters*—because oh, my fabled beast! Your kind has been overrun and wiped out by the Dickmobile. They kill LIFE, then they make a puppet movie about it and give themselves awards, patting themselves on the back so hard their arms just about break. The "entertainment" industry is (as everyone knows) run by males. And people think a new man-President can or will change things? Please! A word to the wise! Get a life! Give me a break! *Grow up!* Take it from Sterling who has watched this show for the better part of a thousand years: Woolf is correct when she says you need a complete change deep-DEEP in the heart of every swilling one of you! Beginning with a purification of media trash and bloodshed from the mass mind, or we're dead.

All right Sterling; there you go again. Nobody gives a shit about your IDEAS. Men are not interested in your MIND! Just CUT TO THE CHASE please. So O.K.—after drinking his fill, my boar lifted his dripping snout—I remember hearing a creak of leather. I looked around. At first I saw nothing. The sun was in my eyes. My boar wheeled and ran. Then, from the shadows of trees—

It was THE WATCH. How did they sneak up on me? Half crazed with loneliness, bemuddled by lack of sleep and deprived of everything I had held dear; woozy me, forgot to keep an ear cocked for the licensed marauders called Authorities.

They popped out of a stand of pine, grinning. Six or eight bastards in all. I jumped into the stream and floundered across — into the hands of two on the other side. I twisted, slipped away. Thought I'd managed to shake them — but no.

They played cat-and-mouse. They pretended to let me go. But grabbed and held me.

"Leave me alone! I haven't done anything," I said haughtily.

One twerp ripped my clothes. I kicked out at nothing.

"You'll get in trouble for this," I threatened.

"From the king?" they teased — exultation on their brutal faces. Yellowed teeth showing in big grins.

Then I was loosed. I ran! A jerk with a harelip tripped me. They laughed. They had strings of saliva drooling from their mouths. I tried to hide my rising dread. I got up with as much dignity as I could muster. Bowing, I made an eloquent plea. I thanked them for taking an interest in me.

I said I was a great Baron's child going through life without the love and support of her parents. I said I didn't mean any harm. I said I'd leave town and never trouble them again. I said flattering things.

They grabbed their crotches, making remarks I wasn't old enough to understand. They got more intense; pushing me from one to the other. Rough hands were laid on me, my rags being ripped off. One or two fingered my breasts and body hair in urgent curiosity; others felt that if they touched me intimately, they'd drop dead — a look of revulsion crossed their faces! The leader or Pointsman then shouldered his way among them. They backed off. Thank God! I was saved!

"I'll never do it again," I sobbed to the Pointsman.

"Oh I doubt that," he said. His unblinking eyes were fixed on me. He smiled. His tongue went in and out; it was disgusting — *wait*. What's happening to me? I had no intention of telling this! To do so would be *out of the question* and I'm warning you, *don't* try to pry out my inmost secrets! I wouldn't reveal this one *for the world!* It's a humiliation never mentioned before, and I refuse to tell it now, because it was not only *mortifying,* but *shameful.* I'm sure I looked a *piteous object* —

It embarrasses me terribly to remember myself bawling and bargaining with those S.O.B.'s as they sneered, grabbed their dicks and talked smut — keeping me in almost unbearable suspense — me thinking I'm holding them off with my vast aplomb; when actually it was the Pointsman's base lust that did it—promising to give me a morsel of food and then release me. *I was hungry!* I was desperate; bread was waved under my nose. I pled, the same way that victims plead to me: humiliatingly. But whether they'd let me go remained a little longer doubtful. More than two hours had passed since they caught me! I thought I'd been smart at least keeping them at bay—grateful I hadn't been gangfucked; but enough was enough! I got angry. I flew at them, bawling commands. I made huge efforts to get The Watch to free me. Then at last realizing they had no plans to do so—real terror gripped my heart.

"Help me, good Virgin of heaven," I muttered.

They'd make a bonfire of me. As a small child I'd seen what they did to witches. The smell. A horrible, burning-hair, frying-skin stench. Or maybe I'd dance on the end of a rope. *Do you know what a gibbet is?* Have you heard of Montfaucon? A high stone pile. Skeletons hang in chains at the top. Wind rattles them, crows circle them. Or maybe they'd boil me in oil! *The worst of all.* You don't have to see an execution like that twice—they lower the bound victim into a pot of bubbling oil; he pulls his feet higher and higher, shrieking—eyes just about popping out—

Paralyzed with fear, I held out my hands imploringly, trying to convince different ones to let me go—then the Pointsman cut short my appeal by seizing me by the hair. He dragged me a hundred yards and flung me into a cage on wheels. It had been hidden in shrubbery.

Getting two men to hold me down, the Pointsman pried open my mouth and examined my teeth *(the incisors curve and are slightly longer than normal).* Next he put a thick rope in my mouth, tying it so tight that the incisors were bared. The cage door was shut (with a clang of rusty iron *I'll never forget*) and locked. Then I was paraded through town as an example to others.

Down winding lanes we went; rumbling over the bridge past the cathedral, past the Mayor's mansion (every stable boy and upstairs maid tumbled out to see what the ruckus was); past homes of the rich and hovels of the poor—a small crowd gathering. My hands had been tied, my naked body exposed to the view of all; absurdly beautiful I'm sure, but unable to answer their taunts because of the rope that cut my mouth.

The crowd grew. Dozens followed, screaming for blood as they threw offal. Dogs yapped; pigs squealed underfoot; vendors sold pie and crucifixes for protection—we went slowly at first, picking up speed downhill. People began running over each other to get a better look or a shot at me; many brought slingshots, others, brimming chamber pots—all under the impression that The Watch had trapped an *Unclean Spirit!* A spirit not keeping its balance too well, jouncing in ruts and kneeling to avoid falling on the long ride to wherever the hell we were going.

We picked up every piece of riffraff on every corner—I'll never forget their flushed, shrieking faces; the ones in back shoving and cursing; the ones in front, eyes wide and excited, gleaming with frantic light, a light that very few people (even killers on their way to the scaffold) have ever seen. The street became a river of writhing, shrieking figures—like a hallucination, turning into a dancing mass of yellow devils, then back into people again—

We went down a passageway, around a corner, and a door was standing open. It was a crypt. They opened the cage, one big fellow seized me by the hair—my head snapped back; I get pain in one cervical vertebra *to this day* when it rains—and threw me out.

In the crypt, they gave me so severe a beating I almost died. They tore me up pretty good, after which the Pointsman made everyone leave.

"A horror like this must never happen again," he said solemnly. "I'll attend to the Ceremony."

He locked the door when the men had left. Then after fingering my vagina and gloating for some time over my half-conscious body *(cut up and spattered with barnyard dung as it was)*, he mounted it, with my legs in the air in a most ridiculous manner, and took his pleasure.

Me being a young virgin, blood flowed. I experienced a deep, portentously hurtful burning the length of my cunt, as the strenuous, in-and-out jackrabbiting of *"himself"* continued; the Pointsman breathing hard as he worked. And although the pain was less intense than when I got buggered by that priest, the act was far more disgusting, having been long-thought-on, it was plain to see.

When the idiot was done, he drove a stake between my breasts. A spray of bright red arterial blood spurted directly into his face, delivered by my still-pumping heart! He shrank back in dread, wiped himself carefully *(it had been quite a gusher)*, crossed himself, said a few Latin words and tossed me into an oaken chest that had been made ready for the purpose. (How do I know these things? I was *hovering. Just like you'll hover* when next you croak.)

The Pointsman called in the others. They lifted the chest. According to sexton's records (that I later went back and checked) the burial took place at midnight in the unconsecrated soil of the sexton's shed.

And poor O'Blivion would have been imprisoned in a state of death, in eternal silence, forever — except for a happy accident. (Of course it was no accident at all; *just Scaulzo licking his chops.*)

Exactly thirty years later, that Pointsman dug me up by lantern light; pried off the coffin lid, stared at me open mouthed *(I recognized him at once* although thirty years had passed. His had been the last face I'd seen) and — prompted I am sure by a desire older than sex — yanked out the stake.

I gave him the nicest surprise!
I'm full of surprises.
Believe me, his bloodcurdling yowl was worth the wait!
And soon; ahead of the game, not only glutted but marvelously avenged — in fact amply repaid by the scream of horrified protest that tore from his throat, I dragged and pushed the soon-snoring Pointsman into the coffin. Then I re-buried the damned thing.

I had by no means drained the idiot. Later I realized what must have happened. He woke up in about an hour, found himself locked inside a casket and began shrieking, crying, blubbering, and praying for mercy as he sobbed, gulped, pounded and begged. If it would help his cause in any way he'd surely get down on his knees and beg my pardon; but — too late, sucker! The Pointsman suffocated to death in my coffin. Slowly.

As for me: I went on to live a life full of rich irony. And now when I hear women whimper about how *cruel* life is, and how they feel *ashamed and degraded,* and they are clutching a ton of *pain and darkness* to their bosoms — I nudge'm in the ribs with an elbow.

"Coo-coo-cachoo," I wink feelingly.

Loaded with New Age trapping as I've rather disgustingly become, I figure: what the hell — these guys all cut their own throat sooner or later, sure. But it is your civic duty, Madame, *not to wait for later!* (I tell them).

FIFTEEN

Five minutes after Abe had left, Douglas MacArthur climbed down the hotel stairs adjusting his hat.
Like any warrior worth his salt he couldn't see that there was any real test of manhood on this planet. How could he know if he was a real hero as everyone said — or a spoiled rich kid in a General suit? For that matter why did Americans think they needed a General as President in the first place? and why did Ike's demographic appeal beat MacArthur's all hollow? Why, *why*, WHY?!!? Was it the old cosmic joke, or maybe...?

Talk about your DJINNI trapped in a bottle! Billions of all-powerful beings flamboozled by the Badguy. And there wasn't the slightest hint that they understood what a trap they were in, or could get out of. And it was no joke for the poor souls in the bottle — who hadn't managed to get the license number of the truck that WHACKED'm.

And as for himself! "Am I a man of steel or an upperclass fop dressed like a rebellious young second lieutenant, as Harry S. Truman says?" he wondered, his head throbbing.

"Unconfessed crimes and assumptions that lie at the root of a Society are what sink it, Douglas," Abe had wagged his beard. "You must go beyond the obvious without letting smaller minds know you're doing it or they'll ask *'So you think you're better than I am?'* and pick a fight; because feeling belittled is the root of all war. A man feels brutally degraded, and has harmed and punished others so diligently that now he's got to make the other guy feel super-guilty, old hoss. I know yours is an incredibly complex task; but this creeping paranoia of yours—"

"Is the very core of my assignment!" Doug screamed, his battered corncob jumping in his mouth.

"Don't be so time-focused. Just BE the guy."

"What the fuck do you think I'm trying to do you blind old windbag?" he wanted to yell—but turned it into: "Mr. President, Sir! Even if war made sense, how could these lunatics wage one? In thirty years the military'll be strangled with infighting and swamped in waste, fraud, decisions by committee, no coherent agreement, competing like maniacs for trillions of defense bucks that they pull out of workers' paychecks BEFORE the workers even SEE their cash! Imagine how *filthy rich* the military is and they STILL have no strategy worth talking about and you tell me to just BE THE GUY? I'm telling you, as a 'fighting force' these maniacs are laughable! They couldn't win a war if it fell in their lap except for one lucky break. The enemy's as dumb-mean as they are."

Lincoln raised an imperious hand. "As humans let's not forget that the clash of swords is what's important to a man, General."

Doug clenched his teeth as the Chief rumbled on.

"Why not reshuffle our cards and try something new? 'See here, you Draconian microbes! *Come up to present time.* We're here to show you the way to Paradise'—huh? Huh? We simply teach mankind to live in peace."

"Let me bring it into focus for you," Doug said as sweetly as he could. "Those barbs may be ferocious but they are masochists! One troop says 'Boy am I steamed!' and he ruptures the lining of his own stomach. Then the guy next to him does the same thing; then they go to a medico who's drugged to the ears after rupturing the lining of HIS stomach while he writes the all time bestselling novel about His Manly Experiences in *The Serious, Important War*! And you claim we can break through that Oldboy Network with mere, foamy-mouthed good sense?"

"You're getting a tic in your left eye."

"*Of course I'm getting a tic in my left eye!* You're giving me one."

"What is it really? Are you worried about your sexual prowess?"

Doug snatched a seltzer bottle off the bureau and let Abe have one in the face, hologram or not.

Abe leaned forward. His lips tightened. "What's that supposed to prove? That *nothing in anyone's imagination* prepared us for a race of belligerent misfits with no gun control law?" He was getting madder and madder. "*Of course* we all prefer the sane exultation of our undersea life back home!" he shouted. "But by punching the Mousehole through this neck o' the woods we stirred up a hornet's nest. Now you *handle it* or turn in your field operative credentials." He wasn't joking.

So what was supposed to have been a fun day on Earth, ended in a foolish quarrel. Which was right on target but oh Lord! How glad Omark'd be to have this job behind him...

Mersoid then had the gall to add: "And don't think because you've had a freeze release you're invulnerable. You are a prime target. Keep your wits about you."

"Whaddaya think I'm doing, ice-hole?" Doug refrained from bellowing.

They argued back and forth but got nowhere; watching each other's pain as they exchanged the sly, caustic barbs that were socially *de rigueur* around here.

"Just be glad we're getting very, very close," Abe said. "I want you to find Woolf, put your heads together and solve this mess. Beat the bush. See what runs out—and I do hope she's safe. She hasn't reported since last week."

That was a stupid idea *(and anyway, hell!* Woolf couldn't be in a deeper ditch then he was), but Doug smiled pleasantly. "Good thinking, Chief. Her on-the-spot expertise has saved my bacon more than once," adding: "I really respected her abilities tremendously until she pulled that fast one on you, Sir."

Lincoln, though, only looked mysterious, strolling up and down by the bed with hands in pockets, head tilted to one side and that much-pictured, enigmatic gaze in his eyes...*What was he up to?* Those burning eyes. So powerful, darkly luminous, remote...a mind that no historian had even *superficially probed* let alone deeply *grasped*—Doug however, knew his Chief like the palm of his hand.

Or thought he did.

Who could you trust? Even as a telepath here, *who—?*

"Relax. You'll get there faster," Lincoln assured him. "We can't kid ourselves or shrug it off. Pardon me, but I must be honest: mass locust irresponsibility can lead only to one thing—but in the meantime I want you to learn how to kick butt real, REAL hard! *You order, they obey.* Nothing to it." And Mersoid blinked out.

It was Doug's turn to shift gears—correcting these rumors that he was putting the Mission at risk because the A-O was jabbing at his brain *(which he was ashamed to admit was true)* and clouding his judgment *(but only now and then, mind you)*. He had to keep it under

DEVIL-MAY-CARE

his hat so as not to get yanked off the job—because *now* was the time to finalize the process of really getting the hang of Earth's endemic, ruinous disease, paranoia—which only proved, more than ever, that no living being would be safe until Scaulzo was DEAD; frozen into his body and then KILLED once and for all! Yet...

Odd thing about these ambitious dudes like MacArthur. They couldn't breathe freely. It was suffocating to be an 'authority figure' and the great mystery was: *Big Names were the saddest of victims.* They shed bitter tears the public was unaware of...'The public'—meaning what? In the U.S. it meant being infatuated with *queens,* their wealth, and their doings, exactly as in 2500 B.C. or 600 A.D. or any date you cared to mention which meant: they only DREAMED they were a democracy. Spiritually they were a MONARCHY. And in REALITY they were THE CHARACTERS IN A CARTOON FAIRY TALE! but would punch you in the mouth if you implied it. The bottom line being: *nobody,* particularly college dons, could DEFINE the words they used. They made lengthy speeches using thousands of words they'd never really root-checked, let alone *boldly gone where no man had gone before* and bravely confronted them in a dictionary. Top CEO's had been tested. Sure enough—none could accurately *(scientifically!)* define words like "is," "go," "the," "into," "communicate," "mind," "soul," any simple word tossed around daily—the alarming fact being: they were a race of people who were terrified of Symbols. They'd bomb you dead in order to avoid being grabbed and dismembered by a *Symbol.* And what was the scariest Symbol of all? WORDS! *Words,* lurking down in the dark under a bridge waiting to eat your head off. Words were THE BOOGYMAN! They had horrible CLAWS that could drag you under and rip your flesh off. Good people had to burn classics off library shelves because classics were *filled* with *hairy, dangerous* WORDS—that could drive NICE people NUTS—forcing them to build a kind of chaos that was hard to pin down—and couple it with such a terrible pressure to CONFORM that sooner or later—KAPLOOIE! They'd successfully greased the CHUTE with their enforced VALUES until WHOMP!!! Chkong. Twanggg-ang ANG, ka-SPLONG! (groan... whimper) and goodbye cruel world.

Doug sighed.

"The prize may cost many lives," Abe warned—maybe he had a point. On a nuts-bolts level MacArthur didn't know nearly enough.

In the political arena he was a *mere baby* and now Truman demanded a face-to-face talk, and might pop in at any moment with his "*The buck stops here!*" bluster and his *choleric rage* that was so *widely admired* — Doug shuddered at the thought — THEN HE SCREAMED!

The scream got choked in his throat.

It happened in the lobby. (*a rude shock.*)

Just outside the dining room, slinking deep into a leather chair, hiding behind a Tokyo newspaper *(the schmoozing little, gonzo bitch!)* was Mr. Spock. This lobby was a tidy place full of leather chairs, sofas, clean ashtrays — they didn't even have closed-circuit TV yet — Doug had been hurrying to push open the plate glass doors —

He only got a glimpse on his way out, but who else could it be but the spidery vampire Sterling O'Blivion — *damn her!* Who authorized the frowsy slut to check out this particular bod? Whoever it was would have to account to Command for it — O'Blivion was a dangerous woman, a smouldering time bomb; odds were that she was in Tokyo to *cause trouble* for the General — this no doubt being her afternoon off for "good *behavior*," the poor dumb cow — *sitting there tough as nails* — he admired that, if nothing else about her — with a watch cap yanked down over those pointed ears. At least she'd wised up that matter doesn't control mind... *but:* she was a person without law or discipline, not interested in logic *(despite the Spock bod)* — not that anyone would *recognize* the green faced Vulcan for another decade or more; so for the moment, *screw O'Blivion* and her spy games. He'd pin her to the wall later. Right now he had *real* fish to fry.

On the street, everything seemed peaceful. He stuck the corncob pipe between his lips and yanked the famous hat down on his head, hoping he wouldn't be recognized...In point of fact, Sterling wouldn't dog his footsteps for long if that's what she was up to. They were shipping her out — *thoroughly trained*, hopefully! Doug had seen smuggled 3d's of the young Sean Fontana and in Doug's book the kid had *Winner* written all over him — even in that slave pit — the future. That "*Just Say No Toxic Amnesia Missile Burn*" that not only the U.S. and all Earth but *this whole Sector* had been turned into — or: *what the world would be like in 200 years* if men continued to misrule it! One *sick*, radioactive *garbage dump* with the most thrilling technological advances, the most wretchedly incurable diseases, and an updated Nixon at the helm. And that's where O'Blivion was being sent. Doug had to chuckle. *Little did the nasty vampire know...*

But now, a more serious problem plagued Douglas MacArthur.

Abe wouldn't let him pack an H-2 unit. "They'd be on you like flies. *Goodbye, Charlie!*" Or: who gives a damn if an armed Sajorian is lurking in this bush or behind *that cherry tree* over there; *Lincoln* sure as hell doesn't...But the day was flooded with sunshine and with G.I.'s who snapped those quivering salute all over the place—*oh crap.* He'd forgotten he was Emperor of Japan—the street already getting blocked with traffic because of him. He veered onto a gravel walk and into a temple garden—listening to the monks chant, but thinking about Sterling. Did her presence mean trouble for him?

Part of the healing process would be to get her killed or, if she lucked out, half-killed. A folk hero, Ster had triumphed over the most childish tortures that humans could think up to do to each other—rape, the water torture, the rack, splinters under the fingernails; small potatoes stuff. Now, she'd have to face the REAL Badmaster. She was about to be tested once more. The (ex) vampire could find a second life as a bona fide crewman when and if (IF!) she could handle what was coming down on her—

"Everybody has to start someplace," Abe said. "Sterling won't crumble under pressure." Did Doug believe that? Sure! You bet. *And the moon was blue cheese.*

On this corner (mused MacArthur, his lips pursed around the stem of the corncob) was a White Slave house—top-secret except for important men who paid to use pretty girls kidnapped out of the Bible Belt and brought here, kicking and screaming along with cute young, chained-up MIA's and AWOLs dragnetted from jungles or wherever—this House had its counterparts in the U.S. of course—but they were a REALITY, not a SYMBOL; so the public was unable to believe in them or take any of it seriously—oh boy— *his mind!* Galloping away. Irrelevant thoughts. *Which had to be—*

Omark really missed his Mary Worth body...the excellent bod he'd worn until just recently. Mary'd been tons of fun, not a hard riddle like this MacArthur guy. Originally a "meddling little old lady" comicstrip character, Mary had arthritis she was easily cured of, then refined into a tough, gutsy, gung-ho guerrilla *battle ace.* Doug picked his teeth thinking—that's what should happen to millions of lonely, sad, abandoned old women. They'd sure as hell make better scrappers than these anti-Mom misogynists from

Military School giving him flak. How does one measure courage anyway? He couldn't prove it but he was sure MacArthur himself didn't possess a tenth the sheer guts of Mary Worth, killed in action against Scaulzo in Argentina. And Mary was not only *not paranoid* but she had *more brains in her little finger* than Doug had in his whole head. Certainly, she was female but—

Everywhere he ambled, he became the center of a worshipful crowd. Was that sweet? *You bet*—especially since his people had A-bombed the hell out of Hiroshima and Nagasaki and imprisoned thousands of U.S. Japanese in concentration camps; yet: adorable tots waved tiny American flags. Timid, gentle folk gave him shy smiles. The ordinary people greeted the General warmly; though there were plenty of brass hats who'd like to see him hung by the heels. But still...

His head kept swiveling for a spectre—Scaulzo. Ever since the Sajorians invented that ultimate, ray-gadget nightmare freakbone poison-beam super-sting glare blast torturegun whose sole purpose was to freeze a being into his body (which would mean nothing to the local Djinnis in bottles, *frozen from birth into meat and didn't know it*)—OWW! Then Benaroya conquered and froze the devil but maybe *thawed'm* on her *unilateral decision* and now—Oh God—

Ever since that day in Naples when the Big S. in person blew him away *(Omark would never forget* how, disembodied, he'd had the "pleasure" of watching his own autopsy performed by a couple of joking medics in an Italian morgue) he saw a Sajorian lurking behind every bush. The first time you died violently it was something of a joke. "So what?" you soothed yourself; reporting happily back to the ship for yet another carcass. But each time, it got more serious. And now—he was straining hard to shield his mind against an unspeakable onslaught—

NOT! Only an attack of jitters brought on by the crowd although...didn't *it always start like that?* An occult WHACK, laced with grim portents. You felt this *consuming anxiety* broken by occasional moments of *false happiness...*

Before MacArthur could stop himself he'd swiped a banana off a stall *(oh lord*...stealing could get a man in an awful pickle) and was peeling it thoughtfully, walking with that stride that commanded respect. There were stale emanations from a tumbledown restaurant—corpses of fish hanging in the doorway *(ugh, UGH!)* out of which a woman came bounding. A woman dressed

DEVIL-MAY-CARE 147

in harem pants and a shiny, jewelled jacket. In one split second she had grabbed the General.

"Fondle and crush me in your arms!" she commanded in her native tongue.

She dragged him down a splintered stairway into a scruffy room with a bed in it.

MacArthur fought her off — trying not to make cries his own troops might hear. Finally he hauled off and punched the broad's ugly face — but the blood-drool only egged her on!

Frantic, Doug prayed she wasn't one of the Enemy dolled up like a perfumed dumpling with black eyes and horrible, herring breath — *oh Christ!* Why hadn't he stayed in the hotel room...He knew he'd regret it but: thrown down by the pert-breasted but hard-muscled dumpling, he let her unzip his pants — *oh God no* — because he was losing both the hat and the pipe; forced to struggle for position as she rolled him right on top of herself, fishing with one damp hand in his fly.

"*Stop it!*" he yelled.

But the dumpling easily yanked out his equipment. (*Oh God no*) She jerked him toward her, clawing with a free hand at his hat (under which was the small bald spot he definitely DID NOT want uncovered) muttering: "No no. Hat off while fucky-fuck! Respect."

"Please don't," the General screamed. These hats of his were regularly put through a fraying machine to make them look battle-worn but that was no reason to get this one all grubby from her fishy fingers — he was already in enough trouble to risk getting the headpiece any dirtier than his aide made it —

Now the damned dumpling went after his pipe. He clamped his teeth firmly; *oh no – not the pipe!* That was one thing she wasn't going to get — he socked her once more in a desperate attempt to seize control without yelling for help; but aside from losing his cherished pipe for the moment, Omark was *delighted* — in fact he was *so glad to be alive* and FREE that he sobbed with relief; overjoyed that the dumpling wasn't part of a Sajorian ambush, targeting him with not only a fat-slugged automatic but with *the unthinkable H-2 unit!* He was so glad, that he went ahead and followed her orders — teeth clenched but lips wide and gasping for air, grinning in relief and gratitude.

He ground his hips against the Dumpling's — she bounced crazily, squirming and bellowing. All at once her legs moved up to clutch his neck. How muscular the sow was! It made him realize, in a moment of insight, exactly why men despised women so much—she grinned up at him like an acrobat—Doug had begun trickling sweat; but felt forced to grin back. Was he horny—*oh, yes indeed!* The brand of horniness you get when a street thug jams a Saturday Night Special against your temple and says "Blow me"—and actually you *do* blow the dear chap—*oh yes, you do!* Exactly as it happens in many a Times Square john or behind some convenient billboard—but the physical equipment worked and he was pumping away and pumping away and pummmm...pinggga...way...*God!* how he hated women.

"Owwww," he sobbed, orgasming miserably—

"Yes! Yes! Yes!" screamed his attacker—lipstick smeared, red-rimmed eyes rolling in their sockets, "YEEEEES!" as (her face sweat-shiny with urgent humping).

"Owwww," she sobbed in awful mimicry.

Finally Doug broke loose and stood, making clouds of smoke as he jerked the hat tightly onto his sweating skull.

"Was good for you too?" sing-songed the grinning, panting Dumpling from Hell. But the worst was yet to come.

She sprang...as again Doug was unprepared; smashing the wind out of his lungs.

"We ride again!" she hooted, dragging him to the mattress.

The hag *(ugly...oh so ugly...spike-toothed...scary)* stroked his cheek with a scaly forefinger—an interminable moment of awfulness! Then throwing both arms around his neck she kissed him—grinding her teeth against his. Doug tried to control his panic. Not wanting to seem Gay or perhaps *semi-impotent,* effeminate, *weak,* or some kind of an unacceptable *White Bread Party Pooper,* he kissed her back exactly as hard as she did, with his eyes shut. Then he opened them wide and saw—

Her eyes. Two gleaming, sinister slits.

(A terrible dread spread through his bowels and genitals and)

He screamed! Shrinking back as—

"WE RIDE AGAIN!"

Doug flopped to the floor, beating at the air with his hands—that terrible scream pealing from his own mouth—

(the mummy).

No. Oh no. *(his nightmare)* The one thing he was terrified of *(oh Christ:* that hideous CORPSE waiting for him behind the slowly

DEVIL-MAY-CARE

opening door) OH NO. NO! *(a mummy in human clothes).*

Cold sweat gushed from Doug's skin—his morale destroyed. But...no! Suddenly he understood perfectly as—The MUMMY bent down, smiling. Its dead lips pulled back. It grabbed Doug by the ears. He felt a sour, stinking breath on his face—*(wormy. Rotten. Mold growing on her plucked brows)*

and whirling in those eyes he saw—something that could NOT be. Just an illusion! Those eyes—they were nothing but empty sockets *(with worms crawling in and out)*

and yet those were not worms, but

(the corpse of every human who ever died in agony on the face of this tortured planet—the heart of all horror)

crawling from the eye sockets of a basilisk face—H.L. Mencken's face: *Beel!* Scaulzo's field officer whose reign of terror bled white the billions...his rotting mouth glued to the General's, and: lifting its skull, it speared him with Images

(of the whole bloody human time track. Incredible errors mixed with hilarious howlers)

as it yanked his ears excruciatingly—Doug twisting, but helpless! *(the wheels within wheels)*

"Wait'll I tell the MEDIA you go both ways," H.L. giggled. "*Oh just wait'll* Truman finds out you performed an Important Crime Against Nature! And did it GOOD. TOO good!" *(grinning into his eyes—that happy, psycho grin*—that Doug told himself wasn't really happening to him but)

Grave-breath puffed in his face. "I followed you two dumb politicos to that bar. *You think you know it all?* You know SHIT!" twisting his ears so bad that Doug nearly screamed. "Your beloved humans—*do they want grossout horror shows?* Tell those morons we'll be pleased to supply their every need until the party is OVER," it giggled.

(oh yes...the Sajorian mind. Omark knew it well)

"And now, you'll wait my pleasure!"

(the old, old writing on the wall)

"Every agonizing second...and it's going to be *sloooow*."

The THING made kissing smacks. A little spittle flew from its lips.

"I'll get my obscene jollies off you," giggled that mortuary horror that made Doug shiver in his bones. "Oh, *you gonna love it,* gone over with instruments of torture—a whole shitload of horrible things behind closed doors—(*it shrieked crazy laughter*) you dumb, human-loving, smalltime anthro APOLOGIST—pretty soon mankind'll be *extinct forever!*"

With a howl, Doug bucked him off or tried to—the "dumpling" drove "her" fist into his face shouting: "Here's a riddle for you! Who's the DUDE whose cumulative EFFECT makes a world of emotional cripples who scream that it can't happen to THEM until they reach a point where they must be reassured and comforted and their fantasies reinforced by either HIM or by ME?!?? YOU ALL LOSE!" unloading its spit-spray of chuckles. "You won't believe what I'm going to do to you—and only THEN will I *use the H-2 on you.* But not today, no; I got something much better in mind. You'll obey me, *on your own will,* under no compulsion, like EVERY real General does," pinching both of Doug's cheeks. "And the best part is—*you'll never know where or WHEN I'll getcha.*"

He grabbed the General's neck, driving callused thumbs into the windpipe. "Nod if you understand!"

Gasping and choking, Doug managed a nod.

Then "H.L. Mencken" waggled ITS dead tongue and let go.

"I want to thank you very much for the intercourse," the THING grinned. "Didn't know you went both ways, didja, dudie? *But any time, eh? We'll do it again often*—first YOU on top, then me!" howling laughter (*her mouth a black, awful semicircle.*)

Now Mencken hopped up, slipped on one shoe, then the other, then belted her harem pants still laughing (*she was* comical—that was the worst of all—comical and *familiar!*) Then blowing a soft kiss, the fiend closed the door behind him delicately—with those wonderful, Sajorian manners.

Doug got stiffly to his feet; throat afire, smashed face dripping blood...the raw degradation making him sick to his stomach as the awful threat made his knees wobble (*time would pass. the threat would remain*) He stumbled over and threw up into a dirty sink. He stood on planks littered with piss-wet papers, cans, fishbones— spitting out a tooth—wincing—then grabbed his pipe, hat and trousers and made fast tracks for the hotel.

(*what had Abe told him there at the end*)—"Douglas," he'd said. "As a boy, my assassin John Wilkes Booth went around killing cats. Can you believe a species *so crazy* it doesn't consider that an INDICATOR? If a person will hurt an animal, he or she will hurt a person, no matter what her RANK or NET WORTH may be. So you can shove the million bucks you spent on a train procession, funeral orations, muffled , *mirrors* draped in black and an *Eternal Flame*. That stuff is *Satanism*. What you need to do is *handle children with intelligence*. Then *adults* won't *murder* you. Yep: sanity is that simple," with a shy little smile)

—blood flowing from nose and mouth—crossing streets so carelessly that angry drivers leaned on their horns. He ran disheveled and panting into the lobby—

No O'Blivion there! Had the bitch tailed him, would she blackmail him, make life unpleasant *(laugh at him)* until Mencken came for the kill? When that shadow fell on you, it was not something you could live with.

Doug ran up ten flights to his room and crawled back into his soft, freshly-made bed with the crisp white sheets—wet and sticky all over.

And yet, *and yet!* The race to the hotel had actually LIFTED his spirits. True, that eerie, graveyard moaning was already surfacing in his mind *(you'll never know where or when)* making him hate and fear O'Blivion and his own troops more than ever but—

Malicious damage could only go so far. Yeah sure, *Beel would never let him alone*—but screw Beel. All the demon had done was REAFFIRM Omark's gutsiness—YEAHHH he was a damn HERO! In or out of a "General Suit" he was CAPTAIN COOL—*unbeatable*. He didn't know what fear was. He had harmed no one and nothing *(but wouldn't hesitate to do so in a just cause, mind you)* and now Beel and his overlord thought they'd put him on a spike—let *them*. The idea is to KNOW what's out there, and use that knowledge NOT to wallow in the *demon-turds* that are *always* floating around to be exploited by anyone who wants to make money off the weak and stupid—which did NOT include DOUG! (Well—*of course*—never forgetting the Sage's tip: *keep alert*. Accidents can and *do* happen here).

(For the thousandth time he wondered how the locals could take the strain).

And as for "terror" and "self-doubt"—don't they very often lead to a whopping success? *You're dingy-dang right they do!*

This was going to be good.

Wiping a last tear, Doug put the phone on his chest and began dialing the number Woolf had left with Tokyo switchboard.

SIXTEEN

It was the dead of night. Moonlight washed over a sleeping neighborhood in a rundown part of town, Sweet Port Alley — musty with age and decay, where a psycho'd stick a knife in you for your billfold or shoes or he'd GRAB a nice person whose folks would never hear from her again *(as had happened to many million innocent Earthies)*...

Was that a footfall? Virginia Woolf looked up and down the street, flattening herself against a wall. Was some fixated clown following her? The average person shouldn't walk here without an armed guard! The place teemed with vermin life, brown shapes scuttling over garbage — men used to run cockfights and crap here before they got shut down — *oops*. Almost walked on a sleeping derelict, paper-bagged bottle clutched in one hand. He'd be lucky if some tripper didn't douse'm with gas and set him afire for the pleasure of it, before this night was over.

Phew. Yucky stench! Woolf had been counting lighted windows — few and far between in a blight zone where vagrants lived on scavenged grub in wilderness of car parts and junked TV sets. She hadn't seen anyone move since she guzzled a Pepsi at a 7-11 ten minutes ago. Pitch dark, too, was the boarded-up warehouse at pavement's end — and beyond it was the freight yard; spooky-quiet as a cemetery.

She turned and swung along, heeltaps reverberating on the walk. Woolf was here on private business — Abe would call it a *dangerous tryst* — because what she'd done had left her with a counteractive decision. The course her own life must take *(not to mention the future of one whole galactic sector)* was now depending on this gruesomely *idiotic*, supernatural, billion-year-old *boobytrap*. A trap baited with mystery like quicksand — that had proved irresistible! At least up to now *(owwww:* even Benaroya was surprised at how muddled her thinking became, *the closer she got to —!*) And yet despite all warnings — despite frantic efforts to link her with a treason attempt —

She herself had arranged every detail.

She, alone, was responsible for what happened here!

Nobody ever went near that old warehouse except bums who slept huddled in its stairwells night and day. They were drunks or mainliners "out of it" to a point where if you were being WHACKED they'd make no effort to help. It was a great spot for the most powerful being *(or so he claimed)* in the universe — now reduced to ruins because of what Virginia Woolf had done to him *(if things were as they seemed)*! She'd asked herself — where would he be 'safe' — and hit on this remote, empty loft that now seemed a smidge obvious. Had the job been too easy? Were her strings being jerked *(or tangled)* in mysterious ways, or???...Such issues were kind of worrisome but not enough to throw the agent off course.

Woolf was wearing white kid gloves and a hat, sling-back pumps with high heels, and a polka-dotted cling dress that set off her lithe, shapely body. She increased her pace; feeling a rising sense of excitement mixed with prickles of dread...

Yoyo emotions often signalled a pleasure fugue to be woven in with ghastly portents of the A-O; so this was COOL! She'd been drilling for it. She sure couldn't risk a bad hit now — but — it was fun to watch her shadow grow huge, then shrimpy, under a line of streetlights as she moved toward the warehouse...

"Hey! Don't go in there lady. It's not safe," called a human figure with its head on its arms, blinking up from a bed of newspapers.

(Whoop...shake the daydream, kiddo!)

The air was cooling, and somewhere a door clunked shut. Woolf thanked the man respectfully, walked inside and took a freight elevator to the third floor.

In the rickety wrought-iron cage she stood wondering if she was really as bent outta shape as it sometimes appeared, but decided: no way. She hadn't gone stupid or soft, or become a hypnotized traitor no matter WHAT Doug and Abe said.

Whether THEY'D been co-opted or not was another story, but SHE'd better not be, because right now she had to control a flood of shifty emotions. It was called "the stuff of drama" — meaning a mashed-up compound of power moves, sex, and violence. She had to juggle two dozen sticks of dynamite while spinning ten buzzsaws and a mouthful of grenades! to get the effect needed for this awful rendezvous — and time was eating her alive —

Woolf walked through an old RCA factory, operational in 1945 for producing phonograph needles. There were crates with the words *Perma-Point* stenciled on them, stacked behind benches and grinding machines that each had a magnifying glass attached; once used by aproned women to hand-sharpen steel needles for the going rate of fifty cents an hour, so the Glenn Miller and Benny Goodman disks could be played over and over by mooning bobbysoxers who were today eighty or ninety years old *(and Woolf could tune in to each of their lives/deaths if she wanted to)* — wow: everything was silty with dust. Then climbing another flight to the soundproofed loft — the agent braced herself.

She paused, adjusting garter belt and stocking seams. She took a deep breath.

(This better come off right, by golly! She better not be tempted to seal her own doom — which *was what everyone)*

Maybe even herself but she hoped not

(seemed to expect she might do under the circumstances)

The prisoner was sitting in a flyblown alcove in the dark. When Woolf flicked the lights on, his expression revealed all the patience of a caged grizzly.

The man was securely locked in and as an added precaution he was chained to the wall. That's how Benaroya kept her prisoner safe — what else could she do? For this was Scaulzo himself, the incarnation of evil in human form.

Billions had killed other billions under his thrust — *criminy!* It was hard to believe there could be ONE source of evil and this was the dude right here. Malign spirit in a goodlooking bod, ow! Better watch your step.

His clothes were rumpled, nails unpolished and yet — one gorgeous guy. He was so...how to put it? *Elegant.*

And these were the forces that stood face to face.

A blush came to Virginia Woolf's cheek, and her breath came faster. Yes, her prisoner was a power-mad bully and the crimes he committed were past belief and yet...*oh!* that disheveled black hair; that calm air of distinction. Even with neck and wrists hobbled and clamped to the wall, he wore the body of the dashing Count de Falke with so much grace.

Woolf had brought the Sajorian a violin, and he spent long hours playing it; also she'd rigged up a shower where the fiend could drag his chains the bare distance it took to stand under a cold spray. Other than that he had nothing. No comforts. No amenities, no frills. Maybe his reason had been damaged by the situation (??); Woolf wouldn't know—she had seen "frozen" beings go temporarily crazy (Omark for one), in fact had gone seriously mad herself the one time she'd been frozen (by this devil after a race and thank God Omark pulled her out of it).

She had to keep telling herself *"He's a merciless specialist in torture and execution, you jerk!* He feels no remorse *ever"* —because: who could believe it? All Benaroya really knew about Scaulzo was that he was coruscatingly evil—so evil that HE HAD TO BE SALVAGED. She knew every being was basically good, even Satan if she could only find a way IN!

One glimmer of truth—it HAD to be done; then ultimately— well for openers, everyone alive would feel the grip of the A-O loosen: And it had nothing to do with the fact that the Big S. was the kind of dashing devil that women lose their heads over—also men, children, dogs and cats and in fact, beings in general—*meaning those of the human stripe.* Never one of the leading field anthropologists from Central Galaxy of course; *don't be silly.* Woolf didn't gloat. She didn't enjoy seeing the Mighty One brought low. She drew up a chair, and scratching one slim calf with a thumb, asked loudly: "Well are ya about ready to listen to some sense, pal?"

"From you, always, my dove; however senseless."

"I've come to warn you that you're living on borrowed time and to ask if you're ready to become good."

"I'm good already, lovely lady. What was it Mae West said— 'And *when I'm bad I'm better.'* Ah, don't cluck and shake your handsome head. I know how trusting your nature is, and swear I won't take advantage of it. Even though it's in your power to destroy me."

"Not while you're locked up, you won't," she brayed.

Yeah, the dude had that Balkan charm all right—a lock of black hair falling on the brow and those cruel, aristocratic features—so hot he'd be called "devastating" by beaucoup women. Scaulzo could make a speech that was lots more entertaining, inspiring, and tear-jerking than ol' Ronald Reagan (Woolf figured it should be flat-out ILLEGAL for a polished actor to run for President—

God knew what damage he might do, all unawares, while being so cute and charming) and the Big S. was a million times more exciting, debonair, and worldly, with the faintest note of mockery in his voice; a sexual taunt that in some quarters would be considered irresistible! And along with the disarming charm, he had... *(ulp)*...super-human powers.

In basic form a basilisk or winged gargoyle, Scaulzo was frozen into this body; but *what a body*. How could Woolf help but find him swooningly *attractive?* Omark, who wanted to gum matters up now that he was being MacArthur, had implied Woolf was "falling for Scaulzo" which was the biggest lie in the world! The silliest thing she'd ever heard. The Sajorian was totally hooked on her, though. She'd known it for a long time.

"To debauch the wholesome. Could anything be more appropriate?" Scaulzo had said. "You are a child-soul; and I, like Humbert Humbert, am fascinated—but far more than Humbert was because YOU are a REAL innocent in adult form but his Lolita was just another wily old demon—*a mere sophisticate*. Personally I *detest* sophisticates. They can be picked like fleas and are even more sexless than whores. *But you* I can't wait until you are consumed in the furnace of my lust, angelic tot"—was *that a trip?* UGH! And double ugh.

Scaulzo was trying to prime her for an "SM affair" that would be unthinkable to say the least. He never stopped judging and gauging *(figuring out lines)* with the barest trace of a knowing smile.

"Sit by me," he purred in that unctuous yet commanding tone of voice that would thrill her if Benaroya wasn't as smart as she was *(but she WAS as smart as she was, so no problem)*. His eyes had a piercing quality about them...this ancient duel had been going on for eons in many venues; the agent wishing-to-jeez she didn't think it as breathtaking as she thought it was, to spar with a malevolent being who was full of tricks...to see if he could force her shield aside...

Which he could, and did.

HEY. That better not happen again! Or she'd be a *goner*.

"No thank you, I prefer to sit here" Woolf murmured coolly and demurely; crossing one silken leg over the other and getting straight to the point despite recurring quivers of excitement.

"Think of this as a gesture of friendship and support," she said. "Me, I'm going to great lengths to whittle away your evilness and turn it around so how about a little cooperation for a change? You can start by getting a EUREKA about how *dumb* it is to be a *criminal*. A criminal works *twice as hard* as an honest, intelligent man, so why be one?"

"I *enjoy* being one. And by your own philosophy that's what life is all about."

"But evil purposes are boring, right? It's a *downer* to blight the hopes of others — where's the challenge in it? Plus which: sooner or later you wind up trapped like now."

He stared at her coolly (Ooh! Little shivers chased themselves up and down her intrigued flesh) before murmuring: "You've changed since we last met. What happened?"

"I've had a conversion experience," Woolf cried. She clasped her hands. A radiant expression lighted her face. "First I got a solid contact with The Supreme Being. Then: becoming involved in every single Earth religion, I love them all. Am I dumb? *Hey!* They are a non-materialist type of local thinking that may *save the day* for the savages."

"Aha."

"Yes: Judaism's swell for them and the Dalai Lama's cool but Scientology, it takes the cake — *and, so!* With a firm belief in God — I know it's not only totally moral but a *sacred duty* to kill bad guys and yet — *yet!* I'm praying that the Holy Spirit will *open your heart*. You, BIG S.! *are a child of the living God Almighty*; one who can think of this remote loft as a *re-education camp* just for YOU. Can't you feel that spirit pouring out upon you? *Can't you feel it?*"

Scaulzo nodded, smiling. "Of course I can. It makes me positive we'll be lovers."

"Naw, that's not what I mean at all."

"But it's what *I* mean. Come sit here by me."

"Uh, maybe later."

Woolf knew what a *sadist* the creep was — he'd fully screened the area against contact with his men — yet Beel managed to track her down. *So O.K.* She was striking out on a risky course, a course that'd be *widely misunderstood* — but the only one she could think up that *might turn the trick* — but suddenly — ooh jeezly! That awful *(sex)* compulsion was returning stronger than ever.

Like a hypnotized bird, Woolf found she couldn't look away from the prisoner — whose eyes glittered with menace...A person'd have to look CLOSE to notice anything chilling in his smile — and people never looked close! You had to be CALM to look right AT the bad dude; *and she was icy calm*, but...Doing it made her want to go to the bathroom or something. A strange, disquieting sensation Woolf had never known before. She was in that space where strange things happen to your mind, and to your body as well. The Count was saying:

"Oh but you're mistaken. It can be wonderfully stimulating. For instance, when I look into your eyes—come on, *look at me*. Or are you such a coward that you don't dare?"

"Don't be crazy." Woolf lowered her gaze, cheeks burning. She was getting light-headed.

"Behold the ultimate power trip," the Count murmured. "I am *cause*. You are *effect*. What an *aphrodisiac* power is. You love being helpless in my hands. Everyone wants to be possessed and manipulated by the silken touch of Satan. Come on. Admit you do."

"Bull dooky" she scoffed, catching her breath. "You better knock that off."

"*Why*? Are you losing control here?"

"Of course not!" Woolf blared indignantly. "It's just not the Lord's way to start a fight you can't win, you dumb creep."

Woolf jerked her hat off and threw it across the room.

Boy—she knew for sure what *Sterling'd* say about this little scene! "You're giving a weapon to the enemy. Why let yourself be sucked in?" Ster would demand, telling Woolf if she didn't have any *better sense* than to *mess around* with a Principality she'd get badly burned and maybe *permanently* screwed, stewed and tattooed not to mention pregnant. She'd say that the Count was *nice as pie* only because he was *chained up!*, and Woolf had better run before something really rotten happened to her. But...to make Scaulzo *good!* Was that not the goal of many lifetimes—the stuff of which crucifixions are made; the whole Jesus story, and didn't it have to be RIGHT for this planet? If she could attract this evil Count into the Lamb's own fold with *love, honesty,* and *whatever else* would get his slimy attention—

"Pleasurable sensations are running through that lovely body of yours," he was whispering. "You can't resist them, can you, my pet."

"*Wise guy*. Go chase yourself." But her voice crackled with pleased excitement.

"Come on...let me take off that pretty silk dress, that you wore just for me, and I'll demonstrate my prowess." And reaching out one finger, he ran it along her silken calf.

Woolf gulped, uncrossed her legs and stood up. "Now stop it! *Just quit that stuff.* You gotta think in a correct order of magnitude—I mean sexuality might be O.K. but it gets *stale* if you aren't PRODUCING anything, any valuable product; know what I mean?"

"That's right, lovely lady; take another step closer."

"I'm gonna lay it on the line. I'm here to bring you to TOTAL UNDERSTANDING! That's what I intend to achieve! And that's the last word I'll have on the subject."

"Then here is my promise. *I swear I'll be converted*—to whatever you had in mind—right after we go to bed together."

"Oh no ya don't. Think I wasn't born yesterday?"

"That's right; one more step. You know what I intend to achieve. *You. Right now.*"

"Not on your life! What you need is *real fun,* such as a goal, some worthwhile, fascinating work—"

"Work? I can assure you that work is the opposite of fun, my dove."

"Naw! Work IS what's fun. WORK should be made the reward instead of mere MONEY. Half this world's problems would vanish." But her voice was thick, she felt a loss of control—she'd been more stirred than she cared to be. And the Count knew it!

"*First you'll yield to my touch,*" he murmured.

"No way..."

"Later on, you'll *imitate* me. The sincerest form of flattery."

"Hah! In your dreams..."

"Soon you will give me your body, Benaroya; and along with it, your loyalty and strict obedience."

"Oh no ya don't."

"Oh, yes, I do. For starters we will have a hot, ongoing sexual affair—an attraction so intense it will burn you alive. You're already crazy for me, Virginia Woolf, and the feeling will grow stronger and stronger until you'll do anything I say and love it—plus, you'll be addicted to it—but no more talk. I see you're already just where I want you to be."

Woolf squirmed uncomfortably; but only on the *inside. Outside* she yawned and buffed her nails trying to fake indifference—it was a dangerous moment. She knew she was in the hands of a he-devil—an *incubus,* lust trap, slick operator, a clever *satyr* stamped with the *cloven hoof*...but she could handle him! And the Count seemed to prove that by falling back and asking questions.

"What's your scheme then? Am I to remain trapped in here, awaiting some sick finale or other?"

"Maybe and maybe not," she shrugged.

"And for how long?"

"For as long as it takes, so don't ask."

"But I'm curious. My life is in your hands. What do you plan to do with it?"

"Well, I don't want to kill you. I LIKE you actually. But if you're *uncooperative* I don't have a *choice*, do I? It all depends on how fast you can become good."

"'Good like you are."

"Yeah, you got it right, Bud."

"I think I understand. You would like me to be sweet, wholesome, and childishly simple like you are."

"Yeah! You got it."

"My dear: let me tell you a story. The story is called *Rain* and it takes place down in the tropics where a preacher gets angry because a whore is quartered near him. He thinks the whore's way of making a living is disgusting, you see. He goes to her house to rebuke her and reform her, and *convert* her, and all that sort of thing; and he keeps trying to convince her to be 'good' according to his sick idea of the word. But all the time, the rain is beating and slashing away at the grass roof over their heads. And can you imagine what finally happens, my dove?"

"No, what?" said Woolf eagerly. She loved stories that had cliff-hangers in them and this one sounded like a corker.

"It turns out to be a fatal attraction like ours. The preacher, overstimulated and unable to control himself, throws himself on the whore and has passionate sex with her. And it turns out that they both reach dizzying heights of wild orgasm after fantastic orgasm, so addictively pleasurable they can hardly endure it! And of course, the whore seldom gets to *come* in her line of work, so she goes crazy for the things they do. And the next morning the preacher wakes up and cuts his own throat."

"Aw! *That's a lotta bull*. That's a dumb story. Why tell me junk like that?" Woolf scowled, tapping her finger restlessly on one heel.

"Because it's exactly what is happening here, only worse,

because I'm your unwilling prisoner and you, in the role of the preacher are saying: 'Become GOOD by my standards when I snap my fingers or I'll kill you.' Am I correct?"

"That's about it, buster," she brayed. "See—in these parts we gotta go by the words of The Sage. Or simple old loving, kind, Jesus. (Not the people who murdered him and made a religion out of him.) *Get it?*"

The Count grinned his crooked, but weirdly come-hither grin. "You are wholly crazy but I enjoy your self-confidence, I'll say that."

"Yeah and it goes *all the way through me* because I'm GOOD! unlike yourself. And that means I'm *guilt-free* and so I can't lose. But YOU? You'll boobytrap yourself over and over because you're guilt-*swamped*."

"So how do I get good like you, my knowledgeable but baffling philosopher?" he smiled.

"Well, first let's get down on our knees and pray."

"Pray. I see. Is it a cheap joke? 'Pray and the devil laughs' is the way I've heard it. Doesn't that moralistic bilge bore you?"

"*Lift up your hands an' praise the Lord!* You an' me—we've always had this appointment with destiny, old buddy." Scaulzo knew better than to laugh indulgently or say something cutting. He knew just when and how to spring a trap...and though frozen (by HER!) into the de Falke body, he was nevertheless not subject to control. There was no reason not to get down on his knees with the seductive Rysemian—who began praying with lofty and sincere fervor.

"Dear God! We've had about enough of this crap here. *This is extremely serious.* Please penetrate this demon's heart with your light and make him good right NOW! And I mean *cold turkey!* Who has time to screw around? Things have gone too far—Shut your eyes, Scaulzo. No fair peeking! Come on! *Cut that out.* Quit looking at me, and take your paw off my ankle—we're talking to GOD here you dope!"

Count de Falke watched her with an amused gleam that vanished when Woolf threw him a reproving glance out of her fine, intelligent *(although perhaps mad)* poet's eyes; and to humor the Rysemian, he closed his own.

SEVENTEEN

"*Oh Jesus Christ!* I can *smell* the stinking embalming fluid NOW!" the vampire howled.

"Unh-uh. That crap wasn't used back then," H.G. said. "Now listen to me. Picture yourself as a *mighty creator*. Got it? A 'little person'—*a mud animal*—would shrink from such an idea. '*Ooh!*' he or she snivels; then curls up, sickens, and dies. But a God must remain *cool as a cucumber*. Got it? O.K. Try again."

"You're making me sorry I was ever born!" she screamed.

"I wouldn't ask," H.G. said patiently, "if this was not a *life-and-death emergency*. Your people are out of control, throwing tantrums as they write *the final page of their Book*. We must break through! Nor do we care how we do it—" Sterling tried again.

A woman looks at her dead daughter in a little white coffin. Even as I watched them screw down the coffin lid, I DENIED IT WAS HAPPENING! Can any of us face the truth? *No!!* So when you say we've got to be *'cleansed and purified'* oh what wicked lies you promulgate—

(Sterling was working hard at her Confession; but she was worried sick about Woolf! whom she knew was in an awful bind. A spider-web that the agent couldn't escape from—)

Woolf needed help DESPERATELY!

But H.G. was making her stick to this hated CURE!

(*even if it killed her*.)

I hope it comes as a nasty shock, you arrogant old goat, that when I was small, Robin Hood was cutting up in a forest across the channel. My town consisted of little gnome houses with steeply pitched roofs, the streets thronged with good folk I knew—we lived in the heart of a feudal country where just about every person who knew me, *loved me*. I was the favorite in my father's stern household—Father (his name was Guy O'Blivion; his father came from Ireland; my Mother was born in France) had been a Knight Templar, brave hero of the Crusades who received such a fat land-and-cash grant that he became one of the world's first bankers—acquiring great wealth for murdering some men and sucking up to others—*which is how every great fortune is founded.* I haven't space to list the dirty deals Father and his gentlemen friends pulled except to say that their money came from plunder, and it was vested, and their privilege defended through what Wordsworth calls *"The meager stale and forbidding ways of law."* But our country at that time *(and God! I am so homesick I could die),* you've seen movies about the splendor of the past; well, they don't show the half of it. A virgin land of forests, rivers and mountains untainted: where a *"loop-hole"* meant a slot to shoot arrows from! I admit that military technology dictated the shape of our home, with its platforms where men could stand and dump boiling water on attackers and there were all sorts of cunning passages, hidden doors, crenellations and machicolations to foil enemies trying to swarm your castle. Which is why we now have a central gov't: so *it* can grab your castle first. And that is what *"progress"* is all about, but don't make the mistake of thinking life is one bit better today. You don't know the half of it.

We had EVERY convenience; we had oranges, velvet, sugar, rice—no General Electric, but the soft, romantic lamplight was *lots nicer* and our three-holer, the third seat small and low for a child, made for good companionship—I can still feel the old, familiar, piney toilet seat, and the joys of sitting there as Blescu *(that great storyteller: She is now dust)* spins yarns and regales me with plots far better than TV; water flowing and moving a long way down— that same water the swans lived in. They shat in it and so did we and none of us ever got sick. Why? Because sickness didn't begin to be widely advertised until later. *(Let's quit kidding ourselves* that our media doesn't propagate illness as well as crime, O.K.?)

I now wish I'd saved a few of our fabulous tapestries, silver table service, canopies, sheets, quotidian stuff that is now worth *museum-piece millions* but at the time, my day was full of familiar routines—and your request brings a memory vividly before me: one childhood day, in which I wake with joy, hop out of bed in reflected glow from sun-drenched fields, and sit for a moment with elbows on windowsill (I can see our stables, courtyard, meadow, town; a leafy bend in the river; blue hills in the distance) and dress, tiptoe down flights of stairs—holding my breath as I pass my parent's room (I'd love to peek in at their lovely sleeping faces but don't dare for fear of waking them: my valiant father, sword in hand—of course not when he's in bed; ha ha—and beautiful rosy-cheeked memere) and sneak across the bridge to the country lane where Greta lives. My adored little friend. And now I see crippled old veteran Andros driving the geese, he waves, I wave, *(come to think of it: old, one-armed Andros was probably 30)*—I cross the goat pasture in balmy spring air, through the woods, then past turf cottages—

To amuse Greta I've dressed as a boy in velvet jacket and tights with a knife sheathed at my waist. Greta needed a little fun—hell: I'd be thrown out next winter and my little chum, after doing all she could to help me, would die. Her parents wouldn't let her go anywhere or do anything and had betrothed her to a rich, ugly, hairy-armed old asshole that she hated. It was me and me alone that she loved; *but money could be made* by marrying your young daughter off—she being an *asset* like a good draft horse, sow, land, or any object some dick considered valuable. The dick was also supposed to be courtly to that object (even while finding it necessary to beat the crap out of it from time to time) and this is what the word *"chivalry"* meant. And it was during the nightmare days between when I was *found* out and was *thrown* out that gentle, faithful Greta died *(of flu, and sorrow)* and for centuries she's been a phantom dogging my heels—

And my parents: the last thing my father said to me was *"You should have been killed at birth"* — but for years I'd look up at the sun or stars (or a clock if I had one) and wonder what they were doing at that exact moment. Blescu is lighting the candles. Mother cards wool (my Mama's spinning wheel: will I never hear that sweetest of sounds again!)...Now they're at church, now in the vegetable patch where I lost my doll, now Father jokes with the New Kids on the Block (a different troupe of players and minstrels showed up every week just as now)—me picturing our enormous echoing hall with bright colored banners and log-sized fireplace and huge table where a harpist plays, servants bringing trays of steaming, savory food; my parents spread a rich feast especially for Knightly friends and visiting nobles, royalty and entourages—*I had been the apple of their eye!* And did they think of me out here on the run, crawling with lice, eating out of trashcans, flea-bitten (some of them got infected and it was the worst), crying for my Mama... picture it! Dark. Winter. Raw cold, suffering "separation anxiety" as the pundits now say. I shiver every time I think of it. How many times I yearned to be home with my loving parents...

In general however, my beloved Papa specialized in injuring and killing. He was very good to me (no beatings unlike other fathers)—a rich baron like Guy O'Blivion would be a shoo-in for President today; because people *fear* him, and think he'll *conquer their enemies* for them, but what isn't apparent is that he *hardly knows other people exist,* and behind the physical grace and clever speeches and state dinners etc., he is strictly out for himself and is 180° *wrong* for the job folks choose him for, out of fear and ignorance. And: shortly (I am sure)—the mold of the churchyard claimed him. And that's what human history is all about. *Sad but true.*

I now open my TECHDICT and see how it describes my dear dead Father to a T. He *"committed harmful acts to resolve a problem."* He and his type are PSYCHO but the public, blinded by fear—and a desperate hope—won't and CAN'T recognize that. Also every man wishes to pick up a few crumbs for himself even if it means the future goes to Scaulzo. It's a tough problem but: as you say—we can lick it with the help of the Sage whom you call SOURCE—O.K., swell! A devil CAN be exorcized, you reiterate. Well I won't argue. I'm too damned tired.

You! Making me remember. You don't realize how exhausting—

Jarred out of sleep by an early warning call from Nancy, O'Blivion kicked that good soul in the buns with a snarled "Take a hike, slut!"

Nancy got understandably mad. "You should be hoarding your strength for the ordeal to come! Want to know why, smart-ass? There's a distinct possibility you'll be tortured TO DEATH this time! Are ya ready?"

Sterling shuddered convulsively but said nothing.

"You should be rethinking your whole life," Nancy scolded primly. "In a matter of hours you'll be off to Weird Chicago of the future where you'll intercept King Arthur, and then if evil doesn't befall either of you—"

"Piss off, mall rat!" Sterling's eyes blazed. "Or as our great master Montaigne asks: *'Is it reasonable* that the life of a wise woman should depend on the judgment of fools?'"

But Nancy'd about had it with the vampire. She posed in front of O'Blivion, hands on hips, designer shoes spread wide apart. "You wouldn't be so *lippy* if you knew what was going to happen to you!" her lecture began.

But I was *(rather distractedly, to be sure)* feeling my oats, to put it mildly *(Sterling wrote)*. I stood up, wiped my mouth and very gently pulled Nancy's Dior wrap down over her arms.

You can imagine her reactions. All those emotions shooting through her poor straight-lady brain all at once—

"Sterling: I'm warning you!"

"Aw chill. I'm on'y looking for info-mation about the King. I mean if we've got to work together as you say—"

"King? What king? Are you referring to Arthur? Take your hands out of there, Sterling! I'm warning you! Young Arthur—to be honest, he's cute but dumb. Not as cute-but-dumb as my Ronnie of course; who could be? And not as ugly-dumb as the Bush or—*stop that!* Do you want me to slap your FACE? H.G. says it's downright *spooky* how humans have no memory whatsoever of their past lives. Even if they happen to be *the Once and Future King*," she giggled nervously, giving me a confused shove.

"My gosh. Feature that," I marveled, doing little things she kept trying to get away from.

"H.G. says the Boy King is a real *straight-arrow* though; wants to be accountable, has not an *ounce* of meanness or sneakiness in him (how dare you! *What are you doing!* You should know better than that) and has actually *evolved tremendously* since he lived at Camelot. There's nothing like a few lifetimes as a woman to show a man what's what and deepen him ethically and philosophically. *Sterling!* Please!"

I turned her around.

I kissed her on the lips.

"Now cut that out," she said—but I could see she was affected, so I nuzzled her neck.

"Tell me about the assignment," I whispered to throw her off track.

"Um...*whew*...Oh God...I wish you wouldn't."

"Just say it," I whispered, my tongue barely touching her lobe above the earring. She smelled good, like a lady.

"Well, the kid's name is Sean Fontana and he's a very *young* kid and I don't believe he's ever even HEARD of Arthur except maybe in a book," she said in rush as I stroked her cheek (and then...one hand stealing downward imperceptibly...her left nipple; which grew hard as a sapphire). "Oh God! *Oh. Please.* Sterling. *Don't...* If Sean really takes H.G.'s bait both of you'll wind up with unlimited personal power—" pushing my hand away firmly. "Isn't that worth a little discomfort, Sterling? So this is why you must be toughened! Your work is crucial." She straightened her shoulders and looked at me; panting slightly, and pale even to her lips. "Omark will be the child's mentor, revealing his past to him on a safe, easy gradient—exactly as H.G.'s past-life therapy is working out the kinks in *you*, O'Blivion. Or at least we hope so."

"Don't hope on my account unless you mean it," I leered, trying to peek down her dress. Nancy shoved me away.

"Sterling! You are overstepping yourself."

"I like it when they fight like wildcats," I murmured suggestively.

"You are insolent. My husband will kill you," but she was already luring me on with her eyes...

Grandfather, I couldn't help myself. I could see why Frank Sinatra fell like a ton of bricks for this woman—and by the way I want to thank you very much for my recent little holiday! It was over in a *blink* though, and I miss being *Mr. You-Know-Who* of the Enterprise for that precious thirty minutes. (Heard on the grapevine that General M. is pissed—*sorry*—only went back to the fifties so as not to be recognized; does MacArthur really think I give a shit about his stupid little affairs?)—at any rate, Nancy was responding like mad, you better believe it; she's the type who'd lie about it though—the original Miss Roachclip just Say No, everything by the book. Sterling, *sit*. Sterling, *stand*. Sterling, take your hand out of my bra before I slap you. I guess it's what you call a love-hate relationship.

"You're having a crisis of conscience and don't know it," she taunted. "You've always played the game recklessly, but this time you're messing with the wrong woman—ow!" she squawked when I grabbed her arm.

"Why you cheap floozie hypocrite, you've been after me since the moment I walked on board this ship and now you're gonna *help me escape* or I'll hurt you *bad*, bitch! I'm dying, damn you! I can't go without a fix—"

She kicked. Right on the kneecap. It hurt! I twisted her arm.

"Don't say something you'll later regret, you slut."

"Ow! Why you f—"

She rolled under my arm, trying to grab my hair. I rammed a sharp elbow into her stomach.

"Oof! I'll teach you—"

"Yeah? See how you like this," rubbing Nancy's face into the floorboards. *She* was the one on her knees now! And I gloated. I jumped on top of her, grabbing her head and twisting. She screamed! but managed to throw me off; so hard I had the wind knocked out of me, and didn't know where I was for a few seconds. Then, I picked up the desk and slammed it at her.

I crushed her like a cricket against the wall! She was all bent over, a tremor or two convulsing her body, that lovely body that great singers and Heads of State had fondled...

I've often wondered. Would things have been different if I hadn't done what I did next? Poor Nan all gooey-nice in her Adolpho dress, upswept hair, pounds of rouge flanking the saccharine smile that seldom leaves those Hallmark lips of hers—

I gave her arm a vicious twist. She screamed. Then with a choked cry—the craving seized me; so overpoweringly that I was forced to play my hand boldly.

I bent Nancy's body over my knees, exposing the slender white throat (which as I've said was not without a certain appeal); and ignoring her shrieks, kicks, and beseechings, sank my teeth into the warm flesh just above the shoulder—expecting not only the greatest satisfaction a mortal can experience, but the *uttermost fulfillment* of all my lustful needs and cravings.

The act was smoothly done. Desperate with hunger as I was, the penetration was as masterful as that pulled off by the late Vladimir Nabokov in his previously-mentioned bestseller *Lolita*: said author, with as fervid a passion as I, proceeding to do the Big Nasty full justice with those three monosyllabic, inflammatory words—

"*To the hilt!*"

But my triumph was brief. Suddenly I howled.

"Oof! *Abominable!*" I wept, as, spitting and gagging, I felt the humiliating tears begin to flow.

"*No wonder people say you're nuts*, you superannuated bimbo," Nancy's slender voice accused as she lay across my knees. "We're in a high-stakes operation! The crummy little appetites of the flesh don't count for shit! What you need is a little *self-discipline* because if you think you know what torture is *now* — just wait till the maniacs of the future get their claws into your lily-white body. They'll probably chop your tits off! Then we'll see who's tough," she sneered, climbing to her feet and adjusting her dress.

Nancy was right, of course. I'm a jerk! Nothing changed in her expression; she has no sense of injury, being a volume-produced servo, one of 87 identicals who have no real lives of their own but do whatever you tell them to do, like a golf cart. (Before the Nancies got popular there were 87 George Bush stewards on Vonderra, each a perfect dup down to the last hair, pimple and spoilt-infant pout but Lincoln had them burnt alive in a disposal unit...a terrible thing to watch...)

My mouth was full of a sluggish ooze: axle-grease mixed with battery acid — Nancy helped me clean up, but like the original she has no capacity for independent thought and although a dead-perfect robot ringer, her body fluids taste awful which I had forgotten in the heat of desire.

"I'm going to make this as brief as possible," she said grimly (I always suspect that my Nancy is *programmed by Gen. Patton himself*; in fact I'm sure of it. She *sounds* like him). "You've got to lick this self-esteem thing! What Scaulzo is doing calls for drastic measures — that crazy occult space scum — he's flying high, trying to impregnate Virginia Woolf with his *furry dick right at this very moment!* So you've got to show some Olympian courage."

"Oh God no! Don't say that. *She wouldn't.* She'd never," I moaned, sick and spent.

"Have a clue. Has anyone ever been able to resist him? Now listen! *You're good.* It's just a matter of getting it under control," she said, washing my mouth out with soap. "Remember, you've been conditioned from birth not to be the powerhouse you really are, because people are frightened of their godhood because they've hurt others for so long — which is just a matter of control; which the great Patton is planning to teach you this very morning, so, *jump!*"

"I can't. I've got to rest..."

"Sterling — to understand the essential absurdity of peoples' ingrained foolishness is the first step to liberation! Now spit out that soap. *Rinse!* When we're done with you, you will know

REAL wonder and delight *for the first time.* Your tenth-rate addictions will *fall away!* They were laid on you from *outside* in the *first place,* get it?"

"But I want my memories. They're *me,*" I mumbled.

"Your memories will be intact but no longer painful, silly! Come on: *do you want to save Woolf* or don't you?"

Then all at once, Grandfather, the weirdest thing happened—maybe not as weird as the slithery sensation (so *new to me*) of passing into another exciting body, leaving mine in my desk chair, then out again when time is up—the easiest, *most delicious* thing in the world; also the most *mysterious,* forbidden, *forgotten* — but more on that later—but this: it was the strangest feeling to come over a stylish sophisticate like me who always ran with a big-money crowd, shopped Rodeo Drive, lunched with Ivana Trump, hung out at Scruples with her trendy pals—but now: at last I realized...what did all that ridiculous tinsel and worldly nonsense mean? Nothing, nothing, *nothing!* Now I looked around me and thought...this is my home. My *future.* With *my woman!* when *(if!)* she gets here—because the past...dear God, the past!...was *beyond horror.*

One time I hid in the catacombs beneath Rome, once fled across the icy expanse of Siberia—a woman of wide reading, voluptuous in a tight black dress, I matriculated at famous universities *(I drove myself;* having no Daddy footing the bills like the modern coed—which made me immune to the hard brainwash that is laid on students to a point where they come out mental cripples—unable to think for themselves—even if they have a so-called IQ of 200. Which leads me to observe that a college degree today is a *mental straitjacket* in my book) but forced to use my own judgment in all things, I escaped this fate. Of course later it was hard for me to sound like an authentic "woman *novelist*"! Women's fiction (as Mersoid says) is forced to *run knock-kneed,* and talk in a high little voice about how *bad* the world is to it; then throw its apron over its head and have a *good cry* like Jane Smiley, Joyce Carol Oates and Doris Lessing do; and *never* talk like a common freebooter, as *I* do; or you won't gain acceptance. And try as I might, I can never seem to attain the despairing, bootlicking *non-awareness* that pockmarks the mainstream channel. All of which makes wide acceptance difficult—because as I have said: *I'm luckier than most!*

Nancy, glancing shrewdly at me as I write this, begins to lay it on with her famous trowel.

"Oh my dear—you have a lot of footwork to do in that megatropolis of the future. Patton'll brief you as to how it might be possible to sneak up on young Fontana (a tough street brat but an excellent poet; on a par with Dylan Thomas, which you should appreciate! *I know your snobbish tastes*) and somehow manage to get him to Vonderra to be nurtured and developed. Do you see what I'm sayin'?"

So I turn, thinking to ask the dumb machine a question about the King; and she gets all excited. *"Ooh the King*—has there been an Elvis sighting?" Which, of course, is *my* fault. My antics have drained her crankcase but soon Mrs. Reagan rights herself—as she's always managed to do.

"Douglas will take him under his wing and our ship will become Camelot celebrating the homecoming of the Once and Future Boy Monarch," she cried excitedly. "Hoo boy it'll be a blast! H.G. says humans will respond to him, and knock off their curlike squabbling—as again Arthur grows into that romantic Welshman, the unknown lad who lifted the sword Excalibur out of the stone so easily when the greatest knights couldn't budge it! The world will unite behind the oak-stout, ancient British royalty—our champion, chosen hero, knight and ruler from the old, very genuine lineage that today is no more—because we all love REAL kings and queens *more than anything!* Even Ronnie does. In fact, *especially* Ronnie does, thirty times more than he loved George Washington who, although trendily large-bodied, had wooden false teeth and was kind of humdrum in an early American way. But you two will be the heirs of the ages," she babbled on and on as...

I was getting a sick feeling in the pit of my stomach.

I might have known it. Virginia Woolf came into my studio and made love to me...why? *Not because she loved ME!* Oh no. *Not at all.* Woolf was after what others have been after. (But if I think that...*my sore heart will break in two*...so I don't.)

But all at once—the thing was turning to ashes.

This hateful Cure! It wasn't for ME they were doing it. It didn't take much study to figure out what was going on—H.G. planned to use my "machine" and from what Nancy had just tipped—*I'd be ordered to pilot it!* And that I had vowed *never to do.*

Anatomy of a rejection:

You know that some years ago I successfully designed and constructed the first TTM, temporal translator of matter, my supreme triumph. My "three puffballs and a clarinet reed" I called it; but it could send a living person to past or future and return her unharmed —

I suppose I was, in a way, a "genius." Brilliant as a bullet in flight, my mind alive with ideas — but even so, it didn't happen in a vacuum. I didn't master the secrets of time without an education of sorts! I told you about the Duke who saved me from a hanging mob. We were married; the Duke allowed me the use of his extensive library, introducing me to the leading scientific lights of the age, who dined often at our house.

After my husband died — with my experience, contacts and knowledge *(not to mention the title and money!)* doors began opening for me. I told you about my early unified field research; then the perfecting of the TTM (which I tried to patent under that name. Chaps in the office were very polite to me, but wouldn't issue a patent; suggesting I find a good doctor and let him prescribe *mind-crippling* drugs) — but I only used it personally that one time...I went to Sibiu at 6 P.M. on a Good Friday, stayed ten minutes and returned 6 P.M. the same Friday — *not a nanosecond* or split-tick had elapsed on the old clock on the mantel-piece of my home in Vienna — but — seeing my native place and childhood home again! The twinkling lights of my own little, N-gauge-railway town that I adored, quaint, droll and rickety, nestled in medieval trappings in a remote mountain pass — but oh so *throbbingly alive* — and me so in love with it, yet scared shitless I'd be busted by *the same rotten sheriff!*

Conflicting emotions are hard to define; but *God forbid* I'd be thrust into the same old noisy brawl of rude jokes or hear one of the dear, forgotten songs — I miss the old songs the most; having so often prayed "Please God *let me live it all over again!* Dark narrow streets, hunger and everything" — but then —

Returning to Sibiu upset me so badly I went to bed aching all over with a fever of 104 and was sick as a dog all through Easter.

I shook my head. "No. *I won't do it.* No way."

"Then you'll never see Woolf again!" Nancy cried.

"You don't know what you're asking!" I screamed — because it's absolutely true, I can't go back. I particularly must avoid that night...

My little daughter so sick, my vain efforts to save her. Sending for the doctor late at night! It was windy, gas lamps flaring, me holding that tiny hand until dawn came and they got cold, so cold, those little fingers I loved. I learned what sorrow was. I began praying in many languages but it did no good. That blessed child was taken from me.

Then, the little white coffin thrown out of the Christian cemetery! That's what made her poor little death so horrifying: me so guilty, my life so cheap and worthless.

The awful, unbearable sadness of it. I wanted to die, wanted to join my baby. Was it a punishment? I left part of myself back there. But that chapter is closed. Many tears were shed. Stephanya was the best thing that ever happened to me—but she's dead and gone—

And I can't reopen the grave of the past!

(Here the page was ripped off, still wet.)

EIGHTEEN

Virginia Woolf was in a big hurry.
If it hadn't been that THE END was coming—she'd have given old MacArthur the *finger!* He treated her bad, *never* answered her calls until the Boss twisted his arm and when they finally did connect he picked a fight.

"Omark. Darling! *Kissy-kiss!* I LOVE you for phoning!" she had said, all excited. "Listen to my discovery! *Religion* may *be the* key to this whole turkey-farm down here."

He'd answered coldly. "Whatever chemistry exists between you and that scaly *basilisk* I don't think it has *one damned thing* to do with *religion,*" in a snotty voice.

So—her scheme was *griping the General's butt*—well that was HIS problem, not HERS. "I'm gonna do what I gotta do!" she repeated firmly. Then the ole spit-polish GI asked her out on a date—but called it *"A clandestine conference* at Checkpoint Janet," the Tokyo aquarium. Boy. *Omark in this role!??!* He couldn't even TALK straight as the big General.

On top of that he was *late.* Woolf had been swimming for an hour with the sharks. Around and around the big glass cage they went: the gorgeous, wily beasts and that great, proud spirit from watery Rysemus—what a lovely change of pace: so homelike! Benaroya hadn't felt any real empathy since Sterling left; but now, with friends—

Armed in the splendor of their huge white teeth, the sharks were lifers without any chance of parole.

Maybe they weren't 'exalted' like dolphins and whales (two species being recommended for sainthood by Hidi's Grandfather due to their *vast understanding...*even under the *torture* they'd taken from sailors viciously at sea). Yet through eons of form-experiments in their ocean, the sharks had travelled a single line;

the line every creature finds, most fascinating by far—*his own*. And now these fabulously graceful beings—*Kings of the Deep*—when not caged-up by cruel Man—trembled in the presence of their kinswoman and shivered with love at her touch—smiling as they glided over and under, and all around the Rysemian in the ancient way—sliding, nuzzling, brushing her gently with their sandpaper tails...

YIKE! MacArthur was tapping on the glass and pointing at his watch, eyebrows raised. Woolf swirled out of the water, shook her hair and hopped onto a stony ledge—wow, the General looked *baaad!* The deep lines around his eyes and bracketing his mouth were somehow frightening—her old mentor was doing incredibly well in his role (Woolf felt a stab of jealousy...Doug was taking being an Earthie with *the proper seriousness* which somehow she had *not yet managed to* do...)

"You're late, ya big lug!" she accused.

MacArthur folded his bathrobe carefully, stowing it well above the waterline. He looked lean and handsome in his fifties swim trunks. Woolf batted her eyes, pouting as she posed on the rock.

"*You're naked!*" the General barked. He had ambled in chewing a submarine sandwich with squishy goo dripping out. He was haggard; puffy circles under the eyes—*cuts* and *bruises*—*bite* marks—looking like he'd been *raped by a demon* or something.

"Yes and YOU aren't being *all you can be* in the army," Woolf lashed right back.

She'd been practicing the long stare, followed by a quick snap of the head, looking up, letting out all your air to show how *dramatic* this moment is; after which the voice comes out in *trembling hysteria*.

"I've been *swimming*, for Pete sake!"

"Let's cut to it, shall we? The mission was supposed to be *in and out*. As little truck with the natives as possible. Then HE shows up, because of YOU."

Woolf twisted slightly, so that her breasts would show to best advantage. She frowned and said: "Are you under the impression that we can keep our *head* in the sand? I mean is Earth a glittering *bauble* for him to pick up and walk *off* with or *isn't* it? With the Terminal so close would he BE here even if I didn't EXIST!??! Or *wouldn't* he for Godsake?"

Doug watched as she picked up a tube of lipstick and applied it. Her brittle words and impatient grooming seemed to prove that she was no threat—Woolf was doing well; sillifying herself *impeccably*—which could mean trouble.

"The following message is direct from Lincoln. Have him confined aboard ship by tonight—or *you're off the Squad!* D'you have a problem with that?"

Humming, Woolf folded her arms, leaned back and let her hair fall across the rock. "What're you so mad about anyway?" she pouted.

"It's been a long, hard day! MacArthur snapped, finishing his sandwich and licking his fingers.

"How long and how hard?" Woolf simpered; as she had seen it done so seriously *(and so often)* in movies, TV and Broadway shows, but Doug only shrugged.

"Look. *I'm not asking you to spell it out.* That would be up to a Board of Inquiry and is, fundamentally, none of my business but my question is—can a mermaid spread them?"

"How dare you!" Woolf's cheeks flamed with color as she jerked erect. "Using O'Blivion's own stuff when she's in—"

"And in doing so—*condemn us?* This mission was originally a nice balance, a *delicate* balance ans in light of that it was wrong of you to take upon yourself—"

"Oh balls, we're all gonna *sit* and watch YOUR puny Earth identity chicken *out?*" Woolf stormed, "SOMEBODY's got to give'm a run for his money and that somebody is ME. Because I have at last found the chink in Scaulzo's armor!"

"Sure you have." Doug's face went sour, his eyes darting sardonically here and there—which tipped her off to how bad he'd been hit. Oh God. It stopped just short of freezing *(or maybe it didn't!)* but Woolf couldn't show that she knew. If he didn't want to talk about it—that might make things worse. Much worse.

"We better get a move on. This place open in half an hour, at which point a million tourists'll—"

But the General was staring open-mouthed at glare waves that rippled, prettily, on the tank wall...

Virginia Woolf reached over, grabbed Doug's neck and began tousling his hair. "Whatever it is you're keeping inside, just let it out! LET IT OUT! Don't keep it bottled up inside," she cried like in some 90 million teleplays.

MacArthur snatched her hand between his, saying all in a

rush: "Isn't it obvious that I'm *jealous?* Do you have to get *everything mixed up with everything else?* Just because our prototypes are *brainwashed* that way, for the love of Heaven?"

"Yes, yes, *yes!* And you, or Abe or George or I—should make a clean breast of it! Just go to their President or somebody; right?—and say *'Hey.* We're here! We *love you!* We have the *answers* to your *problems* if you'd care to lend an ear'—and smile a BIG smile(!) and *wiggle your butt* if their attention wanders."

MacArthur shook his head, sighing. "Baby, let me remind you of one or two things. For example a Vice President having a fight with a *fictional character* in a *TV sitcom* doesn't exactly give the impression that they're in touch with *reality,* does it? Come on. Their deepest urge is to *punish those who deviate, and we deviate.* End of story! But I do agree with you that somehow, some way, we've got to break through."

Woolf nodded thoughtfully. "We've got to show them that metamorphosis is fun—but, how?"

"So we pull together a strategy. The original plan: O'Blivion helps recruit a stable of 2,000 Merlinites—men and women of youthful spirit and pizazz even if they're over 80 and able to pass the Turing test. Meantime we toughen our shields inasmuch as we *never know* when the bastards'll strike, or how," gloomily touching his neck where H.L. Mencken had eaten the skin off in evil passion.

"But Sterling..."

"Forget that bitch for Christ's sake!"

"What is she: our human shield or what?"

Now Doug was mad again—*jeez!* Woolf couldn't keep up with his jealousies. "She's our liaison. Is that a problem?"

Woolf tossed her head. "I notice you don't hesitate to borrow her lines do ya! Who are ya most jealous of, Dougie: *Sterling—or the devil?"*

"That question is just incredibly, incredibly tacky!"

"So hit me! HIT me! Maybe it'd make you feel better."

Doug looked at his watch. Even the way he did it was insulting. "The question everyone's asking is...what will the baby look like?"

She drew herself erect. "How dare you!" she said in cold, evenly-spaced tones.

"You fell for the oldest trick in the book—"

"Is that some kind of a warning or something?"

"Better safe than sorry." Doug struck a match and lit his pipe, pretending to admire the yellow and blue flame. "Or maybe you won't stop until—" he hinted, blowing the match out and staring at her over the smoldering stump.

"Now you listen to me! You say people'll kill us for deviating; well—*maybe the opposite is true!* We could turn ourselves into big business! Start a *bidding* war; put a floor of *ten billion* under it, make 'm *scramble* to sign us! All we've got to do is bring the DEVIL back to GOD, and: find a way to *mass-market it!*" she cried excitedly.

"That's not only crazy but stupid."

"*I mean it!* Even a demon needs understanding."

"You don't bargain with the Supreme Imperialist," he said with bitter wryness, "especially not if he's a walking chancre of psychosexual, military-industrial scatology like the Big S!"

"Love is not bargaining!"

"Oh really? Next you'll tell me love is never having to say you're sorry."

"No: love's a many-splendored gleam except when between two chippies that pass the night; or is a glow that sets—"

"Cadet, you got your work cut out for you," Doug laughed bitterly. "Trouble is, you're fucking with the *spark that could set the whole thing off!*"

"So you got an alternative?"

His mouth had tightened in the grimace she was beginning to know so well—but not like at all. "Abort! Cut your losses. Everyone knows you're having the devil's baby and he's gleefully manipulating your loyalties and genitalia both internal and external—"

"That's a stinking lie!" she shrieked. "Now if we're done with 'Checkpoint Janet' I'll just be running along—"

The General raised his hand. "One more question."

"Yeah?"

"Did you or did you not pump your hips with his?"

"Certainly not!"

"You did it with the vampire!" Flecks of saliva whipped from the General's mouth when he made this accusation.

"That's different! We're in love! We're going to be *married!"* Woolf smiled secretly, recalling Sterling's moans of rapture when they made love mingling with her own...oh, hot DAMN! But she wanted to do it again right NOW! (thinking of wondrous Ster with her thrilling voice like an echo against a craggy cliff...her warm, supple loins in the most excruciatingly thrilling, multiple

two-person orgasming all night long...*yeah*...she guessed that the stuff Scaulzo said really HAD turned her on, at that. *Wow*...she was floating *away*...)

"Well that's all perfectly fine but you're making a *God Damned Fool* of yourself," Doug shouted. "Her appetites—my God! She describes her crimes in rhapsodic terms—don't you ever wonder about a woman who can do the horrible things she's done?"

"No! I wonder about YOU, out for Sterling's blood."

"Nonsense. I just want a clean operation."

"You hate'r! And you're paranoid."

Doug shook his head. "Virginia, you don't know what people *think* of relationships like that. Ask Nancy Reagan! She knows what family values are; she'll put you straight."

"Sterling would merely reveal the truth that *custom plated Twinkies* like Nancy actually have *no truck* with hard-won wisdom; and that if you live life bravely, cowards always think you're a fool."

"Sure!" he yelled. "And do you know why? Because they happen to be *six billion imprisoned souls* under a death sentence, struggling to get out! So for Godsake quit trying to change the subject on me." Doug puffed his pipe. "You heard the order. Bring our pal back in, *frozen*—and that means TODAY before the storm breaks, or stick your resignation on Lincoln's desk. And he won't investigate. Do we finally have a deal?"

"You gotta give me time to think about this," Woolf smiled, flirting warmly with her eyes.

Doug tongued the spot where a tooth had been before Mencken raped him. It was a little sore but no longer bleeding. As a matter of fact...he suddenly felt fine.

"You've got till sundown!" he barked. "Then you're looking at a pretty ugly future."

The shark attendant banged open the door—wearing chinos, a Mickey Mouse shirt and karate thongs.

The man paused, bug-eyed. Japan's new Emperor—with a naked chick? Getting it on in the shark tank? *No!* This could not be. He was being assaulted by demons again.

Doug and Virginia saw a boy bringing two buckets of nearly dead herring to feed the lifers in the tank. The violence of human endeavor seemed so horrible, so needlessly cruel, they forgot to kiss goodbye.

NINETEEN

Sterling had no particular hope that Patton wouldn't beat the bejeezus out of her. It happened once or twice a day like clockwork. She was on her way to her lesson, feeling all blue and worried about her missing lover...usually too proud to bawl, but now: sad tears flowed.

Anyway, thank God she was *outta the chicken coop!* And great gulps of cool air were calming—Ster picking her way slowly along a headland, enjoying the sweep of broad ocean, and getting the kinks out of her legs on a fine morning with the sun an hour over the horizon, the air sparkling clear—her path taking her above a rock-strewn coast: light breezes plowing the Atlantic, and gulls circling; a misty horizon blurring into dim distance—the kind of day that makes you wanna doze under a beach umbrella composing an *Ode to the Nereids* as you quaff Club Soda...but for a sickening fear.

It made her edgy as hell to look down. One slip of the foot and KBLAM! A 200-foot drop down the cliff. Spattered worse than last time. Like Humpty Dumpty they'd never pick up the pieces, which'd be carried off by booming surf that creamed on rocks far below—Ster was forced to grab onto a wind-warped cypress— the idea of bouncing and bursting on sharp rocks made her head WHIRRRRL *(keep eyes open: fool).*

Up above, a fence ran to one side and beyond it was a valley planted in rye and alfalfa and it was quite nice watching shadows crossing the waves; and a breath of sea air did her a world of good—it had rained, too—there were puddles. It was a lovely day but there were storm clouds on the horizon. Maybe later there'd be cold rain and heavy winds. Squalls came up often on this Mediterranean coastline. Bogus ones? *Unh-uh.* Not fake in any way! *Realer than real.* Hard to remember she was on a space ship. And had been, to all intents and purposes, *kidnapped*...

Over that rise was a little seaside town in France; or rather—its prototype ("The muddy lanes remind me of my own sweet day," Sterling wrote that morning)—the dizzying part being that EUROPE HAD BEEN COPIED from THIS continuum a while back. Every frond of seaweed was the original thing (minus medical waste, oil, condoms, sixpack nooses and poison that would pollute every cubic inch of ocean in the days ahead). The mechanism of Vonderra was a no-mechanism—this being no corny little "holodeck," or special effect, or "virtual reality" or any tenth rate Earthie simulation at all; but a flesh-and-blood REALITY. And yet...*and yet!*

("Will I ever feel at home here?" she had to ask. Shee-it! *It made her head spin*) as she groped for the Rysemian answer to her $64-dollar question: "What is reality?" The Sage's answer was: *agreement*. Reality is AGREEMENT, babe. And please note the power of simplicity! It was no stretch at all for people this advanced, to create realities by the yard...Grid 8 boasted multiform solar systems plural-time framed—you could float a raft down the Mississippi in the day of Tom and Huck, or spend your threescore-and-ten in ancient Egypt of the Pharaohs or Manhattan of the early 1900's when Greenwich Village was really worth living in—while every philosopher from Plato to Kant was dutifully mumbling in his beard, "No one knows what the soul is or how it works, *sniff, boohoo*; where did poor little mortal ME *come from?*"—but now: these invaders had brought the answer! "Can I stand it?" you had to ask yourself—hoping you wouldn't fall off the cliff and break your bloody neck—

OH GOD! Right below her was General George Patton. Her heart gave a lurch. Stocky, balding, standing in the churchyard that was their dueling ground as he eyeballed poor O'Blivion up above—oh what an *ass* she'd been! Should have kept the facts of her past to herself; because now—Patton'd use them against her. "Combray beguiles me," she had simpered in her absurd little Confession—and what happened? Today's venue was the actual surrounding that Marcel Proust had set his drama in the fat novel Ster'd ghostwritten for that author in exchange for a haven when the French fuzz were after her! It was the same old story: men stalking her, trying to hunt her down and it seemed easier back then to pen the tiresome *Remembrance of Things Past* for the eager

Marcel, than spend a single day in the slammer but then: first crack off the bat Patton is telling her—"*I'm gonna teach you what to do if you are caught and tortured*" — holy shit. The S.O.B. never failed to awe her—that tank of a body with its bull neck, buttoned into full dress uniform; the jacket resplendent with a gaudy array of medals and topped with epaulettes, the Sam Browne belt set off by gleaming brass, those natty whipcord britches...the engraved scabbard and the *(oh no!! Don't kick me again sir,* PLEASE: I'M SO SORRY!!) heavy hobnail boots Ster's tender ass had connected with on many a painful occasion *(PLEASE! I'll be GOOD!!!)* and to top all—the agonizing little swagger stick *(riding crop)* he carried in his left hand, was busily whacking the heads off daisies. *Whick. Whack. Whup!* — as the very last of her confidence slipped away.

"I see you up there!" boomed the voice—that voice that had scared shit out of his troops! but what scared *Sterling* was the two-edged sword in the General's right hand; and yet...as a prisoner of intergalactic space invaders (which is WHAT SHE WAS! thanks to that traitor Virginia Woolf)—she would now be forced to learn to cope with what H.G. called *"Godhood"* — by which he meant: ever-increasing *power* combined with an intolerably broad *flexiblility—and* that made the vampire *dizzier than ever!* As well it might.

"Get your ass down here and stop goldbricking—you skulking, despicable little *worm!* Cockroachy *blood-lapper:* I know your guilty secret! I KNOW WHAT YOU DO."

Oh God. She'd expected trouble and here it came, blazing fire: George was mad at her! It was always worse when he was mad. He'd flay her alive! thought Sterling, half-sliding down the slope to the churchyard and in her hurry taking a spine-jolting tumble—boink...boink...DOIYYYNG! The worst possible way to begin a lesson—scrambling for handholds among cowflops as she took another pratfall, bumping over rocks that bruised her padded hips, bottom and knees only to wind up—misbegotten fool that she was!—in an anthill at the General's feet.

"*Won't do it?*" he yelped. "Won't use your precious TTM? Maybe you better think that decision over," landing a swift kick on Sterling's anatomy as she leaped up saluting.

"Owww..." But she didn't sob too loud *(or he'd do it harder).* That granite face made the vampire recall the time Patton slapped a GI for "cowardice" or something—she forgot the details but on

Vonderra there'd be NO flood of public outrage to shield her from his Big Brass Bullying! He tossed her a sword *(which she dam-near got cut on the hand* trying to catch neatly) bellowing: "EN GARDE! you disgusting little sleaze who is beneath my, or any decent human's, *contempt*," as he placed a neat nick on her wrist.

"OW!" Sterling screamed, taking the stance: left arm up and crooked: O.K. Right arm extended for the lunge that'd KILL the mofo-egg-suckn coke-sacker *(she hoped to Christ – !)*.

"Li'l scratch. Ain't seen nothin yet." Blood vessels swelled in the General's forehead *(in native form, he was Vonderra's austerely brainy Captain Boolabung:* a horrid drillmaster even to *her,* Woolf said). O'Blivion had to limber up her sword-arm with a few air slices and then it was eye to eye, *whick-whick!* a couple fast ones, their feet shuffling between mossy old French tombstones *(of the late eighteenth and early nineteenth centuries* it looked like).

The churchyard had oodles of quaint country charm – "*Eat steel,* you emotionally distressed chippie-ho!" said the General. "*Hit me!* This is WAR! No quarter given, none asked" – streaming perspiration into his collar as he let Sterling feel the prod of his blade *(and she refused to scream or plead – yet).*

They clattered among marble trumpet-blowers, stony angels, scrolls with carved remembrances – epitaphs graven on pillows of granite many years ago; Patton making his pupil squirm like an eel as he cut air perilously near her tits and ass – going WHICK-whick! as he put steel on *(and IN!)* her curving, fleshy butt and tender parts, until she howled:

"OWWW, damn you! What're you on me for anyway?"

The bastard! He was going for her nipples! Bunching up his ugly mouth, whipping the blade half an inch from – (OW!) her terrified nose! Then inflicting a double-X cut on one cheek – but she caught him a good one too – a painful belly slash that tore his fuckn Sam Browne belt right OFF.

They circled each other, panting.

"We all wanna enjoy some *supernatural nooky,*" Patton sneered. "And your girlfriend's *procured* it for us. WHEE! Get your head smashed open and your eyeballs whirled in a blender," he giggled. (Ster figured he meant he was being harrassed because of what Woolf did; was that it? But she guessed it'd be too dangerous to ask him right now) –

"Shame on you! The most commonplace fact of all facts is that you ARE and will forever BE immortal so don't come crying to ME, General George S. Patton, with your scummy burden of so-called mortality! It's no excuse for the ingrained human violence that must be expunged *(and our Sage shows how to do it painlessly)* before any of you can call yourself *liberated!* It's a cruel — stupid — *delusion* — that anyone dies, you twit. *Death is no excuse!* And it sure as hell is no ESCAPE so you better quit counting on it, got it?"

His eyes bulged redly — the vampire began to plead. "Yessir, *yes yes I'm sorry!* But give us a little credit..."

"Credit. You want credit for your race of pious, coldhearted murdering sons of bitches?" *Whick-whick!* In a sudden rage, Sterling parried his attack; but her riposte was parried neatly. She hip-spun and lunged getting a little flair back into the old arm — but — no score.

"I checked your rap sheet!" Patton puffed. "After prison you got into pimping, petty theft, the rackets — and then you managed a rip-off dance studio," he said scathingly.

"*Lies!* Crap! I never pimped in my life and only stole a little bread now and then to survive —"

"Fine! Now let's see if you c'n *comprehend* that there are things far — far — *worse than death* — come on!"

Sterling blundered at him. Blood spurted from her face and neck; she felt it soak into her shirt — but the Commander of the Third Army, sword clenched in his burly freckled fist, knew how to make this kind of slashing, ringing, sweaty work look easy *(effortless;* GODDAMN his insulting, lying MOUTH!).

"You may maim animals — not recognizing what an animal IS! — unable to recognize your REAL enemy infecting your species with *the greed disease* making 'm leap and giggle endlessly on the TV tube — whores working hard for cash: the *cheapest thing in the world!* Do you get it?"

Ster gulped and nodded. "Sir yes SIR! I GET IT sir!"

"You flat-out *refuse* access to your TTM — yet fantasize that you DESERVE Virginia Woolf, the prize for whom even *Satan* lusts? It's a mystery to me how an old pro like you can take the ridiculous for granted —" *(Whick!)*

His insult was worse than his sword — *her eyes fixated on the blade* — with a diamond flashpoint rippling hypnotically along its razory edge until FWIP! it opened a slice in her thigh. Blood gushed out, a copious flow — it was that old, dark sorrow again

DEVIL-MAY-CARE

threatening to drown her—thoughts of her daughter—*as fresh as the day they happened*—

"I'm disappointed in you. I thought you had more piss and vinegar in you," Patton gasped. "The old man says you're *outta here today!* They'll probably *hang your ass*, but you could just make it. You've got *Attitude*. People get *real nervous* about you. The *very thought* of you running around loose *rankles* in the average human gut, you loose cannon—*whattaya say?* Wanna take on City Hall once and for all?"

Sterling pulled a face. She couldn't stop crying.

"*Hey!* Eye contact here. LOOK at me when I'm talking to you. Give yourself a reality check. *Focus!* Your lips're purple—you look like a goddamn banshee—lie down and R.C.!"

The humid scent of grass was soothing to her nostrils, and Sterling had learned the tech for what the General commanded ("Have a Moment of Epiphany," he was huffing) so she did the R.C. (but QUICK! *to avoid pain*)—O.K.—in all her paralyzing grandeur, Vonderra is only a star cruiser. The REALLY big show is on Grid 8, the Mousehole Terminal—what this whole thing is ABOUT! The spot the Rysemians arrived at by accident (and where they'd by now installed the Canadian Rockies, Paris, India, you name it) at first knowing nothing of the existence of our infinitesimal, dusty globe—

"O.K.—so this awesome hint of the unconceivable vastness of a convoluted universe that hypnotized beings consider their 'reality' is a mockup by a group of original gods, including us amnesiacs in human form—which makes it slightly less than awesome! The Rysemians may be 500 times smarter than Sterling but she's catching up FAST! The important thing to remember being...the important thing is the BEING! not the toys he uses—megatons of matter energy space time and the games we play with these and other knockoff Monopoly tokens—however "complex" and "mysterious" we make it out to be, because the POWER is in WHAT? The power is in YOU! That's what. But remember, Sterling, my love (she told herself feeling much better already)—uh—*revelations don't come cheap*. Bear that in mind kiddo, so you don't turn into one of these pompous Authority Figures that bring death to mankind; the most popular type of death—death by official stupidity—which is what we must try to sidestep NOW!!!

"O.K. you, *that's enough*. Get your sword up. Think we got

all day? Time's trickling out. Frozen into a body Scaulzo *could have been killed* and he SHOULD have been killed! and you know who's FAULT it is that he wasn't. You've got to start cooperating with us right NOW. He's circling. Don't underestimate him. *This is no villain in a cartoon series* — you execrable *couch spud* peddling ersatz *dance courses* to *lonely people* while your world expires with its *ticket punched* forEVER—"

Patton went wild, attacking from all quarters at once—driving O'Blivion over a fence and through the church doors into the old Gothic chapel where sun came blazing through stained glass. (*Oh God in heaven!* Was anything *worse* than having an *advanced race* come to your planet and give you instruction in how to BE?—and!—with the realization that Vonderra WAS the Chariot of Fire her Mama and other good Christians used to pray for—Oh *God!* An undetectable light-leech vivarium; a paragravity-driven, hollowed-out diamond grown in an asteroid seedbelt unthinkably long ago and far away—*help*. The *dizziness!* Must shake it or DIE here).

There was no sound but a frenzied whipping of air, clinking of sabers, shuffling of feet as Patton forced her up a dusty, old, spiral staircase.

"—and you creeps thinking you're smart for making pots of 'money'—as pampered-consumer, bloodswilling tacky human *anachronisms* hardly out of the caves while you make *wreckage* of other species and give each other dumb 'intelligence' tests to prove how *brilliant* y'all are—"

"I'm not responsible for my whole species!" Sterling yelled as he backed her down a gallery.

"*The devil you say!* That's ALLa-ya's big delusion (get that sword up!) and YOU, Trash, have a chemical-dependency problem. I'm here to *get you over it*, degenerate scum, are you *grasping* that this is your ONE SHOT? and YOU are gonna make IMMENSE strides from now on—IF you can shake the local insanity from your brains and APPLY yourself! And don't *smart-mouth* me or you're a *cadaver!*" he bellowed. "Are you comprehending *what is being revealed* to you here?"

"YES! YES!"

"Good! And if you ever *do* get home" (driving Sterling off a balcony down to the church proper and leaping after her) "tell your (puff puff!) *wee leaders* to think it over before they charge into

SPACE waving the American *flag* — you'd be in so *far* over your *head* — humans? *Barbs?* Going glaze-eyed? Over one, *simple, little,* Vonderic continuum — whaddaya think'd go POP if you REALLY saw the Grid on its *own spacetime scale* and not just in your *puny mind* — think about *great open stretches* of plain, glacier, rain forest, tropical paradise, *black space* — stars — even YOU! A *brilliant woman* who lived through the *horrors* of *slave trade* — I know you figured out the *math* to *prove* Grid 8 and c'd go back and *show*'m except they'd *not believe you!* Bunch of baboons swinging in trees—"

"All right! *I got the message!* Shut up and fight! *(you* hairbag!)" — Patton had trapped the now-furious O'Blivion in a pulpit. She parried a blow, dodged the next one and — *the General's sword hit wood.* His sword got stuck! Oh, how *wonderful* that this SMART-MOUTH liked to *express himself warmly* on his favorite subject of how DUMB she was — it allowed her to deliver a FAST PIZZA: *right on the ear!* A nice cut, executed with *flash* and *style* — a big piece of EAR flew through the air and the vampire felt on TOP of the WORLD as, fetching him another, just under the eye — OUT popped his *glaring eyeball itself!* She hadn't quite intended it but THERE the eye WAS, dangling *(oogily)* on his cheek! The socket bubbled blood — Patton scooped up the eye with all the *gunk,* nerves and *blood vessels* attached to it and shoved the grisly thing back in its socket *(somewhat wonky and off center...*which was quite funny). Ster noticed that his hobnail boots, that had hurt her ass, were *red* from *top* to *sole* and gore *gushed down* over the whole natty *uniform,* leaving *no spot unbloody.* Even his once-shiny epaulettes were bathed in blood.

"Treachery rides high!" he snarled as they locked hilts, *faces close together*...Sterling used her knee and then sliced upward — *hey-hey* — she was doing GREAT! Proud of her skill, half-forgotten after a long period of disuse — the General tripped over a pew — he staggered backward. His arms spread out to either side — they began pinwheeling frantically — he backed *right into a plaster saint* — he sprawled full length and ohhhh...YES! The moment of moments: her *sword was quivering at his throat.*

"*Touché,*" she yelled ecstatically. Now she REALLY had a moment of epiphany! Her peformance had been absolutely classic and now, seeing Patton pinned like that, Ster beamed with joy. *She felt so proud!* She had CUT the lippy bastard from gut to gizzard! Now she could slay him dead *(ashes to ashes, dust to dust)* or let him crawl off — an EX-smartmouth and a weeping loser.

"Don't just stand there *gloating,* you ape. *Kill me!*" the General commanded *(there were tears in his eyes).* "Come on. Stick the blade in QUICK. This HURTS."

Sterling shook her head. "I'm not in the mood."

"That's a slap in the face, cadet! The worst insult you can offer an opponent."

"Bullshit!" she grinned. "I've never played by *other peoples' rules* and I'm not about to start now, and here's something I've been wanting tell you AND your stooge Nancy and ANYONE ELSE who feels like laying THEIR stupid rules on ME with no regard for *the most important thing in the world:* MY OWN FREE WILL! Are you ready for this? YOU ALL CAN KISS MY ASS," O'Blivion cried in triumph.

Patton licked his lips. "Wonderful. Throw a little ethics in there and you've learned your lesson for today!" he chuckled, crawling painfully to his feet and staggering to the altar *(but...jeez,* George was all crumpled over. *He gushed blood,* sheets of it — shinier than a bucket of red-hot molten chrome — poured out by mistake — big, steamy jets of glossily cascading hot scarlet MIRRORgoop! — was what this geyser of *chromy liquid* looked like to the vampire) where he boosted himself up and sat, trying to catch his breath.

His wide, dour face turned to her. "So whaddaya say. *In? Out?*"

"You mean I have a choice?"

"Who c'n force a god? Quit thinking like humans. You c'n be snug in your Chicago lair in an hour: say the word."

"And never see Woolf again?"

"Exactly. Or we talk." He patted a spot next to him.

Sterling didn't let on how much it hurt to boost herself up, or how much she *hated* sitting in George's blood, now mingling with hers — *as if they were friends or something!* She was awfully pissed at things he'd said; and yet...of course...*she loved to feel a part of things.*

The General coughed violently and began vomiting pints of blood — she had punctured one of his lungs. *Fine!* It might teach him some manners.

"I know you can't visualize it," he gasped. "People never can, but: your glory days are ahead of you,"

"Meaning me — or all us po' sinners?" Ster grinned.

"All who can open their ears," he wheezed more blood.

"Shakespeare said it, we play roles. That's ALL we do. If you take yourself seriously or think that role is carved in stone—Blurp!" *(Lots of the red stuff.)* "I know you feel a big ache of rejection long-nurtured—thinking 'Why should I help those closet cases who hurt me so bad,' but—"

Patton shook his head and coughed.

O'Blivion stared at him—this hero of a bygone age—was it gonna be a *"We must be kind to each other"* speech or what? And in any case—it wasn't HIM she saw right now because—hey. What the vampire SAW—*and it was another Epiphany thing maybe*—was—that all this red, shiny, *carnal goop*—this SOMA dripping outta both of'm with its hard, metallic glint—no longer meant SQUAT to her. It had no SIGNIFICANCE! deep or shallow because—*it was just blood*. It was no longer a symbol of 87-million other things, it was just ITSELF which is to say: it was JUST blood. It—*was*—*just*—BLOOD!

"And we can make an infinite supply," Patton choked.

As the General talked, a big red bubble came ballooning from his lips. *(fascinating!...)*

"I am one of your true admirers, my dear O'Blivion. Even that pygmy MacArthur knows what a *formidable enemy* you'd make. That's why I'm willing to let you in on a few of the *basic secrets of reality* as they apply to your species—excuse me (BLURP!)" he gasped out.

"The junk the media flashes in your faces is NOT just unreality—" (OH GOD: *the bubble. It was getting enormous!* A great big, sheety pink globe, with the high church windows reflected shinily on one side—*really quite attractive*—)

"It's a Scaulzonically semi-real FILM over a distorting LOOP designed to be close enough to reality to instill the *desperate confusion of a soul in torment* in every single one of you *refugees from a Bosch painting* as you go around *congratulating yourselves* saying 'Oh! Aren't our rulers *clever*—inventing and selling us all these shiny THINGS and brilliant IDEAS?' while all the time—eh! Eh! Eh!" he gargled with a friendly clasp of his bloody hand on her shoulder.

"*Sir! Yes, sir!*" Sterling snapped. She could barely talk; because one corner of her generous mouth had been jaggedly ripped open and she, too, was sliding into limbo—

"For a while there," she mumbled, "all you heard in bars

was Napoleon this and Napoleon that...we were all thrilled to BURGERBITS with Napoleon...like I've seen conquerors come and go with their hi-de-ho and boop-a-doo so I guess I know—"

"No you don't. But no time to haggle—" The big bubble got huger and huger. It POPPED! Blood spattered all over Sterling's face and hair; then as he talked, another bubble started forming.

"Scaulzo's *titillating*, he's *terrifying*, he's *everything the public wants*—the richest and MOST FAMOUS celebrity with top appeal in eighteen galaxies! *But is that good news or bad?* There are no peace talks with the devil—and your weird, wonderful race of men—who are so much greater than they believe *(eh! eh!)* due to loss of memory; do you SEE why they adore war? Do you GET IT that the young King Arthur—rescued by you—then *trained, polished and advised by us*—can begin to begin changing things for the better?"

"Sir! Yes, *sir!*" cried Sterling. But she was lying. What she was REALLY thinking was—B.S. to that! I WANT and NEED to be a vampire because it's what I AM! *Bloodsucking is central to my life!* Without it I'd have no identity—no identity at all—which would be intolerable; so *go to hell.*

The General stared at her.

"And you thought the cattle prod up the rectum was bad," he scoffed. "Poor brute human! You have *no idea* what your 'culture' has done to y'all—excuse me" *(blood drooling from his jaws).* "Oh, if but ONE o' you could look up from the depths of your blinding egotism—long enough to avoid the TRAP about to be sprung and see it is time to WAKE UP!"

Ster flinched when the General reared his head.

"Looky here." He began probing a leg wound with his sword. "This is what gets your attention, right? Cutting through skin and muscle and slicing a bod up—*looky.*"

"That's gross!" She looked away.

"No, you must watch me sever the nerves and ligaments and carve, whittle, and hack the bone underneath—like this; see? These shiny parts, ugh!" He stretched open a deep cut to show her the bone, pulling strips of yellow fat clear of it. "I'll just lop off a finger or two—then my dick—you can mount it on your wall. Then we'll have some toe and scrotum lopping; watch this."

With the sword point he began digging under a severed vein. "Maybe the time isn't right or the machinery's not in place, and you won't accept the risk, beat the odds—" Patton jerked an artery out of his forearm. The round blood vessel stood erect; it was pumping out shiny-bright, scarlet arterial blood in rhythm with the General's weakening heartbeats.

He wiped the sword on his tunic, then ran a hand thoughtfully over the blade. "O.K. So you quit, is that it?"

"Well maybe I need time—"

"Bite the bullet, Sterling," he coughed. "I can't force you but YOU'll force you so let's quit messing around. *Give it a chance!* Soon you'll be *really hooked* on something *great*, not that small-time lying crooked Earthie crap which is all you've known before now. *Sistu?*"

He smiled. It was a gentle smile. "As I say, you're under no obligation—but if you wanna go along with it, here's the procedure. You and I will go to your present-day condo in Chicago; we'll lift your TTM carefully down from the shelf in the locked closet, blow the dust off, have a last-minute briefing and FFFT!, you're gone. You'll materialize in the same place in two hundred years with instructions on how to keep your nose clean, cut your quarry out of the herd and bring him back alive as quick as possible."

"What if I say no right now?"

"I'll respect it."

"Then: no! You don't know how hard I had to fight, forcing myself into the damned thing that one time! I can't do it—"

"Going back to your roots is a terror. *This isn't the same thing at all* so don't dwell on it; think instead of how your *whole tribe'll* be elevated to their past glory—where they can do *wonderful things* with their lives instead of wallowing in pointless frivolities an' *wartainments* – think of the possibilities. Look at the grand scheme of things! And the horror of it is, *history's speeding up*. Every moment is a potential disaster. The alternative is to blow your little fishbowl sky-high. The choice is yours and let me warn you. Never place the words of any Authority (especially me) above your own gut wisdom—unless you wanna get radioactive fast."

A big bubble popped.

"I know you'll do it. You're a good sport," Patton gasped.

It was his highest accolade. He raised one hand in a stiff salute, snapped it at her, and fainted. His bulk slumped heavily off the altar in a jingle of spurs, harness and medals. It flopped on the floor.

Sterling sat there—gazing dreamily at the stained-glass pattern of light. How pretty it looked; catching the morning sun as it twinkled, and flickered, on the General's sprawled-out bod...and on the lovely old, stone floor...that had pools of tacky red chrome drying here and there...*yuck*...

Then she, too, passed out.

TWENTY

Virginia Woolf left General MacArthur climbing into his baggy fatigues, off to a Joint Chiefs clash at the Pentagon—the big palooka was worried GREEN! She'd never seen her teacher so bewildered; acting like he'd been *knocked on the melon*, pretending it's on account-a that dapper little cat Harry Truman—33rd President of the United States—becuz *now!* bigwig engineer Frimble was reassigned as Harry to give his old Coalsack Wars crony the shock of his life; Abe sayin to topple MacArthur off his perch—so Harry'd deliver a cold ultimatum stripping Doug of Emperorhood—yank him out of the Orient—becuz he couldn't keep Woolf on a short enough rein to keep her from abducting their prisoner Scaulzo; thereby setting Doug up for the A-O assault that ESCALATED until now everyone of them was at risk and was—was—

Oh, *who cared?* All this MALE ULTIMATUM crap just made her *miss Sterling all the more.* When, *when!* would this war with Sajor be OVER so they could be TOGETHER again?

(Telepathic orgasms were all very well BUT!—)

Anyway this part of Tokyo was pretty. Woolf skipped along, a towel draped over her bare shoulders, her hair still wet from the shark tank...It was a lovely street with a tiny railed park where pigeons strutted, and wooden benches had been painted a cheerful green. The Japanese weren't a prosperous people back here in the fifties—but at least Tokyo wasn't one of the cities that Harry Truman had dropped his little, old, down-home, Missouri atomic bomb on! but...

Doug had said cruel things to her. He was so mad.

"What are you, *humping the Prince of Darkness?*" he'd ridiculed—ordering her to use a deep probe on her prisoner. "Just find out WHERE and WHEN," he begged.

Even if that were possible it'd betray Scaulzo's trust! Everything she'd worked on so hard; why couldn't Doug and Abe SEE, that *the only thing that held primitives together was religion??* for corn sake—but what happened next depended on Beel. The second in command was *hurting them,* despite all her security measures. She'd been training hard—her shield was invulnerable now—well—she hadn't tested a *really strong one* yet but didn't expect one. But tough times were ahead—things had gotten so weird—*what was Beel up to anyway???*

He had to be thinking some heavy thoughts about his boss. Was Scaulzo out of it for good; had the H-2 caused damage beyond repair? The "ultimate gadget" was too new to have much of a track record; few had been frozen and lived to tell about it *(Woolf was one of 'm* and Doug brought'r out of it). The general rule was to ZAP the enemy into his carcass, blow the carcass to Kingdom Come and *that's all, Charlie;* from here on out your whole Being-ness is DEAD. You are history *(no: less than* that)—Woolf hadn't yet thought about the freeze-and-torture possibilities—nor did she want to; it was too disgusting.

Doug—he hit her with burning questions. No way she could make'm understand—*not this trip*—and NEVER when he was bein' a military dude! But right now—the old John Wayne flair was absent. The no-nonsense certainty—where had it gone?

"That lucky sadist," he had envied Scaulzo. "Gets his kicks yet never feels the slightest twinge of remorse." But *was it true?* Scaulzo was the classic psychotic, and *"psychotic"* meant you felt NO GUILT EVER—if you *felt* guilt you were just another neurotic: very unlike the Big S.—and yet: she knew that *she,* personally, had struck a mortal blow to his evil purposes. She also knew it was a million-to-one shot any change'd be permanent. But did that mean she shouldn't try? NO!

Woolf was working on something that was greater than any single life, greater than any single planet...

On Rysemus they'd long ago found a foolproof way to drive out THE DEVIL, as he was called here. Of course it had to be expertly done, which meant with the spot-on accuracy of a mental laser—NEVER by dudes who were knee-deep in the very mental confusion they were tryin' to exorcise! And actually Omark had got right to the heart of it.

"What Scaulzo rams into a mind is INSANITY. If you try to

figure out insanity and say, 'Maybe this? Maybe that? Maybe the other?' you go ever more hopelessly insane." Boy wasn't that the truth! Yet it was a source of endless fascination to Woolf—this problem of GOOD vs. EVIL because why couldn't you SELL the DEVIL on the plan of being GOOD?

Why not explain to him that EVIL is STUPID because it's the same tired WHACK stuff, over and OVER—like most kneejerk shows that appealed only to *shock cases,* compulsively *dramatizing* their long-past *trauma?* But GOOD: good was FUN! And it netted you *an endlessly beautiful future;* packed with exciting *communication* and thrilling ideas and everything; creative *artforms,* games—of the sort that sick, grownup, abused children were too DEPRESSED even to LOOK AT let alone enjoy. But if Scaulzo could just SEE that!!! All his wonderful talent and skill going down a tube—sneakily *manipulating people* into horrible, dead-end situations that were nothing but BORING! And if such a thing 'couldn't be done,' as some people said—she wanted to *see it for herself,* not just have Doug or Abe TELL her over and over. So THAT'S what she was up to. Not having a dumb AFFAIR with Scaulzo! because—well for one thing—humans knew nothing about the dark art of the psychic WHACK, but WOOLF knew about it—except that...uh...

Hey. This was funny. She was glancing at a nest of cardboard boxes when out of them—like some kinda jack-in-the box—

A grinning tramp popped awake. Through broken teeth he said: "Wa ni gul like oo do play li dis?" *(It sounded like.)* Woolf had been sauntering along, enjoying the sights and smells of Tokyo when—

When what?!!? *(dizziness)* but the utterly crazy part was....getting undermined by—!

A beetle crawled on a wall—it made her smile a little—the sun was drying her hair—it felt good. She better get a move on though. Had a report to file—and maybe Abe'd let her see Ster for one little minute. How great *one, tender kiss* was going to be! if she c'd only—

But—oh God. *Wha—?!!?*

For an instant Woolf didn't know what was wrong; only that something was wrong. She felt her skin crawl. Somehow she'd turned into a weirdly familiar alley that smelled of fish guts, urine and something else—a fume she couldn't identify...

Steps came up behind her; she whirled—nothing there! An A-O wave began to strike lightly—but she'd been psyching up. She could deflect it easily (except for this déjà vu feeling...*that was once again making her head spin*).

"Stand and fight!" she rapped out.

Behind a garbage can, something struck her eye. A glint. Movement! Bursting out of shadows.

All it takes is a split-second of inattention—

Woolf whipped sideways. There was a yell of warning from the tramp—she was looking at orange suits, wraparound shades, a squad closing in—backed by an H-2 unit! Herself looking down its twinkling muzzle in astonishment and then:

BLAM! A burst of fire; first the muted H-2. Then a crack from a Beretta that blew her hand off. Blood and flesh sprayed into the air. The agent came into fighting position.

She had no time to figure how badly she'd messed up. One quick blow, halting the leader with her uninjured hand, thumb to windpipe—then came a battering, knifing punishment that lasted sixty seconds *(but Woolf felt every bit of it;* except for those things that happened after death claimed her...).

What had been Sterling's delight was now—ugly wreckage.

Off to one side, a smiling man puffed a wet cigar.

Sirens howled; the attackers fled. The afternoon headlines were screaming "AN APPALLING ACCIDENT!"—even as the British novelist's stabbed, shot, mutilated body was on its way to the Tokyo morgue.

TWENTY-ONE

Her little daughter Stephanya was much better. Stephy wasn't going to die! Here she came; running to the vampire's arms — smiling, *pretty and happy as always* —

Sterling woke up — with a momentary bitterness *(because the dream wasn't true!)* but fear quickly took the place of bitterness. She'd slept like the dead. That was odd. Usually she slept *lightly* in a strange new place — and this — was her posh suite in the ZATS: a vertical complex thrusting skyward on the corner where her beloved old Drake Hotel used to be. *(But nearly 200 years ago)*.

There'd been another dream, she now recalled: *a nightmare.* Dripping blood. *Woolf was dying!* Ambulance sirens wailed...

"NO!" Sterling had screamed; waking up bathed in tears, *shivering with longing* for Woolf — her eyes, her hair, the way she'd stroll into a room chewing a *toothpick,* so funny, so *alive* — her red nipples...her earthy warmth...*ohhh God!* Sterling's head was pounding. Now she remembered *shrieking at the top of her lungs in her sleep.* Her heart was thudding like a drum —

Christ! What a sick dream. The one about Stephy was wonderful but Woolf's *bloody murder* — that could only be first night-in-a-strange-place jitters! But it'd been so *real.*

All too real. *Thank God it was gone.* The vampire rolled out of bed wiping her eyes — rushing to the panoramic window to gaze at a splintered, shrouded Chicago laid out below —

"Awesome."

A kid's word, that never meant anything up to now.

It scared her — that city down there —

Yesterday morning'd been no different from any other, yet here she was. September, 2123 A.D! A sensational ride better than a roller coaster *(some might say)* except for a cranked-up, "wound up tight" nauseous feeling — Ster peering off toward where the

Loop used to be, shuddering. A fluttery, disoriented feeling (*loosen up. Don't make a big thing of this*) but the sure bet was...Woolf could handle herself. Nothing bad would happen to Benaroya — ever! So don't get all achy-breaky and attract trouble (Sterling scolded herself).

The vampire blew her nose, wiped her tears, noting the thrilled butterflies in her stomach plus shivers of revulsion. *Culture shock.* No biggie. All she had to do was give it a shot. If the quest proved nothing but a pipedream *(as Douglas MacArthur swore it would)* she'd calmly sit down with her TTM she had placed so carefully in a drawer last night and Ffft! *Outta here.*

"There's no need to rush. Give yourself plenty of time," H.G. advised. Well that's *exactly* what she meant to do — after all, wasn't this the great American sprawl that O'Blivion knew like the palm of her hand? With a few little twists. The flag "Old Glory" (according to her briefing by Patton) still had those brave, red-and-white stripes with a blue field in the upper left corner but now the stars were gene-spliced bugs — *jumping orbit* — the theme of the 22nd century, it would seem.

There was no telephone directory in this room where she'd materialized — the locals probably had unique methods and protocol for reaching out and touching each other (Sterling slowly panned the best binocs Vonderra had to offer over the harsh outlines of a once-familiar place whose charm had long since faded) but nothing startling, it appeared, nothing unanticipated. Just the old, familiar monster built by drug makers and their bureaucratty, munitions-&-doc henchmen who needed to add a few more dollars to the bank account at John Q. Public's expense. No big deal — it was only the same old murderous hate being brought to a hellish climax.

Her suite was princely for sure — how different could this Chicago BE from the toddlin' town she'd known in 1999 at the millennium? A loaf of bread now cost $1500 but economics aside...*what unseen horrors awaited her?* What if she couldn't pull the job off — what if *NO sane future* could be set rolling before about 2050 — what if humanity really COULD NOT be altered at its roots? Then: *ka-SMOOSH.* Dear old Earth'd wind up as a *slick, glassy marble.* New weapons could *lick away the atmosphere,* SLURRRP! — as with a giant tongue. Patton called it imminent if she didn't work fast —

But personal feelings were not relevant. The pressure was ON!

H.G. made it pretty clear that she'd either do it right...or go back to her old lifestyle; and once you had a taste of real POWER — *real team spirit* — real EXCITEMENT — she was forced to admit —

"We'll show you that power does NOT corrupt," H.G. said. "It is WEAKNESS that corrupts; and absolute weakness *(as you will now learn)* corrupts absolutely."

Oh boy. Check out that maze down there. An uneasy peek at the Age to Come. She'd have to negotiate those blurry outlines of intricate geometries *(beautiful in their way)*...After the sun was blotted out, the ozone shield had been augmented with filters. The atmosphere — Ster couldn't smell it from up here but she'd sampled a whiff in training: dank, dim, *morbid*. The birds were long gone but PR geniuses made up for their loss by naming places Sparrow Point, Bluebird Ridge, Eagle Museum, Hummingbird Correctional Institute, Grouse Psychiatric Prison...user-friendly labels for landmarks luxurious beyond anything in the past —

Oh, there were big changes all right. Look at Lake Michigan. Wildly tossing waves — *unh-uh!* Only a noxious, slimy glue with a few mutant fish in it. Lights pierced the brown veil over it — yet she was forced to admit that the houses *(houses???)* were posh — cleverly built with water walls on intricate levels — hey! *What the, heck was that?* An airbus that looked like a *living bird of prey*, skimming flat, sparkly rectangles. Beyond it were some retina-piercing fireflies *(a transport system for her to use,* hopefully?) that bustled and wove in and out of massive, dizzy slices of office buildings — if those rotundas *were* offices — and not grim, sinister *Bastilles* waiting to imprison her —

Holy Christ! The vampire crossed herself *(an old habit* that kicked in when she got nervous).

No picture postcard, Chi was still a world of lives. *Stories yet untold*. Sad ones from the look of it. The ZATS was within striking distance of the pile that sheltered young Fontana (if her data was correct). *Weird!* To think that the real King Arthur was out there somewhere — suffering from the same deluding amnesia *(Sterling squinted and focused)* that afflicted every human life. And his rescuer didn't have ONE CLUE what to do next (her eyes probing, assessing) nor could she blame anyone but herself; *her own big mouth* — for starting it all —

Under pressure of Rysemian interrogation, she had rattled off a fairy tale. They bought it! The Knights of the Round Table — an old canard that H.G. pounced on. Snapped at it like a hungry shark. *"Why, that's just what we need!"* he'd beamed, peering through his specs at her. "No question but that Earth people will give their heartfelt allegiance to *King Arthur and his knights*. The Round Table, the KRT, shall be the *talismanic* center as in days of yore. No more Democrats, Republicans, Lawyers, or Political Correctors! One and all, they'll allow themselves to be *unified*, and *purged of psychotic urges* under Camelot's golden banners programmed by our own SOURCE!" he had raved. Now. Ster's job was to map out a strategy to *intercept the Boy King* because somehow she had to *find* the little bugger—even though loose threads were all she had to go on.

Worse, she only vaguely knew the local mind-set—the specifics of what they ate, read, went nuts over as a fad or (far more important): what they'd *jail* and *execute* you for. Did they give you the rope, the gas chamber, a lethal injection, boiling in oil, the Iron Maiden or what??? She'd arrived only last night; had the initial bafflement of ordering dinner to be dumbwaitered up (a marvelous meal of roasted unknowns which she gulped greedily without question) while sequestering her TTM—which by the way, was no sleek, intimidating DEVICE with panels, lights, switches, cables, ionizer-gears clanking seriously and importantly—*no sir.* Her TTM was very ho-hum looking. *Insignificant!* No more complex than a walnut. Harmless as sand dropping through an hourglass. How it worked—from her Drake bedroom she crosshaired coordinates, then shot anchor points *("flitter")* across a span of years toward the ZATS and Sean Fontana's I.D. ridges. Artifacts were sometimes retrieved at this step. *Sterling had managed to retrieve one—*

(She grinned to herself. When developing the tiny TTM there'd been no funded research lab for O'Blivion, you can bet your boots! The field's top men saved the big rewards for their pets who wouldn't embarrass them by turning out to be better than their masters) but—*cutting to the* chase—it's what suddenly *popped into her hands* last night, that just about blew her mind apart.

It was a book of poetry written years ahead of this day *(Sept. 7, 2123)* by the King himself. Sterling crawled into bed where she read the book from cover to cover, and had to stifle her own delight with it. "A deeply thrilling moment. Sean Fontana's name will one day ring with the very greatest!" was her judgment;

and coming from O'Blivion (*who'd read'm all*) (*and wrote the best*) it was high praise. All the Graces seemed enthroned in Sean's work, which blew her away...his essence, freshness, spontaneity, "Is this kid as good as Shakespeare or how about John Donne?" she wound up fretting, hiding the book very, very carefully. *If she was careless!* If somehow a young poet were to stumble on *one of his own works* which he wouldn't write until *years in the future* – it would be like one false step and, WHUMP! The PARADOX ax. Sean Fontana wouldn't exist. Sterling might be caught between two worlds, or *locked into this year* where the corruption was almost absolute, literally swallowed alive by a BLACK HOLE.

After the impact of Sean's book, she drifted off – tossing and turning in nightmares. Now to clear the mind. What had she learned that an undercover operative (and she was no ordinary one) could use? Salient points...*motifs?*

Aside from the "nasty bits" she'd been warned of – obscenities so chilling she simply could not believe such things existed! – were some spectacular advances. Real ground-breakers.

In 2093 it had been established beyond any scientific doubt that MIND, far from arising from MATTER, is senior to matter. The question *"Is there life beyond the undertaker?"* had finally been answered in the affirmative; it was the greatest achievement of the century but – who cared? There was nothing to come back to. *Nothing to live for.* The kids all doted on a moribund cowboy called Radioactive Joe who promoted SHINE ON!, a cellulose derivative that glowed through your intestines and helped you track down *Badguys.*

Slavery had been restored. The 500 million who couldn't compete were fed, housed, given work and drugs and protected from having to make decisions by bosses who swore to tend them in benevolent fashion in exchange for tax abatement.

Another good thing: abortion was still illegal. The anti-abortionists had won hands down! Because a wonderful alternative had been discovered. You could now buy a quivering fetus nestled in networks of spidery, throbbing veins. It *hadn't been killed* and would live a full lifetime. The Right-to-Lifers were *completely satisfied.* Fetuses were so cheap and plentiful that even THE POOR could enjoy one or two on the mantel – a chic decorator item, easy-to-maintain, perfectly legal, and uttering cute little muted cries for 70 or 80 years if its owner enjoyed pin-jabbing or other forms of molestation. Maybe this arrangement was cleaner than growing up to be a cyberpunk/arsonist/sewer rat/rapist/rapee or one of the maimed toads who spat acid that could put your eyes out *(Ster would watch out for them, you better believe it!)* but who knew? And *who cared?*

Nobody. Yep...*nobody*. Rape itself was unimportant. Everyone experienced it. They'd learned, too, that laws were futile. Any law could be bent into a pretzel, and nothing could be imposed on anyone from outside. Not really. The more jails they built, the more crime skyrocketed but voters didn't care any more. They were exhausted, in apathy.

Morale was at a thousand-year low. Sterling would therefore *walk on eggs,* as she smiled her way through the dismal streets—buttoned into a Metallica jacket. She'd think of it as...searching for clues in a tantalizing mystery. "Okay, honey: you said you wanted a big challenge," she growled at her mirror image brushing her teeth...

First stop—hall of records. Practice fitting in. *Adapt quickly.* She was good at that. The risk was part of the game. If there was no dossier on Sean she'd talk to barkeeps—counting on her "quick study" *savoir faire* to avoid trouble. Inner city smarts! That stuff never changed *(fingers crossed).* With luck she'd get a line on a needle in a haystack—whatever technicalities were involved. And after that...

Oh, he'd need some persuading! It was gonna be a messy job. There had to be some way to arrange a one-on-one with a tough reform school brat—who'd kill her as quick as look at her. This was no jewel-clear King Arthur, with the shining shield and famous sword Excalibur—*shit no!* Fact was, King Arthur was BAAAD this lifetime. But the survival of mankind depended on him. He was the needle to stitch it all together; yet—whatever Sterling told him would be bound to sound downright crazy, criminally manipulative, or both.

Wonderful. Still...

Patton said it was her *moral duty* to bring Sean to Vonderra to make up for her own *blood-drenched past,* and if she pulled it off—she and her soulmate Woolf would be together, forever.

Patton swore it.

Together.

Forever!

What a lilt those words had! And they meant that Woolf was *safe*. Nothing could happen to her or the General would be a *liar*, and Rysemians *did not lie*. And because of that totally exhilarating piece of truth—

For the very first time, the vampire wanted to distinguish herself by gallant service. She *needed* Woolf! She needed the Squad— she *needed a future!* And to have one, she had to help avert the *terrible diaster* that was coming.

Only problem was: find this brat, kidnap or make him an enticing offer, while not letting him *(or anyone else)* kill her down there on those ugly streets—right?

Easy. Nothin' to it.

At the Crucial Moment she'd throw a little cold water into her face and slip into her black sequined evening gown with the black net jacket. Good taste is never out of style *(heh heh)* — and she'd take the little Smith & Wesson that Patton gave her. The jacket just hid its black mesh holster.

(You're not getting out of here alive.)

Oh yes she would! She'd pull a rabbit out of a hat.

Just you wait and see.

But first—

O'Blivion stood staring for the better part of an hour, her eyes moving slowly over the complexes...searching for the one clue she needed.

INTERLUDE

CHICAGO, 2123 A.D.

TWENTY-TWO

In the early 22nd century, war broke out between five "Floating Nations" where the drug Just Say No was processed and packaged. It was an economic war—history's bloodiest.

Giant corporations wrote the pattern on humanity's back.

The Refineries Brat Act (as they called it on the street) was rammed through Congress in an effort to help the two-point-nine million orphans that trickled back from ravaged refineries to Earth's main port, Chicago.

The Wild Child population grew, eight to fifteen thousand arrivals daily. Through bribery, kickbacks and money laundering, new corporations were bestowed. These were named "Guardianship," "Loving Hands," "Home Care," "Mother's Nurture" and so on.

A slot machine had been set up. Dynasties were founded; dazzling fortunes were made. Orphans brought top dollar as boy or girl slaves, toys of various kinds—anything a consumer's fantasy hit on. A few lucky ones were even adopted and cared for.

Sean Eric Fontana got caught in this machine. At six months of age he was sent to something called The Bluebird Baby Farm. He was sold at age ten to a man named Mars Peer "The Master" who put him in a well-appointed "home" with fifty other waifs and strays, shipped by sealed ferry to Rat Island on a raw night, foghorns wailing across choppy Lake Michigan waters that looked the same as 200 years ago except filth-encrusted and fishless unless you count the aquarats they call "acid pismires" that can breed for ten years with cancer of the liver.

His parents gone—phantoms of necrology, their boy's name standing alone on forged documents—Sean Eric Fontana began his career.

Mars Peer, among other dubious trades, sold growth hormone processed from corpses. Sean Eric's job was to operate a feeder-tank that channeled 'floaters' into an extraction press while he avoided picking up one of the virus-induced neurological diseases that had killed thirty million Americans the previous year but were pretty well checked by now.

"My power over you is total," Peer's magnified face told the boys at mealtime. "It may be a short trip from mainland to Rat Island but for you it's an irreversible one. Nobody ever escaped from R.I. back to Chicago nor is anything ever smuggled in or out. Kindly remember that you're here for my purposes and not your own. I paid a fair sum for each of you trainees and intend to get my money's worth."

Peer had sallow skin. He wore a clipped goatee and painted-on brows. It had been a fad ten years earlier.

Buddy was the new AI in charge of training. Buddy herded the kids here and there. Because he was AI Buddy never got tired. He said he'd show the boys what's what. He lined them up naked.

"Everybody sing!" Buddy bellowed, cracking a whip.

They all began singing with great enthusiasm. They sang heartily, with gusto, and Sean Eric sang louder than anybody.

"Push mop, haul butt," the AI laid down the law. "If yer defyin' yer dyin'!" Buddy would yell, his pirate's eye flashing fury.

Hard hours in murky green light, tank stink; food so meager the kids went around hungry as sharks, many suffering from walking pneumonia when the lake mist came up. In the darkness at night Sean Eric could see from his cot, beyond stabbing yardlights, the huddled shapes of Kampong where a smiling mile-high Mr. Rogers sang out "I like you just the way you are" 24 hours a day. Or as Holy Writ told them, "America's past is shadowed with discarded celebrities but our sanctified MR. ROGERS obtains forevermore!"

The boy grew up never having felt the touch of human warmth, humor, affection or even interest. But somehow the brutal routine combined with the tedium and pressing nearness of bodies, didn't crush him as it did some other kids.

The Good Life is based on death they were told, in fact Holy Writ put it best: 'One life and no more, is God's way to keep us kneeling.' Every Thursday they were taken to chapel where the world slid away to reveal the true world, a blazing starfield in velvety space. Sean Eric was transfixed by the sight which lasted only for an instant but was said to be a true replica of How It Used To Be.

"The world is an ugly chaos," Mars Peer lectured. "Ugliness and chaos are beautiful. Thus spake our heavenly father Scaulzo, author of The Holy Writ of the Pagan Worship of Bodies when he ordered us to KILL. You will be trained killers, all of you who live. Among others you'll kill those of the evil new religion teaching that you are not your body! These heretics are fools," Peer's voice rang out. "They deserve the worst of deaths. They deserve horror. Horror shapes our minds in Scaulzo's image. Embrace horror! When you dream, dream horror and the most horrible dream of the week wins an Award on Thursday. ACHTUNG! Repeat after me: A Mafia-Gu has no God but Scaulzo and my body is his temple!"

They'd all file to work repeating the sacred phrase.

Sean Eric developed a sense of honor. Where this came from none could say; it was either a genetic imperative or a different kind of endowment. Uneducated, he knew that Peer was totally mad. He'd already made the connection that such madness must pass for sanity among the adults of the outside world.

He grew up tough but wise, with an easy grace marred by serious faults. Sometimes he felt lonely and troubled. It seemed he had a conscience too tender for a Mafia-Gu; and on Rat Island this was unfortunate. Sean had no desire to hurt, maim, confuse, warp, or play tricks on the other kids here. Why should he? They had enough trouble. Worst of all, he didn't even care to dream up horror stories to win an Award.

New sensations woke in him daily; some he couldn't even name. He began having visionary dreams. Or he'd fall into profound monologue with himself at untimely moments.

Other than these faults, his life went through the usual evolutions like anybody's.

The rations on Rat Island were not only stale but putrid, rancid, often inedible. Buddy would bring Sean yellow beans and other treats from the Master's own table. (The boy being softhearted enough to share this booty with fellow sufferers, he was popular with the other kids—those not yet numbed past feeling.)

Buddy, although AI or "artificial intelligence," had a "human" side. He was attracted to young Sean with his straight nose and charming healthy-looking face and Buddy could always make the child laugh by cracking simple jokes, blowing a lightstream out his ears or calling his name and saying funny things on a bullhorn.

Mornings Buddy hiked the platoon across the small island

crisscrossed with paths protected by banks of lasers.

"Your trade is to kill," he'd echo. He meant: get the job done in a fast, workmanlike way—Buddy's unique system being to yank out the spinal cord with a twist of your ice pick, to avoid needless thrashing and gurgling.

Buddy appointed young Fontana squad commander, gave him an honorary commission and had him put the squad through a concentrated regimen. The job began with the careful stalk, followed by a silent paralyzing or decapitation. Each trainee had to carry a scaled-down Bullpup with a beltful of silver jelly johnnies, lethal at 500 yards. (Total load: 98 lbs.)

After target practice the children slashed the throats of self-sealing dummies, then did 500 pushups in acetone-scented crabgrass (the only vegetation that stubbornly resisted being killed off) under a chocolate drizzle that burnt your skin with stinking whirlwinds of what had once been styrofoam. But still: hobnail-boot mentality and all, Buddy kept a sharp eye on his gang. Although he liked to keep order with a fire hose he was considered a fair enough drill sergeant for Rat Island.

One day he half-killed a trainee, he vegetablized the boy for failure to do knee bends fast enough (and cried at the kid's empty place in mess hall afterward). Buddy's was a "corporate approved personality."

As the great Keynes had pointed out, the market gets what it demands. AI, artificial intelligence came into its own about 2065 when people demanded a 'bright companion' or knowledge machine. Then the blue chip companies, the big multinationals, set up design shops to work out the problem however subtle or complex and gradually began tooling up for that market; the smart ones watching the pioneers lose their shirts and then coming along in the slipstream.

The average buyer demanded a friend or interesting pet, especially a robot android to provide some comfort in this barren, sterile and seared world—one not threateningly brilliant, a buddy not too far above the "Go fetch umbrella!" level, a little pal who could make simple, flattering remarks and appear to enjoy being stroked and confided in. Also, Industry needed this type of a Buddy or tireless helper that could be programmed with a basic learning process until it (or he or she) could do any job in a humanlike way; the only rule being to create a shape that would be simple yet elegant, familiar, and wholly user-friendly or attractive to the human that would buy it.

Buddy with his 800-word vocabulary, crude sense of humor, short neck, yellow pantaloons and black hair plaited in a pigtail like an eighteenth century pirate, along with his barbaric certainty of being "Right" no matter what he did, was admittedly a type of insanity but he was a familiar, non-xenophobic type of insanity. Buddy was a beloved stereotype out of racial memory. For a long time Peer was satisfied with the merchandise. As for Buddy's chief problem area, he "knew" "instinctively" that Sean was in some way elevated above the common subset of unwanted boys and he "loved" (in his own limited fashion) Sean for it.

What is Discretion? The word has never been adequately defined, although most monkeys will reject a blue orange lightly dusted with Chanel No. 5. The biosphere had been ravaged—"The stupid thing proved itself intractably fragile and vulnerable!" as a U.S. Senator complained at his Earth-rape trial of 2050 A.D. However, corporate profits were at an all-time high and the people desperately needed a Buddy. Buddy was a fabricated caveman mentality but one who seemed to be (in a perhaps ironic imitation of his model), "kind" when he felt like it. When he *willed it*, apparently. (*"Will"* being another word that has never been adequately defined.)

When an angry Mars Peer ordered Buddy destroyed for offering favors to Sean Fontana, the fat, middle-aged oaf of an AI tried to run away. But being cornered he sobbed and blubbered, begging that at least he—"it"—be permitted to leave a will in Sean's favor.

But as "it" had nothing to leave and could neither summon help nor defend "itself" as the Master pointed out—the unprotectedness of "its" position made it abundantly clear why The Law, fairest of tools, insists that robots should not have high-speed links to each other (smiled the Master).

"Have you learned your lesson?" sneered Mars Peer.

"No," said Buddy.

Buddy was hacked apart on a refectory table, in spasms and a froth of saliva accompanied by shrieks of pain and terror, the students told that despite this histrionic display Buddy didn't really "feel" anything.

But who is to say? When the light in the AI's eyes went out,

Sean felt a gray sense of loss. The funny android had been the closest thing he'd known to the tenderness of parental love.

That night after Lights Out, Fontana risked a beating. He sneaked back to the refectory and stole what was left of Buddy. He had a feeling the AI would come in handy somewhere down the road. And he was positive he could figure out how to restore his friend.

Sean then made one of the mistakes that had been dogging him recently. He left a note stuck to the table with a knife. The note said: "When valiant Buddy was slain, I The Nameless One stole his corpse. Death to ye who seek it!"

He then stashed the hacked-up remains under a rock at the tip of Rat Island.

And the trainees continued to wolf the slop poured into their bowls twice a day, and nearly a third of them lived to grow up. Sean Fontana would one day become the last great American poet—but not until an evil Fate had run its course.

TWENTY-THREE

There was a library at Rat Island, moldering but not off-limits. Along with thick volumes it had jungles of old computer stuff packed in stasiswrap.

As a "commissioned recruit" Sean was taught reading. Constant practice sharpened the skill. Evenings he'd climb an iron catwalk with some moth-eaten text or other, and study until lights out.

"Members of the uranium-radium series of radioactive elements give off gamma rays when they disintegrate to form new elements. In 1950 the Soviets harnessed this gamma, developing an augmented product to control human behavior. When the USSR ended, others took over research—"

Then came a power struggle. With no winners as far as Sean could see. Acid rain dissolved the polar caps, it now cost 10K credits to produce a cup of drinking water. Deforestation was total. Animals were extinct. The last of what they called "deer" was poacher-eaten or trophyized. Illiteracy was state-approved. Sean learned that Earth had been called "the watery blue gem" before twenty billion people used its water as a latrine. Today all water was laced with bad chemicals and human waste beyond fixing.

He learned about Just Say No, the most powerful and effective drug ever produced. A conglomerate called Biolazer by sharing expenses with three nations, perfected an advanced form of the Russian product, spliced it into a program called Blaze that activated Sleepbox that was the source of the far-reaching Just Say No that could pervade any wall no matter how thick, penetrating private homes and working directly on the synapses.

Just Say No was a force so powerful it destroyed its inventors. The street name brownie, sledge, suckeye or JSN, boded a dependency addiction that caused horrible withdrawal symptoms until a fresh dose eased the agony.

Sean wiped his face with a sleeve; the switchpole was thrown — neither laws nor armies could halt a monster adored by Society! A younger consortium gradually brought things under control. These gents called themselves The Kosmic Providers. Their earnings were anything but modest.

Mars Peer used on his recruits (including Sean) a type of *JSN* that had been "liberated" from federal grunts; an outlaw band CIA who started an industrial firm and called it Spytek Ltd. — demonstrating that lack of imagination that was to cause their swift extinction.

Sean was passionately curious about the world outside R.I. and his eyes recorded, his mind remembered. The shelves of dusty books opened up vistas of imagination. "Heading for Apple Harvest" — what sort of event might that be? His thoughts glowed and burned when some old book talked of "early rosy-fingered dawn," or "leaping trout" or "the fifty yard line" or an odd phrase like: "All for love and the world well lost"; or reading about "Cable TV" from 200 years past.

Cubes taught the trainees something different. "To kill cheap is prime. *JSN* can do it but *JSN* carried on amplification wave — only gov't and school can afford that. For you, cheapest and best is your simple razor gash across the throat."

Sean learned well, but failed to extract the fundamental information for the conduct of his life from what they taught him. He'd heard of a hoary tome called The Book of Books, and tried to lay hands on it but learned that Scaulzo the current God (worshipped in parts as Satan) had changed it backward into Holy Writ. And to question Holy Writ was unheard of.

Sean was seeking truth. It seemed there were power plays going on everywhere — the important ones not on any simple, obvious plane. The idea acted like a great magnet to the pupil.

In body he grew lean and hard. In spirit, he was becoming untouchable. He learned patience, to shrug off pain and not be affected by passing upsets.

Peer gave him daily doses of *JSN*, had him taught every way to seek and destroy but could never trap his mind. Sean practiced controlling his body from outside so if worst came to worse there'd be an escape route.

Evenings he was free to use programmers — a ton of junk left over from the old days of computer hacks. He accessed United Brain a hot new database for subatomic DNA manipulation; also multipurpose stasis field that augmented the disease Rottenface used to kill millions in China and Cambodia this year.

Soon he could access Eastbase itself, where the 800 Gulf stretched its greedy canyons. In the same month he fell in love with quantum mechanics, the French Impressionists, a hoary formula that said: "Power Equals Force Times Distance Over Time" — and with God. Soon God spoke to him nightly.

"Read Sir Thomas Malory; read John Donne," God advised.

Malory wasn't there but Donne ignited a fever in Sean.

All this time, a trainee had to sit for ten minutes each morning with the helmet strapped on and the octopus sucking his skull. But luckily hypnotics and the rarer forms of subliminal coercion were considered too expensive for the riffraff at Rat Island.

Learning was implemented by old-fashioned methods: the cheapest and best being flogging, mild starvation or having the hands tied to the feet, and soon the pupil could have infiltrated a citadel if need be. (Unknown to Peer he could "infiltrate" every spot on the island including the subcellar torture ovens used only on hardcases.)

The boy worked, scratched. He wanted it bad — with hardly a notion as to what "it" could be. There was a hunger in Sean; an inner grief as if he missed something but had forgotten what. And somehow this attracted Peer's personal attention.

"Clean him up" said the Master with distaste. "Comb his hair, find proper clothes, get the stink out! " Spitting into a silk handkerchief.

Peer said he hoped much of Eric. "I am impressed. You have the look and feel of a winner."

"Sir!"

"I had your 'Valiant Buddy' note framed," pointing to a wall. "You thought I didn't know which boy did it?"

Peer's lips had been augmented. Today they were a red, shapely, moist Cupid's bow. His eyes were lowered.

"Tell me — where did you hide the 'body'?"

Sean stood quietly, arms folded.

"No matter for now," Peer said. "We prove your effectiveness. Cut you into the bundle. Key to your future."

Sean stood respectfully. "Most humble," he said.

"You'll train as industrial spy. Highest profit potential dealing in information and other intangibles."

Sean said: "My honorable Master does me honor" as he had been trained.

Angry but hiding it. Despising himself for kowtowing.

He was now seventeen, magnificently muscled, with a dark fiery eye. A quiet observer who accepted hardships with stoic endurance.

Peer didn't want to let him go just yet for some reason.

"Welcome to a brutal world. It can be comfy when we learn how to milk it," smiling at Sean over a tall drink.

"Thank you very much, sir."

"A man needs large ambition and burning desire to get the good things in life. Do you want the good things in life, Sean Fontana?"

"I do very much sir."

"Good. Thanks to me you've become adept in all techniques of slaying. Now the simulation ends, the real thing begins so don't let me down, my boy. Sign this paper. A little technicality that came with your original file."

He wrote his name, Sean E. Fontana in the indicated blank.

Peer noted the stubborn angle of the jaw but was convinced Sean could be bought, or intimidated, just like anyone.

But somewhere along the line, Fontana had developed a few crazy, ideas. He dreamed he was the son of an alien King (in fact like all healthy kids was positive of it). With God's help — the old Celtic God in the books — he was going to pull the fangs of this tyrant!

Sean had grown up old-fashioned; believing in some kind of a half-forgotten, weird old, strange, moss-grown, moral justice out of the past. (Maybe because no Religious Rightist ever tried to browbeat the idea into him.)

The Master was a buffoon with drooping mustache, painted brows and now these wet-red-cherry lips of a courtesan. He was also a cowardly bully excessively rich from ooze imports, black market drugs, torture, murder, extortion, kidnapping and more.

The Master knew no compassion for any living thing, and that would be his ruin. Sean detested the man. To get free of Peer had become his sole aim.

TWENTY-FOUR

"Learn the ropes. We'll call you" Sean was told.

He was taken by launch to Pier 81, put ashore and directed to a flophouse in the Wilson Avenue cinderblock slums. His keeve was a closet, unplumbed and unheated but the new Designer Slaughterer (D.S. Degree) considered it a palace.

He was closely monitored. To cut and run would be suicide. But Sean was happy. Drinking the heady wine of freedom. Bent on a course that meant real freedom if he worked slowly, indirectly. But like every orphan he had that scar in the hollow of his left foot where a compellor had been surgically installed.

It was THOTSTIM, electronic thought stimulator not as effective as *JSN* as far as control went but used by Peer as a backup. Sitting on his bunk the boy cut out the compellor with his knife— bleeding and crying like a stuck animal but he did it. Afterward he limped for a week.

His delight was short lived. Chi was a Speedway with a dehuman-language to learn: Speedtalk. He practised in the mazelike streets of a clawing, struggling inferno where ignorant men, having iconized drug world violence, then produced an ever more numbing complexity of tribal rules: conventions whipping in and out, coitus in doorways, impacted trash homes, grotesque dead animals modeled in concrete, INGESTA joints catering to poppers with methane tanks strapped to their backs (humanity had sent its message to the stars: 'Give us your addicts, the wretched refuse of your teeming shores' and the stars happily obliged).

Skinny panderers howled "Take me on a slab!" when you came near, mercs and craunches begged you to "Scarf me tender! or lose the scrote," hookers retailed themselves. There were gangs of ivory skulls, flesh vendors of every stripe, pimps with fly eyes (biopolyterpene grafts: absolute state of the art and worth a pimp's ransom), yokels of baroque description babbling languages that were vaguely unsettling to Sean, he couldn't say why.

He tramped the Nightglow looking at ingenious new devices. Americans had pulled off many stupendous achievements along with degeneracies. Chicago was a fantastic great center of interplanetary trade where under pressure of history, Gov't had become wholly the function of markets.

Sean saw much that was ferocious, nauseating, mawkish or enough to lift the hair on your neck: a cloot (starving illegal E.T.) going through garbage in a vacant lot, twelve foot high with four-foot grab claws and a hide reflecting larval images of the remote parts from whence it came. He watched the dreaded Sapphic Police bust a gang of ten-year-old cyberjocks who were ripping off the soft shop downstairs of him. All rot-faces lived off the gov't, also the skullmugs with acid spit. All malformed lived free. It was poetic justice maybe. But not for the squeamish. It was "very big chic" to have the flesh of the face or head partly removed. The trendies did it. They did it to their babies as well. The little skeletons would grin at you, horribly.

In a month Sean had changed, was a 'new man' among the people, knew the Underbelly like he knew the periodic chart, knew the nuances of street talk along with gutter wisdom and alley sleaze, all kinds of trivia, silly fads (just now the public enjoyed sucking odorous Retro crow eggs through peppermint sticks). Many of his friends were Megapox victims (AIDS 'cured' so the victim didn't die but lived 70 years sick) and others were old, poor, friendless flophouse neighbors. These, he'd bring food and help with little jobs. He'd be called 'foolish' and 'stupid' if some others knew it but Sean really loved these poor, simple, uneducated, unwanted folks and there were a lot of them, among tens of thousands getting fat on crime in this citadel of the damned.

Often he felt lonely. Abandoned. Like what he was: a lonesome kid in a lonely town yearning for real companionship, tenderness, "somebody to talk to" and above all he wanted to make love; not with anyone but with Her, the person he sensed was out there for him.

Sean thought about sex, hope, poetry, philosophy, and God. But God had stopped speaking to him. Maybe he was growing up. But it wasn't as good.

One cold night, "Need help, Zoo Man?" a youth asked.

"If it's free."

"Stink?"

"Sure."

They drank some kind of not-bad civit in round glasses with stones in the bottom and the young man Martin became Sean's guide. He was from Winnetka, had a steel hatchet embedded in his forehead and a living goldfish growing out of his fly, and a friend Loyce a husky very tall Chinese boy who wore his penis in a paincuff and whose girlfriend Emma had a beating heart wired in her lilac hair. Emma was one of the skullfaces with burning eyes, she herself had many friends in permanent bondage, lips stitched, wrists grafted together. They sported pimples, ornate garb.

And they had paralyzed minds. They'd worshipped Horror for so long they turned into it. None would survive another year. They were "the Cool" strung out on neurological painposts. Chi was a deathbed, the dying hanging on through inertia and interplanetary looting.

Martin beckoned.

"Come," he grinned.

Martin lived for taking risks. He knew just what you can do and can't do and how to get around the latter. He looked undernourished but handled himself well.

On the way to Mimi's on North Clark they were jumped by a bejeweled gang out for fun—Sean's prestige soaring when he did what came naturally.

The Jewelies weren't killed but they wouldn't do it again soon.

"You're damned good!" said Martin.

"I'm educated by the worst."

Through the arcade and nostalgia den where you could buy anything, imports, swink teeth with the authentic mold, dried bodies of small ET's, rocks from volcanic Io, insect lust, miraged messages from other worlds, the skeleton of a four year-old child. Black plunder. Spasm logo. The haunting wail of an animal recorded light years away. A "radiator cap" from a bygone era. Chips of the 2002 Bears game. Bones of human-like offshoots, GENETAP. Barrels of KY-jelly, rubber gloves, sex fantods, leather goods, a silk cravat, an old IBM PC stained with real "coffee."

At Mimi's a woman came up to him. "Do you know the force to which all the universe bows its knee?"

"What?" It was noisy in there.

"You seek what is lost."

"Yes, I do."

"And you want to escape the tyrant."

"That's right!"

"Take this, the ultimate magic. Meditate it. Expect a miracle. A fine payoff. Tear up the devil tree!"

It was a small Jesus, real flesh or looked like it—it had real blood running wet and sticky where the wrists, feet and side were pierced. She wrapped it in linen. "No, no money." Sean thanked her, slipped the bloody thing in his pocket and followed Martin who was getting impatient.

"Don't get caught in here," Martin warned. Then he hoisted his body into the blankets. Martin loved taking risks! Sean looked around becoming intrigued—he'd never been in a real nesting place before. Slot yer dick and doan get sick. Mimi's subteen girls 'n boys. (Some much older than the ads claimed.) A jungle-rot of hype, God is alive but She's crazy, somersaulting neon. Try to get one for your home real soon (with a grinning freakface). Drug adverts, Glom is ton but shuddy's yer buddy. WE BUY GOLD. When doors close...SKINDAD.

A hooker wearing antique fur wrap, last of the big cats, grabbed Sean and kissed with her tongue—feet planted ankle-deep in styrofoam kicking around 100 years, can't destroy it or get rid of it, the future feeds on the past—while another puta hiked her knee up and beckoned. She'd been sipping a cherrybulb with augmented lips but now also grabbed Sean and kissed with her tongue, his unscarred flesh attractive to them—They signaled each other.

"Twist. What else matters" the second one whispered in his ear.

He'd have gone with her but fearing disease, wished he had not come.

The first—she had wide maniacal eyes. She felt him and the two made eye signs, looking at Sean's earnest face and the way his muscles bulged under his shirt. They looked at each other, laughed, shrugged, let him go.

He was a bit shocked to learn that Martin had no compunction about gratifying his lusts with any puta free or bonded. Comically maniacal, Martin devoured exotic bowls of glop, blanket hopped and got everything he came for. Then outside, some round-shouldered old looters crooked their rheumy fingers at them and poked out their gray tongues, smack-smack.

This was no crumbling decadence but a flourishing one, a youth culture even though some of the richer 'youths' were well over 90 with the new metabolism. Here Sean learned to dawdle, to loiter; to kick back, to loaf, to hang out, to glom but not to gencrack.

Then one night came the Master's steely voice, "I have a project you'd fit into."

Sean cursed and sweated, he longed for escape more than anything—disgusted with himself for tolerating the iron collar of serfdom but how could he break out? Peer would hunt him down. He needed what the woman said, a magic miracle.

He took out that figure of Jesus she'd given him, unwrapped it, and meditated it. Was this a kinder, gentler answer? Or was it a bloody hoax? He'd find out soon.

Life wasn't worth a squat with Peer breathing down his neck. He needed time to plan something.

TWENTY-FIVE

Designer slaughter. A fine art with subtle components, Peer had taught.

The new D.S. was issued a plinker lasergun now tucked in his waistband, told to memorize the map of Gary that was pinned to a smoky wall and tonight: the dreaded moment had come. Sean walked on cracked cement 200 years out of use (rumored as a "Freeway," it had bulwarks and illegible signs that he planned to come back and study).

Crossing a reserve he heard hoarse shouts, the crowd rushing through stinking air that came from a delousing station. Eight sets of eyes peered out of a cage strung up over an alley—the ground slippery with incandescent vomit caused by the drug Ozolysergimorphine product of splicing, common name Ooze. Sean took pains not to step in any, then on turning a corner found himself at the address he sought.

A tall, gloomy pile stripped of all but the basics. The ground floor was a shoddy glitterworks worked by gangs of subteen pros. Sean was making his way through these kiddie hustlers and johns when a guard, looking at him narrowly, pointed him aside.

Hands on the table.

Sean kept absolutely still while being frisked and was surprised when the cop ignored the plinker and blackjack and waved him on (so what was the cracker looking for? if not a slash-'em-bloody and a new laser pistol, all street legal).

The "job" itself took no more than three minutes. It ran like this:

He went up a spiraling catwalk in this tall shell, nothing but girders in rushing wind, that the gloom of the hour made bleak and eerie, and he saw four men standing talking.

One of them was Sausage, recognized by his incredible nose.

He was a squinty, thin, pockmarked, short-sighted guy with bottle-bottom specs. He never stopped smiling. The others were tall welldressed sullen-looking people, one of whom gripped Sean's hand as he said: "This is the lad who found it, Mr. Chairman."

Sausage's eyes lit up. "So you really have it at last?"

"Yes" the boy nodded, wondering what "it" was that the man wanted so badly.

The other three walked away casually but quickly.

"Let's have it then," Sausage chuckled, holding out his hand.

Sean made a gesture of reaching for something. He closed on the target but instead of handing over the thing Sausage yearned for, what he gave him was the steel finger: a needly shove. Just enough to send the man staggering back.

At the edge, Sausage dropped off screaming—eyes and mouth wide open: Sean went to the edge, looked over (mistake number one) and watched his victim turn head over heels waving arms and legs, thrashing violently for what seemed like a very long time, with a cry that got fainter and fainter as he went down. Then finally, Blap! He exploded on the hard surface.

Sean had closed the books on a living person.

He went down feeling shame for the first time in his life. The Just Say No softened his panic a little, by making it hallucinatory. A target simply went down the air, exploded on the sidewalk and that was it; no remorse, no time to examine your feelings. But he'd bear the scars from now on—as despair, an inability to concentrate. Part of what Peer had done to him that couldn't be cut out.

The Law was waiting downstairs.

The Master had said "You'll be out before they finish booking you" but Sean was interrogated (not intensively. The police always shut their eyes to data concerning political links to organized crime, which this surely involved). He got ten years, served two weeks and was sprung.

His next job would be more in his own control, said Peer who was full of apologies for the slip-up. "But two weeks is nothing is it?" and,

"Give him what he wants! Fancy clothes, drugs, aircar, the medals he so richly deserves. Anything!" Peer cajoled.

Sean refused gifts. He'd learned many things both in and out of jail. He was sick with disgust for killing a "little guy," a low-impact, shabby nondescript who was unarmed and unaware. He swore to get out from under Mars Peer (having a pretty good idea of the method Peer would use to inflict punishment if his suspicions were aroused).

Ten hours later the Master sent him on another run, this time to assassinate a certain Mr. Wrass, head of "Channel" industrial spy network, an expanding operation that had become a threat to Peer's own empire.

TWENTY-SIX

His boots on the stairs.
Outside, raw winter. A cold mean wind. Traffic heavy, the scum of the Speedway panhandling in night shadows. Hydrogencell cabbies raking it in from overflow of jammed theaters.

Something nagged at Sean's mind—the dead weight of the brainwash Peer poured on him.

"The corruption of the human soul is total, boys. Let every cyberzit rejoice! People need a good war; it brings us near the Throne of Scaulzo. His crown is flashing chrome.

"Humans are puppets. Horror lends us the dignity we deserve. The world is a great Mystery we can never know. So don't be afraid to hurt your victims bad. Hurt them! Go deep. Hurt them bad. Bring on the nightmare. People must die. Give them a boost. A man without the mantle of decadence is not a man. He's a joke! Don't let it go to your head. Keep those lips pointing down. Ugliness sells. Hurt your victim. Piss on him every time. Eat ooze. Be like bright chrome. Hurt them bad. Use a nouveau whip. Put them away. Scaulzo's jism is your key to money," and on without respite.

He passed the chapel where they prayed to the giant mainframe brain "that controls us all," a machine with horned temples and an impenetrable security veil. Nobody'd ever seen it but all lived in quaking fear of it. Its worshippers destroyed themselves in exciting ways. Sean smelled burning flesh.

The church next door was bordered on all sides by a 19th-century iron picket fence. It sold religious software and did kabuki howling, praying to the Giant Crystal—next to a holoporn den belching the electrifying excitement of ivoryskulled "death's-head" men accompanied by swivel-hipped silkladies with barlight twinkling on many chains, whips, belts: plus hungry kids with shriveled faces running numbers or working tricks, rubbing shoulders with the embattled political subcult of the moment.

"Are you a cockpit fighter?" a boy yelled at Sean.

Chi was a surface city but N.Y. and D.C. were subterranean (waiting for the apocalypse that would surely come), millions puppetized permanently by consensual images of horror linked with the "Old-New/Religion Body-Worship" — but tonight Sean wouldn't worry about sociology! Just follow orders.

Tinny music roared from open doors.

Feather your nest. Be a corpologist. Get out of hell. Eerie radiance of signs reflected in glowing puke. It was a pleasure neighborhood with bizarre hiding places for moribund junkies.

This man Wrass: he'd been a court eunuch in his youth, Sean had learned, but was rich and powerful now, vast holdings in electronics and reputed to be sole owner of an interstellar cargo line. A whole different ballgame than poor murdered Sausage.

Sean took the beltway to where the specified Calder revolved gracefully, a birddog on his wrist tuned to Mr. Wrass's neural flitter.

He entered the pavilioned luxury of the ground-floor Star Club. No kiddie pops here, only Nice People — Sean had heard of them and didn't trust them.

A clannish circle doted on a naked Erogene in limelight. "She" was singing coyly.

A hostess greeted Sean. He feared getting bounced but no. Took the outside lift to the penthouse. A sweeping view that stunned. This Calder was a floating ziggurat of posh flats and play areas, silken purlieus of a wealth Sean hadn't imagined existed — his first goal being to cope with the culture shock.

He was supposed to be a human murder machine. But without the JSN, he'd cut and run.

The first chamber he sneaked into, happened to be a template at zero g. that fooled his birddog and made his ears go Pop! There was an empty web cradle with underthings including a bra and lace panties (first he ever saw) rising out of it — him bouncing off a wall, somersaulting into the stairwell grabbing for a railing and cursing this rich man's condo that had everything. He lost precious minutes riding drifts, seeking a bridge between grays, his wrist piece locked on source. Its soft buzz said Wrass was very close. Which meant evil tricks would come down.

Then he found it. A woman sat at a console partitioned off by rich hangings. Security guard? Her mind was jacked in so firmly he could have walked up and clubbed the poor cowgirl but it being so simple to glide past, she couldn't be the guard.

Sean verified with his thumb that the knife was still sharp, the cosh still heavy (he'd taken a short length of lead and carved a nice hand piece for it), all backed up by his issue plinker. The buzzer assuring him that he'd indeed entered the personal lair of the tycoon himself.

First an atelier, cave-black. Sean's bloblight picked out a few pleasant objects and one awful one: a man's face, authentic, dry, extremely well preserved. Sean had truly breached the private glitterworks.

He prowled a sauna. The Roman tub was living tissue (he'd never had a tub bath but knew about the pleasures of it) in a room of polished splendor such as he'd never even dreamed about.

Three doll children were sleeping on the leaves around a lily pond. That stunned him! He touched their hands, warm, "alive," he knew they'd be totally real when activated. Bumping into three high-cost "chidren" made him shudder. It was marvelous to see but it set the young killer's teeth on edge.

Through an archway, round a corner, the birddog confirming directions. Then into a passage that curved, the ceiling made of swirling fog. Dark in there except for a luminous strip along each wall.

It seemed too easy. Sean forced himself to stop and listen. His second skin of caution was prickling. He wanted to get out of here. The passage ran about forty yards ahead, ending in a stone wall it would seem. There was a door off to the side that could be a dummy.

Suddenly a light went on. Sean saw that the left wall was a bank of bottles richly gleaming. His eye widened, slid along the row.

A rustle of movement—a hand grabbed his hair, jerked his head backwards, gunmuzzle jabbing into one ear.

"Lookin fer sumthin, punk?"

"Package for the kitchen, sir."

"Drop it easy."

A red explosion went off behind his eyes. Sean steadied his breathing.

"Careful, sir; Mr. Wrass won't like this egg scrambled."

He displayed just enough panache to gain one second, which he used to brace his body and twist, driving the steel through muscle and cartilage avoiding rib bones...a reflex drilled with Buddy so often it had become second nature.

Standing, he examined the corpse slumped on its knees. Flabby bodyguard type reeking of one of the R-drugs, playing the empty flute. Twenty seconds ago alive. Now, limp meat.

This was the second man Sean had killed. He decided he hated it more than anything, more even than dying himself —

The *JSN* was kicking in with its directive. He went on down the hall, mouth cottony from the blow on the head.

TWENTY-SEVEN

The hall dead-ended.

Sean carefully retraced his steps around the corpse and into the bathroom module. He stood listening, nerves tight. No way to go except out. His birddog had been jammed.

He worked off some frustration by slicing a hole in the black glass with his laser—a safety shot. Hate to go scrambling on handholds in the cold but he had to cut a path to Wrass one way or another. He stuck his head out. Bone-chilling! The wind tore, but it was fabulous. And there'd be no guard up here.

The assassin climbed through the hole. His eyes swept a crazy panorama.

Then bang, his habit kicked in.

Sean could easily fall into another 'state.' Feeling high, soaring on air, ecstasy, swoon of rapture, after all he was a poet wasn't he? And Peer was a fool to go sending a mere poet to do a man's job (he grinned) looking out to where the wheatfields had been, and before them the prairie with teepees on it.

"Now" was a seedpod blazing with light, from scintillating Calders rotating gently on cables stretching into infinity, monster edifices built on corroded remains of steel-gut skyscrapers built on historic cemeteries full of lost love grieved over and prayed for until the bones spilled out—

He yelled in the wind. "What is the highest purpose in life?"

And the wind yelled back: "Scaulzo's a liar! Drowning your brain in horror and drugs is for the impotent."

And he yelled, "Hey Scaulzo. The wages of conformity are death! I'm not your mind-blown slave! I can attain ultimate knowledge of EVERYTHING and I swear on this fat decayed old city that I, Sean Fontana, son of an alien King will free myself and my people down there—"

He crawled a few yards. "If I survive tonight, that is," he added quietly. Then taking a chance on location he sliced his way back in.

It was a small room with a cozy fireplace, one door. His bird-dog useless, he put a shoulder to the door and cracked it.

Darkness. Then a snarl.

Through the black sprang a blacker mass. Something ferocious grabbed his boot, rearing so fast it knocked the breath out of Sean. He tightened his muscles and leaped, saving his life.

The attacker zeroed right in, Sean feeling he'd dropped into a cement mixer, fighting for life, trying to avoid those punishing jaws — heaving sideways, firing into the thing's metal casing; armored plates curling away in a whiff of scorched circuits.

He thumbed the blob light.

The attacker had been a vicious-looking mimetic Doberman now blown to smithereens, twitching and smoking. Sean extracted himself from the stinking remains breathing hard, hands streaked with blood. HIS blood.

"Help you over here," said a male voice.

Light came from a high source, revealing a cutaway shelf of opulence that stupefied. This was a mod room full of kinetic sculpture, huge 3.D art, colonnades, two massive staircases curving up flight after flight all decked with real fruit-trees —

Hundreds of off world hides, looking soft as ermine but all of them over thirty feet long, were scattered and piled on onyx floors. The sheer luxury made Sean's jaw drop. A spotlight picked out one man standing at a long table cradling a thunder chicken.

"Looking for action, Beauty? You were expected," he said pleasantly.

The man wiped his lips. He'd been having a meal. It was a giant cauliflower and broiled leg of something very big with two forks stuck in it. Everything was set with silver and crystal on shining cloth.

"Hands in plain sight" he ordered, throwing away the napkin without shifting his eyes.

Those eyes. Sean knew it was the tycoon from cubes he'd seen. Eye muscles elongated so the orb could swivel stylishly. Horrible for a minute but you got used to it. You didn't get used to the lips, writhing like worms.

"Congratulations on destroying my guard dog. A superb job"

said Wrass. The 'dog' had bitten Sean three times bad enough to mention. He was bleeding heavily, cursing himself for letting it happen. Wrass said,

"This is talent. Want to come work for me? At a large advance of course. I can buy your contract. Your boss and I are old friends. Tipple me?"

Eric stared, not knowing what to say. The man looked him up and down the whole time. His weapon was a pulse gray Wesson with a mouth made of red copper one molecule thick; as devastatingly efficient as it was priceless, the young assassin knew.

"Sure, do yourself big favor," Wrass winked. He had a disfigured, syringe-bulb face with those trendy additions, the eyes and lips.

He stared, split tongue poked between those lips. Masklike face, powdered, nerves cut for style, rougy cheeks, leather gloves with rubber fingers.

"You're a man eater?"

"Neg." The intruder shook his head.

"Well shall we sit down and talk it over?"

"Neg," scowling.

"Care to twist then? I've dealt with literally hundreds of young men exactly like you so don't be shy undressing."

Wrass's breath hissed in his odd teeth. Sean had heard the question before.

"Crawl in the hole" he said. He needed lessons in diplomacy.

Wrass didn't show anger but said: "I'm quite serious. What a pleasure meeting a lad willing to take lethal ricks for rock bottom pay. I can do more for you. Give you so much a young man needs. Everything that is valuable. I see you staring at my thunderchicken. How'd you like to have it, or one just like it?" He held the weapon out for Sean. "Come! It's yours. Everything I have could be yours beauty."

What should he do, Sean wondered, lead the devil on waiting for an opening? Tics made Wrass's mouth squirm all the time — when a lip pulled away, Sean saw a double row of upper teeth. That was it. The teeth weren't teeth at all but a new trend, toothlike fingers: manipulators.

"Well?"

Sean gave a resigned nod. "I'll convey the message to my boss, see if he'll sell me."

"He will. I'm sure of it. Now how about dinner?"

"Thanks, not hungry."

"I think I understand," said the magnate in sad tones. "What a heartbreaker this world is. You won't come to me. No. You haven't a grain of intelligence. You don't have the faintest notion what's going to happen to you out there. Do you know what they'll do to a lad like you? You'll be lucky if you're merely thrown into poverty. Shall we say you won't die of natural causes. Are you listening to me now?"

Sean stared at the grotesque mouth that must have cost a king's ransom.

"Yes" he said.

"See my need! Scarf me tender," the tycoon begged.

"Don't put your money down a dry well," Sean told him.

"The importance of financial security is something you may not have had time to consider—"

Maybe there was a smooth way of handling this but Sean didn't know it.

"Get shred!" he snapped.

Wrass shook his head. "I'm afraid you don't have the requisite good manners. And so—"

He stretched out one gloved hand. Sean's whole body went tense but Wrass was only reaching for a glass that glinted, erupted sparks. He tossed off the contents in a gulp, wiped his mouth and said, "Well by God! It's been a pleasure. I've enjoyed this talk with a lovely murderer who is now headed for the little old graveyard behind the church, hey boy?"

Sean jumped, a split second before the gun's hollow stutter. It cracked mirrors, shook the room as a wall and some columns vaporized.

The youth dove under a table that partly shielded him from flying fragments. The air where he'd been exploded and burnt with an ozone smell. Sean rolled and came up behind Mr. Wrass. He shot him in the head, killing him instantly.

TWENTY-EIGHT

Wrass's eye, the right one, dropped off its stalk and went rolling across the floor—a touch Sean would spend many nights trying to forget.

He escaped down a service shaft. He ran in shadows but the law was close behind. They chased him across lawny tissues of a park, cornering him with sharp-toothed cyberhounds.

Captured, he got his bloody gashes sewn up and was questioned for four hours. He was sentenced to ten years in a maximum security prison. He argued that Wrass and his bodyguard would have killed him. The law said that breaking and entering, followed by murder with deadly weapons, were intolerable acts and Sean must suffer.

The doors clanged shut. Suffer he did, for nine dragging days.

Prison escapes can be arranged. This one was arranged; but during his nine days Sean was given a Morality Course by a group of Concerned Citizens.

"You mustn't be bad any more. Crime does not pay," they told him.

"Just say no," they told him, wagging their fingers. They showed him clips of real, green lawns, blue lakes and "sunset" with ranchers laughing as they went home for "supper."

They told him: "Every tree was cut down although trees generated oxygen. Your ancestors did this. The sun used to be unaugmented. You could smell growing things grow. There were viands known as 'pecan pie' and 'sweetcorn on the cob.' There were flowing rivers. Even a dust storm would be welcome to us now. Even a little fly, to walk on your hand."

They showed pictures of couples wandering in something called 'a woodland park.'

"Just say no! If only your grandparents had followed that sensible advice," they told him.

The sorrows of the lost world were piled on Sean's head by earnest social workers; but he could hardly envision it. He agreed that his ancestors should have said "No" to the murder of his planet, but wasn't convinced that the good life was beyond his reach.

Mars Peer made profuse apologies. "Nine days, it wasn't a lifetime. Now whatever you want is yours. Anything at all."

Sean refused the gifts but took the credits, hoping some day to buy freedom. Meantime he'd survive and keep a sharp eye. But then the worst thing of his life happened.

Peer was sending him on what was called a Time hit. Not one person in a billion had made that jump; and he had to do it next week. Peer's client must be richer than the entire nation to buy a service like this.

Sean was appalled to learn that his victim was a woman.

The mark, single-named GUINEVERE, was a singer, a Russian rock star. Touring in the U.S., she had played Chicago about 200 years ago. Sean would have to bring back her head! Or lose his own.

He would do it fast without thinking. Then he'd grab the credits and get out; flee to one of the orbiting cities while Peer celebrated his victory. He'd be in a far better position with three kills under his belt. He'd want to STAY there in the past among all those green trees, rivers, and no Just Say No — but he'd be haltered. The Snapback would give him limited time to do the job, so: no use crying about it.

For I.D. purposes Peer sent a video made long ago in Moscow.

The woman was dressed in tank top and cut-offs. She was working on an old Marine buttkicker he recognized from films. She was swinging a hammer to knock dents out of it. She was drinking a soda. You could read the name on the can. Pepsi!

Why did Peer want this Guinevere dead? Her hair was tucked under a fatigue cap. She had nicely muscled arms, tanned by the clean sun of yesterday. Here she ran along the surf; now walked barefoot in a wet jacket on a rainy night off Red Square as they called it. Here she studied with her parents and schoolboy brother. Now she drove a reaping machine: a golden image with grease on one cheek. Sean longed to touch the back of that neck where the reddish hair curled prettily.

The old film unrolled, Sean eyeballing the Russian's charms—he'd never heard of "rock & roll" or its interim offshoots—this one done to the rebel yell of a poet called Yevtushenko: and the woman, his mark! He had never seen anything so beautiful. Sean played the tape over and over. Guinevere was a few years older than he with fine brows, good cheekbones. Her performance was an electric jolt. The words were foreign but there was no question that she had humor and a childlike sense of wonder. Her murderer was spellbound.

She projected every quality he'd always admired—honesty, vigor, sweetness of heart. Those laughed-at values in a stained, coughing world.

And her voice! Pure innocence but oh. What a paradox. The voice was clear spring water—laced with raw sexuality. An arrow aiming straight at Sean's loneliness with every line drawn clear! No wonder ten million adorers had felt just the way he was feeling—for more than 200 years.

"Give me a day or two to work out an approach," he said to Mars Peer.

"You have until Friday. Just keep the plan simple."

TWENTY-NINE

Studying the video was supposed to help Sean plan Guinevere's death. But could it happen?

He spent hours memorizing the rock star's face, noticing every little thing about her. Her performance was sheer genius. All magic and terror. He exulted in her great signature-sound and body gestures, flaming hair, facial expression, her eyes speaking to him alone. Most of all he wanted to protect Guinevere.

From what? From Sean Fontana.

She was mysterious, famous, glittering and beloved; could communicate with masses of people. She was unattainable—but thrillingly sexy, dead 200 years but mad about Sean. He fantasized until the fantasy became real.

It was no coincidence. They were made for each other. He saw her walk in the door and heard her say "Sean Fontana, I want you NOW! I love your body." Then! Words could never tell how they did it. A sublime coitus! His virgin flesh virgin no more. Guinevere was his woman. Then came ten thousand ever more delirious days together. She enflamed him and made the joy rise in his soul. She needed him with a subtle, burning passion to match his own. But more than that. They'd become a team! They'd do deeds he couldn't now imagine and many years from today—he'd die for Guinevere. But he would never kill her! Never! No matter what the penalty.

He was a lot more afraid of losing Guinevere than of what Peer might do to him.

So what option did he have? Only one. She would remain unmolested, and he—he'd kill Mars Peer. The time had come. The Russian singer's WHACK was set for Friday.

Sean didn't fear death but didn't exactly welcome it with open arms either. He could put distance between himself and Peer maybe but...a life on the run would be the best he could hope for. So there was no choice.

He'd already figured a method to do it.

For years Peer had savaged Sean's mind with the electronic drug, Just Say No. Now the youth would turn the tables. How? By merely accepting that poison inflow—welcoming it even. Then, like an oldtime judo move or computerized wargame from Guinevere's day he would bend the *JSN*, turning it full bore on the "Master." Sean knew such a mirroring effect could be pulled off at least in theory. But the first problem was: the requisite gear was expensive.

He'd need the original program called Blaze and he'd also need a "via," a computer system to channel the *JSN*. Sean haunted the District until he found Martin, that wizard at wheeling and dealing.

"You're mad! For ten billion I c'd maybe line you up with a via if big luck strikes."

"Go out and pray for manna. You can do it."

"How?"

"By not asking how."

"But how? How? How???"

"As fast as possible!"

Martin shrugged. But he'd go after anything the "designer slaughterer" wanted, reasonable or not. The via was absolutely essential. It would tight beam those penetrating short waves that can preserve a soufflé or a corpse, vulcanize rubber, treat cancer, command armies, create matter—or destroy Mars Peer.

"Only extreme amounts of JSN are dangerous" the public had been told. Same old lies. Define 'danger'!

Sean worked at white heat setting up the basics, while practicing the mental "slither" he'd learned at such cost. Then very late next day, Martin delivered the goods.

"Pay dirt. Doesn't come easy." Martin handed over the one precious package with other needed equipment.

"Now it's my turn to ask how," Sean grinned.

"Believe it, no accident. A woman came to my kive. She brought this stuff in weird old plastic bags that I swear were brand new. She had a raspy voice and wore old duds that fluttered from a history shop. An evil broad. Like from another life. I cringed when she said there's info she must impart to you alone."

"What is it about?"

"I barely understood her lingo. It sent chills down my back. She set everything out neatly and whispered: 'Tell your King that Sterling O'Blivion has a business proposition for him.'"

"That's it?"

"She said to tell you 'Arise, Arthur of Avalon. I'm the lady of the lake bringing you a magic sword. But in exchange you must join my HIT SQUAD or croak in your shoes.'"

"She sounds crazy."

"And evil. If you see'r, run! It'd be a cobra's ghost you're grabbing by the tail," said Martin while being shoved out the door.

Sean didn't have time for his chatter. The clock was ticking. It was roasting in the kive today. He set up equipment in every available square foot of space that could be reached easily. He had no time to lose.

Stripping down to shorts, he set himself to doing what had to be done.

Early models resembled a dentist's X-ray machine but this rig Martin had "found" was sveltely desk size, with the game systems veneer of an old rich man's toy, ionized airglow and all. But far from playing games Sean now had to grit his teeth and find out who was really "Master" of this situation.

His hand went out. It turned a selector.

Limbo. Gray, blank. Then: the geometries of polar night soaring.

He was in "the 800 gulf," that assault course drawn from the agreement of brains where the Word could not enter. Sean fumbled—brainwash eating at his mind, but then: a nibble running down the line.

A swelling excitement came. In one flash Mars Peer knew of his presence! This was the chance Sean had waited for: to penetrate Rat Island defense and squash this man, a manipulator who set bombs ticking in children's' brains! But Sean knew exactly how to play this game. Hadn't he been practicing for years? Honing the skill to sneak in, undetected...There. Yes! It was Peer. Breathing. Sean felt his body warmth.

An illusion of course, but so real. They were bodiless here in the gulf but he recognized the "Master" and now must establish dominance—rage sweeping him at what Peer had done, the agonies he inflicted on Sean and the other trainees, destroying many of them; years of struggle to stay alive—all that suffering because of one dirtbag!

Peer was onto him. There'd be no turning back—Blam! A stab that really hurt. Sean studied how it happened, going back to check on how he'd managed to create a connection in the first place. If curiosity had brought Peer in maybe habit (and his own ego) would kill him...

Alone in cramped space he heard voices at unimaginable distances: throngs of them, many men speaking at once—he knuckled down to it. He was the sniper, the hurler of chaos, moving cautiously, concentrating as never before in his life so he could sneak in on tiptoe—

"What is this? An antique Nintendo cartridge? Idiot. Ungrateful little boy. The free ride is over."

Wild emanations! It meant that Sean (if he stayed rock-steady here) might have the inside track he'd worked at for seven long years. Oh yes...he found a gap! There it was. The spot in the "Master's" defense that offered a chance to flush him out if he went in with everything he had.

Peer was hurt. Yes! The tide began running in Sean's favor but...another maze of pitfalls. The "Master" came slipping pain in from all angles. He was responding in fury, hitting with a terrible surge of JSN, delusive paradox that messes up your mind even while revealing so much—

Many things became lucid. Who was Sean Fontana? Kidnapped from colonist parents for profit; sold to a cartel by a power elite under the wings of a great bureaucracy; the youth saw what he hadn't seen before and was rocked to the heart. Aware of the magnitude of the injustice done him but...closing in on a prime source of that injustice.

They struggled. Peer fed him pain, dragged him into the corpse vat where he used to work all day—horrible, stale ammoniac stink he'd grown up with, concentrated MEVs ionizing tissue, the effect sickening. He struck back bringing a shriek from Peer who set up a counterattack of his own with intensity, a focus that wasn't there before. The "Master" was fighting for his life! But—Sean now lost count of the blasts scoring on him—and began hoping he hadn't overrated himself badly.

The effect on him was terrible. Devastating. The "Master"

wanted him first demoralized and then dead and was softening him up, trying to plow him to his knees, dwarfed, then turned inside-out: the Eternity Machine spitting its images as Sean was forced back, back, by slippery jets of energy that scythed him left and right and numbed his senses. He was so tired he could no longer twist the JSN or even tolerate the pain.

Peer began a song of triumph. "Do you know what I'm going to do to you?" he gloated.

A gut instinct was all that kept Sean alive. He clawed his way back slowly, much too slowly, dreamlike crawling out of some kind of expanding frame where horizons collapsed, stunned by what he'd learned, but again looking for something he could sink his teeth in—going against the current but far from broken. He was a knight. And this was his maiden battle. He hadn't waited for the right moment, that's all.

Slight error in strategy! All he needed was the faith, the patience.

More grueling punishment, but it appeared he was gaining control. A grid-coded starburst opened into what looked like home territory; and it was. He knew these canyons, had ridden a few of them all the way down. Sitting at a console he'd once reached this place: the dark, epic ghost land at the root of existence where men create the connection for death, where you can yell your head off and nobody hears: that may be true—but you can also wreak havoc sure as any cavalryman with a sword.

And Sean did it now. Once he'd tried to probe his own past but met with a blank wall. Now, with new understanding he punched in codes linking him to the Unspeakable—he had to tamper with it, even if damaging to himself: signal his presence to powerful but indifferent men making them aware of his existence, sure to bring repercussions later but—Peer's blind rage was hitting him again and again with force.

The pupil struck back. He saw the "Master" writhing, screaming in agony as he'd made others do but then: agonizing pain shot through Sean, a stream of invisible ultrahigh frequency photons assaulting him in his deepest being.

Peer threw an image. Sean face down with his arms lashed behind him, drowned. Mutilated.

"This is your last chance!" Peer yelled. "Leave this area now."

The vision was thrust back haughtily.

"Little upstart. Don't try my patience."

Intense pain, couldn't hang on. Had to hang on. Sean fought with a strength untapped before now, he called on his God — the old Celtic God! — not laid on him by others; except partly by that whore with the bloody Jesus, the puzzle of puzzles — yet it was the great power of his life — the basis of his faith in self, developed in a crucible over many lifetimes.

The net was closing. Peer flying out of control. Sean slicing through flesh and gunk, seizing power to work with his mirrored Just Say No! and the effect mushroomed.

It became awesome even to him, this enormous power he'd summoned up — echoes thundering in total silence, smoke belching from tortured volcano in a distant roar, impossible but there it was, layering the atmosphere, until Peer's scream of agony rang in his ears.

Jolt after jolt in smooth succession. Sean came down heavily, sent Mars Peer reeling, and was calling the tune: Power equals Force times Distance over Time...thrust and riposte in ever-changing patterns until Peer was outperformed.

He grew feeble, flailed, struggled. Sean heard him beg; was positive he did.

Peer was dying.

Under enormous pressure he succumbed.

Maybe it was a trap. Sean waited, listened, tiptoed around the enemy; couldn't detect any indication of movement.

He'd done it.

He cut the power in exhaustion, drank quarts of water and fell into profound slumber. Rat Island was behind him but the scars would remain.

THIRTY

Mars Peer out of the way, Sean went to dig up Buddy. The harsh days of Rat Island Butcher School were definitely over. The patrol guard passed him without a question. Peer's body was lying in state in the auditorium (official cause of death listed as a coronary). The flags hung at half-mast but nobody appeared to be grieving.

Buddy's remains were acid-eaten but intact—Sean stowed everything and left quickly for the offworld site. He found 'honest work' at the gov't installation. He lived with 500 others in a dorm, rented lab space and began 'reassembling' the pirate who once stole beans for him.

It was more than he could do with his own life.

Every night he pored over those videos of the Russian singer who would never know what he'd done for her. Or even that he existed. Dead 200 years? One more cosmic joke.

Sean would spend his future brooding over those old films and working at a rote job—knowing that his true wife Guinevere was out there somewhere waiting for him. Yearning for him as he yearned for her.

Weeks later, the gigantic Holocaust would rip off what remained of Earth's atmosphere and destroy every remaining life form in a matter of seconds, but of course Sean didn't know that yet; he worked, brooded, and thought about his Russian singer...

Dream on, dreamer. What else keeps you alive?

PART TWO

THE GOOD SHIP LOLLIPOP

THIRTY-ONE

"Are you my good little girl?" Darryl F. Zanuck wanted to know.

Shirley Temple cocked her adorable head. Mr. Zanuck, the famed honcho of 20th Century-Fox Film Studios, nuzzled Shirley's bouncy blonde curls with his chin. The child star sat on his lap in his big, super-posh office on the old Fox lot.

Shirley laid one tiny forefinger alongside her chubby cheek (adults always went gaga over that) and piped, with a beguiling upward glance:

"Honor bright I am, Mr. Zanuck dear."

"Well, Shirley, let me finish my little story. I know that until this morning you've been the best little girl in the whole world and that's the truth; isn't it, dear?"

"Ooh, yes, Mr. Zanuck."

"But today—" Zanuck frowned. His fingers combed his thick, rich hair. "I don't know what got into you, Shirley. Is something wrong at home? Are you *mad* at somebody? You're not mad at *me* are you?" He grinned with his shiny, state-of-the-art caps.

Shirley played with his tie tack. "Ooh no, Mr. Zanuck. 'Course I'm not"—but wouldn't look the boss in the eye.

"Then why did you do it, Shirley dear?"

"Why did I do what, Mr. Zanuck dear?"

"Now, you KNOW what, Shirley." Nursing a frosty glass of California orange juice that tinkled with ice cubes (and a pop of Smirnoff) Zanuck tossed the stuff off in one quick, serious gulp. He set the glass carefully on his desk.

He had piercing brown eyes that stared deeply into hers.

"Don't tease your poor Mr. Zanuck so," he said. "Why are you doing these naughty things all of a sudden?"

"OUCH!"

Shirley had pricked herself on the mogul's tie clasp. She didn't mention it (or he'd go into a psychodrama) — but two big tears gathered in her eyes.

"You're acting very strange," Zanuck said. "In every single take today, you sang *'On the scummy shores* of Peppermint Bay' instead of the sunny shores. Why did you use that word *'scummy,'* Shirley? It's a bad word, you know. And nice little girls don't *use* bad words. Do you want to *hurt* Mr. Zanuck? Do you want to hurt your nice *voice* coach? Do you want to hurt your *Mama?* Who do you want to hurt, baby? And...*why?*"

He gathered her closer, his lips nestled in her hair, murmuring: "Come on. You can tell *me,* can't you honey? We're best friends, aren't we, and don't we love each other to *burgerbits?*"

Shirley stroked his hairy wrist. "Ooh yes, Mr. Zanuck, de—"

"Now you stop that 'Ooh Mr. Zanuck dear' shit this instant!" His voice grew suddenly loud and stern. "You're putting on an act with me and I won't have it, you little phony. You don't know how upset I am that you flunked your screen test for the *Wizard of Oz!* Do you know what a *loss* it is to the studio to have the role of Dorothy go to that ugly old, dumb, Judy Garland? Do you know how disappointed your Mr. Zanuck is, honey?"

The child let her tears fall; fidgeting so as not to meet Zanuck's eyes.

"Oh darlin'," he crooned, nuzzling her sweet-smelling scalp, "I'd never have loaned you to MGM anyway but still — it's a blow to the prestige of 20th and a *black mark* against your name, to flunk one of their tests! Why, if everyone did that, what do you think would happen?"

Shirley shook her head violently from side to side, her forehead pressed into Zanuck's vest. Hot tears squirted from her blue eyes — *jeezly beast!* She needed to THINK, and Mr. Zanuck kept asking unanswerable questions and — and —

Oh God, how she missed her Virginia Woolf body! Oh, death was terrible — losing that bod she knew and loved — so warmly, sweetly familiar and her death had been agonizing and — and — no wonder humans wiped-out when it happened to them! They'd go blooie and grab the first infant carc they could reach — never check anything — parents, race, sex, country — *nothin'* — like a drunk forgetting his head on some barstool or battlefield or in a hospital bed maybe — But *thank God for good training!* although, she was getting slower and slower...Each time you lost a bod it got that much stickier — of course human meat was not designed to last more than a few years — but then came the BAD NEWS.

She reported to reembody as usual and discovered — no spare Virginia Woolf was available! They had *ONE* stewing in a cistern but wouldn't be ready for months and all her faves: checked out! Emma Peel — *gone*. Brenda Starr, *nix*. Gertrude Stein *zip*. All on top of the bad death she'd just had — which was as morbid as all get-out and then bang, she's having what the locals called an *After Death Experience!* down the long, twining hall with the lights flashing — the distorted figures you thought you knew — the Sage had identified it as a Between-Lives Incident, or *hypnotic implant* to make you forget who you'd been and then *addle you hard* so you couldn't make good judgments in your new life and *thank GOD for good training!* but still — there was *no Woolf* in the whole megatheater of bodies and she had to get corporatized FAST and keep Earth from being destroyed.

She wanted like mad to be Warrant Officer Ripley from the movie *Alien* but another anthropologist beat her to it, sticking a red flag on that adorable carcass; she was OUTTA LUCK!

There were a few hundred Clinton, Gore, Bush and so on, but who needed'm? No, the only thing at all usable was a Shirley Temple body.

Benaroya asked herself, What am I spose to DO with this cutesy six-year-old dimple box? But having no choice —

Her eyes fluttered open. She swung her cute little feet to the floor. In a moment she was pursing her cute little lips and tugging her soft, golden curls...Hey. It wasn't all that bad! Except —

She felt slightly ridiculous, but: that would pass. It was a letdown — but she'd be brave. She'd make the best of it. Wasn't that just what this cute little trouper was best at?

Shirley tap-danced a few steps. Yes; she would soldier on — she'd be a plucky, stalwart little darling — Daddy's own brave little girl —

Except there was something *crazy* going on in Chicago in the year 2123. Sterling had made a few tiny miscalculations, technical stuff — and wound up where old King Arthur was a teen outlaw — a fully-trained professional killer, which was fine but she hadn't foreseen that his friend Martin would WHACK O'Blivion and — the other thing that upset Shirley right now, was — (the *mop-*

pet gulped.)

"—we'd be in the meanest, nastiest old financial bind," Mr. Zanuck was saying. "As it is we're gonna hafta cut our overhead. I know you don't want to worry your Mother," with a meaningful look that didn't mean a whole lot to Shirley.

"And now this—" he went on, *"this...*I don't know what to call it! What's upset you, honey? Can't you tell me? Pretty please?"

Shirley dug her head into the vest again, sobbing. It was Sean himself who put the kibosh on H.G.'s idea. When the vampire attempted to rendezvous with him, letting him know it was a matter of utmost urgency that she get in contact with him, bad news! Fontana didn't buy it, which meant Shirley had so much to figure out that—that—and she was only a six-year-old child! What did she *expect* of herself? Adult planning skills? Might as well expect a Boeing 747 to fly

("Be careful my darling," was the little thought that Benaroya shot to her sweetheart. "Maintain all your defenses and hurry back to me..." Ster in a CODE RED situation where if anything went wrong—well, the Marines were not exactly on the way. But with luck she and Doug would have it wrapped up by Wednesday.)

Guinevere, who was now a Russian pop star—Sterling *had* been able to contact *her*. Which meant they were still in the game... It seemed Ster first attempted to draw Sean with a magnet of mutuality, in the form of an ad in the 'personal column' of the day. She asked herself: "What have we in common—what *links* us, no matter how remotely?" The link concerned King Arthur's book she couldn't even talk about!

Ster spent days wandering around, her eyes blasted out by mad sights—working and slaving to find the target and then she was *persona non grata!* All she got for her pains was a date with his armed, psycho boyfriend.

But the vampire would go for all. She was healing, getting better by increments and OH—Benaroya just wanted to hold her in her arms again—and *make passionate love!* Ster was regaining confidence as the Cure progressed but—future Earth—out there in the field, unprotected; days before that planet would became a cinder—unless maybe Shirley could—

"Won't you tell your dear Mr. Zanuck, won't you? Pwetty pwease wiv sugar on it," the producer was mouthing wetly in

Shirley's shell-like ear. (*Ick!* It gave her the creeps.)

"You called me a little phony!" gasped the child,

Sobbing heartbrokenly, she wiped her little nose on her sleeve adorably but wouldn't look at the big boss. No*siree* bob! She didn't like being called a phony.

"Oh honey I'm sorry, I'm sorry! It's just that things are...very tough right now," said Mr. Zanuck, pressing her head hard against his suit buttons.

The poor savage seemed genuinely distraught, so, with tears, kisses and promises Benaroya finally soothed him down. She had really thought the word was 'scummy' instead of 'sunny' — how was she to know? She'd been busy! — trying to come up with a solution to the problems facing all of them — Not to mention how shaken she was by her recent death...yes. That was it. Be honest. It gave her the glooms.

Oh GOD how she wanted her Woolf body back! The poor child cried all night long. They kept giving her tranquilizers, she'd palm'm but couldn't sleep or anything — and sure couldn't tell anyone; least of all Mr. Zanuck, because he'd never understand and would be mad and shake her or spank her rosy little cleft bottom or whatever these hypocritical sadists did to disobedient little kids around here.

"You're a great star," said Mr. Zanuck, fiddling with her curls. "You're not only a great star but a member of the family and I love you. And now this—this!"

"I love you too," the moppet piped with her sparkliest smile—

"*Sparkle!*" That's what her Mama always told her to do. And she always did it. But she knew she'd slipped up badly somewhere (a thing the real Shirley would never do; the real Shirley was a real trouper, she was) but was making it right *(she hoped)* with that shiny-eyed, bubbling-over cheeriness of the terminally darling.

And when Mr. Zanuck finally asked, "Now will you sing it right for Mr. Zanuck?," they skipped together hand in hand to the piano and began practicing her singing part.

On the goo-oo-ood ship Lollipop
It's a swee-ee-eet trip, into bed you hop
And dream awayyyy
On the sunny shores of Peppermint Bayyy.

"That's my little trouper!" Zanuck cried delightedly, grabbing the child up in his arms. "Other than what you did in front of Mr. Gable today (and I don't even want to talk about it) you're giving a fine performance. The picture is sure to be loved by girls and boys everywhere, and their mamas and daddies will praise and revere your name, honey."

"That's wonderful! I love you Mr. Zanuck."

"I love you too Shirley dear...but..."

Oh boy — at least it had been relatively quick; but they really gave her nice Woolf body the business — those ten goons in orange suits and wrap-around shades, converging on her in that alley where the nice bum asked what she was doing there — ohhh, she remembered everything about it! It was no accident that the H-2 hadn't worked on her; those geeks were slipshod; shoulda *zapped her hard* into her bod, instead of taking valuable time to *mutilate* the thing, thinking she's frozen into it but lucky she had a freeze release that time! and knew how to handle herself — so she'd taken a big gamble and lost, but not the whole bankroll.

The child heaved a deep sigh. She was still kinda sad about failing that dopy Metro screen test. They made her dance down this ooky, yellow brick road with a dog and two mean goons that played tricks on her (she'd-a sworn one of them had a nuclear device in his shorts) (they were friends of Judy's and didn't want Shirley to get the part) but: it was sorta too bad it happened, because she LOVED Judy. She had a big crush on the Metro star and also, OOH! She LOVED the MGM back lot in Culver City best of all. It had pirate ships, Southern mansions and all kindsa fun stuff like that to play in, and on; and Louis B. Mayer had an even bigger and more fun-filled office than Darryl F. Zanuck and he gave her a whole bag of Licorice All-Sorts — and a new drink called a Shirley Temple was going to be named after her own cute self very soon. But...what's done is done. Oh boy, she'd really get depressed if she got stuck in a carc like this —

"One thing more, Shirley dear," Zanuck began.

Oh-oh. She hated the producer's "one thing mores."

"I hardly know what to say about this. The Legion of Decency wouldn't like it at all, I can vouch for that!" he said rather grimly. "Now, Shirley, don't look at me when I tell it to you. You know how embarrassed your poor Mr. Zanuck sometimes gets, don't you honey?" he blushed.

"What is it? You can tell me," Shirley coaxed winsomely. (Might as well face whatever was eating him and get it over.)"Well...This morning, you know, you pulled off your pretty little dress and your li'l shoes and sockies and undies and everything and sprang right into a duckpond screeching *'Yaaa haaa, EAT my shorts!'* right in front of thirty people including Mr. Clark Gable, which is a very definite *no-no*. What kind of an example is that, for the dear little children who revere you?"

The poor man was so shaken he could hardly choke out the words.

"I don't know what came over me!" cried Shirley with downcast eyes and burning cheeks.

It took five minutes of eyelash-kissing, wrist-stroking and murmured apologies before Zanuck finally got over it and dismissed her.

Whew! She had to hurry, before humanity won the boobyprize it had been working on for about a million years but—

How could a person get anything done around here at this rate?

THIRTY-TWO

Sterling stretched and yawned; looking out her window at blue sky, white clouds, a *clean* Lake Michigan — so happy to be back from the ugly-sick Future that she just wanted (incredible as it seemed to a "rebel" like her) to run down and *kiss the ground* of this delicious, not-yet-ruined America with its rippling, star-studded flag —

What a *rush!* To be back in her Drake Hotel home; resting elbows on her own windowsill, gulping fine Cappuccino and gazing down at the exact angle she'd had from the ZATS — still a bit punchy from three hazardous weeks — her TTM humming faintly on the desk next to the telephone. Chicago looked positively *rural* compared to what it would be in 200 years, if that vomit-caked future couldn't be aborted before the Apocalypse — God! Never again would she be fascinated by low life, *no way!* She now knew what those slick politicians meant when they grunted, "We are gobbling up our children's future: oink!" They were only *telling the truth* for once in their corporate-elite lives.

But here was the BIG NEWS. She was meeting Woolf in *two hours!* In a mere 120 minutes, she'd ride the elevator to the street floor and — *wow!* There'd be time for them to live, laugh and love again. It was so crazy-wonderful the vampire could hardly believe it.

The phone was ringing but Ster lazily chose to ignore it. She had no friends here — a million *acquaintances,* yeah, but no *friends.* She'd been a classy dame running with a big-money crowd — and like her pals had been bored out of her socks. Everyone she knew, was paralyzed by the same old dilemma: shall I be *naive,* wholesome and happy — and be *sneered* at? Or shall I be *sophisticated,* cynical and world weary and be *admired* by everyone but have no *real life?* Sterling sighed. Yep: her glittery pals — one by one, they cashed in their chips—because after a meaningless life they couldn't wait to die, be embalmed, be cremated and be put in a tasteful box with a neatly typed label on it—classified at last! *What a relief.* And the adventurous ones would have themselves strewn over the Great Lakes from a Cessna—but *all were done in* by a litigious, competitive, greed ball system that profited nobody! Wasn't that insane? No: Ster wanted no more of such a vindictive world. All she needed was the strong, pure emotion of her love for Virginia Woolf. AND her job! And now...the Merlinites.

Now that her blood addiction was gone—vanished like any small, worldly dream about body hang-ups—this Round Table plan had taken root in O'Blivion's mind. She was beginning to eat, sleep and breathe nothing but Arthur's Court. She didn't really like Arthur very much; but Guinevere—now there was a woman.

Something KEY was going on with the Muscovite. "A game-saving move," H.G. called it.

Maybe because she spoke Russian *(pick your language, the vampire knew it)* Sterling had been appointed to escort Guinevere to Vonderra; where as her mentor and coach she'd give her a tour and phase her in as the #1 Merlinite. It was a chance for Ster to be at her best—because with the ZATS assignment under her belt she now had a beginner's grasp of the Mothership's capabilities. She'd mastered huge chunks of LRH lore; her tutors were pleased—*now came the fun.*

In videos Guinevere was different in many ways from what Sterling expected. Not a sedate, proper, meekly reserved 6th century British monarch; *unh-uh.* This Guinevere was a brash, brainy, athletic, redhead tomboy with That Look—Sterling couldn't define it but audiences doted on it. She wasn't even "pretty," just cute as hell or perhaps "handsomely feminine" (if there was such a thing), yet with a definite "Don't mess with me" quality you wouldn't want to—well—mess with.

Since Mars Peer had considered it critical to have the Russian pop star destroyed she was probably even more Key than Arthur...it was too soon to know exactly *why*, or where her talents actually lay—but Sterling knew they'd be friends: *real* ones, not like the air-kissing phonies she'd already met thousands of—and that was just the beginning.

O'Blivion had put a list together. She was now a recruiter, a talent coordinator. These people were her quarry—some 1900 women, men and children who, to an extent greater than average, "had it in them" to do great deeds but were being overlooked and wasted in the culture where they lived.

Such neglect was the Red Flag of a demonized society.

Sterling cranked out piles of letters to prospects from all walks of life—chosen, like Fontana, because each of them had a priceless secret buried in his or her past.

But the letter to Sean...writing it was the hardest work Ster ever did. It wasn't particularly difficult to go "BOO!" to people if you had a knack for scaring hell out of them; but...how did you really *communicate* with them?

Perhaps it was a fool's quest, aiming for the "quantum leap in human understanding" that H.G. insisted on—but it sure beat letting a species croak because you lacked guts.

"Listen up, you punk hooligan," Sterling began her letter to Sean (holding an ice-pack against her face from where she tangled with his friend). "Think I'm trying to hit on you, or suck your dirty little *neck*? You can go f—"

Sighing, the vampire crumpled the page. O.K., so she was not an outstandingly successful diplomat—but was the brat worth the effort? A compelling presence, certainly he'd have vassals in any age but this Martin kid? Bad company.

In any case—could an arrogant teenager lead the world to wisdom and sanity? It meant squat that he was a legendary king 60 generations ago. A man could live many lives in 1500 years. He could go sociopathic—under the punishment dished out by suppressive Authorities. Oh sure, she knew what Fontana was capable of—a highly trained killer who could WHACK you with gun, knife, or bare hands, but did that mean he could defuse a tense populace? True, she could hardly blame this *"verray parfit gentil knyght"* for having been bred in a living hell—but that made it doubly preposterous.

She imagined the rage that had to be in Sean—fury over what happened to his parents, himself; the way he'd been mugged—by the self-righteous citizens of the past! So how could he understand the need for loyalty, for trust? Fontana had no way of knowing Sterling wasn't one of the marchers in that long parade of atrocities that grew so naturally out of the mad, Pharisee present...*(shaking her head despairingly).*

To kids like him, life must seem a tiny patch of light surrounded by perilous darkness. That's how she'd felt.

"But how can I trust'm?" she asked aloud.

His pal Martin. A real piece of work. Wild glare in the eye, contemptuous grin on the face—and the slam she'd taken from him ached like crazy. Her nose was all swollen *(oh yeah, it went well with her dueling scars)* – although it had been a mere scuffle. She'd been in worse—

How it happened—after nights of her long-practiced, lean-swift-silent stalking, she caught up with the two of them outside one of those bi-bimbo quickie joints that sprouted everywhere. Ahead, Sean was busy gaping at a gyrating nude four-tit t.s. when Martin (the one with the ax embedded in his forehead with drops of blood trickling out: all the rage) whirled, snapped his pinkie at her and with a dramatic "Eat skut!" smashed her nose. *Ow!* It hurt.

A nice polite lad, I don't think so.

Jamming one foot behind Martin's she cracked him on the skull with her ho-sidearm. He gave a howl of pain and down he went. Sean didn't see it as, fishing handcuffs from her pocket she clamped the dazed and blood-blinded little scumbag to a marquee, a real pleasure.

Sean continued to elude her. But she did find Martin's kive *(a tent on Indigent Flats)* where after he 'apologized' *(at gunpoint)* and so did she, she handed over the program and via. They then shared a horrible-tasting drink. But it was rather sad. The poor kid wasn't going to live long anyway. An elegant weirdo, languid of manner, he'd apparently do anything for his sovereign, but was not Merlinite material; not a KRT selectee. End of story. Martin would die in the coming Holocaust with every man now alive—unless H.G. and Woolf (with her help and Doug's) could put an anti-gridlock, Human Renewal Program together fast.

THIRTY-THREE

Sterling called B.G. for advice. He said:
"We need to capture the secret yearning of the people, which is to be what they really are—not mere voters, but full-fledged gods! Yet here's a rub.

"The mass public won't believe—unless you lie sincerely while hosing'm with porno-violence. But a Merlinite senses the truth. *A true Knight can't* be *fooled for long.*"

The vampire deliberated until the last minute. Then she scribbled a letter to King Arthur at white heat. ("Be sure not to call a longterm amnesiac by a *past-life name!*" H.G. had warned.)

"I need your help, Sean. No ratty little 'reason' not to assist us will suffice. You have slaughtered your enemy with my tools. Congratulations. That was peanut stuff. Now the real cleanup starts.

"My associate, General MacArthur, wants you to spend two weeks with him in a lovely green oasis. You'll witness magical events: a spectacular sunrise each morning amid clean mountain air, vast blue skies, flowing water, a crescent moon hanging between trees as alive as yourself; wild animals roaming a thousand-year-old forest not yet axed by greed—"

Nix. One for the wastebasket.

Fontana'd never buy it. Could these miracles exist for him—in a world eaten alive by hysterical bipeds? No. So...

How (exactly) would a kid *think,* in C-22 on the eve of the Collapse of Everything? If she mentioned "trees," or "animals" or "sunshine"—he'd curl his lip. What was left?

Sterling O'Blivion had a problem. Like every woman, she had been carefully trained that telling the truth is a sin. She'd had 700 years of the usual mixed messages and restrictive beliefs, until she firmly believed that to tell the truth is wicked, naive, childish, unacceptable, anti-God, harmful to others, and either illegal or you could wind up in an insane asylum if you attempted it. With or without a net.

"Only truth can incite the imagination to action heat!" Abe told her. "Men scent the truth, yet always despise it for about, oh, a hundred years or so."

Patton said: "If you can't level with the guy he's too downscale to be of use to himself or us. Give'm the truth."

The truth! Did that mean stripped of the snake-oil in the average huckster's voice—the well-loved "Howdy folks! Aren't I cute, compassionate and sincere in these slick jeans with the rubber buns and a sock in the jock? Thank you for buying this ton of trash I'm shaking in your face, blah-blah blah, nice-and-safe lies, lies, lies—" The *truth!* The alien idea scared the ex-vampire almost to death.

And actually...what WAS the truth?

H.G. said: "No human knows the meaning of the word. Language is a precision tool. Would you operate a punch press or a guillotine without a working knowledge of its parts? You'd chop something off, yes—but *what?* Yet nobody understands what anyone else is saying! Sit a President down. Hand him a copy of his last speech. Ask him to define the words in it. He'll bog down in the first half of the first sentence. Others don't know what he's saying either; but everyone thinks someone else knows so it's O.K."

"You can't expect me to believe—"

"I can and do. You poor savages were long ago hypnotized by Scaulzo, who constantly manipulates the public's loyalty and gonads while forcing them to say they love it, on pain of being thought UNTRENDY. Did you know they joke about you on other planets? Partly because your pundits say 'This desk is real!' while slapping a dream desk with a dream hand, insisting 'And what you call a spirit is not real. It's NOTHING!'—which is why everything blurs together in the untrained mind. And why you can't play by conventional rules and hope to win—am I talking too fast?"

Ogod—when you tried to think like H.G. wanted—
OWWWW!
You'd get WHACKED! for disobeying Scaulzo's laws—
Sterling doubled over. *(here it came again)*

DEVIL-MAY-CARE

(yanking her chain...making her)

scared to death of using her TTM, the little time portal, ever again. Suppose she made a mistake. Suppose she wound up in the wrong place at the wrong time! Suppose she was—

(forced to view her own dead body, as punishment)

walking into the hush of a mortuary.

Sniffing medicated air (UGH! It stank worse than a hospital), feeling the thick carpet underfoot. Turning into a side room. Crossing to the open coffin that stood on a catafalque. Bending over her own corpse.OH GOD! The vampire shrieked aloud— how many times had she bent over a body just like this!

(Whiffs of ancient cannibalism. *Making her faint*)

She caught herself, holding the coffin lid and swaying. There were candles, banked floral pieces—the smell sickened her. It was those flowers! *(The embalming fluid.)*

Her body was laid out in an ornate bronze casket.

She peered into its face. It *(she?)* wore a black formal gown that revealed her breasts—the nipples were erect! The makeup job was terrific; the cadaver had peach-colored cheeks seemingly pulsing with healthy pigment. The hair was an absolute halo

(the corpse was at least having a good hair day)

and long black eyelashes swept the perfect cheeks. A single rose hid her pale, delectable cleavage

(what the fuck did this mean!??! Sterling was no cannibal—and certainly not of *herself)*

and it (SHE) wore costly jewelry: emerald necklace, bracelet, emerald-and-diamond pin set with rubies, and a gold crucifix. (Were they planning on *burying* her in that king's ransom?) The dead woman looked like a statue of a movie vampire: immobile, jeweled, sparkling.

She felt a lump rise in her throat. The tears flowed. She wept for her poor dead self...

The organ began playing very softly. Sterling jumped! Because an oily, stealthy-footed mortician had snuck up beside her as if she was invisible or something.

The undertaker wore black gloves and striped pants. He removed a handkerchief-wrapped tube of stickum from his pocket. His mouth was twisted in a pervert's smile.

What was he going to do to her??? Suddenly she understood.

"STOP!" she screamed, but he paid no attention.

The dead lady looked subtly different from Sterling. She looked like a wax statue of her—face powdered but *dazed;* death had caught her unprepared—she'd been assassinated two days ago! And now, leaning over her, the undertaker busied himself in pasting her eyes shut. Why? Because all afternoon, the corpse's eyes had kept flying open. Two mourners had already gone insane because of it.

Without warning, the organ broke into a wild funeral march. The dead music!

Suddenly the body sat up. The undertaker struggled with it but it was too strong for him. He had to fling himself on top of the corpse to get it to stay down. His assistant quickly brought telephone directories. They weighted the dead woman down with them.

(Actually, Ster thought she looked *cool*. Better turned-out even than in life if such a thing were possible—because medical examiners loved to handle and mess with cadavers more than live bodies, didn't they?) Her eyes half-closed—threatening to pop wide, and stare glassily at the ceiling.

What happened next was horrible! Again the body tried to sit up, *slowly, hideously*...The undertaker closed the lid in a hurry. That prevented it from sitting up. But when Sterling's eyes flew open again in spite of the stickum...

OH NOOOOOOO...

It was all black in this coffin! She was scared out of her wits. She could hear the rats coming down here in the dark. All at once, she saw the face of Edgar Allen Poe take shape before her. *Edgar was crying.* He threw his apron over his head...it was pathetic..."Life is so incredibly tough for us poor men," he sobbed. "Then you die! Quoth the raven, 'Nevermore'—isn't that the saddest thing you ever heard? And now you know why I wrote such awful drivel, Sterling. *Please understand. Please forgive me...*"

Sobs shook the thin, opium-soaked shoulders. Yes: what had happened to Edgar was a *tragedy*...Sterling wept...because...*under Scaulzo's thumb*...

The future was—*her crypt!* And God—it was so *sad!* So SAD... death was all *blue* and *sad* and...solemnly gooshy. The beautiful sadness of her own death. With deft, cannibal overtones...*(Scaulzo working his magic).*

The A-O! A scrambler popping up unwanted just like that

ditzy corpse—basic mechanics of thought control *(and yet.* What kind of awful, cold, chemical lunchmeat would she taste like? Oh yeah: embalmed baloney)—*thank God for her training* because at last she saw that humans did not HAVE to swallow the inflow of poison sewer gas that lay neck-deep all over their planet and The Law said *it didn't exist* and *couldn't hurt you* because you couldn't *see* it or *touch* it—a Sajorian conspiracy—making you go to war—whipped on by the network news, the blues criers, gloom merchants, horror showmen and magpies croaking doom into each other's ears and you were called UNTRENDY if you turned away from it)—NEVERMORE!

Thank God she'd learned one thing from her Cure. When someone *(backed by corpo-bankers)* is hosing you with that *"horror/porn/violence/you!are!your!body!"* abuse—even if they call it *"entertainment"* or *"catharsis"* or whatever—the aim is to *downgrade you* to where you can be *handled*. You bump through fixed, kneejerk emotions: hate, rage, revenge, terror, grief, chagrin, apathy, death *(H.G. said death was an emotion* and there were many others below it!) but Ster had learned a trick or two—for which she thanked her stars.

One trick: you focus and condense your thoughts, *copying* whatever bilge Scaulzo is pumping into your mind. Then run it over and over until you see how *controllable* it is.

This worked for her, unless and until the flow got too powerful. Then she'd automatically collapse—but was getting better and better at not being tweaked by negative input from headlines, political debates, reports of accidents and serial killings and scary fiction, terror shows, gossipy bilge—hell—EMPIRES had been lost by mooning over the mind-poison that some well paid geek was retching all over you! "Come up and see my retchings," thanks a lot but no thanks. Sterling was getting the Agony Organ very much under control. For now. But would keep her fingers crossed—today being crucial.

She tidied up—*mmm!* Six quarts of chocolate and butter pecan ice cream in her freezer—she ate one quart, hoping the rest'd keep until she got "shore leave" again. She glanced at the items on the shelves, and spooned out the last of the peanut butter for a thick, delectable sandwich to munch while she finished that difficult letter.

"Sonny boy, *your world is hanging by a thread.* Open your dirty ears. I shall tell you what every religious doctrine has forbidden since religions began..." *True!*

(People said, "Don't push too hard" — oh yeah? Just let'm all die, huh? She'd been around General George S. Patton too long to be able to tolerate a cowardly side-step like that.)

"Trillions of years ago, there was *a terrible tragedy.*

"It began as the first War to End Wars. Every human now alive suffered cruelly in it *(so cruelly we've been dramatizing it* every second of our lives ever since), along with teeming mega-trillions of others who were literally *smashed to bits.*

"The hopeful part is, the Cure I'm undergoing has helped me remember this War: my part in actual incidents in it, and *I know why our people are going nuts every day of their lives* and have no idea why. Unfortunately, the mess humanity is in cannot be changed by medicos, scientists, politicos, etc. Why?

"These men — the walking wounded even as you and I — got hypnotized by a starry universe that was *(and is)* a mere invention of entities like ourselves. They are deep in a furtive 'affair' with meat bodies which get the hot, obsessive focus, while the spirits who run them are left to moulder away in a wasteland of fatigue syndrome, chronic depression, eating disorders, addiction, disease of every stripe and a pants-wetting *dread of death* with feelings of inadequacy, futility, and alienation. How *humiliating* for an ex-god!

"This mania is whipped on by punishment: the ongoing, hysterical but *totally futile,* manipulative suppression of almost everyone by almost everyone else. But we forget that bullies always die a miserable death! But luckily, such aberration in yourself CAN BE HEALED by the loving aliens on whose behalf I am writing to you..." Highlighted by a couple of chocolate blots.

("*If he swallows this hoopla* — every word of which is TRUE! — he's as crazy as he needs to be," the vampire grinned, taking a big bite of peanut butter sandwich as she scanned what she'd written.)

THIRTY-FOUR

SOMETHING TERRIBLE IS GOING TO HAPPEN
The vampire was amused to find herself scared.
Oh sure. Tell the truth and *get hit by an A-0 bolt* — so what else is new? She had to finish this mad letter and get out of here — or be late for her all-important meeting with Woolf! And the Agony Organ be damned.

"I know what it's like to have a knotted rope around my neck," she wrote. "And Sir, you've got one.

"That's why this letter will grab you. In your heart you KNOW that over the eons our race has been slipping, ever so gradually, to the Dark Side. Now we must crack the mold! that the demon called SCAULZO has cast us in through hypno-pain: until the mass public, snowed and conned, is wholly unable to differentiate. A sociopath appears normal; normal men suspect themselves of being criminals; bad is good; one's butt is, apparently, a hole in the ground — under the growing burden of our hypnotic trance.

"I can't tell you who you WERE, Your Highness, but will give a hint of who you CAN BE in the future. I know this communiqué will strike at a good time. You are at a fork in the road. You desperately need to find an anchor.

Destroying Mars Peer wasn't the satisfaction you hoped for.

A zillion psychos like Peer are being bred in today's world — this being the Devil's Workshop where force only breeds more force.

"I know that you, *a literate man*, will grasp what I'm saying. You exist in a future that is a big mistake. It can be *pre-erased from the record* if 2000 key people can wake up in time. You are one of them. You have two choices, pal.

"You can die there like a cockroach or — return to Camelot and be reunited with Guinevere, your once-&-future mate. When you recognize her, you will KNOW you are that King who can snatch the sword Excalibur out of the stone.

"It won't be easy. I can only promise that as a member of our Special Forces A-SQUAD you'll be awakened to your highest self, where you can do something MEANINGFUL at last. *A new day is coming!* We've got to help humanity GO FREE and that's what this is all about. If your answer is YES we'll know and will pick you up.

"I'm contacting all former Knights of the Round Table along with 1900 bold civilians, to form an elite squad with the goal of *helping people*. We need to break the bonds of the group-enforced limitation, using technology of the sage LRH—the workable *(and thrilling!)* method to free mankind.

"I offer you a sense of purpose, a rich mission; the gleam and glory of a radiant GOAL. Otherwise—be a palm reader, guy. Look in your own hand. And see no future.

"Sincerely: Sterling O'Blivion, Exec Sec of THE MERLINITES INC. LTD."

Now Ster had to get out of here—no time to waste. Her TTM safely locked away (everything she prized was in a huge, well-secured cedar chest in her bedroom), she began packing. The Rysemians covered her needs but it helped to have some familiar things in a new place...

Packing.

But didn't that lead *to...unpacking?*

And then all too soon...packing *again.*

How batty life was.

Packing. Unpacking. Interminable escapes from one doom to another, fleeing by oxcart, donkey, horse, train, plane and now *interstellar cruiser* — but the same tired routine over and over? Her life had been a religious pilgrimage—yet she hadn't known it until this moment!

Sterling frowned, trying to imagine the team of Mary and Joseph actually *packing* to flee from King Herod. Tossing things into a suitcase. His shirt. Her shoes. The baby's diapers—hurry, hurry—*the Bad guy is after us*—

The story of her own life! How many times—oh God, she remembered leaving Stockholm, Johannesburg, Macao, moving to *Cannes*, to *Drain*, to *Weed*, to *Wales*—she sold the restaurant in Vienna that she used to run *(no, not sold. More like gave away. But* at least she managed to get out just before Hitler came to power) <u>and now —</u> and now —

Every once in a while an old friend would come up and say: "Aren't you Sterling O'Blivion from the Sorbonne (or Oxford, Cheyenne, Boston, Tierra del Fuego)? *But no!* It can't be. That was many, many years ago but you look just like — why, it's amazing — would you mind stepping over to the light so I can —"

Then Ster would rush home, throw her stuff together and shove on, panicked because her cover was blown. One of her worst moves took place on the day she left Wellesley; where she'd finally (after many bitter struggles) gotten tenure in the Physics Department —

Stacy Welch, an attractive undergrad from a fine old Vermont family, said she was bringing her (filthy rich) grandmama to Sunday tea "Especially to meet *you*, Ms. O'Blivion! I've told her about your thrilling research," the child beamed. (At least one admiring kid brought a relative to meet Sterling every month. Stacy was an A student; pleasing to look at, never caused a speck of trouble —)

Ster had no clue of the nightmare that awaited her or she'd have got the hell out of there, at least till Monday morning. As it happened, she was giving her brand new Schwinn tenspeed a shakedown cruise around campus and having a wonderful time. It was the first clear day of the week; she was flying up blacktop roads, over grass, around buildings, tearing through puddles trying to get the hang of shifting when suddenly —

Coming around the corner of an ivy-clad dorm, was the eager sophomore and her elderly relative. The young woman pushed a machine that had two thick, black, rubber tires. The contraption actually purred along under its own steam — "A kind of motorized deathbed" was the phrase that popped into the vampire's mind as she sang out:

"What buttons do I push to STOP this thing?" clowning around (later she realized that she hadn't meant the bike at all).

She was pedaling smoothly but a bit too fast

(*grinning*, thinking how fine her article for SciAm had just turned out, and how glad she was to be out of that chair behind the typewriter in her office...and what she would like to eat for supper. A juicy T-bone steak would go fine with a bottle of Cabernet and some broccoli, a green salad with blue cheese, whipped potatoes with country gravy and then for dessert, let's see now —)

It was one of the zillion great dinners of history that never got eaten.

—squeezing the brake levers a bit too hard so that, whoa! Nearly did an endo over the handlebars, but brought the tenspeed to a ragged halt and swung off laughing like a loon.

"This is my grandmother, Cornelia Dobbs," beamed the young girl.

Stacy wore a yellow leotard and leg warmers and was stepping quickly down the walk with her venerable, wheelchair-ridden gran. The chair, with its fawn leather seat and armrests, had hubs of gleaming metal. It was sumptuous. It glittered with more chrome fittings than Ster's new bike had.

And the vampire—she looked exactly like what her resume said she was. A decent, capable, 26-year-old professor of particle physics; at the moment happy as a kid on Christmas morning with her new bike, the first she'd owned.

"This is my grandmother Cornelia Dobbs. We spoke of—"

Stacy's beautifully-dressed gran had to be 90 if she was a day. The sun cast its beams on her parchmenty, patrician face with its alert black eyes under cat-eye specs...She wore a sweater with a big W on it, and a Daffy Duck propeller beanie that some witty freshman had bobby pinned *(no doubt with a giggle or two)* on that old, gray, soon-to-be-dead head...

"This is my grandmother," beamed the girl.

They faced each other. Ster's leg muscles were beginning to burn with unfamiliar effort—she stretched out a tanned young paw *(smelling faintly of 3-in-1 oil)*, leaned forward balancing the wheel, and grinned her sincere grin. Which was the kind of sincere grin that could get a vampire tenure at a ritzy girls' college.

"I'm delighted to meet you! Stacy's told me so much—"

O'Blivion, if truth be told, was the luckiest conwoman on earth because she was a vampire; her lips still pouty-red. There were other risks that she ran, of course, but the hands were not gnarled or arthritic and the face was unmarred by any shadow of a pouch, bag, line or wattle; because what was erroneously declared to be *'natural deterioration'* had never taken place with her—*nor would it!* As long as she got her six ounces of hot Ruby every month.

"Baby, you look like you stepped out of the frame of a very old painting," she'd say with a cocky grin whenever she met her eyes in a mirror. "You're no *moldy corpse,* buried in some European toxic waste dump that used to be a cemetery, with *rats* coming out of your cooze," she would josh the Sterling in the mirror *(by way of a harmless joke)* —

The old lady paused. She stared.

"Sterling?" she whispered.

The light falling on her face — that good bone structure — *those amazing eyes,* now wearing a look of perplexity that Ster knew all too well —

It was Cornelia.

Cornelia.

Oh God. *Oh God!* Seventy years ago.

Nights of Gatsby-style fun — Ster's ex-best-friend: champion downhill skier, winner of essay prizes, double dater, bosom confidante — brilliant sharer of midnight philosophies when thoughts ran free...when the hair that spread across her shoulders was thick amber-and-ash, not scanty white and piled in a bun (Cornelia was called "a knockout" by streams of boys wherever they went) & learning the Charleston & how to drive a Model T & the silly-kid "stunts" on somebody's lawn & — sitting together in their PJ's in the firelight's ruddy glow — and more — much more —

The sun was warm but Sterling felt icy-cold; her heart began to flutter. Gooseflesh broke out all over her body, as if she'd seen a ghost *(and she had)*

The hand that approached hers was a parrot-claw with diamonds.

Cornelia! Whose voice had the loveliest lilt; whose laugh F. Scott Fitzgerald had copied for Daisy's laugh in *Gatsby* (which Ster knew because Scott admitted it — saying it sounded to him like "3 A.M. wind chimes") — but then Life separated them, as Life always does...and Ster would now and then think about trying to find her friend or "Hiring a private dick. Aren't there agencies for that sort of thing?" to put a tracer out. But then she'd think about how she absolutely *did not want* to see the vivacious Cornelia as an older woman (30? 40? 50? 60, 70, 80?) all washed out and faded, wasted, with a thickened middle, her hair touched up and powder in her wrinkles. But the very last thing she ever expected was — oh *God.*

The old, old lady's eyes rolled wildly. She struggled to breathe. She tried to say something — reaching convulsively for the vampire's hand with her clawlike, ringed fingers —

Her eyes flickered oddly; then they glazed, rolling up.

She had died of a stroke in her wheelchair.

And suddenly, *terribly*, Sterling's life was shattered.

Of what came next she had no memory. It seemed she'd driven off leaving everything (including tenure, best pair of broken-in climbing boots and the paper she'd been working on) and didn't stop until she hit Chicago—her soul in turmoil, vowing she'd never go back; "Never, never, *never!*"

Even now she felt a chill of gooseflesh remembering it. No, she didn't stop to glance back—just burned bridges; which included everything that had happened in her life up to that point. The experience put an end to her joy in her own youth *(at least until she met Woolf)*, and when hunger struck—basic hunger, real hunger: hunger for *food*...she answered an ad for a *"Charismatic MGR for franchise dance studio must be able to CLOSE CLOSE CLOSE."*

If there was one thing Ster could do, it was CLOSE. So she grabbed a cab to the Max Arkoff Studio, turned in her app and auditioned and was hired just like that. And was grateful for it. (And if she felt relief that she'd never have to go through that Cornelia experience again, well, wasn't that *perfectly normal* for the love of God?)

Naturally she didn't tell Max Arkoff (the famed twinkle-toes who owned the chain of dance studios) that she'd been taught singing, dancing, acting and juggling by the minstrels and actors who sometimes stayed for weeks in her childhood home when her parents happened to like them—oh, she missed the old songs and speech *so very much!* But this was an O.K. substitute for the moment. A little scammy in a post-modern way, yeah, sure—but she made good bread at the Studio and to be honest, she reveled in the flash and glitter and loved the thrill of the spotlight.

But right now her situation was delicate. The big problem was—*how could Woolf really love her?* Only a fool would presume to think that this entity from a million-years advanced species actually cared for an alley-cat like herself *(who had eaten out of garbage cans!)* and wasn't just using her for personal ends.

"I'm not much of a prize," Ster sighed as she bustled around systematically packing, tidying, securing important papers; selecting a banana from the silver bowl that she and Woolf had bought on a mad trip to Acapulco and meditating as she peeled, bit, and chewed.

DEVIL-MAY-CARE

It was too lopsided a relationship. Woolf had salvaged her but what did she have to give? Why did she matter at all to the Rysemian? Why did...

Uh-oh. She was drifting off on the black cloud the A-O injected into your head, memories crowding in, self-doubts smacking you down to zero—

But Ster had a responsibility to become mentally strong and unflappable. She had a ways to go—and *no mind-polluter was gonna stop her*! Hadn't she'd proved that you can *rethink everything*, bounce back from an unsavory past, make good and "See the light of the spirit within" and all? *You bet!*

Nor did she give, a snap about blood any more. The Cure handled her addiction. It showed a better way. Never had she felt so keenly alive! Being Exec Sec of THE MERLINITES sure beat crawling on high ledges to score Ruby—and the truth was: True Love was—*(uh...hey...feeling woozier and woozier)*—True Love was the only thing worth having.

Sterling had been so lonely, *sad and lonely* and all she wanted was her own True Love...

"I want to be holding you," she messaged, "drinking deep of your kisses—oh Virginia Woolf—we'll be together in one hour—I may not make it—*help*."

Hey! Enough of that *"inadequacy"* crap. *Of course she'd make it!* They'd have a marvelous evening, share a glass of dry white wine, and savor to the full the love that passed all expectations... Sure the vampire was developing a sense of ethics and deep concern for other people but the main thing was, she and her lover were good in bed...*Good?* The sex was *dynamite*! Theirs had been a whirlwind romance because the chemistry cooked and they created a world of their own, which she'd be *in* in about twenty minutes—gazing into the depths of Virginia Woolf's eyes, planning their future together—

Sterling loved the Rysemian with all her heart; sexy, tender, funny Woolf—Yes, things were better for Sterling than she had any right to expect, but was that so awful? At least she was out there with the pro's pulling her share, earning the right to live on a cozy space ship that had everything you could want! Although it would be a total *downer* if humans let Earth slip through their fingers—which they seemed bent on doing while saying the opposite.

Patton's briefing still rang in her ears, "*All you got* is that tiny planet. The void is COLD 'N EMPTY. It'll take you maybe *ten thousand years* to reach Central Galaxy *where the people all live;* and when you get there—!!!"

But—one step at a time. For now, she had completed a difficult and dangerous assignment and deserved a glass of Chablis with the woman of her dreams.

After a moment's debate Sterling wrapped a stewart-plaid scarf around her neck. Then she pulled on a pair of thick gloves. Winter sun was flooding in the window, but the radio said a blizzard was on the way. *O.K.!* She was outta here.

Nothing lasts forever—but their love would last forever.

Woolf had promised it!

THIRTY-FIVE

While Sterling O'Blivion was returning from the ZATS to her Drake Hotel apartment where she would soon pack and go to meet her lover, Shirley Temple was heading into the tangerine sunshine, balancing a stack of fat books and her lunch pail that had Clark Gable's picture on it.

The clock was striking noon; the studio (Twentieth Century-Fox) was crammed with tour buses. Shirley was on her way to the schoolroom that the State of California said must be provided for her — knowing by the hushed chorus of "LOOK!!! IT'S SHIRLEY TEMPLE" that a Mass Public would now start to breathe on her, click Kodaks and shove autograph books in her face (she politely/quickly/smilingly signed a dozen, while tap-tapping for 80 unemployed waiters from Paducah) but here came more — she hadda MAKE LIKE AN EGG & GET CRACKN as they said back here in the Depression Thirties.

The Santa Ana was blowing. That was the desert wind that drove folks mad here in Lotus-Land, where a regiment of Civil War Boys in Blue was now marching past, grinning hugely at the tot — she was appalled to read their minds, so didn't; *holy smoke!* Those men might do anything — her little pink butt was not too safe in a world of towering giants 85% of whom had pea brains and Neanderthal physical urges. No point in exciting these infantrymen more than they were already excited; she vamoosed in the opposite direction as fast as her little legs would carry her.

The lesson after lunch would be history (Shirley waved to some studio policemen and wardrobe ladies scurrying by), probing the whys and hows of *W-A-R!* and she hoped her Teacher didn't check these books too close. They were history books all right but 25 years in the future. Lincoln ordered an in-depth study of Korea to get some historical background on Wartainment in general — and the child needed an angle to help her friend Douglas MacArthur, who was going insane. Doug had to hurry and lay the foundations for the modernization of Japanese industry so it could not only challenge the West, but beat it (part of the S&M sewergas that the Big S.'s men were amusing themselves ladling out while their boss was away). But the NASTY JOLT was, Frimble had been ordered to trash Doug which was sad. The two had flown together during the war (the Coalsack War) and were like brothers — bets were being made that MacArthur couldn't hack the stress and would bail out. So Shirley had to help...because helping adults was the adorable cherub's BAG.

Uh-oh. More autograph hounds! Her little legs twinkled and pumped as the hounds chased her down a Western street into a prairie where she jumped on a moving running board and off it and into and out of a white Cord with superchargers where two employees kissing in the front seat didn't stop to look as Shirley scrambled over them and, head down, ran as fast as — well pretty darn fast and skated across a wet lane knocking over a trash can, trying to catch her breath when a couple of swiftie fans grabbed her dress, half pulling it off; but she bellied under a hedge, hurried toward the side door of her schoolroom, jumped inside and slammed and locked the door — *whew!* That was a close one.

Shirley knew that public adulation was a highly dangerous path but after all, *she did reign supreme* among child stars — a tiny moppet who cut right to your heart with her dimples, baby smile, and chubby round cheeks, not to mention those wide blue eyes that dazzled; plus her cute naturalness that said "I love you SO VERY MUCH!" to everyone. Including psycho-perv kidnappers, child molesters and adoption fraudders which made the job more than a bit dicey.

The public hadn't a clue what a long, hard grind it was. Shirley worked with such professional mastery — a sparkling child laboring doggedly under the glare of lights — everyone saying *she was a wonder* with her concentration and her ability to make a brightly lit sound stage seem like the funnest, most *heartwarming* place in the whole world! But none of it was easy. But later in life her Pa would take her for every dime (under the heading "family values"), she could no longer get a job in pictures and her former fans'd go *tsk-tsk* with their tongues and forget it and soon everyone would die. Then, 100 years dead, she'd be popular again. It was heartwarming.

Great clouds of fragrant Commissary odor pervaded the air; Shirley'd have loved at least one huge, juicy green pickle but no: her tutor always left a lunch for the tot to eat at twelve sharp. And safely barricaded in the little schoolroom on the studio lot, she ate her tuna fish sandwich (not knowing what it was—she thought it was rancid peanut butter or never would've et it being a fish herself and no cannibal!) and drank her glass of milk and chomped her big red apple and her Oreos for dessert...carefully taking them apart to lick the sugar off first.

Then Shirley sat at her little work-desk. She was doing her homework. It was hard! She wore her sun suit and little red tennis shoes with orange stripes. She'd spent last evening coloring in coloring books which was a lot easier than homework.

Her beeper beeped. It was Doug MacArthur. She tried to hang up on him but it was too late.

"Don't call me at the office," she whispered fiercely.

"Your girlfriend O'Blivion just threw a damper on the Fontana kid. She'll screw us out of our Round Table action! What the hell are you doing up there?"

"Get ahold of yourself."

"Arthur won't have anything to do with me," (Doug had tears in his voice) "because your girlfriend injured his friend badly."

"He lumped her nose!"

"She lost her composure! We can't afford to keep her."

"That's nothing but bullshit! And keep your voice down. One of'm's always listening at the door trying to find an excuse to spank me. Or take my temperature and they wonder why kids grow up carrying tubes of vaseline or K-Y around—"

"Have her make amends! We need that snotty juvie right now!"

Shirley sighed. "We've been over this about 100 times too many. She can't just say 'You're the King, now pick up your scepter—'"

"RISK. *She's a risk junky.* A danger to herself and others. She could snap *just like that.*" Shirley heard fingers snap at the other end of the line.

"She's becoming a fixture and you're still jealous? People *like* Sterling. They don't feel threatened by her! Cuz she's not only a *vampire* and a *badass* but *wholesome!* and she knows how to *massage egos.*" Shirley gulped her apple core, she especially liked the seeds. "Whatever happens next, *you* have to orient your emotional life. I bet your fly is open again—"

"Let her show what she's made of! This is a race with the clock. What really counts on this planet is wars, wars, *wars — important stuff!* Men's work."

"You're not making this easy—"

"I firmly believe that if you can discover what caused the war in Vietnam, we'll have the key to the whole puzzle."

"Whaddaya think I'm *tryin* to do, but how could I find that out when nobody in the world knows the answer?" the tot piped adorably. "I mean where do I *start?*"

"Just get those books read and assimilated *fast*. Abe wants a report in one hour. Then you can 'assist' O'Blivion all you want to." His voice was laced with belittling scorn and contempt.

"Honey, we're in the middle of a picture here! I've got a heavy shooting schedule! They're already wondering where I keep sneaking off to." Shirley's heart went out to Douglas but he made her mad too, cuz like 85% of Earthmen he was crazy as a darn bean—

"Just find the wedge we're looking for."

"You're wearing me out with—" but the line had gone dead.

Shirley ran a hand through her curls; O.K., time to deal with the complexities of the Korean War. It would be her school project. Her teacher and Mr. Zanuck would like that—except for the fact that Korea happened in the future but she was sure they were too flaked to know it.

Shirley riffled pages, a cute little frown puckering her face as she dropped Oreo crumbs on the small-print, tomelike volumes—oh boy: the whole Korea deal began, it seemed, with missionaries.

For hundreds of years, Korea was a closed country. All they wanted was to be left alone. And that was bad because: when someone wants to be left alone, it drives all others cuckoo—if, that is, the antisocial hermit has something valuable to take away.

And nations react just like people.

Except they don't get punished, spanked, or have their rectal temperature taken hourly (a few childhood tortures administered like prison sentences "for your own good").

Missionaries grow very fond of countries that have something valuable to take away. Those countries are the ones God desperately wants to save.

So in 1835 a French missionary sneaked into Korea, crossed the Yalu River on a raft at night, crawled through a storm drain, dried himself off and began saving souls.

He saved bunches of souls and was joined that winter by another French missionary who crossed the frozen Yalu disguised as a widower in mourning.

Shirley Temple blinked. Sneaking through storm drains in disguise, *hey!* The dynamic duo sounded like clean, upright lads dedicated to saving souls NOT! And hot on their heels came a disguised Bishop. You'd expect the Pope to come next but he didn't. What happened was, the three churchmen set to work and converted a thousand Koreans! Pretty neat going. You had to hand it to them — unfortunately a new Prince ascended the throne, extremely pissed that "a fast one" was being pulled upon him.

"You can't pull the wool under my nose!" cried the new Prince, deciding to torture the missionaries to death along with their new converts. He ordered a roundup, hunting every single one of them down; women, tots, grandpas, pretty girls, cripples and all. Then he declared a public holiday so that the three missionaries and their converts could be publicly flogged and tortured all day long, and then beheaded. And the heads put on spikes.

So they were publicly flogged and tortured all day, in every way you could imagine and then some. The Prince was using them as an example. He figured this would make Korea private once more.

Only it didn't. Humans fly to where torture is going on (Shirley knew from films and comics) so all it did was titillate a lot of *other* missionaries who went instantly to Korea and snuck in in disguises, no doubt praying for a sensational martyr's death with crowds watching; and there was plenty of tying up or chaining and burning with hot items such as branding irons, red hot coals, and cigars, then some genital-flaying, and body-opening penetration with everything imaginable — *and then some.*

Shirley's eyes were big as saucers! She simply could not figure out why Earthies adored agony so much while saying they didn't. Or why so many missionaries would happily break the law of a land by sneaking into it.

In any case, many were tortured and executed.

Then the French charge d'affaires (French Honcho, she called him) sent a furious letter to the Prince. The Prince sent a letter back. He explained that Koreans were peaceful people who treated shipwrecked sailors and other honorable people in a kind manner, but hated *sneaks*. He said he got upset when people snuck in, so please stop doing it as it upset him to a point where he'd hurt them severely.

The French Honcho was so angry he tore up the note and sent a fleet of 600 men. All but 80 were killed in the battle that followed. The other 80 went and burned the Prince's summer palace to the ground and ran away.

An American schooner was shipwrecked nearby. Its sailors were treated as guests; but another American schooner tried to sneak up the Taedong River and ran aground. Some Koreans came to help. The Americans fired over their heads. The natives ran but came back. Once again the Americans fired. So the Koreans killed the crew and burned the vessel.

Then the Americans sent a fleet of gunboats to establish diplomatic relations. Two boats went up the river without notifying the forts, and were fired upon by the Koreans. The furious Americans considered this an insult to their flag so they attacked the fort, killed nearly all the Koreans, and left in a huff.

Shirley's head was spinning; she shoved the last of the Oreos into her mouth, reading furiously about how there was wonderful timber and mining in Korea in those days and of course everyone lusted after it. But Japan and the Western Powers were smart. They saw what fantastic profits could be made. They kept dropping in uninvited and doing evil things.

The Japanese killed Queen Min of Korea. They did bad things to her. They took her dead body, burned it in a grove and forced Korea to sign a treaty splitting from China so their ill-gotten gains needn't be shared. But the Russians rescued the King. Through him they got a heap of worldly goods along with a piece of the Korean army.

Now waaaait a minute — she read that part again —

"Wha – ???" Shirley wore a new grin of irony; at least it was the *adult men* who did these loathsome deeds and not the women, children or old folks. The Koreans had what she considered a fair curfew. All males were kept off the streets after sundown. This gave the women a peaceful, unmolested time for evening visiting. It made a lotta sense; in America girl children lived in what amounted to *jail* because of morons!

So then Japan got in the habit of doing "policy actions" and crying murder when the Koreans resisted. Russia and Japan divided up a lot of booty and with the help of the U.S. and Britain, cold-bloodedly betrayed their promises of Korean independence. Japan took land away from Korean people to give to Japanese people, then closed all the schools for 20 years, then closed newspapers, then imprisoned writers, censored everything and when the Koreans declared something called "a massive display of passive resistance" the Japanese killed 17,000 of them. Then in World War II they stripped the country, cut down all the trees, razed villages and tortured and killed everyone in sight. And then some.

Shirley Temple found a piece of Kleenex, wiped her eyes, blew her nose; *boy*. History. *Sad?* A real tearjerker.

Then after World War II the events became so crazed the anthropologist could hardly make heads or tails of it. It seemed the Americans appointed a person named General Hodge as Ruler of South Korea. They did this because Hodge detested Koreans. He knew nothing of their history, cared less, and was contemptuous and rude to them, which made him not only a *good ole boy* but an O.K. politician.

When this man landed at Inchon, a flock of misguided Koreans came to greet him, bringing wreaths of flowers and waving U.S. flags. As the two groups met, some Japanese police got huffy. They opened fire, killing some of the Koreans. A happy General Hodge held a ceremony to give the police medals for doing this.

Hello? Anybody home?

This Hodge guy hated Commies so rabidly he said that everything, including monsoons and his indigestion, was caused by them and ordered a crackdown on them. So the country's head Commie fled North where he was immediately shot as an American spy.

"For the luvva Mike!" cried Shirley, beginning to think that Abe Lincoln ordered her to study this mind-boggling mishmash as a form of punishment—but the Chief wouldn't do that *(or would he???)*.

Soon it was 1947 and the "cold war" began. That meant that everyone decided to divide Korea up at the 38th Parallel with the Soviets owning the north and America the south. They didn't ask any person who lived in a little house in either one of the sections, or who had a little garden or a few pigs and chickens, what they had to say about it.

Shirley's eyes were blurred with tears. She could hardly see the page to read about what followed. It included plenty of arson, terrorism, strikes, rape, sodomy, guerrilla sniping and organized violence. Everyone was so upset they hardly knew what they should do next to each other, which was a favorite state of humans because Scaulzo controlled their higher brain function; they then sought refuge in a hysteria that prohibited a search for root causes, allowing everyone to feel not-accountable. This was such a wonderful release that it made the war seemed thrilling, glamorous, and manly, like in an Ernest Hemingway or Norman Mailer novel.

Plenty of organizations and counter-organizations were formed and there were rebels living in the mountains, including plenty of thieves, so that everybody could rip everything off and strut around, grim in the face, showing off their sweat-streaked muscles and being *On Camera* whenever possible.

South Korea spent all its income battling Communists.

No dough was left for farms and schools. The United Nations sent a Commission reporting that everything was hunky-dory and there was positively no chance of war. But the minute the Commission left, war broke out.

It happened on a Saturday night, in a monsoon rain. A bunch of American officers were drinking and dancing when the North Korean tanks boomed through the rice paddies and slaughtered everybody in sight. This made the U.N. feel angry and insulted at being thought wrong! And Harry Truman. He felt that way too. Harry got so hopping mad he declared war and then later decided he might as well tell his Cabinet about it. So he did. He told his Cabinet about it.

The American troops were all kids under 20. They'd been living the easy life in Japan. They thought the whole world was their oyster, and would be scared of them. But it wasn't. Nearly half of these pampered youngsters were killed in the first encounter. That's when General MacArthur got mad and ordered the bombing of North Korean installations and Truman got mad at him. *Zowie!* Everybody got mad! Things were heating up! Both the CIA and MacArthur insisted that China wouldn't intervene. Boy, was Doug ever *wrong!*

It was icy cold. An Arctic front came howling down from Siberia. Peoples' fingers were being frozen off! Doug was in the very act of saying "The war is almost won" in an uplifting speech when the Chinese attacked with rifles and bugles and things, and took the Americans by surprise. They got slaughtered. Then 100,000 Koreans ran from the Chinese and died of cold, sickness, starvation and broken hearts.

Finally when the land was devastated, the animals dead, the trees gone, fields blackened, with human-crammed slums and empty beer *cans* everywhere, the war ended.

The people now lived in beer-can-covered shacks. The beautiful Hermit Land had become the Beer Can Land. For a long time you could hear nothing but the snick of rifle-bolts being pulled back, preparatory to blowing someone's guts out or face off; but soon everyone who was Somebody had been bought off. Then the war ended leaving a million dead or wounded. And also, many happy, newly-rich people. They were like lottery winners! That was the bright side: thousands of black-marketeers and opportunists got a chance to fill their pockets.

One million prostitutes had been newly created.

At home there was a familiar sense of helplessness as people said *"Sniff, boohoo. How sad"* and sent boxes of clothing, shook their heads, experienced a frisson-y 'survivory thrill' and forgot the whole business.

And that was just *Korea!* Vietnam was a thousand times more insane, cruel, and confusing. And it was interesting that at the same time this brutal madness was going on, groups of people in America went around saying "We must *put a stop* to *bad language, gay people, and those who wear a pony tail!"* and burning books for their revelations of injustices.

Apparently it wasn't really *swearing* at all that offended the Religious Right so badly. Those R-R's were in terrible shape, and, slowly disintegrating, they were hallucinating that the Bill of Rights gave them a Right to remove the Right of anyone who dared to be different from themselves *"because God said so"!* — bringing on a crummy mess, as more cries of pain echoed across the countryside.

Shirley slammed the books shut. No point reading on. Wherever you opened a history book was the same old rancid pollution — like when you broke one of those candy canes with a Santa Claus all the way through: wherever you broke, would be the same old guy with the whiskers. All the way through.

Except: this wasn't Christmas.

So O.K.—rolled-up-sleeves time. Now to hop into a warm shower, soap all over with Lifebuoy, rinse, dry thoroughly (especially between the toes as Mr. Zanuck said), get together with Sterling, make hot love, and discuss how they'd go about saving America before it collapsed!

Shirley popped into a warm shower and began singing in her lusty little voice,

"Where the Hoi Polloi can meet the Elite...Forty-Second Streeeet." But all at once she burst out laughing because...

A lot of humans were depending on her.

And that would SPUR HER ON to DO GREAT THINGS!

How? Well for starters—She would give them an awesome demonstration of SUPERNATURAL POWER!

THIRTY-SIX

Sterling knew as soon as she stepped into the taxi that *something was horribly wrong.*
Coming out of the elevator she'd been on Cloud Nine; glowing with anticipation of meeting her lover in just...five more minutes!

The curtain was rising on a whole new chapter of her life; and if the A-O was still pounding her, Virginia Woolf would know exactly what to do about it.

One of the guests was leaning on the marble counter talking to the manager (a good friend of Ster's who always tossed her a conspiratorial wink and did so now) — the guest resplendent in no shirt, a Harvard tie, baggy jeans, red satin high heels and a message-emblazoned baseball cap that said "Nobody Knows I'm Gay" in lavender. His wave sent O'Blivion giggling through the double doors and into a howling, bitter-cold Chicago afternoon — *wow! what a wind.*

Michigan Boulevard was a circus.

The pavement had an icy sheen and the wind blew thick, blinding flakes at her — but Ster was happy — exhilarated! Woolf was waiting out there. The knowledge gave her a swelling thrill (and yet) —

(Was it too good to be true?)

Crossing at the light she got that gut-sick feeling that something was very wrong. Somewhere along the line she'd made a tragically *wrong* decision...The operative word seemed to be WRONG! bonging in her ears, jolting her out of the nice daydream —

Yet wasn't it natural, based on weather conditions? They were heading into the eye of a snowstorm, possibly the worst in local history. Who knew where she and Woolf would wind up today? But wherever it was, it'd be gorgeous. She pictured Woolf running toward her with arms outflung—they were drawing together; closer, and closer—

But then came the twinge again. Something awaited her. Something chilling. Hideous. WRONG—

Where did it come from? Only one place. That fount of bad dreams and wildly stupid ideas, *the Agony Organ*. And she was *not* going to let it spoil this meeting. She'd push the button on it; feeling Woolf so close now, and her lover was just as eager to see her as she was to see Woolf. Sterling shivered with pleasure at the thought—oh wow! The old magic was still there, her heart all a-flutter, the street jammed with people trying to get wherever they were going before the forecast six-feet-of-snow got dumped on the city and the vampire, tacking in the wind, didn't pause for one moment to check out the new books in Brentano's. *Brrrr!* It was too cold for any window shopping or even window-glancing—the streetlights went on with a whoosh, it seemed; people bustling by, steam coming from their mouths—a blizzard was on the way! The icy air was intoxicating.

At least Ster had learned one thing about herself. She was able to love with great loyalty and intensity, no longer craving blood, but gifted with a new sense of herself—really secure for the first time! Walking on an icy sidewalk with her head down, deeply involved in her own expectation raised to the highest pitch *(but she smelled trouble somewhere)* Ster lifted her eyes. To her relief, a cab was sliding to the curb. Virginia Woolf at last! Sterling ran along the curb, the cabbie was holding the door open—traffic whizzed by; a bus boomed past—*(feeling so thrilled except that)*—

For some dumb reason—an icy hand all at once wrapped itself around her heart. She felt weird! Poised on the curb, deliberately waiting until the last moment when a small child waved her in. *(But what did—?)*

It was darker in the cab than outside. Sterling peered in sudden dismay, her heart clanging in her chest. Where was Woolf? Virginia Woolf, *the only one that mattered to her?!!?* She peered into the gloom; uncertain what to make of it when the bus ahead braked, and red twinkles blurred the interior—pale light broken into splinters by dancing snow—

The cab smelled musty and boozy. Someone had left a whiskey bottle on the floor, that Sterling put her foot on and had to catch her balance as she was apparently towering over a tot in a zipped-up bunny suit; queerly perched on a jump seat as it shoved Licorice All-Sorts into its mouth. The area around its mouth was wetly black. *Yuck!*

"Hoo, you look chic. Elegant," the little freak goggled.

Surpassingly horrible, the tot seemed full of life. It cocked its tiny head to one side, leaning forward to paste Ster's face with sticky kisses as it yelped:

"*Gee* you feel so nice'n warm and you smell so good! Gimme a hug. A great BIG one."

The freak ran its hands over Sterling's thighs and belly and before she could stop it — God! They were bumping foreheads!

An exclamation came from Sterling's mouth as she fended off the monster that kept trying to ingratiate itself with her when the cab braked at a light — ordinarily she liked children, but this thing? "A six years' darling of pygmy size," some testy Brit poet had once called the loathsomely precocious of tender years —

"Kiss me!" the infant commanded. "Is there no welcome in your heart for me?" it boomed. Its vocal force was astounding! The weather suddenly turned worse; blinding flurries were dusting a fluffy mantel over buildings and beaches as a lot more came sifting down and the heater didn't work *(brrrr!)* except up in front where the cabbie sat. The cabbie turned on his windshield wipers — the little face poised in front of Sterling's — was the face of — a doll. A *doll, from Hell!*

Sterling had gone into shock. Everything was shutting down. Panic swept her. At the doll's touch, the vampire gave an audible gasp of horror and backed off. All the world could love this monster — she'd seen its films. *She hated it!*

"We must be brave, my darling," the kid said. A vulnerable baby, a flush on her cheeks, she offered the bag of All-Sorts. O'Blivion found herself taking one and popping it into her mouth — oh sure — forget about the steel hand that was squeezing her heart. (A coronary? *Oh God. Not now!* Please.)

The curly-headed moppet nestled against the vampire. "Relax, baby, it's me! There are no secrets, no judgment, you are innocent, loved unconditionally."

At her touch Sterling jumped, flinging herself backward and praying her old prayer: "*Omnes gurgites tui et fluctus tui super me transierunt!*" Her voice tight with hysteria.

"Aw don't get all chokie," coaxed this Shirley Temple — thrusting her hands under Sterling's shirt and cupping both full, high breasts with her sticky little paws, encircling the nipples to caress them delicately—

"What are you *doing*, damn you—!" Sterling squirmed away violently.

"No point weeping over a sad situation—" For a small tot, she had a voice of thunder.

"*Don't you dare touch me!*" screamed the vampire, slapping the vulgar brat as hard as she could.

The child sighed.

"It's an unfortunate turn of events, but for what it's worth I love you till the end of time. Our love is deeper, stronger than before—"

"Oh no..."

"I'd like to sit on your knee."

O'Blivion felt far-away; her voice was a whimper.

"Thank you, no. I wouldn't care for that."

The vampire fought back the tears—a belated realization that this was—*was*—! was too much for her. Her mind stopped functioning.

The child buried its dirty face in her hair.

Ster elbowed it off. It kept trying to open the buttons of her shirtwaist!

"If you touch me again I'll *fuckin kill you*," she hissed furiously.

"Aw come on baby!" piped the Shirley Temple. "I missed my cue, you gonna hang me for it?"

Sterling sat, hands pressed between her knees as she stared out at whirling snow and lights. The child laid a grubby hand on her arm. She shook it off angrily.

"C'mon. Can the stink of Eternity be that bad?" the brat wheedled. "Sure I blew it—it wasn't the first time and it won't be the last but I'm working on the perfect plan. Don't you see it? This'll be even better. I'm a Star! A much bigger star than Virginia Woolf who was just a *writer*, which nobody respects. But folks will *listen to me* this way. I've got to go out and tell them 'The world is ending' if they don't stop being so *tight-assed* and start grasping the true, INFINITE nature of reality, for corn sake."

"Do not touch me again," Ster said coldly, fending off the tiny hands.

"Sweetheart. *The universe* is *not* a *moral tale.* Any rules there are, we invent, so we must VALUE people and not stick knives in 'm as you're doing to me, don't you see?"

Her dream of happiness shattered, Ster looked glumly out the window and laughed a bitter laugh. "So what happened?" she asked in a weary tone of ironical disgust mixed with scathing, grief-laden hatred.

"H.L. Mencken caught me. You shoulda seen what his guys did to me. Talk about gooshy! They cut off — well, later for that. The situation is grim. I gotta prep you for your next step," the tot looked deep into her eyes as Ster twisted her lips in distaste. "And when the mission is accomplished we'll live in a heaven of love, I promise."

"*You promise!*" the vampire spat. She shivered in outrage, the tears streaming down her face. She sobbed wildly as the blonde girl held her and kissed her hair *(or tried to)* and clung to her like an insect, until she slapped it off with a curse.

"I've got a little Kleenex here," the brat muttered.

"Why don't you go back to hell!?" Sterling screeched.

She looked back at the past few weeks and realized what a fool she'd been (*so sublimely happy,* anticipating being with Virginia Woolf...*yeah, right!*) But now she was making a fool out of herself in a different way.

Shirley, tilting her feet up, pranced on the ceiling with the tips of her little Mary Janes, after the manner of happy children everywhere.

The freaky little sprite did have that special air of gracious, iridescent, juvenile pathos — so that O'Blivion was touched in spite of her disappointment and outrage.

"Everything'll be all right, you'll see!" the kid piped. "I will always be there. *You must trust me.* We found a cure for death! and that's the good news. Now for the bad news —

"You O.K.?" she broke off suddenly to ask.

Ster nodded and blew her nose, trying to smile. She tried to calm down by cracking a little joke ("I'd laugh at my own funeral," the plucky vampire always used to say): "You look so *funny.* Not like yourself at all," she croaked.

"Listen to me my darling," Shirley Temple said in fervent tones. "Death's something we all live through — a *terrifying taboo* that *whole religions* have been set up to assure *nobody would break,* and it's happening *right in front of your eyes* so I understand your panic (based on guilt over past life crimes) — but *only good will come of this,* I swear to you."

Shirley reached for her hand. Sterling, in anguish, snatched it away (but no, that wouldn't do. She had to get a grip on herself).

"We just gotta part the veil. We gotta jump right back in the saddle," said Shirley. "Life is for heroes, not crybabies, and don't you forget that! You don't think I croaked on *purpose?* It was a *terrible accident,* the most painful experience I've had, *ever,* maybe. But — it's part of the experience of this planet so if you can't stand the heat stay out of the kitchen. *'O grave where is thy victory, O death where is thy sting?'* Only in the mind!" She slapped a tiny fist into her palm. "Do you believe that?"

"I don't know what I believe any more," Ster said in a hollow voice. She was shaken and dazed...*ill.*

She was developing a nosebleed. "If you'd just hold me once —" A pensive expression had crossed the kid's incomparable face.

"Don't!" Ster shuddered, pressing back against the seat.

"C'mon, you're spose to be a *fighter.* We've got a world to save! We don't have any alternative. Every moment is a slice of holy Eternity called *mundane,* workaday business —"

"Will you for Chrissake *sit still?* I don't feel at all well."

"Hey, we must open ourselves to new experiences forever — certain that those we really love will *return unfailingly* to our arms. *They always do!* Of their own free will, although God exists too."

At that, the vampire broke out in horrible laughter.

"Yeah. Right." Sterling hated the concept of "God" — "God" who had taken a tall, exquisite woman and turned her into a deformed Munchkin three feet tall with black goop on its nasty little face —

"I know I'm only a little kid and little kids have no rights except the right to be abused, but YOU are acting like a member of the Religious Right ready to kill because you can't stand life's staggering abundance!" the child blazed.

"Just keep away from me..." Ster's heart was fluttering, silly things flashing through her mind...aware that she'd been cheated again (dark smudges appeared under her eyes), she'd taken one beating too many, and her life was ruined. It was a LIE to think that things could get better, could actually get *good!* She had made the mistake of thinking the same old awful pattern no longer applied; but it did. This was her rude awakening! She'd foolishly thought that—

"Challenge yourself! You can reach the top o' the mountain!" screamed the hateful tot. *"We have a destiny beyond time and space. It's real and you gotta believe it!" (bumping against her legs.)*

"Just leave me alone..." Ster had pinned her hopes on Woolf and now—she would not recover her balance. When this hideous event registered: *she would lose her sanity.* Crazy comets were mooning the night sky of her mind, memories she'd thought were buried and forgotten...She saw her baby Stephanya's grave, the little cross snow-covered—then weird bits of true gossip.

(Two famous Americans of the nineteenth century had dug up, alone, by hand! the dead bodies of their wives. These men were two of her favorites: Mark Twain and Ralph Waldo Emerson and *Ohhhh God...*why is nothing ever as it seems! Existence itself was unbearable.)

"Don't touch me—"

"You're the one who—"

They were having their first lovers' quarrel! It was wrenchingly absurd. Shirley put her fingers over Ster's lips.

"Don't let me down at a time like this. I thought you were *haute.* I thought you could handle it!" the child cried in formidable tones. "I knew humans aren't in very good shape but *jeez,* I staked my whole rep on your *loyalty* an' *capability* an' LOOK at ya. Where's the exotic, outrageous, *incredible dame* I went gaga over? Why you're just a weak sister like the others."

Shirley was so mad that Licorice Allsorts spouted from her mouth onto Sterling's face.

"Pull yourself together," she snarled in a tone of command. *"Here. Take this."*

"I don't want it." When the butt of the heavy H-2 was shoved into Ster's hand, she went to pieces.

"Take it. You may need it later."

"I can't..." Snapping her head from side to side and rolling helplessly.

"Crap you can't. All right: now here's what you do—"

"Can't, won't take..." frightened into spasms.

"You're dead without it. It'll be our little secret."

The weapon slipped from Ster's fingers, hitting the floor with a thud.

"Pick it up," Shirley barked with authority. "There's a man out

there that's going to kill you. The shadow of death is on you."

But Sterling had gone limp all over.

When the cabbie turned his head, the lady slipped off the seat and lay comatose. Big tears were spilling out of the kid's eyes — her face all red and crumply *(was Mommy OD'd, drunk or dead? Why did this kinda shit happen in his cab* all the time especially in the middle of a fuckn *blizzard?)*

"Turn your head back around, Meatface, or I'll turn it for good!" the child screamed.

(She had the coldest, nastiest, must inhuman expression he'd ever seen—)

The cabbie obeyed quickly.

THIRTY-SEVEN

Three people strode toward an abandoned warehouse down by the railroad tracks at 4 A.M., an hour before sunrise. They were Abraham Lincoln who walked with quick, stiff steps; Harry Truman in a brandnew suit, a toothpick in his mouth; and Guinevere.

Recruited by O'Blivion a month ago, the Russian rockstar had been told that the Merlinites were a lone-gun outfit where she'd be trained to take authority, something like Batman—*for real.* She'd seen the dubbed Batman flicks in St. Petersburg and got off on them; so when Harry Truman sent her an airlines ticket *(along with a pile of cash and ten pair of real Levis!)* just to check the KRT out, she didn't hesitate.

The trio moved quickly through the streets, where Guin was fascinated by everything—the pungent hills of rich garbage, so exotically American! and huge cement pipes brought to drain off flashfloods but later abandoned—it was a creepy neighborhood but Guinevere felt safe with solid, reliable Lincoln and her good friend Harry Truman.

When they reached their destination, a falling-apart old warehouse with bums asleep on stairs, Abe motioned them in and locked the door behind them. Then they stepped into a creaky elevator where Harry punched the button that said UP.

It was H.G. who put Guinevere through a demanding series of courses; but Sterling was the person who ignited her, touching every chord this Russian singer held dear. Guin had always demanded an uncompromising honesty from herself, along with a risk-taking spirit of romantic adventure; and she'd been born with the kind of far-ranging imagination that ordinary conventions couldn't stunt or destroy.

Money was the cheapest thing in the world, said her tutor. What the Merlinites were looking for was that rare, *priceless gem-stone, Spiritual Nobility*.

"And why should you be condemned to be *an object others desire* instead of being you?" Sterling wanted to know. Good question! Guinevere with her classic nose, her blue, widely-spaced eyes and a mouth that—well, songs had been written about Guinevere's mouth; she'd been whistled and clapped at and called "Goddess" and had driven audiences wild. "So what?" she had asked herself in English (learning the shrug that went with those words from fine old Hollywood movies). "Where do *I* fit in, where am I going; *what is my goal?*" she'd asked herself since early childhood.

In old USSR, those questions had been subversive! But how could you help others (which is what she genuinely wanted to do) if you had no true beingness—*no life of your own?*

Vonderra, Sterling explained as she showed Guin her new quarters, would shelter the Merlinites who would change the world *(cancelling war and crime!)* by building communication between individuals that had been undreamed-of in the past.

"Camelot." That's what they wanted, Harry Truman told her. Life on the grand scale. Not some billionaire politician's post-mod spectacle, based on the cheapness of money and what it could buy—but *the genuine thing,* headed by the most gallant knight ever born! Guinevere would fall *dangerously in love with him*; and after a tantalizing but star-crossed romance (as the pair learned to "Cause wonderful futures to come alive" as H.G. put it), the knight would be her husband.

Was it a dream—*had she been hypnotized?* The way Harry told it was irresistible. He knew just how to melt her mistrust and arouse her expectations to a pitch where she wouldn't say No to anything he might suggest; but now—

They were here to give Scaulzo a *"freeze release"* and turn him loose. Mr. Lincoln had grumbled about that.

"You can't keep an immortal penned up indefinitely," he said in his booming, mellow voice. "I hate to admit it but Virginia Woolf may have a point. The knockout punch can only be delivered *when Scaulzo is free*. His influence is so great that he's killing more people from jail than he did formerly—just like your ordinary Mafia Don, ruling with an iron hand from his prison cell."

Guinevere found herself shuddering, despite her strong intention to put on a brave front, because...

In the Rysemian view, Earth was a *paradise for demons*. She herself didn't believe it but after a childhood lived under Soviet rule, well...Guinevere knew what they meant! And Scaulzo was Lord of Devils. She didn't believe that either; but H.G. said no person could be forced to believe anything and in fact: that was the base of insanity, and she had to crack those thick tomes he said would clear it all up—but right at this moment—all she felt was terror.

Harry unlocked the upstairs door. They followed him inside. An attractive, aristocratic-looking man was chained up in there, all alone.

Guin nearly laughed! What had she been so scared of? The man's clothes were dirty but he himself looked clean and "hunky." Enormously alluring, to tell the truth.

He showed no fear. (Guin hoped he was the Knight she'd been promised!)

"Get on with it," the man said. He smiled at Guinevere—*and what a smile! Winning* was the word.

Harry said: "You won't like our little 'procedure' but you'll love the results."

"Will you deliver a message for me?" the man asked. "Just tell Benaroya, 'Leave a light in the window darling. I'm COMING for you.'"

Harry frowned. He was disgusted. That made Scaulzo, reputed to be Top Demon and master manipulator of all, burst out laughing.

But when the procedure began, he wasn't laughing.

He was screaming—and screaming—

THIRTY-EIGHT

Shirley Temple was smokin' hot. Not since the thirties had America lost its head over a little girl.

"I come to you humans from across the void," Shirley roared in pulpits everywhere—standing on a pile of books.

"I'm invitin' you to get out of the sardine can! Join us Superpower players. No more sharp-elbowin'! All that ol' sickness is EEEvil. Are you gonna sit there and TAKE IT any more? ARE YA?"

"NO," people laughed and clapped. They loved Shirley.

When the big drum went *Boom! Boom! Boom!* and the tot waved a tiny fist howling "RISE! RISE! RISE,", her audience (in many parts of the country) moaned and drooled.

"Time is precious. We got work to do! No more media brainwash. Every wunnaya must get to be SELF-determined. You savvy?"

Shirley preached in tarpaper slums, on a grassy hillside at Graceland and in Central Park when frisbees flew overhead. Bathed in spotlights and applause she filled stadiums, packed ballparks and did command shows at the White House and Buckingham Palace. Disney World's "Theater of the Stars" overflowed each night the youngster topped the bill.

"Can we talk, dear?" purred Barbara Oprah during an interview with the urchin on national TV. "People say that behind that clean-cut image of yours is some kind of a *deep, awful secret. Is there a hideous secret, honey? Just between the two of us?"

Shirley hung her head. "No Ma'am! But if I sound fulla crap: it's because the savage mind is *so bafflin'* to a free-swimmer from an upstart culture like mine."

Shirley meant that she longed to translate the Rysemian ethos into whatever the natives would find palatable (heeding H.G.'s advice, "Modulate your tone to a pitch a barbarian can tolerate. Then carefully duplicate its every attitude and inflection") — but not everyone liked her by a long shot! The Fundamentalists got her court-ordered twice. The Skinhead Religious Right sent letter bombs and picketed every appearance and yet: America's All-time, #1 Box Office Champ was once again packing'm in.

"I've come to tell you the true facts, carefully hidden, about your origins on this planet," she cried. "Long cycles of time ago each wunnaya was all-powerful. Then a game got started. The game was to *hypnotize* immortal gods, forcing them to believe they were *poor dumb clucks* who couldn't make things go right, then *laughin' your head off* at them. And: the few people who won big cash awards in the game, were to be worshipped by the others. *Are you tired of that game* yet?" Her words brought wild applause.

"Thank you! *Thank you.* There's a smile on my face for the whole human race, an' it's almost like being in love! I fling myself at your feet to say that *I adore each and every one of you* passionately—"

The audience went crazy. When they quieted down, the moppet went on.

"My assignment is to *wake up the world*! Each of you is an immortal Starmaster, suffering from a common type of Alzheimer's disease! I'll cure you if you come to my ship! This is an ALTAR CALL! Who wants to come up an' be saved? I'll lay hands on ya! That's right—*keep comin'*—I love ya—no crowdin' please; I love ya—"

The most famous girl child in America was knocking them dead from Wilmington to Santa Barbara where crowds of Episcopalians, Jews, Methodists, Baptists, Buddhists and Muslims fought for places at her feet.

Thrusting out that lower lip she shouted:

"YOU created the universe, you buncha amnesiacs! And that's no Eastern Mystic hot oil but the bedrock Detroit truth with sleeves rolled up. If ya don't like the facts—don't let the door hit you in the butt!"

That quieted the crowd briefly.

"The brainwash now going on makes you distrust yourself, your own nature, which is all anyone has! It's the worst thing that can happen to a private individual or a society. Some people make 'money' offa it. *Are they criminals? Huh?*"

"What are you saying?" shouted a man in a turned-around collar. "Is this *anarchy*? Are you telling impressionable people to go live like the *lilies of the field*? What's wrong with you, child? What are you saying?"

"I'm sayin': thoughts must run free! If you are so wicked you need to jail each other's *thoughts,* then you must *all be destroyed* for the sake of the innocent in this universe."

"Are you a *murderer*? Do you want people to *starve to death*? Do you think it's fair to *lead them on,* raise their hopes?" The cleric was indignant. "Your parents should be punished," he glowered.

"We got a Uzi-machine back here," rasped a lady with a nylon stocking over her face.

"Thank you for sharing that with me," Shirley said warmly. "You KNOW this is the greatest country in the world an' you can SEE the vision. YOU created matter. You are all *Starmasters*. The wind that howls 'round the chimney is in *your lungs. Don't wait* for a signal from space. You *came* from there—thank you so much! *Thank you* — I love you, *walk up an' be saved* — walk right up — oh, what sweet flowers."

The floral tributes were taller than Shirley was.

In the Catholic sector congregations argued about whether she should be banned or beatified — the first step to sainthood. Shirley had a tight deadline and wasn't too crazy about being lifted up and kissed or held in some bishop's lap at a press luncheon, but it was all in a day's work.

"Today I want to talk to you about *Religion, Science, and Mysticism,*" roared the cunning little mite. "Science is a *Men's Club*. It has fixed ideas, can't observe, and thinks obsessively. *The definition of psychotic!* As for mysticism — the idea of being 'one with the cosmos' — wanna be 'one' with your *shorts* and a few dead *comets*? Jeez! You are *not* part of the material universe; phenomena are out there that'll prove this to even the dumbest in another 150 years."

"You should be whipped!" screamed a dancing old man.

"I say you *ain't* that body. Would I bother talkin' to a mess of tubes an' gore dead in a few years?"

"Horsewhipped! If your Daddy won't do it I will!"

"Should I be aimin' at a younger audience?" demanded the wrathful urchin.

"You're against God!" answered the giddy buzzard.

"*Now hold it right there!* You wouldn't know God if he bit ya," roared the tot. "Jumpin' from a high window and then blamin' GOD is the suicidal illogic that got your species into trouble in the first place, so clam up."

On a whirlwind schedule she asked them: "*Can humans really find*, after a million years of darkness and strife, that there really is such a thing as FREEDOM? A wage slave doesn't know the meaning of the word. That includes your President. I'm callin' for a far more fundamental change than you can understand. But you can try — *for Shirley.*

"Did you know your President Truman called people *Bleeding Hearts* who said he shouldn't have A-bombed Japanese babies in diapers? From your genocidal viewpoint war is *cute* and *normal!* I'm asking for the greatest change of all, a *spiritual change* so clear your mind of all hypocrisy! Your appalling schizophrenia kills while saying it helps. If you hear a creep telling someone 'Go die of AIDS; GOD hates you' — well this poor sickie must be *rehabilitated*, or *snuffed!* Or your race is doomed. *Is that too hard to grasp?*

"I have shed *many tears* over your history which should be labeled 'Dangerous to your health' — a terrible blow to a good-hearted person. You must not let leaders drag you into wars. The blood of the slain is on *your* head, not theirs! They are psychotic and feel no pain. *Wise up.*

"Are you hearin' me? I can give you the freedom you've always wanted! Set a new tone for your country. Not who is the money-hungriest or other material hangup but: WHO can cause the greatest wonders? Soon you'll mutate mentally into what you've always wanted to be: moral, heroic, and *beloved.*"

Stigmata appeared — not on Shirley's soft little body but on Clark Gable's face, on his picture on her lunch bucket. Open wounds appeared on Clark's cheek! at the exact instant that the moppet cried out:

"You Christians, you got a lot to answer for, burnin' books and startin' wars and leavin' a lotta charred flesh. You Christians: *get outta the institutionalized trap* you call 'religion' and read the Bible yourself! But remember. The First Edition that was destroyed, explained how you aren't your body but have had *zillions of bods* and will have *zillions more* — "

Tomatoes, old shoes, and FAX paper rained down but the bulk of listeners applauded frenziedly.

"*Prove it!*" insisted a stringer from *Scientific American Neuro-Bytes*.

"It'll be proved even to Baptists in 150 years."

Many trashed her, "You are naive! We, for our part, are *sophisticated adults* who *know* we will die and *accept* it."

"I yield the point!" She'd never succeed if she got the creatures angry. Better to start with mutuality.

"*Listen*. I'm alive just like you are, and my craving to go home can get desperate. It's a mess here. Who needs ya? *I'm doing you a favor*. So let's keep the party rockin' all night long! God exists, kids, but the Big Bang came out of *your* hand. You wanna know about it, research your *mind,* not so-called 'space' which is only a viewpoint. *It* didn't bring you into existence! Did the house build the carpenter? This fact won't be headline news because *nobody can make money offa it*. But you don't belong to this universe. You are *not* made of star dust or *any dust at all*. You're Cause, a Prime Mover. A Starmaster.

"And it's *dangerous* to go around thinking your species is somehow intrinsically '*better*' than others. If you mistreat animals and trees you'll soon know *the horror* of loss! Folks are bein' *fed* those ideas. *Drop by drop*. Next drop is the *porno-horror soaking* you're treated to. The object is simple. To keep you from thinking, so you can be *plucked*. Finally, when you think obsessively and can no longer *observe,* then you're *nuts*. See how it works? It's called '*victimization*.'

"Any Convention that cuts you off from *your own identity*, is a *psychotic trick* that must be removed from the picture by *lethal injection* if no other way—"

From the bleachers rang out a crabby, furious voice. "*You in big trouble,* lippy brat! Us block parents is sicking the *truant officer* on you and *here he come!*"

Shirley gaped when a huge, great big black man stood up but she held her ground.

"*Pooh*! I been to Gladiator School," she chirped. "All you gotta do is *get into communication* with each other. *Honest* comm! Not political snow! Not religious ritual! But as the Bible says: you'll be *more than a conqueror*. You'll have a *supernaturally abundant life*. Cuz remember, we're not fighting flesh and blood, *we're fighting Scaulzo!*"

Holy lightning flashed from her eyes. ""So forget going to war like a buncha chumps. *War's a symptom of insanity!* No: an adult should go from enchantment to enchantment, *thrilled with her work* and her friends. If this isn't happening you must *stop everything;* all the *nonsense* you're doing, until you MAKE it happen! Otherwise you're *too dangerous* and the only alternative is, we *put you outta your misery.* But listen. *I owe you a debt of gratitude.* Without you I'd never have known the *depths* to which a sublime Being can sink!"

Shirley fed the hungry and homeless, helped the downtrodden and worked medical miracles; she raised a dead woman in Peoria but the Mortician's Local jumped on her with so many lawsuits she didn't do it again. She delivered the drug addicts and alcoholics and went to steamy ghettoes to *free the slaves.* She put her hand on their head and said: "I free you."

"What you talkin' about Mama?" they say.

But she sees they know what she's talking about. And she travels far and wide and she preaches,

"The human vision of the universe is *so teeny-tiny* it's hard to explain without starting a fight, but don't take my word for anything! Come to our ship and be Cured, and you can bet all your nickels and dimes that *something big is gonna happen.*"

"Ayyymen" shouted thousands of newly-freed slaves, delighted that their Preacher was not only a right-on prophet but a Top Star all dimpled, sparkling, cute as a bug in a rug (*"You'll stop those bad men won't you Daddy?"*) — a charming little girl so understanding, so wise beyond her years and a terrific tap dancer as well; and overnight she became the darling of the media as her popularity swept the country.

"Tugs at your heart" — *The Washington* Post.

"Miss Temple's performance lies within the framework of the macabre, her only saving grace" — *TIME Magazine.*

"One up, one down" — Siskel and Ebert.

"Her winsomeness is as nauseating now as it was in 1935" — The *New Yorker.*

"So low to the ground she was covered with soot from all those tailpipes" — *Rolling Stone.*

"Rabble rouser," "False prophet," "Surgical dwarf in the worst possible taste," complained some periodicals who weren't crazy about Shirley but still:

"I'm out to get back everything I lost! *How about you?* Will ya join me?" the child cried.

Millions joined her in town hall, fieldhouse, jail, riverbottom, AMTRAK platform—hittin' her stride at Wally's Drive-In one moonlit night singin' *Lollipop* to handclaps ("*I swear that you lost, sad souls'll get back your magic properties!*") and at dusk in the Boeing parking lot, Shirley brought the great vision of eternal freedom to engineers and wing assemblers and then: *onward*! Texas oilfield fringe of the heartland, a tugboat during a twister, and under Georgia pines where folks came from miles around to pray, sing, clap their hands and hop on a bus with frosty windows that took dozens up to Washington D.C.: Shirley now knowing she had to *watch her words carefully* assessing how much they'd stand still for. A failure here and Earth would have *no hope of rescue*. She had to talk correctly about religion.

"By an unfortunate administrative error," she cried, "it was stated that God likes to punish people. *Wrong!* He doesn't. Somebody's been lying to you. Whaddaya think armies are all about? A buncha guys far more fascinated by men than by women!

"It took you a long time to get so messed up. *It'll take time to dig ya out*—so come to the altar now. You are *loved*! An' no matter what your sin is, you're *forgiven*! But if you wanna stand on corners shouting 'Queer!' at somebody, go shout at a mirror."

"Then what is hell?" someone yelled.

"Hell is your brainwashing! *You were set up.* But now listen good. Scaulzo has no firm hold on you. Cut loose. Learn to focus and condense thoughts so as to deflect any attack. I made a muddle of everything till I learned how to deflect all but the strongest attacks. I'll teach you how to use a 'shield.' The Devil is just a jerk beaming thought-waves at ya: *Scaulzo's just a bloody little coward.* Why worship a bloody little coward who *talks big*? You are an inexhaustible source of power who considers yourself *weak*! That's the most dangerous state there is. So learn to handle yourself. *Or you're dead meat forever.* Now let us dance around in joy, my brothers and sisters! We will WIN!"

The little girl baptized hordes and she cured more hordes (till the AMA slapped a restraining order on her)—roses in her cheeks.

Often Shirley was met with curses, jeers, thrown beer cans or (in Argentina), guano. She upset hundreds of top theologians, atheists, astrologers and members of the NASA bureaucracy (except the few who happened to love Shirley or had a sense of humor). Reporters asked if she enjoyed bedding prostitutes like many other famed televangelists had done. Shirley said she was too young to know what they meant but added: *"That doesn't mean I'm better than you are!"*

She preached at a summer camp called Winnamookie when the thermometer was topping a hundred. She came running onto the big porch and threw herself into a hammock but unfortunately fell out the other side, which took some of the punch out of her statement.

"I'm *from the planet Rysemus,*" the child confessed while a man put a Band-Aid on her knee. Then standing on the porch railing, she proclaimed:

"Do not tag animals. You don't own them! So keep their territory clean of your junk. It says in Ecclesiastes, *'Man hath no eminence above an animal.'* In Genesis the *'life'* in animals and the *'life'* breathed into man's nostrils is exactly the same *'life'!* Being an animal myself, I know these are important parts of your Bible *overlooked by many."*

It was the Fourth of July, with the crackle and bang of fireworks, ice-cold watermelon and a heat wave. Some kids in the back row were the sort of kids who think that having loud radio volume is cool and makes them cool, so Shirley yelled,

"Settle down! or do I hafta come back there and muss you up?" shaking a pink fist. The boys obeyed grinningly; later getting her autograph on their Bible Camp jackets.

Shirley really spoke their language.

"Jesus said 'Please do not set up important, fatcat churches to me. *Just live as I live* and do as I do' and what did they do? *They did the exact opposite* for two thousand years.

"Why? Well I've been *talking to God* about this and he has commanded me to *blow the whistle* on Scaulzo who has been *manipulating* you folks. And I'm asking you to *help me* because technologies come and go but you, a Spirit, *live on.*

"Here's a message for Christians only. Scaulzo fires *beams of depression* into your mind. The stuff's not from a satellite. *It originates on Sajor.* And here's a piece of news, folks. The Savior is *not gonna return* until you clean up your act here! It says so right in the Bible. In Hebrews 1:13 God says to Jesus 'Son, you're staying here with me until your enemies are your footstool.' Friends, you're gonna *wait a long time* if you think that's happened yet! And in Mark 4:29 it says he'll harvest *when the crop is ripe* and not sooner. The whole point is for you to *stop punishing anyone who disagrees* with *you!* For openers you gotta give women *equal pay!* If you'll do that—"

(Listeners held their breath as Shirley took a bite of Baby Ruth bar)—

"You can have anything you want! *Money,* love, friends, *career;* marriage restored, new *car;* God says so.

"Folks just like you can become millionaires—*Why are you in such horrible shape anyway?* It has come to my attention that Earth's principle industries are whoredom and war. A whore culture *kills. Fake emotion* passed off as *real,* as everyone is *forced to do every day,* does to *you* what dipping your *brain* in *sulphuric acid* would do to your *brain!* If you are to *endure as a species,* the individual must be *self-determined.* Stop tryin' to *manipulate* each other! And for heaven sake: *do not spank!* Or otherwise mess with the butts of, *in any way at all,* KIDS! like you an' me."

"EE-ha" they screamed, copying Shirley's own buoyant warcry that she yelled whenever she got ecstatic telling them about the great change that was now taking place—whooping and hollering all over the place.

That night Sterling O'Blivion sat with thousands of others, counting the house and wondering what it all meant.

What had happened had jarred her—as if she'd had a sharp blow to the head or been shell-shocked, disoriented, wiped out; but now—these expressions of sappy adoration on every face (hers included)—what did they *mean?*

From the rear of the hall Shirley Temple was a tiny, indefinable figure, her hair sticking out like Orphan Annie's. O'Blivion fiddled with her opera glasses.

("I'd love her no matter what," she told herself.)

But *was it true?* Sterling argued with herself.

(I want Woolf! *The woman who taught me to laugh again.*

— her tender simplicity taught me that I can love a woman with *a sublime love* far above anything the Marketplace deals in—

(she took complete possession of my heart. I long to be pressing my body between her knees! I need to bask in her smiles again)

Yet I must remember that we are both *Supernatural.*

(and never forget—like the sailors of Ulysses did, when they heard the Sirens' Song—that you can't ever *ever!* place yourself *between the legs of a mermaid.*)

"I've got to get out of Heartbreak Hotel," she grieved.

And yet *what Presence this kid had;* ah, what power! And when she became Woolf again Sterling would be waiting for her, wearing only a pair of long black gloves, with just a touch of the right scent in her fabulous cleavage...

But on the other hand—*the message!* Sterling shivered in ecstasy, her lips trembling...

These and other thoughts occupied the vampire as Shirley Temple preached on.

Raising her hand for silence the tot cried: "Jesus said over and over that there were SECRETS he's not telling. Way back in 30 A.D. folks weren't ready for it. But you will be ready, he said. *So how about it; ya* ready?

"Nowhere in the Bible does it say you only live once. Jesus said John the Baptist was Elijah *in a previous life.* When Jesus returned from being crucified *why didn't anyone recognize him?* Could it be that he was wearing a *different body?* That's no big deal but here's something that is.

"To say that you live *just one life,* one *tiny little* window of opportunity, is part of Scaulzo's fun; his way of *torturing* humans. He makes you *deathly afraid* of doing the one thing you can never do: DIE! *Is that absurd or what?* Face facts! You don't just croak and fall in a grave. That would be a picnic.

"And I'll tell you something else. You'll still be alive a billion years from now, kids! So quit fearing death. What could be dumber than for an immortal to go around *shaking at the knees* about death? It's counter-productive."

They passed the collection plates that were heaped with hundred-dollar bills. "Take as many as you need, but don't be greedy," Shirley told them.

"What about our technological advances?" she was asked. "Give me a break," said Shirley.

"Sure, the Sajorians are orbiting space up there somewhere but *you'll never locate them.* Will they show up on yer instruments? Puh-LEEZ. Sure you might be able to make visual contact but it would take ninety lifetimes and wouldn't do you a lick o' good in your shape.

"Our sage LRH says that you can be, do, or have ANYTHING

AT ALL! Without breaking a sweat, you can be the God you once were—"

There was pandemonium. The crowd yelled itself hoarse. Shirley had to bang her lunch bucket to shut them up.

"If you're *willing to pay the price* we will furnish the power and everything you need. What is the price? Just wise up! You say you want to 'make something out of yourself,' a cosmic joke. You already have the Power of Nothingness! And as NOTHING you can accomplish ANYTHING—with a little help from your Rysemian friends. AMEN, brothers and sisters?"

"Ayy-MEN!"

"So join in the Game. Stay out of trouble. You have a lot of work to do. *Everybody has to start someplace.* The stuff that repeats over and over in your head? *We can cure it.* All you gotta do is agree to join the Merlinites and come to our space ship. All who want to, raise your hand."

Two hands went up.

"Good! *Take those lucky bums to Vonderra.* All who decide later send a stamped, self-addressed postcard to The Merlinites, Box XXX, Seattle WA.

"So, are ya *ready for miracles* in your life? Are you starving for the Wonderful? Then send in that postcard! Kick your other habits and get addicted to being CAUSE! You'll love it. You'll be given *riches and comfort,* a million-billion times beyond *anything you've imagined.* None can stem the rising tide of the New Retro *Verray Gentil* 21st Century KNIGHTS of *King Arthur's Round Table!*"

"AyyyMEN!"

Shirley took a small bite of slush cone and added, "God said to Abraham: *'I am the breasty one.* I want you to *suck the good milk* from my enormous breasts.' That direct quote from the Bible tells us God is a woman," wiping her mouth.

There was applause, laughter, booing.

"LRH will set me free!" wept a munitions tycoon as he swooned in a seizure. But the tot plowed ahead—waxing ever more eloquent.

"You can change the whole course of this planet.

"So none o' that churchy-minded *'His ways are past finding out'* goo. *Nah!* There is *nothing* you can't know and if someone tells you there is, avoid that person like the *plague!* That stuff comes from *Scaulzo.* Naturally the Big S. is jealous. He wants to *cripple your wisdom.* But your existence is *not bounded* by the laws of a material world. It's the Spirit of Evil that makes folks think so. So, you *don't have to bite the bullet* any more. Death can't hurt you."

She passed out T-shirts that said CAMELOT in 24K gold, above a fairytale King Arthur's Castle, many-towered, with blue skies, fleecy white clouds.

"Never lose touch with the fact that you're an immortal being. For better or for worse, you are on a *voyage into eternity.* You will exist longer than *immense spans of geological time* (and that's a solemn promise from me to you) so might as well make the best of it. So don't judge people by their bodies. You aren't your body. It's only a collection of pipes, sponges, saran wrap and goo. If you were nothing but a bunch of tubey sponges and teeth would I be standing here talking to you? *I wouldn't waste my time* because I've got *better things to do* than talk to pipes and molars. If you don't believe it, *pretend you do!* Because otherwise you're just a *pre-corpse* who'll *wreck* this planet.

"Every boy among you has been a girl many times; does that widen your scope a bit or what?"

"*Coldsmoke the ho!*" shrieked an inner-city queer-basher in gold chains.

"Thank you! *Give'm a big round of applause!* Never forget, dear friend: everything that happens to you, you spent an eternity *engineering.* So do not believe that any human institution that ever existed, can keep the *icy cold* offa you, unless your original nature is restored."

Shirley forgot to buy a license in Milwaukee and had to spend the night in juvenile hall. In the morning she hotwired a squad car and raced it to Campground skidding out on turns, chased by eight motorcycle cops who were mystified because there seemed to be no driver behind the wheel—thus, Shirley was forced to ditch'm. She abandoned the car and ran the last mile and, leaping into the pulpit, cried out:

"*Grace and peace be multiplied unto you!* Depend on our Sage LRH and start gettin' trained today. If you don't know how, just drop me a postcard."

A man in the audience asked, "You say I lived before. If I did why can't I remember it?"

"What did you eat for breakfast last Thursday? *What's your Uncle Irving's middle name?* What did your Mom exclaim the first time she saw you? What did you get for your second Christmas? *How do you spell amnesia?*

"Listen up. Those who scream *'It ain't so'* the loudest maybe can't face what they did. If you used to be an executioner and today you're head of the PTA with a nice wife and kids, would you like to dream about your days as an executioner? *Have a nightmare on me.*

"But there's a new spirit in the land. A tremendous grass-roots movement toward the real American dream! Pass it on to your children! Together we will *reinvent your language* made foul by advertising—*no more slow-dancing!* The excitement will *build.* Your nature will be *restored.* Your life will *explode in blessings.* Are ya with me?"

There was a thunder of applause as they took Shirley to their bosoms.

In closing, the tot said:

"Remember as you go trudging down life's highway, shut your eyes and *send Shirley Temple a little kiss* every now and then.

"Glory to LRH!" she cried. "Now I've gotta put on the feedbag so *that's all, folks.*"

Shirley drove straight to the motel and ate a whole cherry pie and a chocolate shake. After this humble meal she yawned adorably, climbed into her Doctor Denton's with the kitty-face feet, and was asleep before her curly head touched the pillow.

THIRTY-NINE

Three weeks later, the key staff assembled on the lift platform. Shirley Temple had organized a security detail consisting of MacArthur, Truman, Sterling, Guinevere and Sean, with herself as Captain.

Fontana was their second officer. He was a no-show.

Up the shaft they went, level by level. Lights blinked; takeoff was imminent. Doug checked his watch and cursed under his breath. Sterling, for her part, kept sneaking peeks at her new charge, the Russian pop singer.

Guinevere was almost in tears. She'd slightly "lost it" during Scaulzo's freeze release and Abe was mad at her—

Harry gave her a little lecture, standing right there on the lift platform.

"Of course you felt sympathy for the Big S., it's how humans react to him. *He messes with your head.* Folks're schooled to feel *comfortable* with that. He knows exactly how to impress you! Why, Scaulzo is a Rhodes scholar, a longball hitter, he speaks every language fluently, he sings, dances, races cars, ski jumps, is a brilliant quarterback and a great wide receiver, talks beautifully about Family Values, looks great in tights, never says 'shit' or 'fuck' or 'you asshole!' but reinforces your fantasies by being a perfect advocate, the world's greatest lawyer and judge; the one who *understands,* is *compassionate* — AND has a cute lock of hair falling on his forehead. *Of course* you liked him! It's a social comedy that the untrained mind firmly *believes* a demon using a human body is *controllable* by laws and customs. You can't differentiate—*yet.* But that's what our training is for. You'll get rid of the old *buttons* folks have always used to *control each other.* It's the only way to *avoid the boneyard.* And it works; because, you know, people are basically *good!* Not bad as the evil few try to make us believe. Unless the Big S. drives'm completely out of their mind, of course. So just don't let falling for him get to be a habit and you'll do fine."

"But Harry, I..."

"Forget it. It's over."

But Sterling knew it was not over.

Fontana hadn't heard about that; he said he had *"private reasons"* for avoiding his promised wife, the beautiful Guinevere. The young man was a tough nut to crack. Cooperation from him didn't come easy—and after he agreed to board Vonderra things went from bad to worse.

Angry that his recruit was late, MacArthur stared stonily ahead. He'd spent an hour grousing at Shirley about how this encounter was far too vital to be placed at risk.

"You and your schemes. The Chief was right."

Captain Temple kept a dignified silence.

They were bound for a transfer point where the Sajorian leader had arranged for a "hostage exchange"—his rendezvous schedule backed by an all-out threat against Earth.

"When have you been able to handle responsibility?" Doug bellowed. "You deserve such a spanking—"

Scaulzo had notified H.G. as to where, when and *how* the rendezvous would take place but gave no further details. To say that the crew was jumpy with dread that Scaulzo might ambush and wipe the floor with them, would be a whopping understatement; so Doug fumed on—until the Captain turned his heat down.

With a trembling lower lip she cried "I'm a bad little girl and I know it! I should have listened to you, Daddy dear," wiping her nose on her apron.

"Don't you threaten me!" snarled the General.

"No threat. Just a warning," said Shirley, turning to wink at O'Blivion—the ex-vampire keeping her wounded heart under wraps, on the road to recovery, proud and erect in a Starfleet uniform.

Their Captain was fine-tuning the squad according to her usual in-role procedures. It still amazed Sterling that Shirley *(her mouth icky purple from gallons of Goofy Grape!)* could feel fear, or anger, or any emotion, as a *human* while wholly detached as *herself;* laughing inside, with the sweet Rysemian serenity they all had, no matter what complications and compulsions her Earthie role demanded.

But this business of riding a lift-platform with klaxons, flashing lights, fog beepers, thumpy sound of motors churning—such accouterments were necessary *(said H.G.)* because Boot Camp was awfully hard on primitives. You could reach the shuttle deck much faster without the Hollywood effects—ut new people had to be trained on the right gradient. H.G. said it was like giving shiny beads to a stone-age tribe, roaming an isolated pocket of Earth. Because people felt at home with 19th-22nd century gadgetry, a plentiful supply of the relics would appear in their basic training.

Sterling had changed. Today, she delighted in the stripped-down power of simplicity—once hated and feared by her, out of ignorance. It was getting harder and harder to remember her old addiction to techno-obsessive commodities replete with stuff like leather seats and purring, *vroom clank-whang!* Comic book sounds. Only recently had she begun to grasp those 10,000 years of extra evolution! And now that she'd tasted the wondrous lightness of being free of Apparatus, she wanted less and less material junk to slow her down—except, of course, when needed to impress a rookie like Guinevere.

Ster watched Guin looking at everything and wondering about it all—and liked her very much. A magnificent presence with her blue eyes and translucent skin, the physical impact of her could catch a person totally unprepared *(thought Sterling)*. Guinevere had an electric intensity...a power coming off her...she was equally as gorgeous as the early Ava Gardner—wasn't that Fontana kid *crazy* to keep dodging her? What was wrong with him anyway?

Sterling mused on, as the platform chugged them upward...

(King Arthur's wife had dumped him for a knight called Lancelot. Perhaps memories were stirring, somewhere deep within young Fontana...*But that was the past!* New day, new script)—Guinevere looking delightfully formidable in her snappy Starfleet uniform. Abe Lincoln had designed them. They were all wearing them.

"If anyone wants out of this deal better leave now," the Captain had barked as they boarded. There were no takers. Each had sworn to stand up to whatever came, like the well-drilled team they were becoming *(unless today's meeting turned into)*—

D-day! The moment everyone had been dreading.

What Scaulzo was up to remained a puzzle; but whatever this

tryst might mean — the Squad was poised uneasily on a volcano's rim.

"Take a deep breath and try to get through it..."

Sterling's commission had turned out to be such incredible fun, it triggered a wild elation — along with awful fears of losing it. She had a new sideline: *navigator*! A branch of knowledge she'd never explored — but was now happily surrounded by map screens, galactic plotting charts of this particular spatial quadrant (yes: all the *"material junk"* she sneered at — but not being *dependent* on it was the key to *enjoyment* of it) and spent days making forms and numbers go flying across screens, and playing with a new cartochronometer that was a marvel, and thinking "Boy! *Wouldn't Galileo love* this?" — She'd met the old boy once at a market in Salerno buying eels and tried to engage him in small talk, but he walked off, and now here she was, a thirteenth century person, making sense out of the intricacies of celestial plotting; and that was only her *moonlighting* job —

("So this is what life is supposed to be like!" she had marveled; savoring every minute, and wondering why the mass public had agreed to spend years in pointless frivolity.)

— for days now she'd thrown every ounce of energy into headhunting for The Knights; combing the world for a handful of daring spirits more interested in truth, beauty, and creativity than in chasing cash or wallowing in pre-packaged entertainment. She'd interviewed thirty such Type-A Hotdogs and signed nine so far (Guinevere being the only prospect listed as *"rich."* Most were too busy with exciting projects to waste time getting-and-spending when they could be living life *all the way up!*)

A few who rejected the plan called her a *bigot* and said she *lacked respect* for inferring that humans could evolve mentally. Of them, Ster wrote: "Subjects had strong urges to BE LIKE EVERYONE ELSE and do what the majority did, even when stampeding over a cliff. A few said: 'I'm happy. Why should I change?' nor would they comprehend when I answered that question in the Sage's own words." Ster thanked each one politely and went on to the next name on her list.

She and Doug took great satisfaction in drilling the sales pitch they created. The ex-vampire began to revel in that priceless feeling of riding high! Suddenly it was obvious that the Rysemian approach had been kinder, gentler and wiser than she'd imagined;

and to her astonishment, the subtleties Doug pulled off were making it a delight to team up with him. *But then came the day...*

"It is not an easy thing to tell a savage he's a savage," were the first words MacArthur laid on Fontana.

"As an anthropologist I've been half-killed—because even the most bloodthirsty barbarian thinks he's *gentle, honest, and smart!* But in truth: I know of no Earthie who doesn't need a kindly parent to monitor his activities. That includes you, young prince."

Tactful? No; but Sean just yawned. He'd heard hundreds of lectures in dozens of reform schools and thought this was more of the same.

"Evil days are coming! Your world's on the brink of its last Technopop Warboogaloo," Doug barked in his face.

"So you're a prophet?" the boy asked, his lip curled.

"Having your species wiped out should put things in perspective," glowered the General.

"I don't think it'll come to that—"

"You know it will. It's a miracle you idiots haven't destroyed each other long ago."

Sterling and Douglas had bulled their way into Sean's cubicle on the space lab where he worked. They saw a broad shouldered, tousle-haired, moody youth full of dark thoughts. The *Once and Future King*—in plebeian amnesia!

After two months in a thousand-bed dorm, the lad had been awarded this airless, sunless cell—where distrust of them gradually gave way to alert caution.

(*Like rats, people can adjusted to anything,* Sterling thought as she glanced around; remembering how folks had *pinned such hope* on Space Age Careers Solving Our Problem—yeah, right. Were things better here in 2123 A.D.? Not so you could notice! She thought of that famous line from the movie Alien, "In space nobody can hear you scream—" *Yep.*)

Doug, an impressively commanding figure known to Sean through history books, *Humph'd* as the youth walked to the only window and twiddled a knob to let in some brassy, ersatz light.

"It was Sterling who recommended you to our CEO," the General said. "You are, of course, aware that she's the supplier who helped you cancel Mars Peer."

Sterling smiled guilelessly "One other little matter," she said. "There's a woman aboard ship who's waiting for you."

"I don't know anyone on your ship."

"I think you know her."

Sean appeared bored.

"Are you ready for the adventure-challenge of a lifetime?" boomed Doug, flipping through the pitchbook the vampire had compiled to show how great life on Vonderra was.

"Why should I trade one form of slavery for another?"

"With us you'll experience freedom for the first time."

"I've heard all the bunko pitches."

"The 'human condition' is not the only game in town," Sterling chipped in. "We deserve better than goalless media-jive all our lives."

"Let's talk about those nice coffins with flags wrapped around them," MacArthur interrupted. "Let's discuss the fact that your species cannot recognize a serial killer, an evil man with complex hidden agendas, or their own butt maybe—"

Doug pointed the stem of his pipe at the kid, chopping any answer. "You interested in *breaking the cycle of violence,* teaming together on an important project? Want a free ticket out of hell? Want real friendship? Loyalty? *Honor?*" The three were leaning forward and glaring at each other.

"Glamor? Excitement? Wholesome fun not jammed with somebody else's incessant *boohoo/buy-now/whore-bore?*"

"A *meaningful life* instead of an *empty* one? Ya ready to *go to work?* Do you have what it takes to tackle the most crucial experiment of all time—or would you rather stay in this pit and blow up with everyone else? The landscape's gonna be so bloody—"

"Can we build a world without crime, drugs or war?" Sterling asked quietly. "Without sacrificing any rights except the 'right' to be criminally psychotic?"

"And who gets to say what 'psychotic' is?" the kid sneered.

"Just because you were forcibly trained by one doesn't mean you are one," Doug yelled. "You're the man we need!

All this data will be made clear to you step by step—"

"Time is precious. We've got work to do and this isn't about private emotions—"

"Let me tell you about your species, pal!" MacArthur yanked off his tie. They'd been there two hours so far with disappointing results—

But Doug was just getting wound up. "If you set out to solve a problem and the problem doesn't solve: you haven't got to the real problem. Science was supposed to bring a better life. It didn't! Now it must re-examine its basic datum. Will it see clearly enough to do this? Or has it turned sour—i.e., psychotic? And if it has, *then what?"*

"Chop and start over?" Sean folded his arms and scowled (he was all but bursting with curiosity, under the pose).

"Only if you wanna *survive!* And like it or not we're in this together," roared the General. "Stay here, and your desire to be an honorable man will be thwarted. Come with us and you'll have everything you ever desired. We'll not treat any human as a toy—"

"But as a god in crisis, Sterling yelled. *"I was a vampire,* they cured me. They didn't just shove me into some barbaric, twelve-step Recovery Program worse than my dear old addiction—well sure, now and then, I get nostalgic for the days when I prowled the streets with a rapacious eye—cape billowing around me like the wings of a bat, wind flapping my hair and taking my breath away, *how sweet it was!* I'd hit and be gone. Those were the days— *but these are better.* H.G.'ll explain how no spirit can build a future on the cravings of the flesh—and with that in mind we offer an ideal existence; no urban congestion—"

"I'll ask you to go the extra mile," roared the General; "go above and beyond, on an unmarked path; because time's running out on you people—"

"When hasn't time run out on me?" Fontana shouted.

Yes, they were being surveyed through the eyes of a poet, a Mod one—a big handsome shaggy lad wearing nothing but shorts, about to be thrust into a world he was totally unprepared for. Yet Sterling was tremendously excited to be face-to-face with the boy who didn't yet know he was King Arthur! But she couldn't help wondering—what exactly does it mean when you call some dude a *"poet"?* Does it mean he writes bad verses and forces you to listen to him read'm? *Unh-uh! No way!* But—along with a stunning gift unclassifiable by the merely mortal—

It means he is *anarchic.* He's the Seer who expects no mercy. He doesn't live in the delusion lived in by the masses. Male or female, he's a *rough hombre.* He *leads his own life.* He's the exact opposite of the Smug Bourgeoisie in any age *(Ster thought),* and on top of all...

This kid happened to be a *lean-mean murder machine.*

Problem: how do you nail an assassin like this guy, for a job you've got to fill? After four sweaty hours—Doug and Sterling now talking in slow, soft voices, handling every objection soothingly and inspiringly—the mark grabbed a pen.

"What if I want to quit?"

"You take no oath of allegiance. Where one is necessary you've got sickness unto death."

"*You won't!*" Ster said. "I wouldn't have my old life back for every buck in the sleazy society *plus* their awards."

"Visualize, if you can, an immense creative explosion that dwarfs all other endeavors," Doug boomed. "A forum of concepts and thoughts designed to make life better for the people of Earth. Imagine concentrating all your talents on this—the grandest, noblest Renaissance known to man, never before attempted because they hadn't a clue!"

Signed and sealed, Doug took the boy to a piece of Washington Coast owned by Indian tribes—for the shock of his life. Two weeks of the sheer beauty of an untouched corner of a man-ravaged continent—the (once) King grew dizzy with watching buds unfurl, feeling genuine sun on his face, looking up at stars, dreaming a little *(or maybe a lot)* as he vowed to HALT the splat-junkies from destroying the last of this, their inheritance! through more infantile tantrums—spears waving, jaws extruding stale exhortations—

"This is Man's age-old search for freedom and happiness we're discussing here, boy! I won't give you any of that 'long gray line' crap that the original MacArthur loved to spout because I *believe* in America. Your brief experiment in democracy, that fragile hope against hope, is now winding down. I'm sorry to say that you guys lost—in your time frame. The barbarians won."

"But how—" Sean got his answers bit by bit, as they roamed the mountains and camped on Pacific beaches.

"With all of us pulling together, the American Eagle will fly again! You have to fight hard for a good world! Freedom requires constant alertness!" panted MacArthur as they were roped up on Mt. Olympus, "and as for me: I've been a military man for a long time and all I've learned for sure is this. To touch your fingers to a wall, where your friend has his name inscribed in the granite—that may be a wonderfully sentimental, conventional thing. But tears and traditions can't hold a candle to good old down-home survival! Which is what our Squad's all about."

So now *(Sterling wrote)* — the straggler having just sprinted aboard this tiny shuttle with a half-salute no doubt intended as an apology — all of us are glued to the viewports. An unwarlike gang on a tactical mission, we are watching Vonderra (along with the massive ball of Earth behind it) dwindle in the distance.

Sean, turning up at the last possible minute with (I must admit) an expression of grim determination on his face — has just seen Guinevere for the first time. But!

They seem to hate each other. Is it possible?

Both have the KRT requirement of impeccable courage, inquiring mind, and no hidden evil purposes. Will it be a matter of acclimatization, or — ? Either way I'm too busy *(and worried)* to watch those two, I've got my own problems — spelled Shirley Temple! the take-charge urchin who at the moment is pacing the bridge and scowling. *(If I didn't know better I'd say she's scared half to death.)*

The fever in my blood is gone: true. But Shirley? Nature's cruelest mistake! Chugging her Grape crap *(how Virginia Woolf would have hated it!)*, practicing her baton twirling right before everyone's eyes, as the ship plows through space and we wonder what's going to happen next —

Guinevere. She seems guileless but impressively self-possessed — perhaps cast too much in the 'Forgive me!' mold; feeling she has to justify herself at all costs (but that's what women are trained for isn't it?) Is this a self-esteem problem, as I had or maybe still have? Young Sterling, always trying to do something that would make her Mama proud of her; *what irony!* But with Guinevere that too will change.

I'm sure she half-wishes to go back for that shot at the big time. Her skin so tawny, Guin has the freshest coloring along with a smoldering sensuality that bursts out in a sublimely ZOWIE tigerish walk — coupled to a voice that's all purity and vulnerability. You listen in wonder. Naturally she zoomed into the pop charts and grabbed cover-story success. Together she and Fontana are something rare, but —

But what? Guin's lovely eyes surveyed him coldly. Maybe 'hate' is too strong a word — but I'd say this exciting pair have certainly *met their match* in each other.

That, too, is ironic. My satisfying friendship with Woolf has gone on the rocks in a most damaging way; but she says all will be fine. Who am I to argue?

Shirley is no doubt "endearing," but to me an unwelcome intruder. She dances and sings her way through breakfast, dinner and supper — perhaps I'm being mean — she cracks everyone up with her kiddy-pop humor and juvenile 1938 jokes — *she hates movie cliches*. "I just wanna see ONE unconscious person stir and flicker their eyelids and the nurse runs in and says 'Aw shoot...I prayed you were dead.'"

A dopy little sample of our *destroyed romance* —

Just now Sean charged into the chartroom while I was at work; face flushed, eyes bright, an argument had been in progress, the King leaning against a bulkhead and Guinevere standing close; angry words, I don't know what about.

I went so far as to ask Doug about it.

"Human life is a caricature of real life," he said, pipe in mouth. "Scaulzo casts his pall, it's a shame! The inherent goodness of people clamors for something better! But we shall empower them. Right?" And we shook on it. *Yet...*

There is something about being jammed together inside a tiny mechanical whale out here in the vast star-studded universe, that makes you *care mightily* about what's going on with the mates who are growing ever dearer and more important to you — but things were getting better; as a matter of fact we were on the verge of having a delicious time — mostly, of course, I was busy with monitor readouts, learning to use instruments that were new to me and to compute a course with a degree of professionalism that had begun to give me great pleasure. All that honest toil was giving me a wonderful feeling of well-being; a wholeness, an inner harmony I had never known.

Life was pleasant on the shuttle. What more could I want, except to have Virginia Woolf back as she had been? And Shirley promised it would happen soon!

"I understand," she murmured. "Deep inside, I'm exactly the same. I can't wait to be grown up and make love to you again, dearest Sterling..." Hugging her teddy bear. And thus the days pass, en route to God-knows-what —

When I say that the shuttle is "tiny" I only mean by comparison to the Mothership. About our living conditions:

There is a cavernous dining hall *(with a bandstand)* down the hall from my suite; but we prefer to eat supper in the smaller salon which is furnished to be, and I mean exactly in every respect *(town, streets, weather, everything)* a San Francisco boardinghouse in the year 1890.

We wear the clothing of the period—

(In case some stiff, grim-jawed helot gets mad that the Manly Dignity of an Interstellar Cruiser is being shat upon by our architectural enhancements combined with our innocent, childlike fun—*come to the party!* You don't have to sit snapping commands or plotting police actions in order to move a craft through the dead-cold nothingness that is Space. In fact—*that's a disease*)

At any rate we made our boardinghouse livable, and at once began to feel homey like a family. There's nothing like candlelight on a space ship to make you feel cozy! At first everyone walked shy and cautious; treating each other with that conventional social veneer (the phony "kid gloves" strangers use to keep from getting close, right?) but soon it melted—

The rain drummed on the roof. We were totally at ease with each other, freed from anxiety (I kept expecting a chill to creep into our comradeship but to my surprise it didn't!).

Chow over, we'd amble into the den where a fire blazed. Or go and cook our good grub over it; beans, potatoes and all (Shirley opening a huge jack-knife to carve the protein) and when the chores were done, crickets singing, owls calling (we'd brought everything you could want; saguara cactus, guitars, harmonicas) and we were sprawled merrily around the warm gleam, we'd each tell a tale or sing a crazy ethnic song (Guin was the best of course; Doug and Harry did Coalsack chants, I pulled off a rousing number from the 1242 Hit Parade that wasn't too shabby), forging links that were going to endure forever—*or as long as we survived*—which was the iffy part.

Often we sat in companionable silence, and that was good too. Now writing this—looking around at my buddies, my heart swells with affection for them.

We seem a bonded, welded group in a charmed atmosphere. The ship a little luminous cave; us sitting around the glow of a cheery fire after work—there's plenty of work and that makes it really real. Or Shirley'll climb up on something and sing *Lollipop*, strutting and tap dancing—recreating her roles in a tough little voice, towering over everyone—being a mobster being Shirley Temple or something; sticking out her little tongue, so darling and cute she is disgusting.

Doug would tug her curls—and at bedtime, in her pink Doctor Denton's with the kitty feet—she knelt and said her little prayers *(so cute!)* Then made the rounds kissing each one goodnight *(kissing me a long, swoony kiss,* traumatizing though it be); wringing everyone's heart as she makes her sleepy way to bed, yawning the cutest of yawns.

Insufferable! *(But a wise Captain for us.)*

Unfortunately these halcyon hours were not to last unbroken—

Tonight, after we sat around the fire's warm glow swapping yarns as usual, and when the others were asleep; myself being the only one still up—I made some coffee (decaf), many new thoughts rocketing through my brain. My love for my comrades was beyond mere words; but I wanted Woolf back—had a little dream that she was back, and I was so happy—

There was a flash of light. "Nah, just my eyes," I told myself. "Everything is under control..."

Suddenly there came a series of bone-crushing jolts. Then an awful commotion as sirens began wailing and *ba-Blam!* The kind of jolt that tears your insides out—

The ship swayed and buckled.

Scaulzo had nailed us!

FORTY

"*Holy crap!*" yelled Shirley tumbling from her bunk. A punishing series of jolts knocked her down. There was a sound of glass shattering, then screams of tortured metal as sponsons gave way — MacArthur trying without success to get into his pants; hopping around one leg in and one out, howling curses —

"Now see what you've done, you filthy brat," he yowled.

We scrambled into our uniforms *(me trembling like a leaf!* Bits of straw in my hair from camp) —

The bloody Sajorians were out there but we got no clear view of them. They were mere blips on a screen *(and behind them the sky was crammed with stars)* — our shuttle taking major hits.

"We're unarmed," Harry Truman yelled. "Now you see why I A-bombed Japan, you goddam buncha bleedin' hearts—"

"Oh shut up both of you!" Shirley snapped. She'd torn her foot on a bulkhead and her size-one kitty-slipper was dripping blood. "It's time to scout out the terrain, so chill and lemme think, dammit."

"He's pulling your braids," said Arthur at the viewport.

I saw what he meant: a bona-fide Scaulzo WHACK! Wispy threads of light spurting flak at us: red tracers closing the distance with terrifying speed! Little packages of murder that came zinging. Most of it barely deflected by our shields.

Doug was pissed. "*You sold us out.* If you hadn't of wore those skimpy shorts — with your underpants showing — he wouldn't have FIXED on you! That's how women bring on—"

"As I've said on a number of occasions, your mother wears army shoes," Shirley said scathingly.

"Don't you insult my mother!"

BLAM! More glass breaking — this time I had an awful feeling what it was: my new carto-chronometer. Oh God (*I began praying*) get us out of this alive! I *love* these guys, I don't want to *lose*'m now that I've just *found*'m and while you're at it God, keep my navigating tools safe too, amen...On second thought *cancel that amen!* It's an Egyptian word. It'll bring a curse down on our heads—

(*Odd thing about going into shock.* A sudden trauma can make people do and say foolish things—when they know there's no hope. Nothing you can do to save yourself and your friends, nothing at all and you're all scared, mad, helpless)

"Get set for the thrilling seconds ahead!" Guinevere said in the calmest, throatiest voice imaginable—Arthur gave her a sidewise glance with his eyes wide.

We're all sitting watching blurry junk on the screen—

"You hear that?" Shirley cupped her ear.

"What?"

"At any moment—*Hang on.*"

The rippling PTWHEEENG sounded over and over, a vicious firestorm. Then *Whappo!*—Scaulzo raddled us with black ice, *rocks* streaking past, huge *boulders* that slammed and rebounded with enormous force, rocking us.

Shirley hopped into the command chair.

"Wow. That was too close to home," she frowned at the next PTWHEEENG! that all but buried us.

It was followed by the craziest bunch of missiles I ever saw: *enormous blips* that were nothing but the rattle-blam of gigantic L.A. Gears, Pumas, Adidas, Nikes, Reeboks pinging us—big running shoes the size of condos in Palm Beach—mixed with frozen underwear streaming by, bones of every shape, mirrored grapefruit growing legs—

"What the hell!" squawked our leader.

"Doesn't seem real," I yelled.

"Oh it's real all right. Any one of those items could do the job."

Cans of tomato soup came at us in spirals. Out of nothing came bright green shrimp, linear accelerators and wrapped deli sandwiches! Shiny convertibles—yachts—diamond rings—designer duds—mansions, screen contracts, awards, money/power/influence packages wrapped up in satin bows—thrones, medals, diplomas; shitloads of heroin—

"The glitter o' fool's gold!" cried our leader as every gleaming symbol in the Consumer's Wishbook came flying at us—every gadget we sold our souls for!

Multicolored walnuts smacked us at top speed and fell burning.

That broke the spell. We all got the giggles, burping, yawning, clowning around, sheer hysteria maybe: but then—

"*If and when* Scaulzo shows up there will be no fears, doubts, or panic expressed," the Captain said quietly. "And *whatever I say goes*. Any problem with that, Squad?"

Hard-muscled Fontana stuck by her side—the rest jumping to our posts where for hours we were conscious of nothing but flashes of flame and the angry beating of rocks, shrapnel, and Consumer's Nifty Stuff on our hull which was tough enough (I hoped) to withstand it.

Gradually the attack petered out, and stopped.

We braced ourselves for another onslaught but none came.

"Transfer point can't be far off. Let's get a little sack time," grumbled Shirley.

Truman peered at her over his wire-rim glasses. "Is he preparing a death blow?"

"'Course not. You know what the sucker wants."

"And will he get it?" (Owlishly.)

"Ask me no questions Mr. President—"

Then putting her lips close to my ear she whispered *(actually it tickled not unpleasantly)*: "Listen up, Sterling. You've got to do the right thing—no matter how lonely. We will love again together, we two, signed and sealed but hey! If we should lose a million years, *what's a million* years in *eternity*?" Throwing her arms around my neck.

She was funny, small and warm but—I didn't know what she was talking about. I wanted, in fact desperately needed the full-grown Virginia Woolf! But meanwhile we slept, woke, reassured each other; and passed the time roaming up and down corridors (or roller-skating in them) between attacks.

Our "little traveler" shuttle (as I've said) was equipped with a dining hall and two theaters that were never used. Captain Temple had ordered a chapel with an organ that had enormous pipes where she could play Bach at clarion fullness; now we retreated there to drown out Scaulzo's noisy taunts.

While Shirley sat serenely at the keyboard, I hovered at the back of the chapel sipping black coffee from a thermos and listening to the rolling chords of the old, familiar *Toccata and Fugue in D Minor* booming out; the echoes dying away in the depths of the ship—thousands of candles blazing all around—

It would have been a moment of burning inspiration if only Shirley'd been a yard taller, a generation older—the real Virginia Woolf. But suddenly I got the message.

"No; *no no no,* you *can't* go off with him—"

"I set this deal up. Now I've gotta work it out."

"Not that way!"

"Remember what I said—always the right thing—"

PTWHEENG! the heat was back, I didn't care! How could I struggle on without her. *What would be the point?* All that's left of my life—adrift, without my guiding star! But we were going to die here anyway. *Fine.* Dying would be better than losing her—

Shirley ESP'd my thought. A grim smile made her face look so strange.

"Thinking like that is OUT!" she snarled. "Start *thinking like a human* and *your world ends* or weren't you listening for chrissake?"

"O.K....you're right..." Scaulzo was taking a vicious pleasure in peppering our smoldering hull. He was rubbing our face in it. We weren't in deep space yet—this was solar system space out near the Belt beyond Mars—I joined the others; moody and upset, wondering in what form disaster would strike.

MacArthur and Truman sat with their feet up on the railing of the old iron stove, spitting tobacco at it now and then and talking, cracker-barrel style as if they might not die at any second.

"Yep, that bunch is *made* for war all right. How long can they go without a war? Peace'd be an evolutionary step about as far away from them as they are from monkeys, that's why we've got to bomb China."

"That's why we *bomb* and *bomb,* yep: you take away the boys'-club sexual factor and, hell. War's only about money."

We were at the forward viewport. "Lookit that asteroid belt, a stone's throw from Earth and the most valuable thing they got," MacArthur said.

"Now you're talkin'. Every element you can imagine is floating out there, just sitting waiting for'm. And it would bring on all the fighting they love; the piracy, thieving, promotions, lawsuits—the flag-draped coffins shipped back home with booming ratings for the eleven o'clock news — what a resource! Makes the American continent look like a pea."

"I can see it now!" Doug said excitedly. "Just fly up and saw a piece off. Set up your little factory, progressing alongside a nice chunk as it eats it, smelts it, dumps the pollution out the back and the product out the side; every schoolgirl with her own little refinery; nobody ever hungry again. Is that the ideal solution for Earthies or ain't it?"

Meantime the enemy drummed away — like the old playground bully throwing rocks and trash. And us gawking out viewports didn't help — the whole Squad exhausted, tired and tense, the Rysemians sniping at each other —

"It's all your fault!" Doug accused.

"Shut up, shut up, shut UP!" screamed Shirley, hands over ears.

"Turn in your oak leaves the botha you!" Truman yelled.

...To watch these alien beings whose lives are a paean of love, mimicking us chain gang prisoners from Earth — as part of a training gradient; to make us feel at home! — this was something I couldn't quite wrap my mind around. And I saw that Arthur and Guinevere couldn't either.

At Harry's insistence that we needed a hot meal in our bellies *(to face what would surely come)* — we all sat down to an old-fashioned stew for dinner as a family, perhaps for the last time. Then came the gathering at the big viewscreen to watch the missile onslaught. We had a bit of poltergeist phenomena in the main cabin, plates smashed against walls, the sound of doors slamming where there were no doors — a few typical A-O chain-yankers, best ignored.

King Arthur (*I was under orders to call him Sean*: he wouldn't learn who he'd been until the Cure), stalwart figure in a bubble-suit, went out to check our hull that we could see was dulled with space-dirt and much pockmarked with burning holes; he reported only minor damage. Sean was barely inside when there came another PTWEEEONK-*thwonk!*

We were enveloped in blinding light, possibly the glare of a crippling blowout...the Squad froze.

Then came an ominous silence as the light faded.

We were back to normal. Everything gratifyingly quiet. But two minutes later, the hairs on my neck began bristling. Suddenly —

A flourish of trumpets! It was most effective; our whole attention was taken up by the big surprise they heralded. Then another blare of horns—brassy echoes dying away in awesome silence...

The silence broken by a dry, suave voice that terrified me worse than anything. My teeth began chattering.

"*I've come for you, Benaroya,*" purred the demon. "I need you where I can keep an eye on you."

Scaulzo's voice! It radiated menace—goosebumps broke out all over me—visual contact was zero; nothing onscreen.

"I've been waiting for days. Why're you late?" our Captain asked in querulous tones *(to my amazement)*.

"Don't waste time trying to jerk me around. I'm not putting a gun to your head. Just come at once or Earth is destroyed as per our agreement."

"Aw don't talk like that, you know how much I wantcha—Mm! Your aftershave smells good."

"Let me reassure you on one point, Benaroya. Any subterfuge or counter-measure will result in immediate—"

There was a broken connection: wows, crackles—I tried to catch Shirley's eye but she'd hidden her face behind an outsized pair of sunglasses *(to me the worst possible sign)*.

Scaulzo's voice purred again, "You've been luckier than you know. *You know who to thank,* Virginia Woolf; now are you ready for *the big one?*"

"You mean the big, cold, *furry* one?" the sly tot piped.

"—Earth's instant annihilation—" (more crackle-crack, sounding like the fiend was chomping peanut brittle)—"crew in no danger if you follow orders."

"Orders, who needs orders! But hey, who's gonna run Earth with us on our honeymoon?" Shirley asked in smarmy tones *(her voice chilled my blood* — at that moment I *hated* her!).

"Beel is in charge for Satanists to adore. I'm moving on. I insist that you come with me immediately, no tricks, is that understood?"

Shirley Temple put her fists on her hips, lower lip thrust out. "Now hold your shirt. I *said* yes didn't I? I need a couple days—"

"A bargain's a bargain. One hundred seconds and counting or Earth gets blown off orbit!"

"*Ooh!* I'm so caught up in passion for you that I—" squealed the moppet, frowning in preoccupation. "Gimme a minute to think."

"You have one minute."

"At ease. Make it an hour O.K.? I got somethin' to confess."

She smoothed her little apron and began thoughtfully, "Sure I wanna come, why not? My career is goin' nowhere except in the toilet, everyone hates me here and you were right about BAD bein' better than GOOD. But one thing must be made clear: because of you, I'm an *outcast,* rejected by my own people—"

"Not because of me," he said in firm tones. "You know I would have trained you, taught you everything I know but instead you chose those namby-pamby human scumsuckers. Now you'll suffer and die for that choice unless you throw in with ME! And I mean whole-heartedly. You must SWEAR you LIKE great big, ice-cold, furry ones, is that clear?"

"Oh, do I ever," the tot cried; quietly smiling behind her hand—me so jealous I could have killed her!

"Thirty seconds."

"Not so fast. Will you guarantee the safety of my crew?"

"Do you EAT ice-cold furry ones?"

"Oh, yummy! *Gee* I like all this attention—you know I'm a woman of my word, Scaulzo; if I say I'll do something I'll *do* 'er. I am *swooning* for the consummation of our love, as fast as possible. But first I've got to make sure that you won't hurt my friends."

"You have my word—and my compliments on a wise decision."

I couldn't keep quiet. *"Oh God!* She's going away with that creep!" I yelped. "No! No! *No!"*

"Calm down, schweetheart," Shirley muttered out of the side of her mouth. "Are you wholly without brains? Scaulzo's the original, plodding, linear rationalist; a complete, Authoritarian, dimbulb *suppressive.* He has *no* unstructured imagination, no magic—*no faith!* And powerful as he is, we Merlinites can WHUP him! And if any of you don't understand what I'm sayin' maybe you belong in *his* camp, not mine," she finished with a furious glance at all of us—her pudgy fingers poking at buttons, making a stab at picking up Scaulzo's image.

"What are you telling your men?" came his fussy voice.

"Just that I can't wait to hop in the sack with ya."

"Thirty seconds."

"And tellya how I ADMIRE you for making humans think that

sleaze is good, good is unsophisticated, junk is to die for, innocence is ridiculous, ethics are situational, markets are all that is Holy—ohhh, you're good."

"Congratulations on the insight! You had me chained up and were taunting me. Then it happened, as you knew it would: first I swore revenge but then—I got addicted to those chains! You are my Dominatrix! And we'll take turns DOING IT to each other. Does that sound hot?"

"I can't wait," breathed Shirley Temple, her hands moving over the controls. "But before we choose who gets to be the Marquis de Sade first...there's one other thing I must confess."

"Well?" A note of suspicion edged his voice.

"You gotta understand somethin' about me. Your goons *froze me into my body*! and you know how MEAN people get when they get stuck in bods; it's nothin' but grief, shame, bickering, frustration and a maddening, ever-present *fear of death* — what I'm sayin' is, I'm much *crueler* than I was when I was free! I can't wait to see you and get my hands on that whip, and crack it briskly on your buttocky parts and all those curvy places," her childy voice oozed lust.

"And...can we take pictures?" Scaulzo panted.

"Absolutely the filthiest! In every position!"

"And can I...*you-know-what*? As often as I want to?"

"All night long, until it bleeds," the tot murmured.

I could almost hear Scaulzo lick his lips as he said: "Time's up. Beam to my vessel and we'll get started!"

"Oh...I can't wait...My little body is throbbing...the giblets in particular. From now on I'm yours body an' soul, except for one request."

"And what can that request be, my playmate of the month?" the demon purred.

"I insist upon seeing you on the screen right now."

"What for? I don't propose to—"

"I just wanna tellya how *crazy* I am aboutcha, *in front of my friends*."

"You mean as in a Bushie marriage ceremony?"

"Exactly."

"We'll do it on my turf, pet."

"But I want us to be face to face—in front of my crew, see? Then they'll understand what an *emotional impact* you've had on me; they'll *know* I'm not being coerced; they'll know how *right* they are to reject me, *me:* a craven nymphet—a shameless, redhot mama who cannot control her hysterical, insatiable cravings!"

"I prefer to—" *Ping!* At last her fingers hit the right combination. We looked toward the dark screen—

And for an instant were staring at the demon *in his basic body!* For one lightning-flash there he was, Scaulzo, the basilisk. THE ancient Spirit of Evil.

Gargoyle head. A hideous, scaly face that showed his curved teeth dripping slime. The hooflike feet, the bulging eyeballs—green blood, beating through a pair of filmy wings that sprouted from deformed shoulders—you could *smell* the wretch! Gagging sulphur. Brimstone. That nostril-wrinkling, acrid stink of the Big S. right out of history *(and I'm sure he didn't know we saw,* or we'd be dead).

Then almost instantly he was everybody's favorite again: the slick, handsome Count de Falke and now—

Pitching her voice as low as she could, Shirley Temple began panting and groaning like the soundtrack of a porno movie combined (to some degree) with that of The Exorcist.

"Ohhhh. *Ohhhh, Scaulzo!* Your big hard furry thing feels SO GOOD...Can I help it if I'm overcome by this steamy craving for your forky tail and stiffened giblets as Tom Wolfe calls them? Tom is of course no relation to Virginia, but in any case I can't wait to be seized in your massive (but knighted, titled, and exceedingly refined) arms with your big—Oh God—*Whew*—Ohhh! My little body is so turned on...*Just thinking about it* is doing the strangest things to my little pink whaddaya callit—pudendum or sumpn—"

"What do you mean your 'little' body, Virginia? There's nothing little about you. You are bigger than huge. Last time we met you were a heavyweight in the literary world—"

"Well, uh, I'm still defining myself—which is why I gotta tell ya that—" *(Was the child playing for time?* Would I be putting myself in a position of humiliation by hoping and praying that she was?)

"Ohhh Scaulzo, I'm so hot forya that...I wanna sing you a sexy little song, and do a copulative dance that'll drive you mad with erections, because we have an *audience,* and I know how you *love audiences,* Big S.! Will you grant me this small, prenuptial favor? I'm comin' onto your screens right now! EE-hah! O.K. boys, roll'm!

Ready, set, *go!* Get them cameras crankin' — *(whew).*"

I'd have sworn I heard the Prince of Darkness catch his breath in delight or perhaps fear. And in a moment Shirley was dimpling up, beckoning us into one of the empty theaters, and signaling for music.

"Don't try this at home, turkeys," she said, rolling her eyes.

She started with the waltz clog, an elementary tap dancing step that gradually became more and more complex until...Glory of glories! Shirley was tapping up and down a long flight of stairs, her little patent leather shoes all a-twinkle as she launched into the opening bars of Lollipop with a toss of saucy curls.

Her flying feet in their shiny black Mary Janes began going TAPPY-taptaptap-taptaptaptap in a blur of inspiration ("What a grand little trouper and heartbreaker Shirley Temple was, back when I was alive," Truman whispered sentimentally)

There was no mistaking that signature style of hers; all she needed was Mr. Bojangles Robinson's hand in hers as they came tapping down the stairs of Scarlett O'Hara's burned-out mansion in the Georgia boondocks, straight into the arms of the Union Soldiers...thus ending the War Between the States and bringing peace and plenty to a blood-soaked nation...Oh boy. The kid had talent. She'd go far! But not as far, I still hoped beyond hope, as the wicked planet Sajor...

When her number was over the six of us applauded frenziedly, Arthur and Guinevere whistling and stamping for an encore. The pair of them was utterly charming — now whispering together, heads bent toward each other (did that mean something?)

Shirley smiled and smiled. Her nose was running; her teeth all purple with Goofy Grape — I kept thinking of something she once told me. "A truly heroic act must be imbecilic."

"Huh?" I had said; believing she was pulling my leg.

"Every victory is not some Trillion-dollar Dickmobile production where the brave lads plant some flag or other on the blood-soaked soil of some defeated enemy or other, thereby making themselves look good, *unh-uh!* The greatest, most stunning of victories will seem idiotic, absurd; or bad, wrong and punishable, to those who have neither wit nor imagination to see what is being done, by the most magnificent of heroes, against the greatest of odds, ya see what I'm sayin?"

But the minute her act was over...very sadly, Shirley Temple went to pack up her little clothes and go away with Scaulzo. Forever.

My eyes stung. It was goodbye. Our love just wasn't meant to be. I couldn't keep from weeping there in the back of the room where nobody could see; when all at once...

The viewscreen! A glimmer of light.

The light grew brilliant, dazzling. An imposing display but what was it?

We watched that ominous blur on the monitors. The Sajorian fleet was still nothing but faint streaks beyond visibility. But from them a fireball bloomed; heading straight at us, twisting as it rolled at tremendous speed!

The fact that the motion was soundless made it all the more terrifying. I ducked, pure instinct—expecting destruction to break at any moment.

That fireball or whatever it was—missile, torpedo, what? Rushing toward us like the finger of doom—closer and closer it came; whirling, corkscrewing, spurting incandescence on the blackness; expanding until it dominated our screen—

Then in mid-trajectory, PHHFWAM! It burst in pieces.

Some kind of a banner began unfurling.

Yards and yards of bunting were unrolling—spreading out for miles across the black vista. Satiny stuff—just like in those old-fashioned storybooks about knights, dragons and castles—or like the sash on that funeral wreath I saw before I fell, back on Vonderra.

It unrolled to full extent, drifting there gorgeously—swans and roses alternating along the borders.

On the colossal banner glowed a message of two words.

YOU WIN

We were alone in space with that enormous, spreading sash. The Sajorian ships were gone.

"He'll leave Earth alone now—or the time bein'," Shirley Temple proclaimed.

We thought of reeling the banner in but decided to let it stay. Maybe some crew of the future will stumble upon it. And maybe—out there in the cold, dead silence—they'll feel like winners.

FORTY-ONE

Officer Spock, in dress uniform, presented himself (or *herself*... his? hers? *it*self? Sterling didn't know what to call it when she wore her Spock bod) at Oak Street Beach at first light, one morning two weeks later.

Today was the day that she and Virginia Woolf were scheduled to meet, at last! "If Woolf can get away," H.G. had warned.

The "First Mate of the Enterprise" hadn't slept all night—she was too elated and excited. She missed Woolf so much, and had waited so long! What a thrill to know that the waiting was over.

A full-fledged liaison officer, O'Blivion could now check out this body whenever she pleased. It was always fun, even though the first exquisite pleasure had worn off. A bod was just a bod— it couldn't change who you were; and each carc had liabilities you were stuck with when you checked it out. But this morning Mr. Spock's heart was beating fast. Would Woolf show up or wouldn't she?

"She's got to come," Spock muttered.

Once upon a time, long ago and far away (actually it happened in Paris on April 13, 1923) Sterling O'Blivion had waited and waited for Virginia Woolf in a park under some chestnut trees. They'd made the date at a party the night before—where the vampire first met the real Woolf, a world-famous novelist.

Poor O'Blivion had stood near a row of horse-drawn buggies that kept picking up fares and galloping off and returning to the end of the line, all morning long. She waited for hours! She walked up and down peering into every passing face; once or twice *absolutely certain* that Virginia Woolf was just now coming over the brow of the hill. But it always turned out to be some stranger. Woolf never showed up.

And really—why should she? With all her grace, strength,

glamor, and international reputation she certainly didn't need some ragtag, woman-of-the-streets *vampire* as a friend!

Of course that was a long time ago but...

Hooooo...that Chicago wind was cold; the lake choppy, the water black, a few snowflakes drifting into it. Spock had walked for miles wearing the knitted cap pulled down over her pointy ears, glad that nobody recognized her *(him?)* (it). The city was all but deserted this early in the morning...

Spock looked sadly at her watch.

"I love you absolutely always," Benaroya had vowed, promising to return as her own adult self — so *where the devil was she?* Spock stamped his feet, blew on his hands. Maybe something happened! Maybe Woolf couldn't make it and had left a message with Nancy Reagan back at the ship...

Spock began to move toward the water, hoping against hope that Woolf (45 minutes late!) would show up and end this empty, bleak loneliness. He gingerly crossed the frozen sand to the lake, picked up a couple of rocks, pegged them in and walked on — hoping and praying it would be Woolf who showed and not "Little Miss Marker"! If Sterling had to listen to another chorus of *"Animal crackers in my soup, monkeys and rabbits loop-de-loop"* she'd go *bonkers*. But even so...to have Shirley Temple present herself right now, would be a lot better than being stood up. At least they could go have a latte and get swept up in plans for building the team —

After Scaulzo's defeat they had made a tour of inspection; then, warping out and heading slowly home to the Mothership (Vonderra still orbited 200 miles above Earth's surface) — a burst of cheering went up: they were on their way again. Jubilation! After a bonfire, feast, dance, and a long, cozy sleep, it was back to work for the whole Squad.

New Merlinites were arriving every day; to Ster, some of the most fascinating and intelligent people in the world. How she got them together, dividing her time between Earth and Vonderra — now *that* was the *story*. Everything was hunky-dory except that she longed for Virginia Woolf and could never be happy without her! Even the wonders to come couldn't take her mind off her friend.

A Round Table capable of expanding from a three to a 160-foot diameter had been installed —

"Your membership begins with an official welcome," Sterling would tell each new recruit. Then the fun began! She had put everything in order—the only sour note being: humans didn't have many more days to watch the stars sink and the sun come up, because after 2123 A.D., except for Merlinites the species was extinct. Crushed by the shadowy hand of Scaulzo, all that remained was a whirl of ruddy haze where Earth had been.

"It's all over," Abe Lincoln announced sadly.

"Even the name 'Earth' is soon lost," Patton clucked.

"Oh well," H.G. consoled the devastated Sterling. "It's true that humanity is wiped out, doesn't exist, is nothing but a memory; but look on the bright side. What a miracle it lasted as long as it did!"

Poor souls—the Rysemians had tried their darnedest to save them. Even today, in the late 1990's, as she stood on this wintry beach, they were sinking deeper and deeper into chaos. There was a slight possibility that the end could be headed off; perhaps with a new set of dreams, a total transformation of human society, they could cut new grooves more satisfying than the old. Of course to do that they'd have to take an honest, unflinching look at themselves—but hey—that would be asking too much of a primitive tribe.

But the ship was full of unexpected delights. Sean and Guin were deep in a whirlwind romance, everyone charmed with the burning-eyed King and the flame-haired beauty from what had once been the Soviet Union—both of them splendidly endowed, meant for great things. So the Squad had a delicious time; they all saw eye to eye (more or less), enjoying what seemed like an extended holiday, totally at ease with one another—"And what else is life FOR?" Sterling asked herself. The Cure worked! That's what counted.

She had gained a power unsuspected...but available to any human who genuinely sought it. Oh sure, she had lingering feelings of inadequacy and a cheesy self-image; but H.G. said it'd pass ("It takes weeks, sometimes months, to strip off the guilt when you've lived on blood for 7 centuries!") as would her jealousy and other non-optimal emotions and yet—

It got a little thick when Doug MacArthur, squinting, pipe in mouth, took Shirley Temple on his knee and she covered his face with kisses. Could that possibly mean...?

Spock chewed his lip, watching a wave lit up by one ray of sunshine. He listened to foghorns moan. He looked back at the solid outline of buildings along Michigan Boulevard.

Nothing.

He could wait no longer. He turned to go—

Then far down the beach, a low racing car pulled up at the side of the parkway and a figure sprang out.

Spock came to unmoving attention, his eyes riveted on the person approaching. Whoever it was—it sure wasn't Virginia Woolf! But it wasn't Shirley Temple either. Spock shaded his eyes, frowning.

Who the sam-hill could it be?—muffled to the ears in an overcoat; wearing galoshes, and a pulled-down gray fedora of the type worn by Bogey and hoodlums of the forties.

The galoshes flapped. The figure was halfway across the beach before Sterling had an inkling of who it was that came rocketing toward her with outspread arms—galloping on the wind!

Spock scowled, shoved back his watch-cap, broke into a trot as he moved toward...*who*? Some unknown stranger. A guy without sense enough to buckle his galoshes. A muscular man, pretty fast, light on his feet, waggling his fingers—

Then suddenly mad with joy, Spock let out a yell and sprinted to that unforgettable figure—arms wide; the pair of them laughing like maniacs and swinging each other around, giving forth hoarse yells of delight and amusement.

It was Captain Kirk, in the flesh.

ABOUT JODY SCOTT

b. 1923 – d. 2007

Born in 1923, Jody Scott, or Joann Margaret Huguelet as it says on her birth certificate — Mr. Scott came later closely followed by Mr. Wood, two characters out of P.G. Wodehouse (if Wodehouse had happened to marry Jean Genet) — was born in Chicago of an old-settler family of Fort Dearborn (as the toddlin' town was once called) with loose ties to the underworld.

Ms. Scott attended Daniel Boone grammar school, Senn High, North Park College, Northwestern U. and U.C. Berkeley before crying out in clear, ringing tones: "Enough of this crap. If you wanna be a writer, never, NEVER go to college or you'll come out a brainwashed zombie who offends nobody but writes like everyone else...or as Monty Python used to say: 'Dull, dull, dull!' - the L's sounding like W's."

Our subject then worked as a sardine packer, orthopedist's office assistant, *Circle Magazine* editor (knew Henry Miller and Anais Nin), artist's model at Art Institute of Chicago, factory hand, cabbage puller ("in Texas where I was arrested with my buddy Don Scott for hitchhiking and slapped around, then thrown in jail for eight days; how stupid can 'The Law' be? Its reasoning was: my gay friend — close pal of Leonard Bernstein and Tennessee Williams — had long hair, therefore we must be criminals"), blue movie maker, headline writer for the *Monterey Herald* ("that's where I got my spare, lean style"), bookstore/art gallery owner, vacation land salesman and at many other fascinating trades, spent six months in Guatemala ("in Antigua enjoyed a night alone with Gore Vidal at his house both madly talking") and lived in Seattle in a falling-apart house choked with ivy and blackberry brambles a stone's throw from Puget Sound and was the winner of the 'America's Ugliest Couch' contest upon which she wrote every day from 9 AM to 2 PM Pacific time.

Jody died in 2007.